Animals Don't Pray

By Michael Reinwald

Library of Congress Cataloging (pending) as of.
ISBN#-978-0-692-22444-1
Animalsdontpray.com

Index

Acknowledgements

I could not have written this book without the help of these people.
Thank You.

Anthony and Brandi Katagas
Mark Maiocco   Mike Covino
Damon Testani   Brian Riley
Seth Tallman   Sid Cohen
Alan Blassberg   Stephanie Swartz
Steve and Shirley Nemchek
Shaun McMenamey   Peter Cartwright
Sean Markham   Dr. Wayne Michalka
and
Mike Koch

ANIMAL

My name is M. Wolfgang Klein.

I am not a writer.

I am 38 years old and I'm on the verge of putting the barrel back into my mouth and pulling the trigger for real this time.
But first I decide I am going to write down the last 20 years of my existence, to the best of my ability.
Then we're going to examine it. We're going to go thru it piece by piece.
We're going to rip it apart, so maybe then I can truly discover what is really going on.

I have been dealing with depression and some sort of chemical imbalance as long as I can remember. Now I am done. I'm tired and I feel old. I'm alone. I'm broke.

I go by Wolfgang because my father said I had an uncle named Michael and he didn't want to get the 2 of us confused. I never met this uncle. My father is Irish with a German last name that people sometimes mistake for Jewish, His dysfunctional family of 9 is from Hell's Kitchen originally and when he was 2 my grandfather took the family to Bridgeport, CT. My mother was born in Naples, Italy. She came here when she was 10 with my grandparents and settled in Bridgeport.

I grew up in a normal blue collar household, the middle child and only son. I grew up in Trumbull, Connecticut and spent my young years playing in a 350 acre nature preserve located in the middle of town. Life was easy playing in those woods.

I had no idea how fucked up things would become later on in life. Back then the only thing I feared was having my father find out something I did by the police or school teachers. Because he was old school, beatings happened. The only thing it taught me was how to be a manipulating motherfucker and lie. So there'd be no consequences.

I was never right even as a boy. I was crazy. I was out of control. I hated school and was a bad kid. I couldn't concentrate and fell thru the cracks. I was happy if I pulled D's on my report card. I was a young free boy that wasn't interested in a structured system led by useless assholes. Now it's diagnosed as A.D.D and every kid is on medication for it.

I'm tired of the lies. I'm tired of the bullshit. I've grown a huge dislike for anyone who preaches religion or even talks about it. I believe it's fake and made up by man for power and control which I believe is evil in itself. Religion poisons everything.

The government is fucked up and corrupt. I don't vote because I don't care and it doesn't count. Politicians and lawyers are sleaze bags in my bible. Fuck the Pharmaceutical and Health insurance companies. They only benefit the wealthy and drug addicts. Fuck the media and the asshole conglomerate that runs it.

Fuck your material objects and your status.

Fuck You.

I am an Outlaw.
I am an Animal.

I am not a part of the machine.
I hear voices inside my head.

CRIMINAL ACTIVITY 101.

I went to a community college in Tampa, Florida. They would accept anyone and it was very cheap for my parents to send me there. It was Florida and I was from Connecticut. The value of money was way different back then. And my parents could afford it, considering my siblings got into four year colleges and had real tuition to pay.

I pull up into the parking lot of the dorm I'm staying at. It is private housing for USF students - meaning the campus dorm wasn't patrolled by USF security; it was private facility where all these wealthy Jews from Long Island and Miami were staying. The parking lot explains everything to me. These kids have money, I come rolling up in a ten year old Honda. Two pairs of jeans, four shirts (one tie died), one pair of leather LL Bean 3/4 inch boots. My Parents gave me four hundred dollars to last four months

Do the math.

They said everything is paid for, books, accommodations and food was covered by the facility I was staying at.
I had five bucks a day to live on AND for gas.
ARE YOU FUCKING KIDDING ME?

This is how it all started or so I think.
I had to fend for myself.
I had to fit in.

I literally walk into a building of criminals. Drug dealing, robbing, and scamming, hustling all done by these crazy 18 and 19 year old wealthy Jews.
If you are weak you get preyed on.
Just like in life.

The moment I walk into my room I see this dude outside of my window, scaling the wall 2 stories up. He opens my window, climbs in and goes to my roommate's closet.
"What's up, I'm Mark"

Then he starts going thru my roommate's shit frantically and finds a brand new $175 Polo shirt with the tags on it and heads toward the window and climbs out.

"Hey dude, what's up?" I say.
He replies "Have you met your roommate Russell yet?"
"No"
"You'll understand when you meet him, my room is 334. Come hang out"
And he's out.
He must know I am no rat.

Russell comes into the room and introduces himself. I can immediately read this guy. He's rich, Jewish, and from Long Island. He's is a mama's boy, he's on serious medication, he bitches, he moans, he's dirty, he sweats, he cries, his hair is greasy and his face is filled with pimples. Russell comes from money - I can tell by all the shit he has; TV, VCR, phone, jewelry, and a lot of nice clothes.
But he's weak.

Mark becomes one of my good friends. (Still is to this day. He lives in Miami, makes a million dollars a year, and never married.)

I meet two other guys that I immediately become friends with Bob and Keefe. Good guys, crazy fucking people, MY kind of people. I spend the rest of the semester learning the craft of scamming and hustling and robbing with these guys.

My first day of class. It's English.

I'm a well-groomed, good-looking guy. The teacher is a tall woman with real short gray hair and real blue eyes. I guess she was around 48.
Old for me back then, but sure, I'd bang her.
She begins her introduction, but then she looks at me goes, "Most of you young people will not get thru this class. Some of you people might not get thru this SCHOOL. And I guarantee you some of you will be frying fries at McDonalds." She is looking at me.

WHY the fuck is she staring at ME? Does she want to fuck me? I think not. She has blue, deep blue eyes. She will not take her eyes away from me and it has become a stare down.
What the fuck again.

Then she passes out the assignment, team up with a partner in class and write a mini bio about each other. Typed.

Typed? Wha..?.

I get teamed up with this Long Island Jew, short, big tits, Silva was her name.

Silva suggests we meet that night to get started and I'm cool with it. Since I didn't have a computer or a typewriter I figure I can get this chick to do it for me.

Just get a little booze in her.

We meet at the local college pub. I'm feeding her beer and shots, and we're havin' a good ol' time. Not only am I going to get laid tonight I'm gonna have this chick do my work all semester long. Great, excellent, wonderful...

The next thing I know I'm standing next to my bed getting clawed in the face by this fucking beast. My cock is swirling piss around all over my bed and on the girl. She doesn't return my calls. I can't get the work done.

I don't have a typewriter and the teacher is a real cunt of a person.

How will I be able to face this girl in class?

Fuck it.

I return my books, get cash and buy a bag of the Crippies, high grade bud.

I will deal with that crap later just like everything else.

I soon end up dropping out of all my classes, losing interest because I really don't know exactly what anyone is really talking about. Can't concentrate, just like high school, always day dreaming. So I end up hanging with my pot dealin' brothers Bob and Keefe at Clearwater beach, sippin' drinks on white sand during the day and hittin' the bars at night.

Debauchery all around.

But these things cost money and I don't have it. So I have to make it.

I have to fit in.

So the mall becomes a bank. MY bank.

Bob is a Miami boy. He likes steroids, the gym, girls and pot. Bob took one class a semester at USF, held on a closed circuit television once a week on Sundays, and he could watch it in his dorm room. He never did watch the fuckinmg thing and at the end of the semester he pays someone else to take the test. Bob sold pot and always keeps it in his fridge and he had a snake living in his box spring that would only come out to feed. He stood about five eight and always wears gym gear tank tops with gold bracelets and diamond earrings. Bob is a low key kinda guy unless provoked. Bob is a good man. This is 1990.

Keefe is from Boca Raton. He also digs steroids and pot. Keefe is a good student and does well at USF. He comes from a wealthy family and loves to steal. He had blond hair and some freckles and stands about five eight. This guy has an outfit for every fucking occasion and he always has to have the best of what's out there, like some sort of competition within himself. He's nuts like that. And that's why he's sort of the ringleader of our litt'e badass gang of thieves.

The mall closes at 9pm during the week we show up at 8:45. We walk to the southwest corner of the mall, enter a door into a maze of back hallways. I assume it's used for security and employees. It was the back door to all the stores. The door to this hall has no lock on it, you just have to know where it is. Keefe knew.

We go and wait, and wait. It's now 10:15 and we're alone. We walk out into the main corridor and start attacking the stands left unguarded. Polo cologne for men is a big score. A $60 dollar bottle we could sell for half. There are 134 bottles. GONE.

Next we go clothes shopping for ourselves. All these stores have pull down grates, but with a screwdriver in the hole it works every time. I help myself to the latest apparel and steal a few women's items I know I could sell. Then we walk right out the door and hike it 3 blocks to my car, all of us carrying a large gym bag of loot.

Just over $1300 I make after we sell everything in one day.

It's easy and it's fun.

This type of adrenaline rush is something new.
I now fit in with the right clothes and a little bit of pocket cash to flash.
Right?
Wrong.
This is bad and I know it. You know it. We all know it. But no one can know. This is the beginning of some real scumbag shit.

But I don't care. Fuck it.

God has other plans for me.

You would think $1300 would last. Nope, blew it in a week on everything you could think of.

This becomes a pattern I keep running for the rest of my life.

My friend John Jay from Trumbull comes down to visit and we drive to New Orleans for Mardi Gras with Bob and Keefe. I have no money, maybe a hundred bucks. Gas is cheap and we're in the south. I have no worries. I let my boy John Jay pick up all the bush and while he's getting laid I go thru the chick's purse. This happens every night and I leave Louisiana with just over $ 800 bucks. John Jay had no idea.

Bob and I decide to put our money together and with Mark's connection out west we decide to buy a shit load of pot.
3 pounds. Now with the sale of this load I'm able to sit back the remaining weeks of the semester and collect my cash. I have my boy Aaron who is computer whiz in graphic arts print me up a fake report card to send to my folks. So far things are running smoothly.

Every week these Jamaicans from Tampa come by on Thursday and pick up four ounces. They love the bud. We get it Fed Ex'd from northern California and just double or triple the price. It doesn't matter because no one in Florida is getting bud from Cali. It's exotic to the Jamaicans. Plus these fuckers will break it up and sell fucking nickel bags. It's working out. For 3 weeks in a row it was fine then week number 4.

I'm getting ready to drive back home, car packed, and I go up to Bob's room to collect my cash for the rest of the bud. I knock. The door opens.

I enter and three bigass Jamaicans with guns are standing in this tiny dorm room. Bob is sitting in his chair with the look on his face like, dude why did you come up here NOW?

These savages open up his little fridge and take out the last pound of pot. They make Bob take off his jewelry and hand it over. And all the while this crazy Jamaican who we've been dealing with, Sampson, is saying, "Don't worry Bobby mon, this isn't personal it's just business". Bob replies "I understand." Then they tell me to empty my pockets. Am I in a fucking movie? I have $1700 cash on me. ALL my money. Then they decide to take every item in the room. The T.V, the computer, the phone, answering machines, cd's, the stereo, they rape his wardrobe. Luckily for Bob it's all of his roommate's shit.

I now have nothing. Not even gas money. Can't call my parents and tell them. Bob asks to use my car, I tell him then I need to use his car, we agree and swap. I don't really want to know why he wants it, I know it's for nothing good.

I go back into my dorm room and Russell is in the shower and his things are packed away in boxes and footlockers. Fuck Russell. I take all of his shit, everything, and load it into Bob's car. By the time Russell gets out of the shower I'm long gone.

I arrive in the pawnshop 20 minutes later. I negotiate a price on everything and all I can get is $350. I take it and get out of there before someone sees me. Because at the end of the semester everyone is robbing and stealing and pawning before they leave for the summer.

Bob and I agree to meet inside the strip joint to exchange keys later that day.

"Bro, thanks for keeping cool. That was some fucked up shit," he says. "I wasn't going to start dickin' around with these crazy fuckin niggers with semi-automatics. I knew it was too be good to be true."
I raise my beer and we toast.

In the parking we are saying ure goodbyes and Bob says, "Yo Wolfgang, open your trunk". I do and next to all my luggage is a half-pound of weed.

"I did what I had to do and that's your cut."
"I don't even want to ask but THANK YOU, brother." I give him a hug and we head out in our own directions.

Two miles later I see that fucker in my review mirror flashing his lights like a madman. I pull into the strip mall parking lot. Bob rolls down his window.
"Bro, I forgot something"
I'm thinking real quick is this a set up or a sting? Bob opens the door and jumps into my passenger seat. "Dude hold on Don't move!"
He reaches under my seat and slowly pulls out a cocked 22.
He laughs to himself and says, "Dude I almost forgot."

This is the last time I ever spend any time in Florida.

I drive straight to Connecticut without any sleep. It takes me 19 hrs. I stopp at my parents house in Trumbull around breakfast time, had a quick bite with the family and then off I go to UCONN for their spring weekend. Meet up with my boys and sell a half pound of pot in 90 minutes. 64 eighths times 50   I end up leaving the weekend after all expensive paid with $2600. I move back into my parent's house.

I leave my criminal activities back in Florida, except for a little pot dealing. Stealing is a big no-no here, it's a Florida thing
I did it to survive.
I justify it.

Elizabeth arrives back in Trumbull after her freshman year in college, she is a Jewish princess. She has been my girlfriend since we were both sixteen. She is good. She is innocent. She is the first person I ever loved.

A job never entered my mind for the summer. I figured I had enough cash to float on by but not really. I work at College Painters with my friends and after two weeks I decide it's not for me. It's not the work, it's the wage. I'm being exploited, taken advantage of.
I see a promotion at a bank where they are offering student credit cards without a co-signer. All you need is was a school ID, and I have one. Thank you. I fill out the forms and in two weeks had a credit card with a $2500 dollar limit.

Elizabeth and my family think I still work for College Painters and so do most of my friends. I withdraw $800 from the credit card and go straight to Jersey to see Mark from Florida. He's home for the summer, still dealing pot thru the mail. I buy some. I sell it.

My summer is spent vacationing from Maryland to Montreal. I tell my family and Elizabeth that College Painters use us all over the country to train other painters because we are THAT good. The rest of the time I spend with Elizabeth at the beach.

No one questions me, I always have cash. My parents and Elizabeth think I do real well that semester considering I could barely make it out of high school. I tell them I had a 2.8 GPA. Lie. Have a bogus report card on my folks' fridge that reads all B's. More lies. Had told Elizabeth at one point that I got a score of 820 on the SAT's. Lie. My score is whatever you get for signing your name.

On the surface to everyone, things look good for me. I'm able to live two lives. But the summer is coming to an end. And I have no plan, it's all just bullshit. All lies.

The last memory I have of that summer is being in Canoe Brook Lake on a real hot August morning. Early morning.

Elizabeth and I are the only ones there and we play like teenagers do when they're in love. After an hour or so in the water (she likes to swim the length of the lake), we come to rest on a dock in the water and dry off. We just talk and hold one another and kiss. Neither of us want to be anywhere else, not ever again.

I never need to be at any other place in the world than there at that moment. And I'm still looking for a way to get back there.

At the end of summer I tell my family and Elizabeth that I want to go and work in the "real world" for a semester and I go and work at my uncle's printing shop. Elizabeth goes back to college.

After one month of being a delivery boy and spending the weekends at UCONN with a lot of my Trumbull friends that went there, I get a DUI. I lose my license for a mandatory six months because I refuse to blow into the Breathalyzer. I deserve it. I was driving my car on sidewalks. Cutting thru the campus on the grass, driving down a one way street the wrong way. It was a short cut to where I had to go and I said fuck it.
So no license, no job.

My last day of work at my uncle's plant and I stay late. My uncle Joe has a brand new state of the art color printer. This is 1991. I now graduate from petty thief punk to counterfeiter. My last day of work for my uncle and I decide to print money. First one bill at a time, then I'm doing sheets of 20's.

Once my license got revoked, I lost my job and spent the next six months depressed at my parent's house. I sleep Monday through Friday and go out on the weekends with my friends and I buy drinks with the fake money. Well not me, actually. I go up to a group of chicks and ask them if I could buy them a round. They would always say yes and I would give one of the bills and send them up to the bar to order. I never show my face to the bartender.

The rest of my peers are getting educations at real colleges. I am wasting time. I don't have a plan. I become frustrated with my situation and take out my insecurities on telephone calls to Elizabeth. I become jealous.

I become a complete sociopath felon punkass who is no man.

I am lost.

CALIFORNIA 1

Spring.

I get my license back and a painting job for the summer with a friend's brother 6 years older than me and also from Trumbull. My friends are home from school and Elizabeth is still hanging with me. It was a good summer.

In August I leave across country with four of my buddies to Yellowstone then from there we would go our separate ways. Me to California, and they would go to Durango, Colorado.

I have a cousin that lives in Santa Monica, met him 4 or 5 times in my life. He is a registered nurse and sort of stale. He is 6 years older than me as well.

Once I arrive I have no idea what I'm going to do. I have very little money. I can't find a waitering job anywhere. All the Mexicans do the labor out here. So no painting or landscaping jobs. I spend a month on his couch really depressed. My pot dealin' friends Fed Ex me pot anytime I need it.

Then one day I see in the paper as bold as it can be: German looking men wanted for television and film work. I think.

I fucking think.

I have German blood. I'm pretty good looking. I have shoulder length dirty blonde hair and blue eyes. I'm only 5 foot 6 depending on what shoes I'm wearing but fuck it I call the number.

"Hello. Yes, my name is Wolfgang Klein and I'm calling about the ad." The person on the other end invites me down to Hollywood for an interview.

I'm feelin' pretty good.
I am young. I am naive.

The office is in a building on the corner of Cahuenga and Hollywood Blvd. 9th floor.

The sign reads *Jerry Foote Casting*. I walk in and the waiting room is filled with every new transplant to the city. I get an interview and they sweet talk me. They say I have the look they are using now for Bugle Boy jeans commercial. All I need are headshots and I could start working. They tell me it will be six hundred bucks for a portfolio. I tell them I need to think about it and I leave. I don't have 600 bucks I have 300, that's it. The next day I get a phone call from Jerry Foote himself saying he would really like to work with me. He is a homosexual. This is clear right off. I explain my situation and he agrees to accept 300 for now and I could pay him later for the photos. I go to a photo shoot with 15 other actor/models wannabes and one photographer and one make-up artist. I have seven different outfits I was told to bring. We spend the day taking pictures on the streets of Hollywood. It's fun. But I still don't have any pictures and Jerry Foote wants 300 hundred more and he will release my pics. Then it will be 100 bucks for each photo blown up to 8 1/2 by 11. I'm starting to think I'm getting fucked.

I tell him I will work off the pics by being the receptionist. He agrees.

It takes me one day to realize that this whole casting operation is bullshit. It's a front to sell headshots. It doesn't matter what you look like, if you're fat or short, teeth, no teeth, these people convince you that you need headshots and then they could get you work. They don't turn anyone away and they feel people out, seeing how much they can con you for.
The waiting room is always filled, people thinking their dreams were coming true when in fact they were being preyed on.
It's been a month and I have no money and no headshots. Jerry is still holding my prints hostage. I am eating Ramen noodles and sleeping on my cousin's couch, this is not how I thought California would be. My depression deepens. Rage ignites.

I miss Elizabeth.

I decide that I'm all set with California. I walk into "work" and I go straight to the file cabinet in Jerry's office. I open each drawer looking for my prints. I find them and grab them. One employee, Janet, a real piece of shit, grabs my arm and tells me to put them back. I'm a little startled because I wasn't expecting anyone to put their hands on me. So this fat little piggy gets hit in the mouth by my elbow when I swing it away. She starts screaming, "He hit me! He hit me!"

Other employees come out of their offices to see the commotion and Jerry walks in from outside. Our eyes meet. And at that moment he knows what I was capable of.

"Did you get what you want?" He asks with his lisp.

"I got what was mine, yes." I reply.

"Then please leave."

As I walk down the hall and into the reception area I can see the look of shock on all these people's faces. I walk up to the desk and unplug the TV/VCR combo (they used it to show fashion gigs), put it underneath my arm as I walk towards the door I tell everyone, "This place is a scam. They will take your money and lie. And Jerry Wood tried to molest me, God bless you all." I leave and one block down on Hollywood Blvd is a pawn show. I receive $75 bucks for the TV/VCR combo.

Old dog, no new tricks.

Back in Santa Monica and my car is packed, I'm leaving, but I don't have any cash, not enough to get to Colorado. I tell my cousin I'm leaving and he insists that he takes me out for dinner and drinks before I go. Since we haven't hung out at all and I had no money, free food and drink would be great, I agree. We head out downtown to some Mexican joint. I don't really want to tell him my situation, so I just listen to his shit and suck back Margaritas. I'm getting my cousin drunk because he can't drink. I am pretty buzzed.

Enter the criminal thoughts.

I quickly scan the place and look at all the purses hanging from the back of chairs. The place is crowed and loud. If I do anything I have to do it quick and now. My cousin is getting ready to pay the tab and I tell him, "I'm going to the bar to order two more shots of tequila" He says, "No none for me, you go, I'm going to the men's room."

I walk up to the bar behind two girls. I lean in and ask the girls if they mind if I stand here while I order a drink? I already have my hand in and out of one of their purses and the wallet down my pants.

The two girls welcome me in between them so I can order a shot, I buy them shots and tell them, "It was nice meeting you and thanks." It always pays to be polite. I leave and meet my cousin in the parking lot. The poor girls has no clue.

The next day I wake up early and depressed and feeling guilty, I scored $180 cash. Why do I do this?
Why can't I live a normal life God?

I take off without saying goodbye to my cousin or thank you.
I am a piece of shit.

I'm too depressed to talk to anyone.

I drive straight to Durango.

BUG JUICE AND STRAY CATS

Durango is beautiful, different then California.

My friends from Trumbull live in the Floridian apartments, the ghetto of Durango. It is semi furnished and the only utensils they have are the ones we used when we were camping in Yellowstone. No food in the fridge.

And cats are scattered everywhere around the building.

There are about 24 people from Trumbull living in Durango, all living in better conditions that what we have. My crew of guys: Cheen, he sold pot that was Fed Ex'd in from New York. John Jay works at a hair salon. Jimmy works at the mountain as ski patrol and Jsole was a student.

What am I going to do? I need money.

Always need more money.

The few restaurants and bars aren't hiring, The Mountain isn't hiring. I can't find a job.

One night at Farquarts restaurant I go into the kitchen and steal a huge side of beef. It's too big to walk out the front door, so I push it out the back and drag it to my friend's car in the snow. Once we get home we throw it directly in the oven. No pan. Set the oven at 350 degrees and wait. It takes 2 days to cook that fucker. Then it sits in the oven for days on end while we rip off pieces of meat.

Animals.

But animals, they don't need money. Not like I need it. Americana Beauty College is located in Durango. I go to investigate. I figure everyone's got something to do except me. I would like to try to become a hairdresser at this point …or so I think. I go in and get a tour and act like I'm interested. A lot of women. Shelia the Owner of the school mentions I could qualify for a grant. On the condition that I finish school, I would not have to pay it back.

Yes please, thank you.

I apply and I get accepted.

Now at some point the paper work is fouled up because I receive a check in my mailbox for $5000 made out to me. I deposit the money immediately and never mention a word about it to Shelia. I start classes and it sucks.

I buy skis and a season pass to Purgatory Mountain.

A month into it and Shelia is asking about the grant money, I tell her I have no idea. What do I know? I fuck four girls from the class and I hardly show up. I don't like touching people's hair, I decide I don't want to be a hairdresser anymore.

I spend my days with Cheen. We wake up at the ass crack of dawn and head up the mountain, the first ones there every day. We ski the backside of the mountain through the woods to a manmade fort. There we pack the bong with snow and get kooky. These are good days.

Shelia is calling my apartment nonstop, she knows. She found out. I have my roommate John Jay answer the phone. He tells her I left for Connecticut and no, he doesn't know my address.

Fuck her.

We drink every night and ski during the day, sometimes on mushrooms. One night Cheeen comes home and throws a fire extinguisher through the picture window. For fun.

The next day when we return from the mountain the sheriff is waiting for us with an eviction notice. We have 48hrs to vacate the premises or charges will be filed.

Jimmy's girlfriend lives downstairs. Nikki, from Texas.

We all move into her one bedroom apartment. It's small. Four sleeping bags laid in a row in front of the TV. Jimmy sleeps in the bedroom with his lady. It's becoming pathetic, the way I'm living. All I do is ski during the day and drink at night. My family thinks I'm still attending Cosmetology school. I'm going to have to figure that one out, but I have a few months to chill in the meantime.

Nikki is a diabetic, she has to shoot insulin. She has syringes.

Our friend Kevin who lives up on the mountain in a phat log cabin, has satellite T.V and a bunch of new 4x4's in his driveway, he supplies pretty much the west coast of acid. He sells most of his shit when he goes on tour with The Grateful Dead and Phish. He manufactures in Durango.

Cheen and I, since we don't work, spend a lot of time at Kevin's pad. It's nice. He always has a fire blazing, food, and all these crunchy Deadhead chicks living there when not on tour. I love it. I don't mind hairy girls.

One random day, Kevin pulls Cheen and me aside and gives us a Tupperware container filled with 3 cups of "BUGJUICE".

Acid, mushrooms, madam, peyote, all combined in liquid form. He was brewing it for few days. Kevin tells us to only take a pin drop of the stuff on our tongue. He says we should soak sheets of paper in it and then cut it into little squares so we can figure out how much we should take. We don't listen.

As Cheen is about to dip his tongue into the container I hit his arm. He swallows way more than anyone should.

Now it's my turn.

The same thing happens.

Cheen hits my arm and I swallow.

Not good.

Our roommates have to endure a laughing fit between Cheen and me for 3 hours, and then we grab our skis and head to the mountain.

Over the next couple of weeks I dose my roommates without their knowledge.

Things are getting out of hand.

One day I wake up from these fucking cats that inhabit the apartment building. No one in the place gets these cats fixed or even claims them. I want to kill them, all of them.

When I see these cats all the time, every day, all over place, it makes me depressed because it reminds me that I had to live among the poor and filthy Native Americans that occupy these apartments.

So I go and open a can of tuna and put it on the deck. In five minutes I had five cats on the can. I go over to the Bug Juice and fill up a syringe. I grab one cat off the deck and bring it inside. This is no domesticated cat, it starts growling at me. I try to hold it down and the fucker is clawing me til I bleed. I grab the needle with my right hand and go to plunge it into the cat. It squirms away and I hit my left hand with the needle.

I scream and run to the sliding glass door and open it. I kick the cat out. Literally. Shut the door and pull out the needle.

Fuck.

It was going to be a long day to say the least. But I figure I deserve it. So I roll with it. I'm fucked up for 18 hours.

The Bug Juice sits on top of the fridge next to Nikki's syringes. No one wants any part of it, including me.

It was the end of March and Durango is still covered in snow. I'm getting bored of not doing anything. Elizabeth is home for the summer in 7 weeks and I want to see her.
I miss her.

I turn 21 in April.

I drive back home to Trumbull. I have no plan. I have to act like I've been attending hairdressing school and the reason I haven't graduated is because in Connecticut you need five hundred more hours of schooling than in Colorado. That's what I tell everyone.

My parents enroll me in hairdressing school in Bridgeport, hoping that I would finish. It costs them $700 for one month.
I go maybe a total of 3 days in that month. I would leave my parent's house in the morning and pretend to go to school, just like high school.

I spend my days hustling pot back and forth to UConn.

One day I go to the casino with $15, stay 8 hours and make $825 on blackjack. This guy sitting next to me is missing 2 fingers and he pretty much coached me all day, told me how to play.

The next day I show up at hairdressing school and the owner starts screaming and bitching, "You're not gonna come and go as you please and disrupt my class, Mr. Klein,." This guy brings me into his office and writes me a check for $700 in my name and tells me he doesn't want me as a student. Great. I cash the check.

I tell my parents after the month is up that I want hold off on going back and they should save their money. I want to take the summer off. My parents are again disappointed.

I spend a couple weeks at URI with Elizabeth, when I wasn't driving pot up to UConn.
I see a commercial on T.V

It's an ad for Nantucket Island, I had no idea that Nantucket existed up until that point.
I need to go to Nantucket, something tells me.
I need money.

The money I'm making for driving pounds of weed from Norwalk to UConn is only a couple hundred bucks per ounce of bud. Frank-o is a major bud dealer and is introduced by my friend's crazy cousin. He's connected. He moves sixty pounds one time, once a month. The two or three pounds he fronts me and my friends are no big deal to him. So I think.

I cancel my phone line at my parents' house.

I take 2 pounds of weed from Frank-o and instead of dropping it off to his people, I decide to drop it off to my people. I lay low for 4 days and collect 3 grand from my boys at Uconn.
Frank-o doesn't know where I live and I no longer have a phone. Fuck him.

I tell my lady I'm going to Nantucket for the summer and she is cool with it.

Elizabeth is doing an internship in New York for the summer, commuting back and forth from Trumbull. She always works hard and is not really into the whole bar scene. She would rather read a good book then deal with assholes at bars.
I trust her.
Always.
But I have a mean jealous streak, I'm insecure. I don't want anyone to corrupt her. No one is worthy of her.
It's hard for me to leave when I just got home 6 weeks ago. But I have to go and she understands. She's my girlfriend no matter where I was in the country. I get a ride to Hyannis Port, Cape Cod, and board the ferry to Nantucket

This is May 14th.

I spend the summer on Nantucket Island with Elizabeth visiting a few times. Again, no place else ever I'd rather be.

I come back to Trumbull at the end of August.
Now Elizabeth tells me she wants her freedom during her senior year of college. It freaks me out. I rage.
I try by best to accept it.
I decide to move to New York City and I enroll at HB studios.
I study acting with William Hickey and I move into an apartment on 2Ave and 12th street with two girls, NYU students. Heather and Beth. I am a poor

student. I can't pay attention, I keep daydreaming about the Swedish chick next to me.

I work as a bus boy in an Italian restaurant in Chelsea, I make shit money.

One day this gay older guy befriends me in Washington Square Park. We start talking small talk then he propositions me. He wants to give me a hundred bucks if he can suck my cock. I don't have to think about. I tell him to give me the money now and meet me in the public bathroom. I will be there in two minutes. He does. He's stupid. I walk off and jump into a cab.

I spend my days reading Howard Korder plays. I am lonely, I am depressed, I have no friends here. I think about my girlfriend. I drink and spend what little money I have in bars. I buy weed from the Jamaicans that hang outside of my building.

I live on the 7th floor with my window facing 12th street and I have a pump bb gun.

Just for fun I turn out the lights and open the window a crack. I stick the barrel out and aim at the crackheads smoking rock in the doorway across the street. I shoot their hands and watch them freak out. Just for fun.
I call up bullshit sex lines and run up a phone bill that I have to explain to these two girls. I hang out at porn shops late at night. I know all the hookers and drug dealers on my street. I fuck random girls at random.

I try to live a normal life without being a criminal.

Acting becomes too hard because I can't follow through on anything. I need headshots, an agent, SAG card. It's impossible for me to come up with these things.

I lose interest.

Heather's boyfriend Alex is graduating NYU film school. He's finishing up his senior film. A documentary called HATED with his buddy Todd. These guys always hang out at the apartment while working on their film.

I constantly pay attention to these guys any chance I got. And when they invite me to the screening at Ticsh, I'm blown away and now I become very interested in making movies. Like a light bulb finally goes off in my head. All I do is think about and watch film from here on in. But I have no background, no education, and no chance of ever going to film school.

No money. No rich uncle. No trust fund.

Alex, who is on his way to being a famous director, tells me, "Dude if you want to be an actor, you should get to know the directors that are studying at NYU because they are going to be the ones making the movies very soon".
I reply. "How do I do that?"
"Sit in on film making classes at NYU, get to know the students, tell the professor that you're an actor and you want to study behind the scenes. Learn the background of production."

Like it's that simple.

It's March 15th and I'm home for my mom's 50th surprise party that weekend.
I see my friends home from school in a bar the night before the party. My boy Sean tells me he and his friends are leaving tomorrow to Bahamas for spring break.
I have no money, but I do have a credit card. Credit card companies would send me cards even when I haven't paid on any of them.
I have collection agencies calling me.
I leave the bar and go back to my pad in the city, party, then jump on a flight at 7am to Paradise Island. I spend $700 on a ticket at the last minute. I have $40 dollars cash on me. I never tell work I'm leaving.
The Bahamas is filled with white trash southerners doing their spring break thing. I hate it. It's below me.
I borrow a hundred dollars from Sean and head straight to the casino. I spend 2 hours playing blackjack and bank $350 after I pay Sean back. I have to go back and forth to the casino every other day to make vacation money. I do O.K.
Victor the cab driver used to be a cop but he says he makes better money at driving a taxi. He becomes our personal chauffeur for the week and takes us on a tour into the REAL Bahamas where tourist do not go. Victor sets me up with a coke connection 30 miles from our resort. We go. I buy. $350 worth.
I go back to the hotel and smash it up. Then I sell it off to all the spring breakers at the resort. Gone in one hour.
Triple my investment.

We fuck a couple of pigs from Virgina and fly back to New York.

My work fires me. I have two weeks left of classes at HB.
I don't go.

Heather and Beth are graduating and leaving in a couple of weeks and giving up the apartment. I have no plan. Depression is lurking. Summer is around the corner and I have no intention on sticking around. I can't spend a summer at my parent's house. Again I have no money and I'm trying to get back to Nantucket for the summer. Just because.

I end up getting a painting gig and I'm able to save $700 in three weeks then I split for the island again.

While in Nantucket I write Professor Charles Milne at NYU, he teaches Narrative One filmmaking. He grants me an interview in the middle of August and I take it.

I say, "Professor I'm just an actor who wants to learn behind the scenes of filmmaking, would it be cool if I sat in?" He says, "If you can get into my classroom without having any school identification. I will put you on attendance."

"No Problem."

I show up the first day with a coffee tray in my hand filled with coffee cups and a book bag over my shoulder. I approach the school's doors and gesture to the security guards to open the door and they do. "What's up, gentleman, I got some coffee for ya." They immediately take it.

"My name is Wolfgang Klein."

"Hey Wolfgang. Thanks, I'm Felix and that's Johnson."

"Can you tell me where Charles Milnes Class is?" They point right and say,

"Up those stairs and turn left."

"Thanks guys."

That was it. After that I was never asked for an NYU ID.

I sit in and I have no idea what the fuck is going on. First, Narrative One is not the beginning of filmmaking; it's like second year filmmaking. I'm lost. But I go with it.

The professor divides the class into 5 groups of six. Each group gets to make six short films, one for each student. Everyone gets a turn of directing their own film. And then you work various positions on others. Sound, lighting, producing, editing, camera, tech.

I watch what's going and sort of float by for months. Maybe holding a boom. Finding locations, running errands. But when it comes my turn to make my own short film on 16mm, I get to write it, direct it, it's mine. But I can't come up with the thousand bucks for the actual film and it's embarrassing.
I disappear.

I move back to Trumbull.

All my friends are graduating college, moving forward. I have no plan. My plan usually consisted of partying and women and in whatever order, didn't matter.
After spending months apart, Elizabeth calls. She misses me. I miss her. She invites me to her graduation but I decline. Still we get back together again.

I don't work.

My friend Mike is taking summer classes at UConn that summer so he can graduate. He is living in off campus housing with some of his bullshit frat boys. I don't like frat boys, there is something gay about them. Mike was from Trumbull and he could care less about his fraternity.
It's June and Mike's roommate just got a shipment of 14 pounds of pot. In two days' time the pot was going to Buffalo, New York. I get the phone call from Mike at my mom's house. "Bro, come to my house at 11:30 I will be at the bar with my brothers".
That was code for break into my house and rob these motherfuckers. I do and ransack the fuck out of the place, I grab the 14 pounds of pot and in two trips I load up my trunk.
Mike leaves UConn with his degree two days later.
Back in Trumbull we split up the weed and that's my income for four months.

September rolls around and Elizabeth gets a job as a personal shopper at major retailer in Manhattan. She and her friend Pam get an apartment together in midtown. Pam's boyfriend Johnny moves in and so do I. We don't work.
Johnny's a trust fund baby and gets ten grand a clip whenever he calls his father. I'm broke. We spend the days playing video games while the girls work. I can't do any criminal activity because I live with Elizabeth and she wouldn't approve. She supports me. I feel like a loser again.

I try to get a waitering job but I give up after a few interviews. I hate myself and it shows. I split on the weekends back to Trumbull to hang with my friends, then Sunday I return to New York. I do this for 7 or 8 months. Elizabeth can sense that I'm not happy and I'm sure she's wondering what kind of man I am. I am an unstable man. Sleep all day, jobless. Depressed all the time.

Spring is here and my boys rent a house in Newport, Rhode Island for the summer. They use it as a weekend house. I spend the whole summer there working as a painter.
Elizabeth comes and visits a few times, but I have the feeling that this is the end. I don't blame her, I have no future. I could never give her what she needs.

After a few weeks I don't show up for work because I'm always hung over and the shitty wage I'm getting isn't worth it. I'm being taken advantage of.
Fuck it.

I can survive with nothing and do. I party just as hard as if I had a job and fuck more girls.

Depression is now is a daily feeling. I fucking hate it. I tell my friends this and they can't understand why. My buddy Dave says, "How can you be depressed, you're at the beach every day, in the bars at night, and you have women all around you"
He's right but I can't escape this feeling.

I start to loathe myself.

Elizabeth and I break up but still hang out from time to time. When I see her it just reminds me of what a loser I am, that I can't get my shit together enough to make her happy.

The summer ends. I go back to Trumbull.

I need to get out of here. I don't want to be seen. I don't want to see people I know and have them ask me, "So what are you doing now?" I don't want to lie. My parents open my mail and every time it's an argument. I can't get a job. I can't work for minimum wage.

Fuck it. I'm goin back to Cali.

I suck it up and get a painting gig with a few guys I know. I hate it but do it anyway.

I save some cash, not much.

On Friday I get a call from my buddy Bud.

I met Bud in the fourth grade in Trumbull and after 2 years his parents moved to Westport, CT.

I always saw Bud through the years and when he went to UConn we reunited. Bud is one of my friends that traffics pot with me. He is one crazy mother. He is very smart, good looking, and cunning. He does not come from a modest family - both his parents are lawyers and well off. The weirdest thing about Bud is that he will never let you know what he's thinking.

"Hello."

"Hey guy, it's Bud."

"What's up my man?"

"Seeing what's going on with you."

"Nothing. I'm trying to get out of here, Bud. I want to take off to California"

"What's in California?"

"I'm gonna try to sell a script. A screenplay. But first I have to put some of it on paper...'

Pause.

"Bud, Bud. You there?"

"Yeah yeah. You're going to do what?

"I'm going to try to sell a screenplay"

"That's what I thought you said. How are you going to do that?"

"Well I have a laptop with a screenwriting app. Hopefully by the time I get out to Cali, I will have a good portion done and then you know, try to sell it."

"When are you going, Klein?"

"Trying to get out of here next week sometime"

"Call me the day before you leave. I'm going with you."

"For real?"

"Fuck yeah."

"Cool..!"

I beg my father to please by me a laptop. I tell him I need it if I want to be making movies. Then I tell him I'm moving to California again. He has heard all this before. I beg some more and start doing chores around the house. Then I hit my mother up. I badger her until she can't take it, then she convinces my father to buy me one. He does because he's a good man, It's the cheapest laptop you can find and I'm grateful. I then purchase the screenwriting cd.

The last time I see Elizabeth is at her apartment the day before I leave, we had gone out the night before for drinks and I slept over.
On the couch.
My heart is broken.

She is being very nice and kind and sweet and in the morning she invites me into her bed. That's the first time in a long time we make love and the last time. While we lay next to each other her phone rings.
"Hello, oh hi," she goes. "Yes. Ok, Apartment 34M. 7ish? Sure see you then. Bye."

My heart drops

"Who was that?
She doesn't say anything for a second, then: "This guy I met in the Hamptons."

FUCK FUCK FUCK THE HAMPTONS.

"Oh really? Is it something serious?" I'm trying to be calm but all these images are racing thru my mind, I can't handle this.
I take a deep breath.
"Nooo," she smiles. "He just asked me out and this will be our first date." She can see I'm about to break down
"Wolfgang, Wolfgang. Listen, you're moving to California tomorrow, you're going to do great things .We have spent eight years together and you will always have a place in my heart."
I look at her dead in the face and say, "You going to tell that guy tonight when he goes to kiss you where your mouth was just a few hours before?" She looks at me with hatred.

I look away.
I open the door and walk out. This is the last time I see her. As I walk down the hallway I break down. Why Why WHY did I do that. I am the weak one. I am ashamed.
It's too late to apologize, I said it. It's done.

I hate myself.

California2

There are no cell phones, Bud and I are driving our own cars, he has a Toyota Land Cruiser and I've got a Volkswagen Jetta. In the middle of the night we lose each other in Pennsylvania. That's it, how are we going to find each other? We don't even have a destination. I drive two and a half hours before I see his truck on the interstate. We sleep at a truck stop in our cars and all I can think about is Elizabeth. I don't sleep. I have $1383 to my name.

We reach Boulder, Colorado with no problems so far. We meet up with my buddy Chris from Trumbull for a day. We party, but just the usual - pot, mushrooms, booze, one hit of LSD, and a fuck load of nitrous. Everything is right for the moment. Finally.

Morning comes and we say our goodbyes still high from the night. I jump in my car and head onto the Interstate West with Bud behind me. A few hours go by and I blow my water pump.
I guess it's the altitude.

My car barely makes it into this one horse town, Idaho Springs, Colorado. It's one road in the center of town that's surrounded by mountains. It's nothing.

One or two motels sit on the side of the road. Up from them is a gas station. The mechanic says he can fix it but it would take a day. It's 11am. Fuck, the mechanic had eyeballs tattooed on his eyelids.

I think shit, don't fuck with this guy. "So, when you say a day do you mean 24 hours?" He blinks, flashing me the tatts.
"That's what I mean, by 11am tomorrow you'll be ready to go."
I ask him how much and he spits out, "Three-hundred and fifty dollars."
Fuck. Plus I have to pay for a motel room. $59.
"O.K. guy, it's all yours," I say.

Bud is nice enough to split the room.

"Since we've got time to kill let's work on our scripts," He says. I say, "Yeah but let's walk to the sandwich shop and grab some lunch first." He agrees and we go. Our view from the window that we eat at displays the town. More nothing. Openness with a vast mountain range, blue-blue sky. Warm. It's October 3rd 1995.
"Bud you know what we're going to do today?"

"Tell me."

I point out the window to the lonely blond 18yr old girl selling fruit on the side of the road and say, "I'm going to fuck her today."
He believes me.
In three minutes I'm buying fruit from this 18yr old white trash chick, she's got tattoos on her back and possibly has a meth problem because she's so fucking skinny.
"So me and my friend Bud here had a little car trouble and we will be stayin' here for a few days. Do you know where to party?"
She stands up and sticks out her chest. "Well we usually rent out rooms in those motels and drink there."
"Really, that's great because we have a room right over there. Room 31. What time do you get off?"
"3," she says.
Great, what's your name?"
"Mandy."
Mandy, I'm Wolfgang and as soon as you're done with work you're more than welcome to come on over and have a few beers."
I walk away with a cantaloupe but I don't have a knife to cut it.
Now we are sitting in the motel room with time to kill before things get ugly. Bud is typing.
I'm smoking pot, thinking what did I just get myself into. I feel that this girl is bad news and I made a mistake. But fuck it, we all dig our own graves.
And so deeper I dig and it's ugly and ridiculous.
And then off we go, shaking that Nothing town with its shadows off our stiniking hides like the animals we are.

It's my second time in Vegas. The first time was when I was living in Durango.

Bud and I can't find a hotel room anywhere so we head down to old Vegas. That's the spot you want to be at anyway.
We get a cheap dive off the strip for 19.99, it's a piece of shit but who cares, we're here to make some money. Bud had made prior arrangements before we left to meet his friend Renat in Las Vegas. I've met her before at Phish shows and at Uconn. Renat is down. Renat's two friends she brought with her, not so cool.

At the Horseshoe.

My method to blackjack is this - if I could down my full drink of gin and tonic by the time the dealer is done dealing, I would win that hand. Bud likes my method and does the same. It works up until the 11th hand. Renat is sitting between me and Bud, watching the antics unfold at 2 dollars a bet. The dealer is an Asian of some sort, and she no like us. The more we drink the more belligerent we're getting and my method no longer works but I continue on drinking and gambling. Bud and I don't leave the table for 5 hours. Not even to piss.

The dealer says in her Asian accent, "I dink somebo'y spill their drink."
I quickly put away my cock.

She looks under the table and says, "I dink sombo'y peeing on me!"
I see Bud squirm and put his cock away.

Renat is just realizing that these two men have been urinating on the dealer all night. She gets up and leaves and at that moment the pit bosses walk up. "Guys, we are going to comp you food at our casino restaurant. Please get up now and follow us."

I'm so fucked up I leave my chips on the table and stumble into the restaurant. Buds eyes roll back in his head but he is still holding a conversation with the hostess. Renat and her two friends join us at the table. The waiter walks up.

"Now what can I get you?" he's looking at Bud and I shout out "YOU CAN SUCK MY DICK."

In a second I'm being dragged from the table and literally thrown out of the casino and onto the street. No joke.

The next day we are so hung over we decide to sleep in and leave the following day. Renat and her friends had enough of our bullshit and wouldn't return calls.

Since we have the room for another night and we are feeling much better by 8pm, we decide to gamble a little bit so we can recoup our losses from the night before.

We won't drink and we will gamble smart. RIGHT.

By midnight I'm seeing double and trying desperately to fuck Kay the dealer. She is amused by this and playing my side with the cards. I'm up. I'm feeling good; this chick is into me. Bud's makin' money. California is going to be great. Life is good.

I get caught up in the moment and I'm standing at the table and I unzip my pants and pull out my dick. No one sees. I begin to piss and I can't stop. I see piss trails coming from underneath the table onto the open floor. I can't stop pissing.

It feels good so fuck it.

Next thing I know, I'm on my back, my cock like a loose fire hose spraying everywhere. I look up to see the bouncer that decked me and two cops. They pull me to my feet and I make eye contact with Kay, I can tell immediately tell my chances are slim now. As I'm being dragged away I scream, "BUD TAKE MY CHIPS AND THROW IT ON BLACK"

I beg the cops not to arrest me, "Sir, why did they keep serving me when they know better? I'm the victim here. You guys poison me to the point where I become impaired so you can take all of my cash. I was literally in a comatose state, I thought I was home."

Another gentleman walks into the room. He tells me to sign this piece of paper.

I do. I don't read it.

"O.K. Mr. Klein. This incident has just been documented. You are no longer welcome in any of Binions casino. You are barred. If caught on the premises again, you will be prosecuted."

"Thank you sir."

Around 3:30 am Bud comes back to the room.

"Look what I got, Wolf. $823 for you! I like how you always bet on your race."

We decide a strip joint would be the best thing to do and we take off. Again with the booze and now I'm spending the only bit of money I have to my name on lap dances and hand jobs. I've got to get out of Nevada before it sucks me dry.

Daryl Patterson is six years older than me, his younger brother Dale is only two years older. They are from Trumbull. I painted with Daryl's best friend Sean for a summer and he hooked me up with Daryl who now lives in Pacific Beach, San Diego.

So that became our destination.

L.A. would have been the smarter choice but we don't know anyone.

This tall beautiful Pilipino girl answers the door. Holy shit.
"Hello, is Daryl here?" I ask.
"No I'm sorry, he's not." She starts to laugh "You guys are Wolfgang and Bud..!"
"Yes."
"Daryl is at the Jimmy Buffet concert, should be back soon."
We walk into the house and start drinking.

Daryl and his buddies return from the show and it becomes a party, Bud and I wake up on the couches the next morning.

I see Bud flipping the pillows because he pissed himself. Daryl wakes up, cooks us breakfast, and says, "I will help you guys get on your feet the same way someone helped me when I arrived here 10 years ago. We pay it forward here." Daryl is a real nice guy, soft spoken, kind, and generous. He has his own construction company. You would never think that this guy is the ultimate scam artist.

After weeks of lying around the house and getting fucked up every night, Daryl tells us we've got to go. We have one week to get our shit straight.

Gumby is Daryl's roommate. He is a sales rep for a power tool company. His girlfriend Dawn works for a commercial contractor. She gets me a job painting apartment buildings for 10 bucks an hour. I work with white trash skin heads from Palm Desert. I hate it but I need the money to get a pad for myself.

Bud and I go apartment hunting and we come across this pad 3 blocks from the beach. The girl tells us that her roommate moved out and she is taking off to L.A. She's got to break the lease unless she can sublet it. She tells us we can also keep all the furniture for a price.
Bud and I can't afford it so we move on.

We move closer to the ghetto and a block from the beach. We live at 10591/2 Hornblend Ave. The rent is $675 a month for two bedrooms. We have no furniture, no beds, no silverware.

We celebrate at the bar across the street called Stingers. We never pay for a drink, never. The bartender is from Stamford, CT, and never gives a bill, we don't even tip him, we just drink.

A week later we are driving by the first apartment we looked at, the girl is in the process of moving out. All the furniture was being stored outside in this bullshit open carport. We noticed that her car wasn't there. Trip after trip we are able to steal every piece of furniture during the day. We had matching couches a television stand. I got the bed in a coin toss and Bud got the dressers. We had a shower curtain and towels, sheets. Blankets. Bud found a mattress and box spring on the side of the road and brought it home and wrapped it in cellophane then put a sheet on it. We stole a city garbage can and used it as ours, we went to Goodwill and bought dishes for a dollar. Bud brought a T.V from CT in the back of his truck along with his stereo and cds. We had a nice apartment. Home sweet home.

After 3 weeks I quit my job. I can't work like this, I hate the uneducated simple minded fucks I work with.

White Trash.

I quit. Fuck you.

The apartment building I live in is a two story U shaped building with a courtyard in the middle. You can see everybody's business. My door is right next to Keith and Dave's, 40 yr. old coke dealers. Everyone in the complex tells us to stay away from those guys.

So one day I need to borrow a vacuum cleaner and knock on Keith's door and introduce myself. This guy looked the part. "Tall, skinny, gaunt and wirery. We make small talk and he gives me his vacuum.

When I return it 15 minutes later he had a gram of coke wrapped up in a cigarette wrapper.

"Here this is for you," and he hands it to me.

I take it and say thanks not knowing what's inside. I enter my pad and show Bud. He says, "The first one is always free. As soon as you do that you'll always be buying blow from that crack head." I have never done cocaine up until this point. I'm 25.

I do it and it's nothing. No big deal.

We have no jobs and everywhere we apply turns us down. Bud has a degree, I do not. I try every place for a job - rent a car places, pizza delivery, bartender, waiter, Mason work, nothing,

We end up working for Daryl. He's putting a draining system in a house in La Jolla, plus remodeling the whole interior. It was a three million dollar house. Over time we realize he is just winging it, he doesn't know what the fuck he's doing. He gives Bud and I a job, digging ditches alongside illegals, jackhammering hard clay 8 ft. down.

My parents were right. They said my whole life if I didn't pay attention in school I would be digging ditches. Well you win. You're right.

I dig a hole so fucking deep that Bud and I can sleep in it. No one can see us. We drink Jack Daniels every night in our apartment then go out to Stingers. We hide in 100ft pine trees at work so no one can find us. We get paid 7 dollars an hour. We have to get paid at the end of each day. We are always hung-over. We raid the women's refrigerator who's house we work at. We work maybe 5 hours a day 3 or 4 days a week.

STILL BROKE.

Bud works on his script in his free time, every day he goes to the coffee shop and works. I follow but can't write, my mind can't concentrate so I chat up what girls are in the shop.
And wait for night to fall.

We buy day old chicken because it's cheaper, we figure just cook it longer. Two sisters from Boston move to the left side of my pad. We fuck them whenever we want. And they cook us dinner. Good people. We still have no jobs. Daryl is fed-up with us and only gives us shit jobs to do. I decline most of the time, unless I really need it.

We drink Jack Daniels and Coke every day. Our apartment is decorated with Jack bottles. We seem to always have pocket money $10 or fifteen dollars. Never rent money or electric.

At the last minute I put an ad in the newspaper for Michael's Painting. I get a call to paint a bathroom and a small kitchen.
Great.

I do it in two days and make $550 cash. I pay my share of the month rent. Bud is always a better money manager than me and works more often with Daryl.

I pay $335 and the rest is for partying. I like how things work out. I buy Jack and Coke and no food. The refrigerator is empty. We have electric bills that we throw out. Every night is a party. We still drink for free at Stingers and at this point I buy my first bindle of cocaine.
I like it.
I really, really like it. The euphoric feeling, everything positive.
I feel invincible.

Of course only for a short period of time then I need more. The next morning I have $65 left. Not bad.

We make it last a week and we spend our mornings at the coffee shop.

Bud writes, I give up.

Then we go downtown. Not downtown San Diego but *downtown*, code for the Porn Palace. We could kill a good hour downtown. The Porn Palace is a huge porn shop that sells everything porn and in the back they have real nice porn booths.
Clean, way cleaner than NYC.
They have nice leather seats big enough for two.
They have one big screen with smaller multiple screens and multiple channels underneath it. There is so much porn being thrown at you, it's porn overload. You spend 10 minutes searching hundreds of pornos and then the last two you go back to, the ones you checked off in the back of your head. It's fun.
I'm trying to jerkoff when something catches my eye. A little piece of paper slipped under the door. I pick it up and it reads, "FREE GOOD HEAD". I wait and crack the door and I see these little Asian fucks slipping notes under other doors. I shut the door and go back to business.

On the drive back, neither Bur nor I say a word.

I start buying cocaine from my cracked out neighbors, they would sell me $10, $20, $30, however much money I had.

One night leaving the bar a local comes up to Bud and me, asking us where we're from. We say New York. We can see this guy is tweaked out on crank. He has PB Vermon tattooed on his neck. He tells us that he doesn't like east coasters coming out for the winter and showing no respect to the locals.
You've got to be kidding me.
He follows us to the Circle K parking lot and now he has a few of his boys with them. FUCK. "Hey man, " I say. "We moved here 3 months ago, do you know Daryl Patterson?"
"Why the fuck would I know him?" The tattooed freak says.
"I don't know, what's your prob..."
The fucker clocks me dead in the nose. I hear the crunch. Blood all over my face and shirt and in my eyes. That's the third time my nose was broken, I will not get it fixed.
Bud has a glass beer mug the whole time, he left the bar with it and is sipping it until he pours it upside down and bashes it into this motherfucker's

face. The guy couldn't stand up after 3 shots to the face. His friends run off. And so do we.

Circle K has cameras, need to lay low now.

I'm a scumbag.

I call my mother and tell her I was in a fight and I'm going to get arrested if I don't make restitution. I tell her I was playing pool with some local piece of shit and I was winning, so the guy became threatening towards me. I told him to get out of my face but he didn't. So I whacked him with the pool stick in the mouth. And now I have to pay for his teeth. Oh yeah, try not to tell Dad.

She sends the money and I'm positive she doesn't believe me.

I shop at Goodwill. Never go to the beach. Mostly out every night. Give up on the job, can't write shit, Bud can write. I feel guilty all the time so I escape that feeling by catching a buzz, everything is in perspective when I'm buzzed.
Money is low again, but I do my best work under pressure.
Things look good on the surface but they are far from it. Weeks go by with no ambition. Days of paralyzing guilt. Can't get out of bed. Got to get these horrific thoughts out of my mind. I miss Elizabeth and hate that I can't live a normal life. I have night terrors all the time unless I pass out. I always see the sunrise from the night before. I try again to get a job, any job, but no luck.
I take a road trip to Rosarita, Mexico with the Boston girls and their friends from home. I have 10 bucks. We drive Karen's car over the border. I'm the only male in the group (Bud stayed back because he's smart). We spend the day at some beach bar where they serve 1 dollar tequila shots. I do ten of them and then suck back a few of the girls' beers. I convince them to let me drive back.
I have one eye closed driving really fast down dark dirt roads. Everyone is screaming. Finally I pull over a mile from the border and let Karen drive her own car. We get to the border and she is pulled over for suspicion of drunk driving.
Shit…
I don't speak Spanish.

I tell the girls to give me forty dollars and I will get them out of here. I put twenty in my pocket and approach the border patrol. I motion with my hands that I will drive and flash him the other twenty. I walk over and escort Karen to the front passenger seat, and shake the Mexican's hand, sliding him the twenty.

We drive thru.

Everybody hates me.

I drive calm back to the beach and then bust out partying once I meet up with Bud.

Our lifestyle consists of booze, bush and blow. Every night is a bigger and crazier drug fest. How can I sleep or hold a job when all these fun things are going on?

The bar closes at 2am and then reopens at 6am. Kind of odd. We were wondering what type of people show up at a bar at 6am. So one night Bud and I drink til 2, leave the bar to go get the cocaine, and in a matter of no time the sun is up and we're back at the bar, 6am on the dot.

Not the usual bartender, it's now some old guy, maybe 65 or so. He doesn't like us.

We call him Coach.

By 6:15 the bar is packed again and the only time you see the morning sun is when someone opens the front door.

We get thrown out at 8 in the morning. I guess the old guy didn't like our antics.

We go home and drink till we pass out.

Rent is due again. And that really depresses me. We have no food. Our friend Mike from Trumbull is coming out to S.D. to do a lighting gig for some corporate company. He will be here for five days. The first night we take him to the usual joint. Stingers. We drink all the gin in the house. Then he asks me, "Can you get pharmaceuticals? Pills?"

"Where?" I ask, really not knowing, no idea.

"Go to Mexico, my boss will pay a shit load for pain killers, morphine, percs, oxy, benzos. Whatever. Do you think you can get them?"

I think about for one second. "I need the money up front"

"No shit." He says.

The next day I get $700 cash and a list of pills I need to get.

I know this is a bad idea. I don't think anyone in my family would be proud. I tried to get a job. I would like to work but right now this is my only option. I can't call home again.

Bud wants no part of it but he's willing to come along and watch. Fuck it. If God didn't want me to do this he would not have put the opportunity in front of me.

I justify it.

I park far away from the border and walk across. We are in Tijuana walking up Revolution Ave. Every Mexican is trying to get us into their bar for drinks. Loud music and a few under age gringo girls, I mean under 21. We go in. Immediately this fucker is pouring cheap tequila down our throats. Then I order two margaritas so we can get our heads straight and think of a plan.

Two blocks up is a farmicia. The deal is whatever price I can negotiate the pills for, I get to keep the rest. But I'm going to keep it all. We drink two more margaritas and go. It's a shithole drugstore and the little fuck behind the counter makes eye contact with me and instantly he's in my face. He knows what I'm looking for.

"No Espanola," I say.

"That's ok, my friend"

"I need to go in the backroom."

"You have prescription?" he asks

"I didn't need one last time, man. C'mon you know me. I aint no gringo tourist." I'm lying. I was never there.

"You need prescription!" He points across the street to a doctor's office.

"How much?"

"50."

"No,' I pull out forty from my pocket and put it in his hand. "Fuck prescription."

He takes it and leads me into the back. Bud is standing by the door. A shoe box emerges from underneath a floor board.

HOLY SHIT.

Bottles of Valium, Oxycodone, liquid Morphine, Fentanyl patches. Somas. Diazepam. Vicodent.. DEMEROL.

I'm trying to negotiate pills and now this fuck doesn't understand English. Each time I pull a bottle out to look at it, I stick one in my pocket.

Bud starts a little commotion up front by knocking into a stand.

My guy takes his eyes off me for a split second. And that's it. I grab all the Fentanyl patches and stick them by my balls and I grab a bottle of Demerol.

I give the guy a hundred bucks and tell him I'm taking one bottle of Valium (90 pills) and one bottle of Vicodent (80 pills in 2 bottles). A half bottle of Percs. (40 10mlg pills) and 60 Diazepam (in 2 bottles). And hurry my ass out of the store and take a few lefts and rights to get off the main strip. That 700 hundred is now 500, 60 on drinks and 140 on pills. The rest is mine. I have rent money and a little left over for food. I have 6 pill bottles filled to the top and 8 Fentanyl patches in my jeans. I don't wear underwear. Every time I walk I can hear the pills shake.

We go to a strip bar to celebrate our semi victory. Dirty Mexican whores are on us as soon as we sit down, "Cervaza! Cervaza! Buy me cervaza!" Seven whores vying for attention, I don't mind but they keep putting their hands on my cock and rubbing my thighs.
They can blatantly feel the pills.

I'm freaked out a bit. Bud could give a fuck and keeps on buying these whores drinks. I need to get the fuck out of here. These whores want to get fucked and that's what I'm going to do.

I leave with the hottest one and as soon as I walk into the sunlight my buzz kicks in. Bud is right behind me with his own toot. We sneak into a shithole bar, no gringos. I go into the bathroom and crack open a bottle of Valium, I swallow four.

I go back to the bar and make everyone do shots of tequila and order a round of margaritas, all the locals are laughing AT me, I think they are laughing WITH me. More shots and some Mexican shit beer. I finally feel ok, my nerves have calmed down. For now. These whores take us to a motel made out of rock, stone. It cost a dollar for the room and $24 for the rubber.
Things don't feel right.
The border is about 4 miles away.
I don't speak Spanish.

Bud and I are sharing a room with these two pigs and everything is made of stone, the walls the floor the steps, the shelves, the fucking bed frame. Bud's chick decides to take a shit with the door open and converse in Spanish with her friend.

The more I look at my chick the more she looks like a man who had a huge tit operation. I got a bad feeling. Why is that chick taking her time taking a shit in front of us? Why are they killing time? They already felt me up and know my pockets are filled with narcotics; you'd have to be stupid if you can't see the outlining of plastic pill bottles bursting out of my slacks. We're about to get robbed.

Bud and I don't say a word to each other. I pull up my pants. He opens the door and we bolt down two flights of stairs, jumping eight steps at a time.

It's dark out and we stumble into a clothing shack down a side road. The woman is selling suede leather jackets. The real deal. You could tell by the stitching and the cuts that she made them. I take the terracotta color. I buy Bud the dark brown one, these jackets have no lining in them its straight rawhide. One of a kind, we look good. It's 83 degrees.

The border is in our view. We have to walk thru both Mexican agents and U.S. At this point a few drinks sound like a good idea so we turn into a bar. "Just tequila please and none of that cheap tourist shit," I tell the bartender. "I'm paying cash. Hook me up, amigo." He brings over his best bottle which tastes like shit and it's warm. Bud and I drink the last half of the bottle just by passing it back and forth.

The Valium is making me feel woozy.

I give that Mexican 60 dollars and run outside and violently puke on the street. "I swear that guy was serving us gasoline."
I have to piss, and I can see the agents 30 yards ahead of me. I'm in line and I have to piss. I'm wearing sunglasses at night. My body shakes with pills every step I take. I have long hair covering my eyes. My white v neck t-shirt has dirt and puke on it. I look shady.
"Bud, do you see that McDonalds on the U.S side?"
"Yeah."
"If anyone tries to put their hands on me going thru the turnstile, I'm fighting until I get on the U.S side."
"You think that's a good idea, they can see right over there."
"I rather be arrested in San Diego than fuckin' Tijuana!"
"Good point. You're fucked."
"Thanks."
I take the soda cup I was drinking from and pop open the lid. I don't say anything and put it down in front of my crotch, I unzip and poke the head of my dick in the cup and fill it to the top. I put the lid back on with the straw sticking up. No one knows shit. Every step closer, my heart beats slower.

Every time I hear it beat, I have a childhood memory. I think of my parents. I walk closer to the line, I see the agents ripping apart a car to my right. I think of my Elizabeth and how she wouldn't approve of this.

I don't show any emotion, I'm in a trance. I act like I am a sipping thru the straw. I walk right thru. Never taking off the sunglasses. No nod of the head, no thank you. And no looking back. I walk straight to the parking lot a quarter of a mile away. Bud was few hundred feet back to see if I was being followed. Nothing is spoken and we drive 27 miles back to P.B.

I got a shit load of pills spread out on my bed.

I separate the pills and fill two bottles with a variety of sorts for Mike's boss Jahean. I tell Mike that he owes me more money because the pills were more expensive this time. He laughs.

I have just over $200 left, not enough for rent. I could sell the extra drugs I have, but what is the point, as soon I get cash I'm going to turn around and buy more drugs. Plus I got the real good shit. I trade some benzos and a patch for 4 grams of coke. I'm all set now.

Gotta make rent.

After getting jacked up on coffee one morning at the shop, I can't sit still as always. Bud can type fast and he is moving along on his screenplay. I act like I'm working. I have my laptop out, a cup of coffee on my right. Any chick that walks in and buys my bullshit sees that I look the part. I write nothing. I am wasting time. I am full of shit.

I need to get rid of my anxiety feeling so I'm going downtown to jerkoff. The best way to spend five bucks.

Bud declined. "Dude it's only 10:30 in the morning, save that shit for the evening before we cook."

"No I gotta go."

It's hot as hell outside and the parking lot is filled. Don't people work? Who the hell is jerking off in the middle of the day?

I park across the way at the Jack in the Box parking lot. I walk in and browse the video wall and try to make up my mind which movie, which 100 movies I want to scan through. Then I see these little Asian men roaming around the store.

Are they gay? Or are they pimping out girls? What's their deal? I make sure I make eye contact with one of them. I walk into a booth and slide in a ten dollar bill. That's gives about 17 minutes of porn play. I wait. I turn the volume up as loud as it can go. My minutes are going down so I put another five in the machine. My dick isn't even out. I wait and then I see the little white paper slip underneath the door. "FREE GOOD HEAD." I unlock the lock. And it's loud.

The Asian steps in and puts his finger over his mouth, "Ssshhh." It's tight inside this 4x4 booth. I shut the door and he motions for me to take off my pants. I grab him by the throat with two fingers, my thumb and pointer, and apply such force he starts squirming. I take my right hand and grab the back of his head and smash it into the television screen. BOOM. This guy drops, dead weight.

I have to move his body away from the door and prop it up on the seat. I fish in my pocket for more cash and pull out a five. Time is about to run out and I slide the bill in. I have about five minutes of movies going. I reach in all of his pockets, take his wallet, and $215 in his jacket. Then some thing tells me to take off his shoes. I slip off his loafers and I can see a wad of cash in his sock.

I take it.

I peek out the door and the coast is clear. I walk over to the sex toys and mingle a little with the cashier. My heart drops and I begin to shake. I don't see anymore Asians anywhere. Kind of weird.

I walk outside into the bright light and cross the busy fairway. I walk behind Jack in the Box and count the money. That fuck had 7 hundred in his sock plus the 200 in his jacket. Not a bad score.
Wallet I throw out.

I walk into the backdoor and sit inside while eating a cheeseburger. I watch across the street. Twenty minutes later I see the Asian fuck leave with two of his little buddies. They drive away in a Lexus.
No Cops.
For some reason I don't feel so bad.

Everyone I know is starting a career, some friends are even getting married, but everyone has a good job.
And I am always one week away from being homeless.
I don't understand why I can't get a job. I'm clean, no tattoos, well dressed, a pretty good made up resume. I have all my teeth. But I can't find a job worth shit. That's not true.

I'm sure I could find a job at the supermarket for minimum wage. Fuck that. I can't be confined to one spot for a certain amount of time. I would be staring at the clock all the time. And minimum wage is not going to support my partying ways. My time is more valuable to me.

Can't sleep at night, all the ruffling around in Bud's room is keeping me on edge. His bed is still wrapped in cellophane, it makes the worst noise. After a month Bud decides he doesn't need the plastic on the bed anymore. Every time he pissed his bed he said he would always wake up in a pool of piss, and he told me he was afraid of drowning in his sleep. Now he just saturates the bed, which he says is also a good thing because of all the lit cigarettes he falls asleep with are definitely out because the mattress is so soiled nothing can stay lit in that thing.

I need to start writing a script. But I can't. Can't do it. Nothing to write about. I'm a farce.

Bud is working everyday on his, and I must say I'm pretty impressed on how he can just bang this out. I have something wrong with me. I can't concentrate long enough to sit still. I make up excuses. The girls at the coffee shop think we are the shit. All we do is talk movie crap to them and tell them how we go back and forth to L.A for meetings. Bullshit. They eat it up. Free coffee every day and sometimes a pill here and there.

One by one I see everyone in the apartment complex eventually knocking on Keith's door. He has the complex hooked on his crappy blow including me. But I don't really pay for it. I scam two other guys I know who ask me for coke, I just double the price.

Haven't met any nice girls here. I see them, I just haven't met them yet. I have no wrap. I have no money. I have no confidence. I never once went into the ocean but have two surf boards on are wall to impress chicks. We took them from Daryl.

The days suck. Try to sleep the sunlight away. Always have an unsettling feeling. I told my family I was coming to California to write scripts and haven't done shit.

Big let down. I'm full of shit.

It's Christmastime and everyone I know is leaving to go back east. New York. Trumbull. New Jersey. I tell my family I'm not coming home. Even when they offer to buy me a plane ticket I decline. My mother gets upset. My father says I'm on drugs. I don't want to return home, it will remind me too much of Elizabeth. It will make me lie to friends and family when they ask me, "So what are you doing now?" Because the truth would scare the fuck out them.

3 days before Christmas and I'm all alone. I receive a care package from my folks, some baked cookies, package of socks and underwear (I haven't worn underwear or socks since I was 13), shaving cream and an envelope with $400 cash in it.

I go straight to Stingers and start sucking back Jacks, in my own world when this chick and a dude come in and sit next to me. The girl is in the middle. We make small talk and introduce ourselves. Her name is Laura. I forget what other bullshit I said. But she asks if I'm going to be here for a while. I nod and say I believe so. She leaves with the dude she came with. I drink. Strong drink.

When she returns solo I'm in the dark stages.

She tells me she is a student and she's going back home to Cherry Hill, New Jersey in 2 days. I tell her I have no home, I tell her my parents were killed in a plane wreck less than a year ago. She starts to tear up. I embrace her and tell her it's ok. Laura is a skinny brunette with tits too big for her frame. She's hot and she doesn't wear any underwear either.

I wake up and look to my left and can't believe I got this hottie in my bed. I must have blacked out. Can't remember shit. We are both naked. I wake her up by going down on her.

We go out for breakfast and she tells me she has to go to her apartment to do a few things before she leaves for home the next day. Cool. Then she returns while I'm vacuuming my pad.

What a good holiday it's been so far.

We take off in my car to Tijuana for lunch and drinks. We find a little hole in the wall Mexican joint and drink Margaritas. She is all over me, on my lap, constantly kissing me. This chick might be a nympho, I fuck her standing up in the dirty bathroom. We drink more and then eat. It's now ten at night, I'm pretty juiced.

We walk back over the border towards my car and I see that Laura's cold so I buy her a sweater. We get back to my apartment around midnight and get naked for a few hours before we fall asleep.

I wake up realizing that I spent pretty much all my money on this chick and she is leaving tonight. I take her to breakfast and we go back and sleep and fuck the rest of the day.

Laura drives an old 1968 Volkswagen wagon. It's pretty cool. She says she wants to take me to this huge sushi place, so we go, she drives. This place is fucking huge and filled with a lot of people, I don't like the smell. But I deal with it. We sit and order.

I can't believe I got this smoking chick sitting in front of me, she's a little stupid but I can get over it. She takes off her flip flop and starts rubbing my balls under the table. I have to get her back home for one last sex session before she jumps on her 11 o'clock flight.

My big left toe is in a full cramp. I've never had this happen before. It's the worst Charlie horse in my life and it's in my toe. Very uncomfortable, Laura can see I'm uncomfortable. I get up to go to the men's room and I look like a gimp.

She drives me back to my apartment and at this time my whole left leg is cramped. Hard. I can tell this is going to be a problem. I've never felt anything like it, so I try to fuck her missionary with a stiff leg and it doesn't work out too well. It's getting late and she's got to leave. She hugs and kisses me and I walk her to the door. When she is leaving, my friend Barry comes walking in. "Dude what's wrong with you?" he laughs.

I'm hunched over because now my lower back and legs are so cramped I'm almost paralyzed. He says, "Shake it off. Let's go get a drink." "Fuck you, Barry." I start cleaning my pad, hiding the bong and the coke mirror, putting a bag of pills in the ceiling, I start vacuuming again. I am in pain and I know very soon I'm going to have to call the ambulance. It's getting worse. My neck and shoulders I can't move, my hands and fingers are so cramped they look like claws.

I dial 911 and Barry takes off.

The operator is being a douche. She keeps making me repeat myself.

The flashing red lights freak out the crackheads next door and everyone comes out of the complex to see me being carried, literally carried by this big burly EMT guy down the stairs and into the ambulance.
"What did you take?!" They keep screaming at me.
"What are you on?!"
I'm in the fetal position and they're ripping off my clothes.
"Sushi."
"What?"
"I ate sushi today."
They don't look too impressed with my answer and carry me into the hospital and throw me naked on a gurney. The doctor comes over. I'm in excruciating pain. The bright light over my head is blinding me. I'm naked.
"What did you take?"
"Nothing!" I start screaming "NOTHING! NOTHING! Except a Valium I took before."
"WHY! WHERE DID YOU GET IT?"
"I took it because my back was killing me and I got it in Mexico."
Wrong answer.
"Mr. Klein if you can't urinate in this cup we are going to send this tube up your urethra."
With the help of 2 nurses they walk me over to the bathroom and hold me up. I squirt out in agony just enough of dark orange piss, the nurses made some comment on how bad it smelled. Now they finally give me a hospital gown. Put an I.V into my arm and pump me full of electrolytes and

nutrients and vitamins for three hours. Plus they give me two huge horse pills of Percocet on the spot. After a while the Dr. comes by and asks me, "When was the last time you drank water. "

I have to think. Honestly the last time I had a glass of water? I can't remember.
"Never."
"Never?"
"Well you can't drink the water from the tap, its brown."
"You can buy bottled water or juice, you know?"
"True. But we bought Jack Daniels and diet coke; we are sort of on a budget."
"You depleted your system and could of done major organ damage, you need to rehydrate yourself every day. Take vitamins and eat fruit. And take better care of yourself."

I fall asleep and when I awake the nurse is giving me instructions. No drinking alcohol and gives me the number to AA. Gives me a sheet of a healthy diet with all the food groups. Then she gives me 8 Valium, hospital grade, and 10 horse pills. Painkillers. I don't really know what they are except they're great. My body was wrecked with pain so I needed them. She tells me to drink a lot of Gatorade every day and eat bananas. She calls a cab and the hospital pays for it.
Later on I get a bill in the mail for $3500 bucks. I throw it out.

It's Christmas Eve and I'm feeling good.
I'm at the bar but I make sure I eat a lot of bananas and drink tons of Gatorade, plus the pills I'm on really help me lift my spirits.
Not the usual crowd in the bar, sort of empty. I'm high. I think of Laura, I think that things could be looking up here in San Diego. I don't need to go back east, ever.

This biker chick sits next to me at the bar, it's early, about seven. We start the usual bar talk bullshit. I lie. I tell her I'm a screenwriter, but she doesn't seem interested. She's like 35. She asks me, "Are you on something?" I smile and say "Oh yeah, this doctor just gave me these heavy pain killers, is it obvious?"
"I can tell. Do you have any on you?"

I point across the street and tell her that they're there in my apartment. She buys me a drink. Tells me she's got four kids at home with her husband and she was just stopping off for one drink after work.
Great.

We finish our drinks and she asks me if she can come by and pick up a pill or two. We leave and walk across the street and cut in back of the Circle

K to my building. She walks in and looks around and comments on how nice it is, she's nuts.

I take out the pills and give her a variety of sorts and tell her, "Merry Christmas." She is really happy and it shows because as she is thanking me she's rubbing my cock on the couch. I pull it out and she grabs it and plays with it a little, teasing. Then she gets up and locks the front door with the dead bolt. She walks over to my bedroom and pulls her pants down and gets on all fours. "Fuck me Now."
I do.

I notice her whole entire back is a huge tattoo of angel wings. She tells me to cum inside her, I do in a minute. She gets up, pulls up her pants and as she is walking to the door she says, "Merry Christmas right back atcha."

I feel good right about now, I do bong hit and head back to the bar. The bouncer says, "You didn't just fuck that woman?"
"No, why?" I crack a smile
"Her crazyass husband is a Hell's Angel"
"No, no, I just gave her a Valium. She said she had cramps."
I have one drink and leave. Pass out.

I stay in bed on Christmas day, I don't answer the phone.
Depression.

I don't do anything for a week. I sit on the couch, I barely eat, I watch T.V. I don't change my clothes. Then New Years Eve comes around. I shower and shave. I'm going over a buddy's house during the day to celebrate then to a party at night with the girls from Vancouver. They do not do drugs. They don't know anything about them. They are straight.

It's one in the afternoon and I do my first line of blow with Brucey. We watch Apocalypse Now. My heart is beating very fast so I take a shot of brandy to calm it down. Doesn't work.
Panic sets in.
I take another shot of brandy.
I don't talk for the whole movie. I'm sweating. I do a little bit more thinking. It might calm me down. I was wrong.
I leave and go home.
I'm all freaked the fuck out.

I shut all the blinds, lock the door. Unplug the phone. Cover the picture window with my down comforter so no light can escape. I take off all my clothes and lay on the couch. I start saying soft little prayers to God. I swear I will never fuck around with drugs again. I will be a better man. I will tell my family I love them. I will do anything. Please God. Please.

I get the courage to show up at the party at 10:30. Everybody says I look flush. I tell the girls I fell asleep and didn't hear the phone. I grab the bottle of Jack from the table. I recognize this little Japanese guy, he's pudgy and short. He recognizes me. "Hey aren't you from Bridgeport?" I ask.
He says, "Yeah, Wolfgang right? From Adrian's parties"
"Yeah dude, what are you doing here?"
"I go to medical school here."
REALLY.

"John right? Listen, I hit my head in the shower before and ever since my heart has been beating really fast, can you take my pulse?"
We walk into a bedroom and he grabs my wrist and his watch.
"How much cocaine have you done?" he asks. "Don't worry, I won't say anything."
"I did just a small line about 9 hours ago."
" NINE hours ago? Your heart rate is at heart attack range. You must of snorted meth, cocaine doesn't react that long."
"So what now?" I ask.
"Go to the emergency room".
"Fuck no, I was just there and nowadays after they treat you for drug overdoses, they have you arrested."
"I haven't heard that."

"Well, John, thanks for your help. I'm gonna ride this one out. Good luck in school. And Happy New Year." I shake his hand.
I walk downstairs and drink the bottle of Jack, 3 quarters of the bottle I kill in 15 minutes. I figure I'm going to slow down my heart with booze. I pass out before midnight on the couch.

I awake to one of the Vancouver chicks on me, fully clothed.
It's 5am. I get up and go back to my pad. I take off all my clothes and lay back down on my couch. I don't sleep. I don't eat.

I see the sun go up and down 3 times.

I can't piss or shit. I have bad thoughts. I really think about suicide for the first time. On the third day I convince myself to go to the hospital. I have chest pains. I drive myself this time. They hook me up to an EKG machine. Everyone is giving me dirty looks. After two hours I'm sitting in the Dr.'s office.
"Mr. Klein, do you have a drug problem?"

"No."

"Well then everything looks fine. You should have nothing to worry about."

That's it.

After that visit my chest pains go away.

Bud comes back a day ago and Laura was supposed to arrive two days before that. If she did she isn't returning my calls.

We party all over again. Our friends Cheen, Ritchie and Edfucking G are coming in on a Thursday from New York. I have about $200 cash on me and no rent. Fuck it. We pick up these animals at the airport and start drinking; we don't stop till the early hours, fall asleep and then take a road trip to Hollywood.

My friends do well, they all are self-made successes, they have a suite at The Standard. Bud and I are along for the ride. A package is waiting for Ritchie at the front desk, it's from Fed Ex. That crazy fuck shipped his drugs right to the hotel. We never stopped partying.

At the Viper Room we drink heavy and take Ecstasy, all five of us own the corner of the bar next to the stage. I'm sitting next to a 38 year old from Texas. She is visiting her friends in Echo Park. We are fucked up and not one of us uses the bathroom. At one point Edfucking G is dancing with his cock out, pissing directly at the stage. No one says anything, the band keeps playing. I see the bouncers are on their hands and knees mopping up our piss. They can't figure it out. The bartender is giving us pitchers of gin and tonics. We don't get thrown out and I end the night by going to Echo Park with this lady. Those guys go back to the room and get blown out.

I start saying off base shit as soon as I enter this army hanger on stilts in the middle of nowhere, "You can get away with murder in a place like this." She is not impressed.

I go into black out mode and next thing I know she is driving me back to Hollywood and I'm apologizing for shit I don't even remember. I could care less, but I haven't fucked a 38 year old from Texas yet. I convince her to stay and now I have to pay for another room. Fuuucckk iittt. I do it. I keep ripping off the condom until she gives in and then I could fuck her properly. I phone the guys' room to let them know where I was and Edfucking G came right down.

You can see it in his demeanor he hasn't slept yet. He pulls off the blankets and says UGHHH. "Do you feel proud about that Cougar?" He's a dick. "Get your shit together and let's go. Meet us outside and don't forget to kiss your mother goodbye."

I fuck her real quick one last time and run up to the suite. No one has slept and they are drinking Bloody's. The sun is up. We do more coke and lay out at the pool. This is the way I should be livin'…in Hollywood, livin' the dream.

It's unobtainable with 34 bucks to my name.

By night fall we drive back to P.B.
Loaded.
But the cocaine is mellowing us out, it's keeping the balance.
We pull into the pad and head directly to Stingers. We hook Edfucking G up with a chick who is half black and half Mexican. He calls her a Mexi-coon, she doesn't get it and he ends up fucking her. Cheen and Ritchie are still at the bar when Bud and I leave to go to a party we heard of. They decline because they can't pull themselves out of the corner of the bar. It's a neighborhood party I heard about for weeks. It's three houses on the beach, lots of chicas in bikinis.

One house was a bunch of hardcore surfers that sold smack and coke. The other house is a punk band that took the drugs the surfers sold them, and the third house was a bunch of college girls.

I stay for an hour and rob the surfer's house and get a half ounce of coke or meth, I can't tell at the moment. I just walked into the house and directly into a bedroom. I acted like I lived there. The bedroom was empty and in the dresser draw was THIS. I knew it because I leave my shit in a dresser drawer, I leave and motion to bud.

About 150 people partying.

I weave in and out of the crowd and get into a cab on Garnett Ave, just to make sure I wasn't being followed. I meet up with Bud and do a few key bumps. It's definitely coke. Good coke. We can't tell our Trumbull friends, they wouldn't understand. They have jobs and bank accounts. And besides, robbing from drug dealers is just part of the game. It's not like they're real people.

Daryl comes over to our pad.
He never visits.
He wants to know if we know anything about the coke that was stolen at the party. We tell him no.
"Don't fuck with me guys, I don't care. But people are saying you guys are selling coke, which you never did before. It's a small town. Get rid of it or get out of town."

We give it to our friend Paul to sell and make whatever he wants, just give us $800.

He does. Quickly.

I never hear from sushi Laura again. Oh well.

Two movie studios exist in San Diego. They shoot a shitty cable series. Low grade. I put together the best resume I can, I use other people's student films as my own credit. I dress really conservatively; pull my hair back in a ponytail. I wait two hours before I get called in for the interview. I was inside for less than one minute. I didn't even say anything. The guy took my resume and put it on a pile of others and told me he will call if anything comes up, good bye. Fuck the job situation.

They shut off our power for lack of payment.

Fuck them.

I get a drill from Daryl and drill straight thru the wall into the Boston sisters' pad. I plug in an extension cord and we only have one choice for electricity. The refrigerator or the T.V. We go with the TV. Candles are good enough lighting for night. We drink and are six weeks behind on rent.

We go to Vegas with a hundred bucks. We sleep on the street. We drink for three days with no money and no room. We get asked to leave Lady Luck because a mother and daughter think we are stalking them. We are filthy looking. We reek of booze. It's a hard 3 days, it started off great then went downhill fast.

We only have enough gas to get us to Bakersfield. A mile before the station I get out of the car and put a dirty towel over the back license plate. I tell Bud to go inside and use the bathroom and buy a soda with the only 75 cents we have.

He does.

I scan the station and I see no cameras. I pump the gas. I see Bud paying for his soda and then he walks out. I pass him and tell him to just top it off, I will be right out. I walk in and ask for the men's room. The cashier can't be bothered and points. I walk out and ask him, "How far to Vegas?" He says without looking up, "About 2 hours."

"Thanks." I walk out and jump right in the truck and take off in the opposite direction. Ten miles down the road we take the towel off from the plate.

San Diego sucks.

The billboard on the bus reads, "One in Five People in P.B have an STD. DO YOU?"

God I hope not.

Bud and I have a bet. Who can go the longest without showering or changing clothes. He goes 14 days, I go 17. I bang more women in those 17 days than I ever have before. It must be the pheromones.

I stay up for days at our crackhead neighbor's place listening to old vinyl albums and drinking big glasses of vodka at 8am. Peeking out of the shade every once in a while.

It's Tuesday.

I know this is not good behavior. I get sketched out. I spend my days filled with guilt and shame and I drink to feel numb at night. I smoke pot daily, hourly. I fuck pretty much every girl I can in the complex. All I do is drink and take drugs for weeks, now daily.

I toss and turn and for some reason my eye catches my laptop closed on my desk. It's dark but I can see it. I see water all around my desk, I get up and open the laptop to see it dripping wet. What happened? Someone pissed in my laptop. Ruined. Who could have done this?

Big disappointment.

The apartment is trashed.

No screenplay.

Bud is finished with his and he registers it with the Writer's Guild. We exhaust our moneymaking skills here. We live like scumbags, instead of going to the coffee shop nowadays, I sit in front of the T.V and jerkoff to old vhs tapes of porn. So in debt, I don't think we will be getting our security deposit back. Bud decides he is going back east, he wants to take summer classes at NYU on film.

Now what.

I'm not staying in this shit hole by myself.

I tell him we need to raise money to drive back, and that plus my car probably won't make it. I need three days before I split with you. The car is easily worth six grand. I just bought it 3 years ago. Fucking Volkswagen. The used car guy gives me $2300, I'm robbed. But I don't have much choice.

Daryl's roommate Gumby sells tools for a huge tool supply company. He ha\s stock in Daryl's garage. That's how Daryl makes money. He sells off these tools worth thousands of dollars for half price. Brand new, in the box. Gumby has so many different models and demo tools; he doesn't know what the fuck he has. Bud and I take a few when we say our goodbyes. The next day we sell them at the pawn shop.

Fuck Gumby, he was always a dick towards us anyway. Plus it wasn't his money. We made $1500 to get home.

Fuck the landlord, Mr. Wong, just because. He was well aware that these white trash neighbors of mine were selling blow and responsible for my drug habit which I did not have before I moved in.
All I do is pack the little clothes I have and leave everything else.

All the furniture. The phone, the mattress, the rotten food in the fridge. The empty bottles of Jack. The lamps. The holes in the wall and the broken bathroom door. Fuck the landlord and all this shit in Pacific Beach.

Hey Man, Nice Shot

We jump in Bud's truck and head east. Trumbull, here we come.

The sun is setting as we are pulling into Scottsdale, Arizona. I ask Bud "How do you know this chick?"

"She's friends with my little sister from Trumbull and now she's a sophomore at ASU, I called her before and told her we would be arriving tonight. We just got to meet her at the bar; I hope I remember what she looks like."

I pop a Valium.

The bar is packed, as packed as can be, but I make my way up to the bar and grab a stool. I don't move too many fucking people. Bud and I drink and piss for a couple of hours before Alisha finds us.

It's not hard, we don't look like college students.

No boys allowed at the sorority house we were staying at. That's what she said. We said we will be quiet and sneak in. I see a bottle of tequila in her roommate's closet and take it. Bud and I kill it and start smoking pot in the room. Everyone freaks out. We wrestle for the rest of the night and this poor young girl is almost in tears by morning. We say thank you and act real nice but she hates us.

It's 85 degrees in the hot Arizona sun at 9:30 in the morning. We see a school fair of some sort and decide to check it out. I have shoulder length dirty blonde hair, I am wearing a white v neck Hanes t shirt and that terracotta suede Mexican jacket with black dickies and platform shoes and sunglasses. Bud has long brown hair. He is wearing a white crew neck t shirt with his brown suede Mexican jacket with brown slacks from Goodwill. He also has platform shoes and a chain for his wallet that drags on the ground. Everyone else is wearing shorts and summer attire. The fair sucks and we decide to get a drink.

We end up at IHOP because first we need some food. Everything is bright and I don't remove my shades at all. As we walk in I see 3 girls sitting in a booth. We walk up and sit down then I say, "Ladies my name is Wolfgang and this is Bud, do you mind if we join you for breakfast?" They are a little bit taken back, but say o.k. The girls are young, 20 maybe. All in good shape but they have that Arizona white trash flavor about them.

"Hey girls, Bud and I are from L.A and we are going to shoot a movie Bud wrote in New York, He sold the rights two months ago and now we start pre-production. We have a few days to kill so we thought we would hang out here."

"Do you girls know of anything for us to do while we are in town?" "You guys wanna play pool? That's the only thing open now that serves drinks," the tall chick says.

"Ladies, if you accompany me and my friend here, drinks are on me all day."

They smile and oblige. Bud and I order breakfast, never removing our shades. Kelly, Sherri and Luann tell us their boring stories, none of them go to college, they are working now to pay for it later they tell us.
Riiight.
I think they might be strippers. Or have stripped at some point.

We play pool and buy these girls drinks and shots. It's noon. Bud hits the pool lamp by accident and cracks the light and we get warned to calm down. We drink this jerk out of Jack, he only has one bottle. These girls are trying to choose between them who's hooking up with who. Bud and I start on the gin, and start sword fighting with the pool sticks. The jerk behind the bar tells us "enough is enough" and is about to walk from behind the bar. I run up to the bar and give him a fifty dollar bill and tell him "That's for you." He takes it. Good thing because if he came out from the bar he would see all the piss on the floor.

Luann tells us she has a new roommate moving into her house today, she needs to go. Bud and I pack everyone in the front seat, girls on my lap. We drive to Luann's sister's house and we see a moving truck and people moving shit out of it. We are bombed and can't get on the highway to head home. We tell the girls we will help you ladies move if we could spend the night on the couch. Luann asks her sister, who is my age. And then I come over and introduce myself.
"Hi Keri?"
"No Carrie."

"Oh sorry. My name is Wolfgang Klein and that is Bud Larsen. We are from L.A. on our way to New York. We met your beautiful sister this morning and had a little too much drink. I was wondering - if we help you guys unload this truck, could crash on your couch until early tomorrow morning?"

Luann tells her that we are movie producers and have been buying drinks and food all morning. Carrie walks over

"I don't know what kind of shit you told my sister.

"What, wait!"

I run to the truck and pull out Bud's script and run back to her,

"Here read this and tell us what you think."

I KNOW SHE WON'T.

She doesn't think we're bullshitters anymore and I show her the wad of cash in my pocket and say, "When you're finished here I would like to take you guys out for dinner."

"Alright, no fucking around, you can help us for in exchange crashing here one night."

The new roommate has no idea how we got in the picture. Carrie tells us to say we are her cousins down from L.A for the weekend.

We start moving furniture.

Drunk.

Nothing I hate more than anything is moving furniture.

I ask to use the bathroom and walk around back. I see a very clean in-ground pool. I take off all my clothes and jump in. Bud is still working. The truck is almost empty as I walk back with dripping hair. Bud curses me out and I tell him I'm going to the liquor store. I ask the girls what would they like, it's on me, a little party for your new roommate. They give me a list of shit.

Tequila for margaritas.

Vodka and mixers.

Jack Daniels.

Fuckin' Corona and Bush beer.

And frozen mudslide mix.

And smokes for all 3 girls.

These girls really take advantage of me.

The sun is still up and I'm making out with Luann in her basement, then I go outside and try to fool around with Kelly. Drinking and drinking, no cocaine. Just hangin' out at this pool with strangers I met at IHOP 5 hours ago. I tell these girls I will take them out to dinner and they choose Olive Garden.

Typical.

It's Bud and me with these 5 chicks at a huge round table. Something doesn't look right. I see nothing but families and children and old people looking at my table. Then I realize I'm with a bunch of cigarette smoking foul fucking mouthed whores dressed like sluts. I feel uncomfortable so I drink more. The bill is around $400.

I better get laid tonight.

We go back to the house and a few more of their friends show up and start partying. I find a phone in the back bedroom and whip out my little address book and start calling all my friends back east, I even call this chick in Norway. In San Diego we didn't have long distance service, so any chance we got to use it we'd call everyone we knew.

I drink too much and now we are going to a bar. I'm so fucked up, I'm saying the most fucked up things to the bartender and she won't even serve me. I put my head down underneath the bar and violently puke all over the floor. It won't stop and people are starting to scream. Bud thinks it's funny and starts kicking me in my ass as I'm bent over throwing up my guts. I clear the bar and it wreaks something awful. Of course they ask me to leave and everyone in the bar comes with us. I tell the bartender, "See what happens when you don't serve me..?"

The girls are now having a pool party at 1am at the house. I'm trying to hook up with this chick Kelly but she wants no part of me. The scene I made in the bar. So I go after Luann, easy prey. I should have brought a rubber.

In the morning I walk into a bedroom to see Bud in bed with 3 chicks. One girl had the tattoo of the SS on her wrist. White trash. I kick his feet and he wakes up without waking the strippers. We want to leave before they make us clean up. We are so hung over, we go and sleep in a parking lot at the university for a couple of hours then we go back to IHOP.

We drive fifteen minutes out of town when we realize that we left our only cassette tape at the house.

We have to go back.

It's FILTER we have been listening to it over and over and over. Sort of insane. We have to go back.

We arrive at the girl's house and no one is home so we jump the gate and go in the back of the house. I see the tape on the table and grab it. Then I decide to stick my head in the pool to wet my hair.

When I pull my head out of the water I see Carrie standing there. "What the fuck are you guys doing back here, you left hours ago without saying word, we were wondering if you guys stole anything?"

"Come on Carrie we came back for our tape, we rang the bell and we didn't see any cars and no one answered the door."

"I was in the bathroom and they went for breakfast."

I got the vibe she didn't trust us.

"Well thanks again, Carrie."

We jump back into the truck and take off with
"hey man last shot"
blaring.

Wait til' they get the phone bill.

We drive, we sleep in rest stops.

Bud is excited because he has never experienced New Orleans and we should be there in about an hour. Louisiana State Police fly past us, until they realize the truck we're in has Connecticut plates and Grateful Dead and Phish stickers all over it.
They slow up, we slow up.

Bud will not pass the trooper and we have the Interstate behind us at 35mph. The cops pull over on the side of the highway and wait a minute then they fly up on our ass with lights flashing. We pull over and two big black troopers ask us if we have been drinking.
It's 10:30 in the morning.

He said Bud swerved, he was full of shit. He thought we had drugs in the truck. They separate Bud and me and they find my head bag of pot. Bud says he doesn't smoke pot. I admit to it. The cops want to know if we have anymore drugs in the car before they call in the dogs. I have about $1800 in a back pack if they find it. I know they will take it.

"Officer, I mean Trooper. I am the only pot smoker here and that was a bag I bought in California. You can bring in the dogs but that is the only pot we have"
The Troopers empty the bag and let us go.

Holy Shit.

Down on Bourbon Street we immediately start drinking.
It's Monday, no special occasion.

We get a room in dead center of the French Quarter, the only one available is on the 12th floor and only has a king size bed. We take it. Razoo is the closest bar and we go, and we stay.

People are drinking everyday all hours on Bourbon Street, and so are we, Bud is dancing with a group of ladies. I've never seen the guy dance in my life. He's pickin' up change and doing it well.

I meet a punk chick with fire engine red long hair. We chat and before you know it I'm driving her car back to her hotel in the Garden District to smoke some pot.

It's 7pm.

We make out in the elevator and go inside her room and I see her guy friend passed out on the bed. She rolls a joint. We smoke it in the bathroom and start laughing. Her guy friend wakes up and kicks us out.

I don't know her name but she is from Texas and came down with a group of friends. She says she is German and Mexican. She has a hot ass and tits. I drive to a bar in the Garden District and I see Bud there dancing. (The next day he tells me he was never there.)

The next thing I know I'm telling the girl my rubbers are in the truck in the parking garage. She says O.K. and I fuck her without them. She has a tribal tat around her left nipple and three steel barbells thru her hood, she told me to be careful. We fuck all night.

Bud stumbles in thru the door, stumbles over to the bed and plops down and he is out. Snoring.

The chick freaks a little bit and leaves when I pass out.

Bud wakes the next morning and wants to know - why is there hair conditioner all over the sheets?

We travel south again to visit a friend in Plaquemine, Louisiana.

Dave Karageorge, he's a Trumbull guy who came to Mardi Gras with me in 1991 and never went back home.

He met a Greek girl, married her and had a family. His wife's brother is the Mayor, her other brother is the Sheriff and her other brother owned the only restaurant in town.

The town has only one traffic signal.

Dave put us to work for a few days, light painting and dump runs.

This is a great little southern backwards town, I like it here. Dave pays us well for the little work we do and we take off to the Smokey Mountains in Tennessee.

We drink at this shithole and some chick I'm talking to asks to see my fingernails. I show her and she is disgusted. They have paint and dirt in them. She gets up and walks away. Kinda weird and she was kinda fat. Wake up in the morning with the phone book out to the escort page. Bud comes walking in with a smile, he hooked up.

We drive fast and hung-over. We make it in 13 hours.

Back in Trumbull, at my parents' house, total disappointment. My father made me pay back my mother the money I took from her over the course of my "little adventure" as he calls it.

I work with a piece of shit coke head painter, he's like fifty. He didn't pay me for a month and one Saturday morning before I was leaving to Newport for the weekend (my friends still rent a summer house there). I ring his doorbell at 8:30 in the morning. He's white trash.

No answer.

I ring again.

No answer.

His wife fucked some black guy a few years back and now this 2 year old little black girl is looking out the window. I feel bad for her.

I bang on the door. BOOM. BOOM!

No answer.

I kick the fucker in and that gets Peter's attention. He runs to the door. "Fucking pay me now," I yell. "I'm calling the cops," he yells back. "Go ahead I will tell them you owe me drugs and they will have a dog here in a minute."

He tells his wife to go into a back and take the kid. He is in his bathrobe. "You owe me two grand Peter. Put your pants on, I'm taking you to the bank."

"No no, hold on! "

He comes back into the living room with an envelope and hands it to me.

"Do I have to count it?" I ask.

"No it's all there."

"Fuck you, Peter."

I walk out and jump into my friend's car I borrowed because I don't have one yet. I get down the road and count the money and that piece of shit shorted me 100 bucks.

I use the money and buy a 1985 Jetta, It was a bear. Burgundy, sun roof, it never breaks down. It's a good car for $1500. I spend the rest of the summer jumping from one paint job to the next. Never making enough money and whatever money I have I spend on the weekends in Newport.

Partying, women, drugs.

I hear Elizabeth gets engaged to a Jewish lawyer.
My heart sinks.

Rollin' In the Benzo, Hangin' with Lorenzo

Bud in the meanwhile is in New York taking film classes and I rarely talk to him throughout the summer, but at the end of the season I get a call from him, He's shooting his student film and wants me to act in it.
GREAT.

It's the 3rd weekend in August 1996.

My parents are on vacation and I decide to take my mom's Mercedes (my dad bought pre owned) to Newport Rhode Island on Friday.
I have to be in Central Park by 10am Sunday to act in this film. No problem, if I leave Newport Sunday morning at 6am, that should give me plenty of time. My parents don't come home until Tuesday.

I act like a big shot and hit it hard on Friday night. Saturday I pull up at the beach in the Benzo, I make sure I'm seen at the beach bar for a while then do a couple laps in town before we head out for the night. I'm a douchebag.

It's going to be a good night. We have a crew of 18 with us at the house. All animals.

It's a beautiful summer night.   We party as usual. I hook up with a chick at the bar and leave around midnight. I fuck around with here until 3:30 or 4 in the morning, she won't let me have sex with her, so I leave.
Back at the house I see Freddy Knuckles sitting on the back deck. Alone. Everyone is gone or in bed.

Freddy has a Frisbee turned upside with a mound of blow in the middle of it next to him on the table. He makes me do some. Of course I do a little, then a little more. Then the sun is coming up and a do a shit load.

It's almost 6am and I have to take off. I have to be in New York. No excuses. I run up to the bedroom to pack my things and my buddy Dave is in bed and tells me, "I don't think you should be going anywhere, just lay down for a minute. You're really whacked, dude."
I don't listen and grab my shit and jump into the Benzo.
It's a beautiful morning. I'm so High, I don't even know it.

Newport has one way in and one way out. It's a small road with a double yellow line. Speed limit is 25mph. I have the stereo real loud and I'm going about 55. Sitting in the gas station on my left, just before the Newport Bridge is a cop.

I 'm over the yellow line and speeding.

He pulls me over right before I get onto the bridge. I don't wait for him to come to the car. I get out and put my wrists together. And say. "I'm not doing any field test so just arrest me."

He slaps the cuffs on me and starts to go thru my pockets and pulls out rolled up bills.

"We're going to test this for any narcotic residue."

I say, "Go ahead, I just licked those bills clean 10 minutes ago, good luck."

They throw me into the cop car and have mine towed. I pass out for a few hours in a cold concrete cell. They put the air conditioner on high and don't give me a blanket. They wake me up to fingerprint me and blow in the Breathalyzer. I do. The cops think they recognize me and they should - 3 years before I was arrested for throwing a fence post thru a window on the main drag. I was really fucked up on Jack Daniels. The judge told me to pay restitution and the charges would be dropped. I never paid because I couldn't find the owner, nor could the prosecutor. Charges were dismissed.

I ask the cop if I can get a blanket as he is walking me back to my cell. He throws me an old wool blanket. Inside the cell there is a closed circuit camera high in the corner staring on the cot. I put the blanket over my face so I can't see the camera and leave the rest of my body exposed. I jerk off so all these fuckin' pigs could watch. I don't hear the door open and when I am about to bust a nut I get whacked in the face with a baton, the folded up blanket takes some of the hit. But I end up with a bloody nose.

I get released the next day and have to pay to get my mom's car out of impound. I have to appear in court in two weeks.

Fuck Rhode Island, I'm never going back. I never go to court.

I don't tell anyone what happened except Bud. He understands the situation.

For a graduation present Bud gets an Arri BL16mm film camera, his parents are good that way. Bud is going to make an independent feature film. The script he wrote in San Diego is the one. *JIMMY'S STORY* and he asks if I want to help him. I'm more than ecstatic to help make a movie and have no other goals except to see this thing through.

I live at my parents' house.

During the week Bud works as a handyman for his family, His family has a huge estate and he takes on the duties of keeping it up. That gives him money for the weekends to buy film and shoot.

We start with a casting call in New York. Just put an ad in trades and watch all the headshots delivered in baskets to your door. After we find a crew of people that work for free. Some good friends like Sean Shaun, he becomes our sound guy. The actors, of course free. The cameraman is from Jersey. Free. Bud does the lighting. I have to find locations to shoot at. Then convince the owners of these locations for permission to shoot there for free. I tell them all that I had permits and everything will be fine and we'll make you famous… blah blah blah.

I never have a permit or insurance and I make up fake documents and credentials and a business card the reads, *"Wolfgang Klein. Producer- Jack in The Box Productions- phone number."*

Whatever is needed for Bud to make his film, I do.

I know a guy at Kodak film that gives us reels of film for free. If the can is dented at all it is thrown away, and usually nothing would be wrong with the film. I can't say his name but he would give us all the free film we wanted.
Great.

Then we find a guy in the city named Norman. He's about 80, a friend of a friend tells us about him, if we pay him cash the price would be half to develop. But we have to drop it off at his house on Sunday night in Brookfield, CT.

It's a drive. Every Sunday night after a weekend of shooting, Bud and I take the ride.

I don't work. I run errands for the movie and hustle a little money on the side. We shoot Friday night, all night, then Saturday from dawn til about midnight. Then run out to the bar and get shit faced for two hours, bring a crowd back to Bud's parents' compound and continue to get loose. All the actors and actresses and crew come from New York and they stay at Bud's parents' on the shoot days. They don't party. They sleep, as they should because we work long days and they are professionals. On Sunday we always work till 3pm so we can get the film to Brookfield and have it developed by Wednesday.

Everyone leaves by train and Bud and I left on our own. We drop off the film and get fucked up at every bar on the way back and return to Fairfield at 2am Monday morning.

We do this every week for about 9 months.
It's getting out of control.

We drink and get fucked up with some townie chicks and end up fucking them in the woods, this sort of shit goes on.

The lead actor sucks. We are too far into the movie to shut it down, Bud won't do that.

After awhile the cast and crew were afraid of us because we would treat work like a party and start with beers and move on. I fuck the makeup artist and she quits. I fuck a few extras and they never show up afterwards. Fuck it we have a movie to make and we do a damn good job.

We are near the end of filming and have one more seen to shoot, which would be shot in Vermont at Bud's parents' ski house.

Bud, after this last weekend of filming will spend the summer cutting the film. Literally. It will take 3 months or more to edit an hour and a half feature film. He says he doesn't need me for a while. Now I will have nothing else to do, no more production after this weekend.

It'spring. May, and we shot film 3 weekends a month since October.

I am losing my mind. I need to make big money and I convince myself that we could sell this movie, but when and how, I don't know? The money is already spent in my head.

I've got to get away for the summer. I really got to get away.

Elizabeth is getting married June 28th and I can't be in the country, I still have dreams about her weekly.

I'm still living at my folks' and broke. Still depressed.

I land a painting job with this commercial painting company in Bridgeport, and work one month before I quit on good terms.

I save $1600 and the next day I buy a ticket to Prague, to depart June 28th at 9:37am out of JFK International. It's an open ticket. It costs me $800.

I can't be around here when I have been telling people I've been making a movie and then they see me painting houses.
No way.

I'm a Producer.

Smoking bugs in Prague. 1997

Mike Kotch has been my friend since Junior High school. He is about 6'2. He used to take steroids in high school then he discovered pot and acid and mushrooms and became a dreadlock wearing drug taking animal. He paints and does carpentry. He is good with his hands. He deals pot. He is a conniving man. He fucks a lot of girls. He is the kind of guy that will shit in your pool. He simply doesn't give a fuck. He also lives at his parents' like it's a flop house. But we're good friends and we don't pull that shady shit with each other. He calls me up on a Sunday in June around noon time and asks me if I want to go to "The Gathering of The Vibes" Croton-on-Hudson, New York. I say yes but I don't have much cash.

I jump in his jeep along with Mudman and head on up to the show. We have enough money between us to get in then we have to scam drugs and beer.

NO problem...

Within minutes we run into a hippie we know from Monroe.

Robby the Whack Job.

He tours with Phish and sells tons of drugs. Right now he is bugged out on acid.

"Hey Robby, what's up?"

Robby is carrying an ice tea bottle with duct tape taped all around the cap. "Dude," he says. "Two nights ago I got pulled over by the cops on the way here, way upstate. I'm in my Saab and it's filled with shit. And I know these fuckers are gonna bust me just based on the way I look."

He takes a deep breath and continues.

"I have a sheet of acid on the side of my seat near the gear shift. I take and unscrew the new ice tea bottle and stuff it in."

"Good idea."

"The cops end up being cool and just give me a warning for speeding, considering. A few hours later I pull over in a rest area to get some sleep, I wake up at the crack of dawn. All my windows are shut and the sun is blaring down on me, it's fuckin' hot. Without thinking I grab the ice tea and crack it open and guzzle. Not a big deal, right? I end up tripping balls at 7:30 in the morning. But I did the same thing again last night, forgetting. So that is why I have it duct taped."

Kotch and I look at each other and say "How do we get some of that." Robby tells us he will only give us a little drip in the cap and then he is going to wrap it back up. The drip becomes a shot. All three of us take our share.

I'm wearing denim overalls with a white Hanes v-neck all the time. We trip and dance.

We find an old tire tube and rope and we're giving chicks rides on it. We run real fast over the grassy wet knoll and pick up enough momentum then swing them off, everyone wants a ride and it's a big hit for a few hours.

We have no tent, Kotch can't figure how to put it together even though he had done it hundreds of times before. So we have to find some ladies to keep us warm.

This crunchy girl Kotch hooks up with says she will be in Vermont next weekend and we should meet up. We tell her we will be in Okemo on Friday night and hook her up if she allows us to stay in her tent. That never works because we're so fuckin' gone on LSD.

After a while this girl hates us. We won't shut up, make up songs about huffing paint and sniffing glue.
The whole campsite is fed up with us.
People begin to hate us.

We become obnoxious and when the sun finally comes up it's warm enough to sleep in the jeep so we crash out for a few hours while everyone is leaving the festival.

It's Monday and we can't understand why there is so much traffic on the Merritt Parkway. Where are all these people going? Work perhaps?

I leave for Prague in a week. I have no contacts there. I don't speak the language. I don't know where I'm going once I get off the plane.

I have one more scene to shoot in Vermont. I tell Bud that I'm going up early to Vermont and I will be staying at Kotch's parents' cabin in Groton for a few days, I have everything organized for the shoot this weekend. I just have to make it to Okemo Mountain by Friday night for the first take. I can do this.

Wednesday after the festival we track down Robby in Monroe and demand that he gives us half of the bottle of acid. He is a pussy and gives in, and we pay him a few bucks. We try to divide about 200 hits into 28 oz. of ice tea by measuring tablespoons. It doesn't make sense. We end up with half the bottle or 14 oz. of strong liquid acid.

We pack up the jeep and head up to Groton.

Kotch's cabin is on 97 acres of land next to a neighbor who has 345 acres. We are alone with nature, alcohol, pot, guns and acid.

We wake up early Thursday morning, the sun is out, and it's real warm. You can smell landscape and hear all the things in it. I walk over to the kitchen sink and stare out of the window, long stare. I turn and see the bottle of ice tea on top of the fridge. I grab it, pull out a table spoon from the cabinet and take my first dose of medicine for the day.
It is 8am.

Kotch and Mudman soon follow, ten minutes later.
Then we cook breakfast and go on a hike. We hike for five hours deep. Gone. Then we come across a road, a paved road, a highway maybe, we don't know. Next to the road is a raging river with rapids. We decide it's a good idea to get in that thing.
I'm wearing sandals and shorts. No wallet.

I go right in and the current just BAM. Takes me down about 300 yards to a nice calm patch. Kotch and Mud jump right in and we meet up down in the shallow pool.

We are tripping balls.

Lying on our backs having the water rush over your body is the best feeling at the moment.
"Hey you guys alright down there?" We all open our eyes and look up. It's a Vermont State Trooper. "Where's your car?"
"We hiked here!"
"From where?"
"Over that little mountain pass in Groton." Kotch says.
"I don't think you guys will make it back today, it's over 8 miles. Where are your back packs?"
"We didn't bring any, sir."
"No water, any snacks? Well what the hell you doing in the river?"
"We just wanted to cool off."
"Well. You know that's illegal, what you're doing?"
"No sir."
"Get on up out of there I will drive you back to Groton General store."

He makes us stand around a good fifteen minutes so we can dry off a little. He has no idea he is about to let 3 heavily dosed animals into his car. We are all in awe of the leather seats and tell him they don't make cop cars like this where were from.

"And where is that?"

Kotch jumps in and tells him that he is from Groton for the last five years and we are visiting him. Then the Trooper asks, "Why were you in a cop car?" I tell him 3 of my cousins are on the force, 2 state police in Connecticut and one Bridgeport cop.

He likes hearing that and loosens up. I bullshit, I only have one corrupt cousin who is a Bridgeport cop. It takes the Trooper 8 minutes to drop us off and we say thank you and walk back to the cabin.

We take another dose of medicine and start to cook meat. We drive around on Quads until dinner is ready and then after dinner we decide to go night hunting with his father's elephant gun and assorted rifles. We are going into the wilderness packed to the teet. We discuss killing a bear or a moose over dinner, and how we will chop it up and use every part of the animal. We will be able to eat and make coats from whatever we kill. We tape flashlights to the barrels of the guns while we finish up the last of the Wild Turkey. It's dark as shit out, the moon isn't even around. We talk too much to hear anything so we decide to split up from one another.

Bad idea.

I walk south, Kotch goes north, and Mudman west. Less than one second later I hear Boom boom boom!
Boom boom!

I go running towards a light pointed up at the sky. I think Kotch is down. I hear laughter getting louder and then another Boom!
I see Kotch laying on his back firing the elephant gun up at the sky….just to see the flame shoot out the barrel.

We can't see Mudman's light.

So Kotch decides to start rapid firing into the sky to get his attention. We both break out in hysterical laughter when Kotch mentions maybe he killed him with a stray bullet. Then things get silent and we can hear gunshots in the distance. I pull up my rifle and aim for the sky. I shoot and the kick back puts me on my ass. We start to laugh again only to be interrupted by more gun fire, this time getting closer. I hear bullets cutting thru the trees above me. Mudman sneaks up on us as we are lying on the ground with our lights out. We all start to giggle again.
More gun fire.
Real close.
It ain't Mudman.

Kotch takes off yelling in the direction of the gunfire on acid "You want me, come and get me!" Boom! He fires right in front of himself. We can see the flame.

It's like a movie.

I catch up to him and Mudman is on my side and we all start firing straight forward like we are in a gun battle in *Tombstone*. This is dangerous. The gunfire stops.

"I think we should get back to the cabin before anyone gets hurt," Kotch says in a moment of sanity. "Does anyone know the way?"

We decide to lie on the ground and wait for sunrise so we can see where we're going. No one has any idea what time it is. I lay the gun down next to me and stare up at the sky. No one is talking at this point. We are all lost in our own minds. I don't remember if I fell asleep or not but when the sun comes up we see the cabin only two hundred yards away.

We find out later that the neighbor was drinking and playing with his guns when he heard us shooting.

We eat breakfast and wash up in the river.

I crack my first beer at 9:30am.
Kotch is packing the jeep to head o Okemo Mountain.
Mudman takes the ice tea acid bottle and says, "One for the road animals?"
Kotch takes the tablespoon from his pocket (I don't know why it's in his pocket). "Sure" he says. We all take our morning dose.
We drive with open beers and open minds.

We arrive in town and it's dead, it's summer time and just locals hanging out. Mudman suggests we stop over at the pay phone and call the girl from the Vibes. While he is doing that Kotch and I are taking little sips of the tea. He says we have to meet her at some restaurant in town.
It's around 5:30pm and I have to meet everyone from the film crew at 10 at the condo.

We take another tablespoon at the restaurant bar while we're sippin on beers waiting for this girl to show up so we can sit down and eat. When she does finally show up we are already in a laughing fit. Each of us hiding behind our menus, trying not to laugh but we can't help ourselves. The waitress is not impressed.
The girl is not impressed.

We all order a round of beers and the house hamburgers.
We still can't stop laughing enough to complete full sentences.
No one touches any food.

While the crunchy chick goes to the bathroom Mudman doses her beer with a drop of tea. If she wants to hang out with us she best be on the same boat.

Bud's condo is on the mountain. Literally you can ski off his porch and down the slope. Everyone is arriving, five or six car loads of people and equipment. It's going to be a night shoot and then we would all split in the morning back to Connecticut.

I'm with a terrifying bunch of people, my friends…on acid.

Everyone on set is excited to see me; they stop what they're doing and come over to greet me and my friends. They can see something is not right. Mudman is tripping over lights.

This dirty crunchy chick is starting to bug out. She doesn't look good. Kotch is telling people about the tea then he pulls it out. Bud is not happy and pulls me aside.

"Dude what the fuck, you are supposed to be the producer. This isn't a party. These people don't know you like I do. Be professional. Look around." I do and see a big fucking mess of shit.
I mean all the equipment, the camera, the lights, the cables, the audio gear.
Too much stuff in here and not enough space for me.
I've got to get outta here.

"You're right Bud, I'm sorry. I will take the animals away right now and meet you back here at six in the mornin'." I say good bye to everyone quickly, gather the clan and head out.
Bud gives me a thumb's up on the way out.

I have seven hours to kill before we take off, we go for a hike up the ski mountain, staring at the dark sky with the whitest stars.
We lay down.
My mind drifts off.

In two days I will be on a plane to Prague and Elizabeth will be married. I don't like these thoughts but they won't leave my mind at this point. It just keeps getting faster and faster, more and more bad thoughts, sad thoughts. I look like I'm sleeping from the outside but on the inside is a violent war.

All these questions I ask myself over and over.

Why did I take acid today? Why did I show up on acid? Why do I take drugs? Why do I want to escape? Why am I an asshole? Why do I act the way I act? Why can't I marry Elizabeth?

I dated her for eight years on and off and she meets this guy and marries him in less than two fucking years.

What is wrong with me!

Why has it been two years and I can't get this girl out of my mind? A half conscious scream is let loose from my gut, and I open my eyes, the sun is almost up. I look around and see Mudman cuddled up with the crunchy chick and Kotch is gone. I walk back to the condo and fall asleep in Bud's truck for a bit.

The car ride back is just Bud and I. I tell him again that I'm sorry for the mishap and he says, "Dude not a big deal, you did all the ground work before hand and I told you that you didn't need to come up. So it really was no big deal. Anyway, everyone was happy to see you before you left for your trip."

Man, that makes me feel good all over again after the whole bad acid trip a few hours before, now I am ready to party. My conscious is clear for the moment.

I get dropped off at my parents' house and sleep for a couple of hours. I am supposed to pack but don't feel like it. I grab my money belt and put it on, it contains my passport and an airline ticket and $750 cash. I take off my unwashed overalls and put on a pair of black slacks with a black leather belt with a clean white V-neck. My shoes are black with one buckle each. I then put my overalls back on over my slacks.

I'm packed.

I tell my parents I will be back later on and jump into Bud's truck. We go to the Seagrape Bar on Fairfield Beach. All of our friends are hanging out there getting fucked up.

I just have to be at the airport by 7am.

We all drink and piss on the floor. It's normal there. For some reason no one can walk the 30 feet to the bathroom so every time someone goes up to the bar, they piss. Just pull your cock out then put both hands on the bar with money in one hand and order a drink. When done, slip it back into your shorts or pants and zipper quickly. The bathroom is just used to do blow in. And we wonder why the place always smells of piss.

It's June and I'm wearing two pairs of pants and sweating my balls off. I'm sitting in a chair next to Kotch when he pulls out a cigarette and lights

it. I immediately smell pot and the bartender does too. He comes over and looks at us and says, "You guys smoking that shit in here again?"
"No."

"Man, I smell it real strong, like it's coming from right over here."
He points at Kotch and me.
"Budda, I swear, we are not smoking pot in your bar tonight."
Budda walks away,
Moments later the whole bar now wreaks of weed.

Steve the owner comes up to us and he has always been a dick and says, "I've had my eyes on you two clowns and I'm surprised that I can honestly say it's not you two .I haven't seen you guys smoke anything except your Marlboros."
"Hey Steve why don't you buy us a drink for being such good citizens in your bar?" Kotch yells at him.
Steve pays no mind and goes back to the kitchen. Kotch is laughing.
"Stupid asshole, that guy has never seen a stunt before?"
"You're fucked up dude"
"I spent an hour rolling this bud into cigarettes with filters; I had just bought a rolling machine and had to use it so I rolled an ounce with it. Looks real, right?"
"Yeah, except for the smell."
"I haven't been able to figure that one out yet. I smoke them in public and no one knows. It's called a stunt."
"Good for you."

I get up and walk away from him and never ask how and when did he leave Vermont. I don't really care. The guy is whack job.

I walk over to Edfucking G who's at a table with a bunch of young girls from home. Perfect. I sit next to this chick with dreds, her name is Holly and she will be a senior come September at UVM. She has a beautiful face and small little petite body, and she has armpit hair, which I like. She smells of coconut oil. She is wearing a bikini under her sundress, which I also like. She asks about my get up, "What's with the overalls at the beach?" And I tell her, "I'm leaving for Prague at 7 in the morning and in case I don't make it back to Trumbull tonight I will be somewhat packed and just catch my flight"
"Where's your toothbrush?"
"I will buy one there."
"I have everything I need right here" I tap on my waist where my money belt is.
"Why wouldn't you make back to Trumbull tonight? It's not that far?

"Well I might and I might not. That depends on you."

I say excuse me and walk back up to the bar and order a Jack for me and I buy Holly a beer. I sit back down.

"You didn't have to buy me a beer "she says.

"I know. I but I wanted to because I want to get you buzzed enough so I can take you for a stroll on the beach and possibly kiss you under the moonlight."

"You're crazy. Do you use that cheesy line on everyone, It's soooo baaad. You're being sarcastic right?" She's laughing

I lean over and whisper in her ear, "Hey Holly, don't embarrass me in front of my friends. I was serious. I think you're great and beautiful and what guy wouldn't want to make out with you. I'm sorry you thought I was being cheesy."

I lean back and can see the look on her face is one of hurt. She thinks she hurt my feelings.

Which is impossible.

I play the victim.

I get up with a sad look on my face and say, "Sorry about all this, I feel like a dick." I walk up to the bar I hear "Wait!"

I walk around to the other side so I have a view of her but she can't really see me. My friends know what's going on, I got this girl. She is going to mull around for a while before she decides to come and find me.

I drink more with my buddies.

It's around one in the morning and the bar is still packed, ladies everywhere. I lost track of Holly when all of a sudden she appears right by my side.

"You wanna do a shot with me?" She says in her little voice.

"I thought I was cheesy."

" No. No, I think we misunderstood each other."

"Oh I see maybe I was a bit cheesy now that I think about," I lie.

"No really, it was sort of flattering."

She orders two shots of tequila and we do it. Holly doesn't leave my side for the rest of the night.

I win.

I need more booze if I'm going to try to close this deal. I keep my eye on Budda. When he has to go back to refill the ice bin, I lean over the bar and grab a bottle of vodka. I do this so quick Holly doesn't even notice and I put the bottle inside my overalls.

The bouncer starts announcing last call and I ask Holly if she wants to go to a party afterwards on the beach. My friend Edfucking G lives on the beach with a few other animals. But there is no party tonight, I lied. Holly says yes and I tell her we will walk the beach to his house, it's about a quarter mile.

The beach is well lit with the moon and we can see each perfectly, I stop and take the bottle out of my overalls I tell her Budda gave it to me. She rolls her eyes. I take a swig from the bottle and she declines. But she starts kissing me. I take another swig and fall on the ground with Holly on top of me. The sand is becoming a bitch so I tell Holly to wait right here while I run up to the houses on the shore to see if I could grab a blanket.
I run thru 3 yards and find a beach blanket on the back deck of a cottage. I take it and run back to only see Holly's sundress and flip flops in the sand.
"Come in."

I look up and see Holly topless in the water.
I can't get all these clothes of fast enough. Finally I'm balls naked and run into the water.

I can't believe the rack on this small little girl, she must have back problems. We make out some more. The blanket didn't really matter considering I have sand all over me; it's in my ass crack, on my balls and in my mouth. It feels like she is jerking me off with sandpaper.
I bring her back in the water and fuck her.

The sun is coming up again and I barely slept. I leave the girl wrapped up in the blanket and walk back to the bar and use the pay phone across the street.
"Bud, what up man?
"You're an asshole, what time is it?"
"I don't know. Time for you to drive me to the airport?"
"You're on your own, guy."
"Come on, Bud. I don't have time to go back to Trumbull and beg my folks and I am not going to spend 150 bucks on a cab. Come on dude, I will owe you one."
"Where are you?'
"Seagrape parking lot."
"Fuck. I will be there in fifteen minutes. Later." Bud hangs up and I walk over to the deli and grab a coffee.

I'm just about to drift off on the bench in front of the store and I hear a loud screech. I open my eyes and see Bud. He is wide eyed. I know he hasn't slept yet. He is driving his father's brand new 120 thousand dollar Mercedes coupe convertible. His parents must be away.

"Wake up fucker and grab me a coffee."

On the way to JFK international Bud is telling me about the two chicks he picked up and that they are asleep at his house right now and how I should postpone my flight til later in the day and go hang out. He is talking a mile a minute and driving about 100 mph while looking at me and not the road.

He seems more excited about Prague than I am. He is starting to freak me out. "Don't worry about the movie. When you get back I will have plenty of post-production work for you, we still have to score it and sync it up. Don't worry, plenty of shit to do. Plenty of shit"
"Great, thanks, just watch the road, dude."

We pull up to the terminal and Bud hands me 5 Valium. "Take these. It's a long flight, and here." He gives me his tin of chewing tobacco. "Did you pack any rubbers?" He says as he is driving off laughing.

When I check in the lady behind the counter gives me shit for not having any luggage. She doesn't believe me when I tell her I'm buying my clothes there. She wants to know why I have an open ticket. I tell her it's open because I'm in the process of selling a movie and if the deal is made I have to fly back on a moment's notice. She could give a shit. I ask her to point in what direction is the bar at. She ignores me and I walk off.

I chug 3 nine dollar pints and eat all five pills before I board the plane. Once I get on the plane I put a dip in my mouth and sit next to a German couple.

I pass out before takeoff and I am being woken up by the attendants at Heathrow airport. My mouth is dry and I still have the chewing tobacco lodged in the side of my cheek. I have to piss so bad my dick is hard. I'm a little dazed walking around Heathrow and after I piss I walk over to the gate and lie down and sleep for two hours before my connecting flight to Prague.

I am really, really shot. I have not eaten in over 24 hours and my body is beginning to shut down and I'm in an airplane going to a country where I don't speak the language.
I need a beer.

When I land in Prague, I notice the airport is chaos. I don't know why or where I am going. I find a taxi driver that speaks very bad English. Fuck it, I jump in his car.
"Take me to the center."

He just nods and says O.K. The drive is about hour from the airport and I'm wondering how am I gonna pay this guy I haven't converted my money yet and all I have is $20's. We pull up to a museum, the center of the city. I give the guy a twenty and say thanks. I get out of the cab. I figure an hour taxi ride is worth twenty bucks. Anyway I can't deal and just walk away. I hang out in the city.

Eat a sidewalk sausage and try to find a hostel. It becomes an impossible task so I grab another cab. I look for one that could speak English. I jump in and say, "Bring me to a hostel." He says "O.K." I relax in the back and check out the scene. In about 15 minutes we arrive at a place up in the hills. I see 12 or 15 buildings that are each 13 stories tall. Across the street I see this enormous stadium.

(Later on I am told that the stadium was built for the 1936 Olympics but because of the war it was never used. It supposedly could hold a hundred thousand people. At the moment the dormitories were hostels, it was like its own little city of travelers.)

The cab driver drops me off and I tell him, "I gotta go inside to get change."
"No," he says
"Do you have change?"
I show him the twenty and then he grabs it quick out of my hand.
"Hey fucker wha…"
He starts yelling in broken English, "Twenty dolla!" and gets back into his car.
I just got fucked, welcome to Prague.

I walk up to the reception desk and ask if I could have my own single room. She tells me it will double in price and I say how much and she says 8 American dollars a night. Great I will take 30 nights now. I pay her up front $240 dollars.

The bathroom and showers are down the hall and the bar/ breakfast area are directly across from my room on the second floor. I check it out and push the two beds together. I take off my black slacks. I can't remember when the last time I showered was. I walk outside and introduce myself to a group of backpackers sitting on the grass. Some Australian girls, some English girls and a couple of dudes from Wales. We all meet and greet and they let me tag along into town and join them for dinner.
My adrenaline is pumping.

This one chick shows me how to convert my cash and I realize things are pretty cheap here. After dinner we head into some club way underground with no windows and the walls are rock. It's some sort of cave. Packed. Music blaring. We grab a table and people are everywhere. I can't stop chugging these warm beers. And I keep buying rounds for everyone. Some

dude lays out some powder on the table and I ask him, "What is that?" I can't understand his accent and it's too fuckin' loud. He says something but all I can understand is, "…..it comes from the border of Poland…." It looks like fish scales. I roll up some Czech bill and snort a lot of it. It burned.
And instantly I was full of happiness, all jacked up.

The next thing I know, I am on the outskirts of town with 3 Australian guys in a local bar and the fucking sun is up again.
Randy tells me that we have been snorting speed all night. Fuck that.
"I don't do speed" I tell him. "Well, mate you were doing it last night. For fuck's sake, a couple of hours ago."

Beers are cheaper outside of the city so I keep buying rounds for everyone. I am exchanging American dollars at this shithole pub at 7 in the morning, Fuck it. I keep drinking.

Next thing I know I'm wearing a sheet from my bed and just my money belt underneath it sitting outside the hostel on a picnic table. This Australian chick from the night before can't believe I'm still awake and she convinces me to go lay down in my room, which I do.

I wake up at 3 hours later, take a shower and put on my black slacks and go out on the town again, this time by myself. I learn the subway system in no time and the bus schedule. I stay away from the clubs and hang out at a joint café Gula Gula, It's an artsy place with eclectic music and smoking hot staff. I like this place.
I meet other backpackers mostly from the states and I hate them. They're from the midwest and they have that stupid accent, they dress like assholes, rude to women and have that whole fraternity thing goin on. I keep my distance from any Americans.

That night I meet this girl from England named Fiona, she is traveling by herself for a few months around Eastern Europe and hangin' in Prague for a while. She has long black hair, great green eyes, big boobs and a tight body plus her accent makes her better. She is intelligent.
We start talking the way you do when traveling. And then she tells me she knows of a great restaurant we can go to.

This is great, I'm in Prague 2 days and I have this incredible chick askin' me to dinner. I must behave. No drug talk. Be a gentleman, Wolfgang, she's nice. I would make her my girlfriend in a second but that doesn't happen, she has a plan, an itinerary with her. I pay for the meal because it's cheap and I want her to think I'm a big shot.
I'm loser.

We plan on meeting up again the next day or the day after that and she splits to her hostel and I go to mine.

The bar is right across from my room and I can't pass by it without going in.
Ever.

I meet these Swedes and all they do is drink and drink.

They take me to go buy hash at 2am in the city.

I haven't seen a black person here at all and then I walk down a street next to Chaparouse and I see all these Nigerian blacks selling hash and kind bud. We buy it and eat a gram of hash each. Fuck it, we couldn't find any smoking utensils.

I end up in this club and I hate clubs. I hate club music, it's not for me but I make the best of it. I fuck this little Goth girl in the men's room, I prop her on the edge of the urinal and fuck the hell out of her, no rubber, but her huge platform shoe is nailing my back and I can't take it so I stop. I don't remember her name so I ask her and then I ask her where she's from. She says, "Inga from Holland, you just ask me that."

I must be really fucked up because I can't remember how I even started talking to her. She looks young. "Inga," I say. "Did you come to Prague with your friends?" She replies, "No, I with my parents visiting my brother."

Really.

"How old are you?"

"16."

I pull up my pants and pull her off the urinal. I ask her if she wants me to get her a drink and she says yes without even looking at me. I tell her I will be right back and walk off, straight out the doors and into a taxi.

I meet the Swedes back at the hostel and we start drinking again this time in one of the guy's room, Jonas. I walk in and I see his garbage can completely full of piss.

"Dude, the bathroom is right across the hall from your room."

"I know but fuck it."

"I understand, but how are you going to get rid of that, it's filled to the rim. If you pick it up it will definitely spill."

"Watch!"

This dude takes off all of his clothes and props open his room door with a book and picks up the garbage can very slowly. He is taking small little baby steps towards the door and I can see the piss flowing over the top on to his hands and floor. We are both laughing and he takes the bucket of piss and just throws it down the hallway.

Piss everywhere.

The loud noise from the garbage can wakes a few people up. I decide to tiptoe thru the piss and go to my room. Then I hear the arguments and the yelling and then the fight in the hallway I don't leave my room and now I have to piss. I shut off the lights open up the window. I have to climb 3 ft. up on the heating vent in order to piss out the window. I do. No one notices. I try to go to sleep and the sun is about to come up. What am I doing in Prague?

I get a phone call from Fiona at my hostel which is weird because I didn't know you can do that. She asks me if I would like to go to the community pool this afternoon. "Sure." It's not like I have a plan or anything. I don't have shorts so I go to the lost and found and actually walk away with some nice surfer shorts and an old 70's style leather coat.

I take the bus a half hour to meet Fiona, on that bus ride I meet 2 German girls vacationing in Prague for a week, I saw them at my hostel before but they looked young, so I didn't talk to them. So now they come and talk to me. We do the introduction and they tell me they are alone traveling and they are each 16 years old. I am blown away that someone's parents would let their young girls travel alone abroad. I become friends with them in the big brother kind of way. They are also going to the pool.

I get off the bus and meet Fiona. I greet her with these 2 young chicks and tell her that they are staying at my hostel so we came down together. They introduce themselves and a little small talk before we all decide to sit together on the grass. I realize I left my sunglasses on the bus. *Bad mistake.*

The pool is enormous, old, but big. There must be a couple hundred people here sunbathing and swimming. It's nice.
Fiona lays out a huge blanket and she brought some fruit and cheese.

The German girls' names I can't pronounce, so I call them each "sister". They also brought some fruit and vodka.

It takes me a minute to realize that 80 percent of these people are naked, fully naked. I turn around to see the two 15 year olds naked on the blanket next to Fiona.
I am freaking out.

Fiona takes off her top but leaves her bathing suit bottoms on. I am lying in the middle of naked girls. No sunglasses. Everyone is acting completely normal. Except me. I have to lay on my stomach because my dick is so hard it will pop out my shorts. I shut my eyes because I feel like someone will catch me staring, I end up falling asleep for a while and I awake to the girls giggling.

They are sitting up, passing the vodka bottle around discretely among themselves. They take a quick swig then suck on a peach slice.

Fiona can drink that crazy English chick. The German girls stand up and walk over to the pool, I can't help but to look. This is too weird for me. Fiona tits are perfect.

I take a huge gulp from the bottle. Fiona grabs my hand and we walk into the pool.

This is great.

I never want to go home.

Not once have I been depressed. I love my life.

Fiona is in my arms in the pool.

I am holding her legs while her arm is around my shoulders. I am slowly spinning around, almost like dancing. It's a very romantic moment because neither of us say a word, we just feel good in the sun, in the water. I try to kiss her and she laughs and says, "No".

Playing hard to get? Then the two Germans jump on me, they are both trying to dunk me and rip off my bathing suit. I am afraid to wrestle with them or have any physical contact so I get up out of the pool and go lay down. Fiona is already there.

Fiona wants to know if I want to go out to another restaurant again tonight. I say yes but feel bad in front of the Germans so I extend the invitation, they tell me they can't afford it and I tell them my treat.

So, dinner and drinks with these girls.

At the restaurant sitting at the head of the table with two shots of Jack Daniels and a pint of warm beer. No one believes in ice in this country. I eat very little and drink a lot. I am sort of bored with these chicks. Fiona is great and all but I need more. When the bill comes I pay and tell everyone I'm tired and going home and they seem disappointed.

I walk the German girls home and Fiona is with me, when we reach her hostel she gives me a big hug and a kiss on the cheek and says, "Thank you, Wolfgang, dinner was excellent. Should I give you a ring tomorrow?"

"Yeah, sure, good bye."

I'm thinking what the fuck with this girl.

Whatever.

I go back to the hostel bar and this is where I meet the three Irishmen; Nicki, Johnny and Delroy. Nicki and Johnny are brothers, Delroy is their neighborhood friend.

We spend the rest of the night drinking Absinthe and enjoying each other's company. Nicki tells me that they are traveling around Europe for the summer and they just came from Amsterdam. They have pot and mushrooms. The first time I smoke pot from Amsterdam I almost throw up.

It's about five in the morning and I'm in the basement dorms of the hostel, I'm so fucked up on Absinthe, my vision is becoming blurred. I take a hit of this weed and lose all sense of everything. I kept asking, "Where am I?" the Irishmen said.

A few days have gone by and all I did was lie in bed. My body was shutting down. The sweats. The cramps . The lack of sleep. The long and over extended jerkoff sessions.

The depression was eating at my mind again.

I have $300 dollars left and I've been here for only ten days.

Is this movie going to sell? And how?

Too much to think about.

I take a shower and walk over to see if Fiona is at her hostel. She's not, she left. I grab some pints at a bar and feel good again. When I get back to my hostel I see the receptionist and she tells me I have a bunch a messages and she says in her Czech accent, "Where have you been Wolvgang?" It's nice to hear the concern in her voice. "I was in my room," I said. "Vee vere knocking for days and no answer and then vee open the door and nobody there."

"Really? Maybe you had the wrong room, I'm in 208."

"Yes vee know, Wolvgang."

I take the messages and shrug my shoulders and walk away. Fiona left me four messages, she is going to Budapest for a week or so and she will return to Prague soon. She also left her address and email.

Two messages from the German girls wanting to know where I am.

The Irishmen left a hand written note. "Wolfgang we are in room 4 in the basement. Nick."

Things are good. I like the fact people were looking for me. I go to the hostel bar and I see the Irishmen. They are happy to see me walk in and we start drinking warm pints before heading to Café Gula Gula. I need to watch my money if I want to stay here for the summer. The Irishmen are good a buying rounds.

As we sit and bullshit they ask me if I'm going to travel anywhere else in the Eu. I tell them no. I was just planning on staying in Prague. I don't want to tell them I am running out of money.

We drink for days and nights at café Gula Gula, I get to know all the hot waitresses and the bartender. I convince them to let me run tabs. It's my home away from home away from home. We can't leave, ever, because every day is new backpackers. New opportunities.

So many girls.

I run into the German girls on the street while I'm with the Irishmen. The Irish get a little weirded out when they see these two young girls approach me and start hugging and kissing me. I invite them back to my hostel bar and they come. My Irish friends don't say anything. The German girls tell me they are going home tomorrow. I'm sort of happy. But in the meantime they are drinking like Germans. I buy shots of Absinthe and that puts them overboard. They end up retreating to my room to pass out.

I stay out until dawn again with the Irishmen and we rob a bakery truck that was making morning deliveries. We don't take money. We steal all the Danishes and muffins without getting caught.

I now have 12 racks of breakfast treats stacked in my room, it's daylight and I pass out next to these two drunk underage girls snoring next to me. It's so hot in the room and it smells of body odor and booze.

I sleep for four hours and I am woken up by someone jerking me off. At first it feels good then I realize who is doing it and I freak. I tell the German girls, "No. No. No." I jump out of bed and throw my overalls on and forget that it ever happened.

The girls have been drinking coffee and smoking cigarettes and eating my Danishes all morning. They don't have to leave until night time and they need a place to hang while they wait. So I let them stay.
I leave and go back to the bar.

My money is real low.
I drink for free or on my tab.
I get fucked up. Quick.
I pound warm pints and go back to the hostel and meet up with the Irishmen. I say my goodbyes to the Germans and we exchange emails.
(I will still be in touch with these girls 12 years later.)

We decide instead of sitting in bars all day we will go out and do the tourist thing. We go to the bus station and find a couple of tours to go on, outside of the city. We see an archeological expedition going on 2 hours away we take it. Now we have one hour to scramble for road drinks and food before we depart on this bus.

I notice that there are a lot of chicks going on this tour and that is a good thing. I also run into the crazy Swede, Jonas. Jonas is very good looking; he is about 6 foot 5, blue eyes and brown shaggy hair. He has a bottle of vodka with him and he is already drunk. The tattoo on his arm reads "who is your god" with no question mark and it is written in French. The bus ride is a rather enjoyable experience. The bottle of booze is being passed around and a bunch of Canadian chicks are singing some Elton John song that I forgot the name of.

Johnny pulls out a bag of mushrooms. The bag is sealed and it has "Magic Shrooms" printed on the label. It's from Amsterdam.
I say, very serious, "Dude, are you sure that's a good idea?"
Johnny replies, "Tell me the difference between a good idea and a bad idea?"
I have no answer.

I think about it and watch as he pours out a couple a caps and stems and throws them in his mouth. I put out my hand and gobble up a few pieces. Johnny passes the bag to his brother Nick and he eats some then gives the rest to the Swede. I turn and tell Johnny, "Now THAT was a bad idea." He agrees.

Kat was hot for an English chick with a snaggle tooth. She is wearing a sundress and has short, short brown hair. Everyone on the tour wants to fuck her. She is our guide.

As soon as we exit the bus we are given a list of rules, the Swede crumbles his up and throws it as far as he could. I can see that this guy is gone and this whole event is not going to go so well. Kat sees this and immediately asks him if he is intoxicated.
"Only on life baby," he replies.
"Why would you litter? The first rule is no trash. Carry your own garbage."
"I was trying to get in the trash bin over there."
We all turn to look and there is no trash bin in sight, anywhere.
The mushrooms are kicking in.
Rule number 2. Do not touch anything.
After that I couldn't read anymore.

We get on site and I'm not impressed. It's a shit load of dirt and holes. Kat says the soil is from the 15th century. Who really gives a fuck, I want to say. Nick is throwing up and laughing at the same time and walks off tour. The Swede gets kicked off for pissing on the site. Johnny can't speak and Delroy is in the bus sleeping. We don't belong there and decide it would be in our best interest to get the fuck out of there as soon as possible.

The real problem manifests itself when the bus driver refuses to take us back. We have to wait until the end of the 5 hour tour. The Swede is crazy at this point and puts his hands on the driver as to pull him out of his seat.
I can't believe what I'm seeing:

The driver pulls out a pistol and points it at the Swede and directs him off the bus. I start to giggle a little bit and that starts off a laughing fit between the Irishmen.

We are fuuucked uuup.

The Swede is on the ground, crying in the dirt. The driver is screaming in Czech or whatever. The rest of the tour group is watching from afar. I realize we are in the middle of nowhere and we NEED this guy to bring us back. I walk towards the man with my hands up and a huge shroomed out smile on my face.

"Excuse me, Sir. Sir, do you speak any English?"

He just looks at me.

"I want to give you money for our friend's behavior."

Now he listens.

"Sir. We will leave now and go sit quiet and abandon the rest of the tour as long as you bring us back to Praha at the end?"

I lean down towards the Swede who is still lying in the dirt face down, and I go into his front pocket and pullout his cash. My back is turned to the driver. I take half the money and stuff it into my front pocket.

Quick.

As I turn back around I extend my hand and give the guy about forty American dollars in Czech currency.

"We're sorry about this and we will see you soon."

The Irishmen pick up the Swede and the driver gets back on the bus and shuts the door.

The tour disappears somewhere.

Delroy is still sleeping on the bus. Nick suggests we walk off into the forest for a while and try to get our acts together. We do. We still have a bottle of Black Death vodka from Russia and it tastes like fucking gasoline, but we still pass it around.

I am trying to drink as much vodka as I can so I can offset the shrooms because they are really starting to bug me out.

It doesn't work.

We keep walking and bullshitting and realize no one knows how to get back to the bus. And no one has a watch. The Swede is so fucked up, he hasn't said a word in a couple of hours and his facial expression is pure evil. We come across a road in the back country and we watch as the Swede flags down the only car coming our way.

The car stops and we watch the Swede walk over to the window and say a few words in a different language. Then he takes a step back from the car and gaggles up this big lugi and spits it in the guy's face..

Great. Now what.

The guy, who is built like a hockey player, kicks open his door and jumps out right in the Swede's face. The Swede clocks him so hard and quick on the chin, it sounds like two rocks being banged together. The car dude becomes dead weight and drops right where he's standing.

The Irishmen drag the car guy onto the grass next to the road. The Swede starts laughing as he is revving up the engine from the driver's seat. "Who has a driver's license?" The Swede says.

I jump in the back seat with Johnny, and Nick is in the front.

The Swede wasn't kidding.

He can't drive.

I don't trust anyone behind the wheel and my perception is still distorted. Nick jumps into the driver's seat and takes control. I am afraid to ask him how fucked he is so I don't. We have no clue in what direction we should be going in and it's only a matter of time before this guy wakes up from his nap and reports his car stolen.

We drive for close to an hour now and now we all have to piss. We pull into this little town and find a petrol station. We all get out and go to the men's room and Nick goes inside and tries to get some information on how to get back to Praha. We start losing it again in the men's room, laughing fits. Uncontrollable. That crazy fuckin' Swede pulls a folded up piece of paper out of his sock.

This is no good.

It's that whacky speed from Poland and I tell him, "No fuckin' way, I don't want any of that shit."

Then I take two small little key bumps.

Just so I can get back to normal. The Irishmen do more than their fair share. The Swede is blown out on it already.

Nick tells us that some woman told him that the train station is 3 kilometers away and that we can jump on a train to the center of Prague.

We ditch the car in a shitty neighborhood and walk to the nearest liquor store, then grab a taxi to the train station.

I spot the Swede for a ticket. He tells me "I don't know where all my money has gone, maybe it fell out of my pocket?"

"Don't worry dude, I got ya. Just pay me back when we get back to the hostel." He doesn't know I'm paying for his ticket with his own money.

On the train we keep drinking. I'm amazed that no one has brought up the events of the day. Not a word is spoken about it. Like it was the norm.

Animals.

I get back to my room finally. I can't live like this. Everything is getting a little out of control. Everyone I meet is off the wall. Do I attract these people? Am I the whack job? What the hell am I doing here? For real.

Anytime I can remember a dream it consists of tornados.

I can feel my body shutting down as I stare at the ceiling. My thoughts are in battle again. Positive vs. the negative. Elizabeth is now married and on her honeymoon somewhere and I am here. I am in the country called Crazy and the state of Delusion. People my age don't take summer vacations for the whole summer, like school kids do. Everyone back home is working, getting on with their lives, and I am dicking around in Prague.
I feel guilty and the depression and shame soon follow.
I got to start drinking again.
I need to poison the demons inside my mind.

Days pass and the usual shit takes place; drink, fuck and take some sort of drugs.

I am officially out of money again. No nothing. No one to call and I wouldn't anyway.
Fuck it.
I can get a job teaching English and try to live straight on the little money I could make.
Be responsible.
No way, it's just a bullshit thought.
I am on vacation, why would I work?
I just need to find the right opportunity in the next twelve hours.
And I do.

It's 1 am and I am at the hostel bar next to my room. I have been drinking pints and Absinthe. Surge the bartender lets me drink on a tab as long as I pay it before the end of each week. The Irishmen are draining beers at a good rate. The room is packed with backpackers and cigarette smoke. As always I'm at a table with some girls and the Irishmen when out the corner of my eye I see these two unsavory guys lurking around. I notice that the bartender notices.

These girls from New Zealand just arrived at the hostel and are a day early. Vary was one of the girls name, I don't know if I knew the other one. They have all their bags with them and no place to stay for the night, due to check in at 10 am the next day. I tell Vary that I have a double room and she and friend could split a bed if they want to. Of course she says yes.
We continue drinking.

All the girls' bags are in the corner of the bar on a bench filled with other bags and coats. It's only about fifteen feet away from us. The place is loud and Depeche Mode is playing on the system. I am trying to get to know these chicks better when I see one of the unsavory dudes kick one of the girls' bags from the bar floor into the hallway.

It's hard for me to get up because I am stuck in the back of this round table with my chair up against the wall. I push the table away from me and jump over a few chairs to get out. This causes a big commotion but I get out the door and the bartender is right there with me. These two dudes were already out the door and running thru the parking lot.
This was my opportunity.

I am less than twenty yards away from these guys when the Bartender gives up running.
I still give chase and the dudes stop on the grass. They start yelling at me in German as they are approaching me.
I am alone.
Alone alone.
I am surrounded by woods. I can see one of the guys have a purse under his arm. I point
"That's not yours," I say almost out of breath.
I get clocked in the face by the other dude and fall right there. I hear them laughing.
I am thinking what the fuck am I doing here.

I take a softball-sized rock into my hand as I slowly get up. When I get to my feet I turn around and whack one dude in the face with the rock. The rock never leaves my hand and I hit him repeatedly until he is down.
I don't feel the kicks to my chest.

My adrenaline is high and I love it. My left eye is almost swollen shut and my white v-neck t-shirt is red with blood. I stand up and I get clocked again, this time in the chin and I bite my tongue. I fall back down. I'm on all fours and I can see the bag on the ground next to me. I am getting my ass beat. I'm trying to cover my face because I don't need any teeth kicked out tonight in Prague. If that guy picks up that rock I am a dead man. I grab the bag and curl it into me while I go into the fetal position. I am getting kicked in the back and then it stops.

I open my eyes and see Nick has this guy in a chokehold on the ground. I get up and slowly stomp on his face until he starts coughing up blood. I go into his pockets and pull out a few crowns. Nick is standing over the other guy. "This guy isn't moving," he says as he nudges him with his foot. "Fuck him," I say. Then I see Nick go thru the guy's pockets and pulls out a little cash. He looks at me and smiles. I smile back.
I thank Nick.
Finally, I get my hands inside the purse.

It contains the girl's passport, Euro-Rail ticket, flight itinerary. Address book and camera. Phone cards. Then in the side zipped pocket is five folded and crisp one hundred dollar bills.
I take it.
Nick doesn't see this and I don't tell him.

It takes ten minutes to walk back to the hostel. I didn't realize how far I ran.

I limp into the bar and everyone is cheering. I hold up the bag. I am the wounded hero.

I am a scumbag.

I hand Vary her bag and ask her to check if anything is missing.
"Passport is here. And my ticket, wait where is..? They took my money."
"Everything was thrown out on the ground when I approached them," I say, wiping off some blood with a bar towel.
Now the bartender is handing me a bag of ice for my eye.
"Well, Wolfgang. Thank you sooo much!" says Vary.

I fuck her that night while her friend is in the bed next to us.
Watching.

There are no curtains on the window and the sun comes up around 4:10 am. The room is well lit.

At one point the two of them are having a chat while I fuck Vary from the side. I won't fall asleep until they leave the room because I don't want to get robbed (back).
Only a person who steals thinks this way.
I am a bad man.
At least now my swollen and bruised face shows that I pay for my sins.

The next day I meet up with Nick and he tells me that Delroy has not slept in 3 nights.

"The fucking guy is staying up writing in his journal. Backwards! We had to read it all in the mirror."

"Really," I say because I think what an impossible thing that is.

"The shit he has been writing ain't good, mate. He's talking about Jesus and himself being, like, as one."

Now I'm really interested.

"Take me to him," I tell Nick.

So I travel down stairs to a crowd of people and I see Delroy beating up a bus driver. Nick and I break it up.

"Delroy, what the fuck man?"

Delroy stands off and is completely calm and says, "I'm sorry I thought you were the devil," and walks off.

The poor bus driver only has minor bruises on him. Johnny picks the guy up and explains to him that his buddy ain't right and they are very very sorry.

We go to the bar and Delroy is supposed to meet us in an hour or so. He never shows.

We drink and try to analyze the situation at hand. After a few pints we are split up, mixing it up with a few chicks. Delroy is on his own and not my problem. The night is just getting started and Johnny, Nick and myself all find women and we're going to a restaurant when we see Delroy. The streets are bustling with people and the sun close to setting and we walk up to him, and he is just staring at this church in front of him.

"Dude, Delroy!" Nick yells at him.

Delroy slowly turns around.

He doesn't say anything but he has this glazed look on with a huge grinning smile. "I feel like I'm on Ecstasy," he mumbles.

We all stop and gather around him. "Delroy, did you take something?" Johnny asks.

Delroy replies, "I don't need to take anything, I just feel good, I am in touch. Wolfgang understands."

We all look at each other.

Johnny takes Delroy by the arm and we proceed down the alley to the restaurant with girls in tow.

I have my chick to the right of me and Delroy is on my left, next to Johnny. I can see that this kid is going thru some sort of trip. Delroy gets up and I can see that he's handing out his possessions to other customers in the restaurant. He gives away his passport and his credit card.

He gives away his room key.

Then Nick jumps up and starts collecting the things back.

I can't be bothered and I tell Johnny, "Fuck him, if he wants to act crazy, let him."

Johnny understands that his friend is being a buzz kill and lets Delroy run off into the street while we enjoy our meal and company.

We drink.

We eat.

The next morning I am walking back from another hostel when I see these two Australian girls I know from my hostel.

"Did you see what happened, Wolfgang?"

"What?"

"Delroy was taken away in an ambulance"

"No shit."

"He stripped off all his clothes and was yelling that he was Jesus Christ. When the staff tried to calm him down he went balls and they called the proper authorities."

"What do you want me to do about it? I only met the guy 2 weeks ago."

"Have you seen Nick or Johnny?"

"I have not. But I will go and look for them."

I get into the Hostel and go straight to Nick's room. I bang on the door a few times before it opens to Nick half asleep.

"You seen Delroy?" I say.

"He never came back last night." Nick says, rubbing his eyes.

"The Aussie chick told me that the cops grabbed him for running around nude."

"For fuck's sake man. You ain't lyin?"

"Go ask the chick."

Nick wakes up Johnny and explains what's up. They dress and go out to get a cab to the police station. I wander upstairs to my room, piss in a bottle, lie down and fall asleep.

I over hear these Australian chicks talking about Delroy. I'm sitting in the dining room. She says they're able to get in touch with his parents and when Delroy was handed the phone to speak he said,"Mom, don't say anything. I can read your mind." And then he hung up the phone. I hear her tell her friend that she thinks he went schizophrenic.

I eat cold cuts with no bread and order a pint.
When the Aussie sees me in there she rushes over to tell me that Delroy was assaulting the police and they had to restrain him and not in a good way.
I really don't want to get involved.

Nick and Johnny go down to the police station, trying to find out what happened when they tell them Delroy was sent to an asylum. Nick gets directions and meets me back at the hostel.
"You've got to come with us," he says to me.
"Bullshit I do," I say

Then I realize these guys need support and I have nothing better to do, so I decide to go. Nick being the oldest of the group has told Delroy's parents he would look after him considering it was Delroy's first time away from home without supervision. He was much younger than the two brothers.

I've never been to an insane asylum.

Yet.

The bus ride is about an hour outside of Prague. It's a beautiful ride thru the country. No one really talks. I could see Nick and Johnny are a bit stressed out when we pull up to this huge 16th century castle sitting on plush grounds. It's something like out medieval times. I cannot believe this is a looney bin. We literally have to use steel knockers to bang on the front door. After a few big bangs a woman answers the door.
Her English is horrible.

Nick hands her a card that the police gave him and she takes it, looks at it, and welcomes us in.

This nut house looks medieval on the inside as well. You can hear people screaming and laughing, echoing down the hallways. The woman brings us to courtyard that has trees and picnic tables and fire pits.
She tells us to wait.
Everyone is feeling a bit sketched out in here.

The woman locked the only door in and out of the courtyard when she left. No one says anything, we all just look at each other. I could tell by the sun that it's getting late in the day and I don't want to be here when it gets dark. I hear the doors open and we see Delroy walk out. He is in a light blue tattered robe with dark blue pajamas and slippers. He looks really fucked up. He has a huge grin on his face and a long piece of drool hangs from his lower lip. I can't believe this shit, it's just like in the fucking movies. He is accompanied by a better looking woman than the last and her English is understandable. She explains to us that Delroy has a chemical imbalance, that he was prone to having a breakdown of sorts.

God like feeling.

He went schizophrenic but not paranoid. He's elated. She says he is highly medicated and they need to get in touch with his family for arrangements.

Delroy sits next to me on the bench. "Watcchh, I will make the fire." I can barely understand his drugged out mumbling.

He snaps his finger slowly.

"Watch meee make the fiiire."

I don't say anything and I watch him attempt to start a fire with his mind. Everyone is staring.

The woman interrupts and grabs Delroys attention and ours by fuckin' screaming, "Delroy! Delroy! Delroy! Delroy! Delroy!"

The kid ain't paying attention because he is out of his mind.

And then the woman is grabbing his arm and screaming again, "Delroy! Delroy!"

She's pissed and this starts a bit of tension among the Irishmen. They don't look too pleased on the way Delroy is being treated.

I need to get out of here before they lock us all in is what I keep thinking.

I tell Nick we've got to go because the last bus back to Prague is about to depart in 10 minutes.

He just looks at me.

I could tell he's a ticking time bomb.

He asks the woman for contact numbers so he can give it to Delroy's parents. Fuck this place.

I wait outside while Johnny is pissing around the corner. Nick appears with a few pieces of paper in his hand. We start walking to the bus stop and not a word is spoken.

Fiona is back.

She tells me she is heading back this way and did I forget. I am wearing the same clothes, a few pounds lighter and now I have a beard.

She comes into my room. "Look at you" she says. "Look at this PLACE," she continues while pointing at all the piss bottles in every corner of my room.

"Yea" I say as I am in the fetal position on a bare mattress.

"Wolfgang, you really should get out of here and come with me, I am going to Austria for five days."

I stop listening to her because I can't get my mind out of the gutter.

"Come lay down next to me," I say.

Fiona walks over fully clothed and lies down on her back on the corner of my bed. I lean over to listen to her.

Fiona is still talking. "I would like you to come with me to this restaurant tonight."

"I don't know," I say.

"Did you meet any boys on your trip?" I ask her.

"No," she smiles. "And what about you, you're always whoring around."

"Fiona, why would you say that? I'm a decent guy saving myself for a woman like you."

She laughs. I lean over and she lets me kiss her.

Later that day I clean up my act and go and meet Fiona. I'm excited because I really like this girl.

I would marry her.

At dinner I give her the whole run down about the Irishmen. I want to let her know that I spent my days helping these poor guys. (Of course this is only half true. The other half of the time I was getting fucked up and trying to fuck anything that moved, but I won't let her know that.)

"Wolfgang, have you decided if you want to come to Austria with me?"

"Well are we going as a couple or friends?"

"Why would you ask such a thing?" I could hear bitchiness in her voice.

"Fiona, I like you and it would piss me off a great deal if I go with you and along the way I have to watch men flirt with you and try to pick you up. I know what I am talking about. You know you're a beautiful woman and you like the attention of men."

Her eyes are squinting at me, I can see she is a bit taken back.

"So, no. I do not want to go with you as 'friends.'"

"Wolfgang, I like you but that's it. I like your company, I like your personality. I like your generosity. I think you're entertaining and I even like your I don't give a shit attitude. But we are FRIENDS. That's it. "

"I don't get it," I whisper to her. "And I don't see the point, I could care less about fucking Austria."

"See."

"See what?" I say and I'm getting pissed.

"Wolfgang, I know you better than you think I do. I am attracted to you. And I know once we get romantic you'll get bored of me. I can't keep your interests and the only reason you stick around is because I haven't fucked you."

"Man. Fiona, you are good," I am grinning. "If I go to Austria will we have sex?"

"NO." She screams.

"O.K. O.K, I was kidding you know that! Come on."

"You're an asshole."

"I know."

The waitress drops off the bill and I am surprised to see Fiona grab it from the table. I don't say anything. I have paid enough for this girl.

"Are you going out?" she asks as we are leaving.

"I'm going to café Gula Gula to get drunk, yes."

"You're already drunk," she says.

"No you're wrong. I'm ALWAYS drunk"

"Can I come with?"

"Yes," I say as I grab her in a playful headlock.

Before we step foot into the bar she gives me a peck on the cheek.

"What was that for?" I say.

"I like you, Wolfgang Klein," she whispers in my ear.

I see the Irishmen in the bar and a few other faces from the hostel. I turn to her and say, "I'm not going to Austria with you and after tonight we probably won't see each other again so stop fucking with me."

I walk into the bar and I can feel the rage inside trying to slip out.

I drink hard.

I want to kill someone. Who does this girl think she is toying with my emotions? I ignore her the rest of the evening.

The Irishmen tell me that Delroy's parents are flying down in a couple of days and that they have to charter a private plane back to Ireland because Delroy could be a risk on commercial airlines.

Fuck that I say.

I blackout for the rest of the evening and I wake up with Fiona in the spoon position. She is fully dressed. I am naked. When she awakes she gives me a peck on the cheek. I really like this chick. I keep pressing her hand down towards my hard cock and she gently strokes it once then gets out of bed. "I had a lot of fun with you, Wolfgang Klein, but I must leave now." Fiona's telling me this as she is writing something on a piece of paper she grabbed from her purse. "We will talk soon," She says as she is hugging me and then she leaves.

I feel the pains of my black heart breaking just a little bit. I am naked and I can smell myself. I instantly think about Elizabeth and this puts me back into a stage of depression. I am living like an animal while she is out cruising the Mediterranean in style. I live like a pig.

I am a pig.

I do bad things and feel bad about them but still do them.

I loathe myself.

What am I doing here? Why do I have it so hard? Am I really a bad person or just using my instincts, my survival skills?

Where are you God?

I am afraid to sober up because the withdrawals are terrifying. The night terrors alone scare me to death. I call on the Irishmen and tell Nick, "I don't feel right, and it's not a physical thing. I'm starting to have fucked up thoughts." He can tell by the look on my pale face, I'm scared. "Listen mate, you need to get yourself healthy, we'll go and get some fruit and juices at the market. You can't drink 12 hours a day every day for a month and not have repercussions," he tells me. "You need to eat and only drink beer and water. Stay off the spirits man, that shit will kill you."

I don't want to tell him that I've started to think suicidal thoughts.

Nick grabs a beer from his bag and hands it to me as I sit up. I open the lid and once it touches my lips it never leaves. He tells me that Delroy's parents are arriving tomorrow.

That beer made feel only a little better I need about 15 more.

I put on my overalls and Nick and I go into the city.

I feel all this debauchery in Prague has run its course and it's time to go back to the States. I need to get healthy and sober up and try to see this movie through. But I know that once I get home after two hours of being there I am going to regret it, so fuck that idea.

I lay low for five days, I keep my drinking to a minimum of six beers at night. During the day I drink a gallon and a half of water and take walks to and from Charles Bridge. I eat plenty of Bananas. I try to think happy thoughts.

I clean my room and do my laundry for the first time since being here. I plug up the shower drain and let the hot water fill up a couple of inches. Someone gives me shampoo and that's what I use for detergent. I let the clothes get nice and wet and then pour half the bottle of shampoo on it. I try to use my hands and rub the clothes together as if that will do something. It doesn't and the water turns black, not gray. Black. I unplug the drain and let the shower run on my clothes for a good half hour before I pull them out and hang them to dry in my hot as hell room.

I have $278 American dollars left.
If I am smart I could make it last.
As long as I stop acting like a big shot and buying drinks for everyone I should be fine.
I feel rejuvenated.
My room is clean my clothes are cleaner than before and I am clean. My head is clear again.

I meet up with the Irishmen and a few other dudes from France and we go to Chapparouse. The place is packed, real packed. I know the waitress and she hooks us up. She brings five cold beers right to us. I make my way across the room and find a seat on a couch. There is so much smoke in the room my eyes are burning. The girl next to me sees that I'm tearing up and offers me her scarf. Its summertime and this chick is wearing a scarf, that should have been a sign right there.
Foolish me.

She speaks English and is from Larchmont, N.Y. She went to NYU and is taking summer classes in Prague. She is tall and Jewish. Great body and her face isn't bad, but she always has this pissed off look on it. Her name is Alice and she is fucking crazy.
"Are you sure?" I ask.
And Alice replies, "Yes. Yes, take it!" And hands the scarf to me. I wipe my eyes.

I spend the next two hours pretending to listen to this crazy as she tells me her whole life story. I bear through it because I really want to fuck the whacko. She tells me she is leaving town tomorrow night but she will be back in a week. I could give a shit. I am putting on the act and she has no idea. I will say whatever it takes. I will do whatever it takes to fuck this girl before she leaves. I put on the charm and nice guy act and tell her that I'm not looking to hook up with anyone, I could do that anytime, I tell her. I say "I just want to have a girlfriend I can hang out with, you know, a good friend… someone I deeply care about and also get to screw."
She looks at me.
I am stoned face.
I count to the number 4 in my head.

She breaks with a huge sigh and smile."Awww that is the nicest thing I have ever heard a guy say."

Really.

"Well I'm just trying to be honest."

I ask her if we can see each other when we get back to New York and that seals the deal.

I start walking her back to my pad and we walk through the square past this bar/sidewalk café. I see this dark haired tattooed chick staring at me as I walk by. I can't stop looking at her. We lock eyes for longer than a moment and it seems weird that we are both staring each other down. This image is burned in my head. This is the woman I've been looking for in my fucked up dreams. She is the one. I must find her again soon.

I get back to the hostel bar and it's the same ol' same ol'. I don't even want to fuck what's her face anymore, so I let her in my room, tell her where the bathroom is, and then tell her I have to make a phone call to the States, I will be back in a bit. And with no guilt I walk back into the bar. I can't get the tattooed girls face out of my head.

I start drinking Jack Daniels and soon one by one the remaining Irishmen come in. And they brought some pussy with them. Irish bush and there is one for me too. I don't have much time so I immediately grab the girl's hand and we start running down the stairs and outside into the woods. She must smell my pheromones because there's not much talking when we meet. I just say, "Oh your name is Wendy. Wendy my name is Wolfgang." We shake hands but I don't let go. I lean over to her ear and ask her, "Do you want to go outside and make out?"

In a matter of minutes I'm on my back in the dirt and this Irish chick is riding me like a pro. I'm good for 2 minutes of hard penetration before I'm about to blow. I tell her to get off and she won't. She bucks faster and I try to throw her off and she leans forward and pounds herself harder against me. At that point I'm done. And I forgot the condom.

We both walk back smoking a cigarette.

I left Alice 23 minutes ago.

I don't wash up. I just go back to the hostel bar. No one notices that I was gone. I grab the Absinthe bottle and start pouring shots of it to all my friends at the bar. I'm feeling good. I'm in high spirits.

From the bar which is located across the hall from my room and four steps down, you have a perfect view of my door. A few backpackers and the Irish chick say, "Hey did you see a naked girl leave that room?"

I look up and wait.

I see Alice returning from the bathroom and going back into my room. She is wearing nothing. I look at everyone in the bar and say, "Gotta go guys." I smile at the Irish chick that I just fucked. She smiles then throws her beer in my face and tries to hit me. The bartender grabs her and a little scuffle happens before the bartender kicks her ass out and I ask the Irishmen, "Where did u find this nut bag?" I leave and walk up four steps to the naked girl behind my door.

She tells me her nickname is "Puddles".

I don't really get it until she starts squirting all over my bed. I have only seen squirters in porn, and now I have a real live one. I have sex with this girl all night and by morning my room is covered in bodily fluids.
Alice tells me she is leaving for a few days and when she returns can she stay with me for 2 nights before she flies back to the States. "Sure," I say because this is the craziest sex I've had and I'm not finished with her yet. She leaves and I finally take a much needed shower.

I'm exhausted, lying on my mattress.

My thoughts are becoming scary and I don't want to let those negative vibes take hold of me. I am also running low on cash again. I have a few hundred bucks left but that is only good for a couple of days.
I know I'm going to have to pull some shady shit again and that thought doesn't sit well with me.

I decide I will worry about these problems when I'm broke and sober. Right now I'm going to find the tattooed girl and get fucked up. I get out of bed and go looking for her.

I meet up with the Irishmen and the usual happens.
We start drinking.
It's noon.

I'm sitting in the windowsill at café Gula Gula and I see Billy Corgan of *The Smashing Pumpkins* walk right past me. It's eighty degrees outside and this guy is wearing a black turtleneck and black pants with his pale shaved head walking with his guitar player. I yell "Yo Billy boy!"
He turns around, never takes off his sunglasses, and looks right at me. I raise my fist in a Black Panther sort of way.
He pauses then turns back around and continues to walk away.
The Irishmen think I'm an asshole.
They're right.

Now that I'm buzzed I am on a mission to find Tattoo Girl.

I walk past the place I saw her. She's not there. I stroll around for a few hours jumping from pub to pub, getting nice and juiced up.
I remember thinking I really love this lifestyle.
No work, all play.
If only I had a boatload of cash.
I go to the town square and it's so fucking crowded I have to sit down. So I make my way to the Church steps and lay down instead. It's hot and I shut my eyes for what I think is a minute but it's longer because when I wake up, it's dark out.
People are still packed in the square to check out the clock and the steps I'm on are littered with bodies. I stand up to stretch and that's when I see her. She is about 30 feet in front me.
I hustle down the steps and grab her arm.
"Hey," I say as she turns around. I let go of her arm. "I have been looking for you all day." The girl is a little startled. "My name is Wolfgang. I don't mean to scare you, I saw you yesterday in that café and all I did was think about you since then. Are you alone?"

In a real strong Austrian accent she says, "Hello, Wolfgang. My name is Katy and yes, I'm alone here"

"Katy, it's too crowed here. Can I buy you a pint in a pub somewhere and talk to you?" She grabs my hand and I follow her thru the crowd to a side street that's less packed. We walk into a bar and I order two drafts.
"Did you see me yesterday?" I ask her.
"Yes I did I see you walking with that girl past the café last night."
"Yes that was me. I saw you too and I wanted to stop but that girl I was with was staying in the same hostel as me and she was so fuckin' drunk, I wasn't going to let her walk back alone."
"Uh huh," she goes, not buying this bullshit for a second.
"So do you live here?"
"I live in Vienna and my father lives in Prague. So my brother and friends came down for a week's holiday. My brother is off doing something else and I'm pretty much on my own. What are you doing here?"
That's a good question.
"I'm here on holiday for a couple of weeks." I say.

I can't believe how beautiful this girl is, just stunning I can't take my eyes off of her. "Where are your friends?

"Everyone sleeps all day and then they go out late at night, I prefer daytime to night."

"Can I buy you dinner tonight, Katy? When are you going back home? Are you staying close to here?" All these questions come out rapid fire. I'm getting a little nervous and I don't know how to tell her I want to spend the rest of my life with her.

"Really do you…"

I cut her off before she can say anything else, "Katy, listen. I don't want to sound crazy. I know we just met but I like the way I feel when I'm in your presence. Once I saw you I couldn't get you out of my mind and I spent the day looking for you. I'm telling you it's fate that we met."

"Wow," she says sarcastically. "Ok Wolfgang you can take me to dinner. My brother and his friends leave tomorrow and I am staying another 4 days. My father is in rehab and I have to wait for him to get home before I go back to Vienna."

"Tell me about the art work on your arms, did you do it yourself?

"Well I'm an artist, sculpting and paint. These are smaller versions of my work I had put on my arm. I actually photographed them to a certain size and had a friend duplicate them onto my arms. Do you like?" she asks.

"I do. A lot. Anywhere else you have them?

"No just my arms. How about you, Wolfgang, any markings or piercings?"

"No, clean, I like them but I know once I get them I will probably regret it a few years later." She looks at me with a raised brow and says, "I could understand that."

I think I hurt her feelings.

"You know when I came here, I packed nothing. I only have what you see - and a dirty pair of overalls. I grabbed some things at the lost and found but nothing good." (I'm shooting to change the subject of tattoos.) "Do you know any 2nd hand shops or vintage clothing stores?"

"Yes I do," she says. "I was there this morning, if you like I can take you now, and it's not too far."

"Most definitely"

We down our beers and before we leave I ask the bartender for 2 shots of Jack Daniels. Katy shrugs her shoulders and does it. I do mine because I need it to calm my nerves.

This chick is great thank you God.

I ask her where I can get a chain wallet like the one she's sportin'. We walk together holding hands and I can't believe all this is really happening. I just saw this chick yesterday and thought about this subconsciously. Is this for real? Am I awake?

Something must be wrong with her.

"Yellow looks good with your tan," she says as she is handing me a1960's polyester golf shirt. I put it on and button it up. "Do you like?" "Oh yeah, nice old school cut." I say.

"Good, it looks good on you." She takes it off me and says, "I will buy this for you since you bought the drinks."

"Come on now," I say .

"Wolfgang, I could afford 2 crowns on a shirt. You spent more than that on drinks."

"Fine." I don't persist.

I walk outside to light up a smoke and I am looking thru the glass window at Katy as she is waiting in the checkout. I am thinking what a cool chick, what a great day. I will marry this girl tonight if she wanted. Then I see her put the shirt on, she was only wearing a white wife beater. As she walks up to the cashier I see her say something and then point and walk away. I don't really pay any mind to it.

Katy walks into the bathroom for a moment and then comes outside to meet me wearing the shirt. "Okay let's go," She says and grabs my hand and we get lost in the crowd of people.

I think she stole the shirt but I don't say anything.

I don't care.

I bring her to the hostel just to show her off to the Irishmen and everyone else. It works.

I take a shower while the Irishmen are entertaining her and then we all go to dinner. At the restaurant the waitress is being a douche bag. I don't think she likes Americans, I don't think she likes ME because I keep coming in repeatedly with different chicks.

No tip for her.

After dinner and drinks I realize I have maybe enough money to last 3 days, maybe.

Shit.

We are all at a club getting down when she plants the first kiss on me. I grab her and leave and we start making out on the street. "Wolfgang come with me to my father's flat, he doesn't live far."
"Let's go."

The place is huge. It's trashed a bit with broken guitars and amplifiers. And some holes in the walls.
"My father is a Czech rock star, and this is 3rd time in rehab, we did some cleaning when we arrived because the place was destroyed. My father went nuts and the neighbors called the police. He had a choice of jail or rehab because they found drugs in the flat. He chose rehab."
Katy shows me her art, which is hung on every wall. I like it.

I spend the next 3 days with her in the flat. She cooks and does some painting when we aren't making love.
I am sober.
I don't want to ever leave this girl.
    I invite her to come to the States and she says, "I would love to but can't afford it." I open my big mouth and say, "Don't worry, I will pay for it, you just have to give me a few weeks when I get back home to get organized."
"Why don't you come to Vienna and stay with me for the remainder of your holiday?"
    I don't know what to say. How can I tell her that I'm broke when I told her I've been making a movie?
"I told Nick and Johnny I would go back to Ireland with them but don't worry baby we'll see each soon enough."
    I have nothing waiting for me back home, I can't even afford to support myself and I don't think she would be too impressed with living at my folks' house and I still have to figure out how I am going to get cash for the remainder of this trip.
    We lay in bed for most of the last day, holding each other.
I can feel her need for someone as she could feel mine. I don't want her to leave because I know I will never see her again. We exchange addresses and I take her to posh restaurant. She is dressed in a black tight sleeveless dress that runs to the floor. It accentuates all her assets, she looks like Morticia from the Adam's family with sleeves of tattoos. She is smoking hot and every head in the joint was checking her out. Man, this was going to be hard to leave her.
"Katy, do you think I could get work in Vienna?"
    I know I can't, I don't speak the language. I have no idea how to get a visa or money for one.

She smiles. "You want to work in Vienna.'

"I want to be with you."

"What about your movie, Wolfgang?"

"Well it's in post-production now, not much I can do I'm not an editor and it's going to take some time to piece together and then try to sell it."

"Aren't you supposed to be over seeing things?"

"Yeah I guess but...but fuckit I would leave it all to be with you."

"You need to finish your project and not let me get in the way, when you want me to come visit you call or write me."

"What if it takes longer then I thought. What if you forget about me?"

"Trust me darling I will never forget you. When you get settled I will come. We will keep in touch always."

I start drinking wine. A shit load of it. I didn't want the feeling of loneliness to set in yet.

I am already depressed.

The bill pretty much wiped me out of cash. I have twenty American dollars left and that won't even get me out of the country.

Two hours later I'm pissing off the Charles bridge Katy is keeping a lookout because she's cool like that, then I see her rush towards me, she grabs my cock and puts it back in my pants and then starts making out with me viciously. I open my eye to see two undercover cops walk right past me and bust the vagrant drug addict ten feet away from where I'm pissing.
I love this girl.

We walk back to the flat and shower together we have about five hours left. We sleep and at the crack of dawn we both hug and part our ways, she's going to the airport and I'm going to make me some rent. I return to the hostel and it's around seven am. They are serving breakfast and I am demanding a drink of absinthe on the rocks. The bartender is hesitant but gives in because he knows I won't leave. I get the Irish up from their beds and make them start drinking with me. I'm going to spend the last money I have getting as fucked up as possible. I don't want reality to happen.

By ten in the morning we are searching for drugs downtown, stopping in every pub for a drink on the way. When we reach the part of town where all the Nigerians sell weed and speed. I tell Nick "I don't have any cash for it."

He replies and says "Who does." Then I see him walk up to the drug dealer and they proceed to walk into a narrow alley off the street. As I approach the corner I see Nick smashing this guy's face against the stone building, the 5foot8 Nigerian was no match for 6 foot 3 Nicki Welsh. I see the guy fall on the ground and then Nicks brother Johnny ripped the guy's clothes apart and took all the hash and money he had on him. We all take off running and laughing into the metro. A few stops later and we are in another bar. It's on the out skirts of Prague not many tourists at all except for this pig chic from Florida.

We grab a table and sit outside Johnny will buy the drinks with the Nigerians money. We roll tobacco and hash joints at the table and smoke them and this seems to annoy this pig from Florida. "Are you guys smoking hash? I smell hash." Nick tells her to mind her fucking business and then this pig stands up and calls over the waiter to rat us out. We put out the joint and act like we don't know what the fuck she is talking about. Everything goes back to normal for a moment and I order a shot of absinthe and have the waiter bring it over to the pig. She doesn't know what to think so I stand up with a shot in my hand and walk over to her table and I say" No hard feelings, my friends are a little rough over there and I just wanted to apologize." I hold up the shot and cling her glass and we both put em back. "My name is Wolfgang." Hi Wolfgang I'm Sharon."

This girl is your typical fat, low self-esteem, stupid angry ugly cunt. You can tell her family has money because she is dumb enough to wear expensive jewelry and carry $900 purse.
Johnny whispers in my ear "What the fuck are you doing man are you crazy? Let's get the fuck out of here."
 "Wait. Sharon where are you going to night." I ask her as I am standing up. "I don't know."
I blurt out as Johnny is pushing me to the door "Meet me at Chapparouse at midnight."
"You must of gone nuts that girl isn't even a girl she is a beast. Are you that fucked up mate?"
Nick doesn't say anything because he knows.
"Relax Johnny, I was just havin fun with her. Sometimes you got to kill them with kindness you know." Johnny just looks at me with disgust and Nick and I start cracking up. We go to café Gula Gula , I love all the waitress and they adore me but today I think I'm going to say my goodbyes. I need to make some sort of cash to get home and I won't' be back in this joint. I have already made up my mind. Katy left, Fiona left. I have no money and I can't keep on doing criminal acts to get by. Well one more so I can leave this place. I have partied myself on to the verge of a nervous breakdown and I'm starting to have suicidal thoughts.

I tell the waitress and bartender I am leaving and they all start hugging and kissing me. They hand me telephone numbers and addresses. If I had known a couple of these waitress were interested I would have been all over them and that could have changed the outcome of things. But no go.

Nick says "You're full of shit but what a great scam?? You're getting free drinks and numbers too bad you can't come back here again."
"No dude I am I tryin to get out tomorrow or the next or the next as soon as I can get a flight, I've had enough of this I can't party anymore I feel like my body is shutting down."
"You're a Pussy." Johnny says.
"Fine, you buy all the drinks and I will drink your money gone you Irish fuck. Let's Go."
Its late afternoon and the table is littered with shot glasses and pint glasses I have the waitress on my lap, I am feeling no pain.
"That's it."
'What do you mean Johnny?'
"Drank all the money, Nick has to go to the bank and exchange some pounds."
"Fuck that I can't see … plus it would take a couple of hours. I have to first go back to the hostel then take the metro back down town, fuck that."
"I can give you guys a few rounds, stay." The waitress says.

We do and they end up feeding us also. Good people those Czechs. I have a pocket filled with napkins with numbers and names on them and not a cent to my name. I am bombed. I hug and kiss again and say my Thank yous. On the walk back to the metro we decide we need speed to continue this journey. So I walk up to the gypsies in the town center and they are all hot Romania Prostitutes. As I walk thru them I am getting groped by all these girls, I know they are trying to pick pocket me but I have nothing so I don't care. I ask one girl if she would like to come back to my room and she said yes and then gave me a price. I told her she was "too beautiful to be whore and I don't pay for sex but do you know where I can get some speed?" We had no money, I figured we would do the old lets taste it first and see if it's real. Then I would blow as much as I could up my nose then tell the guy I don't want it its bunk fuck you. The Romanian chic brought back two big Nigerians. Are these guys also pimps I said to myself? They were uneasy looking and I immediately felt like we were getting set up for something. My instincts kick in and I start to walk away. Nick and Johnny followed. I shuffled through the packed streets and felt like at any moment I was going to get shanked. We hustled down into the metro. I know undercovers are all over the place so I feel a little safer.

"That was weird." Johnny said as we wait for the train.

"You think so; you don't remember that guy from this morning? I saw him a block before we jacked the nigger."

"Great. That guy travels all over the place. What are the odds that we ran into him? Do you think he recognized us?

"I think so." I said.

We all sat in silence until our stop.

Back at the Hostel and the receptionist informs me that Alice came looking for me.

"Yeah" I say.

"She was waiting awhile. So I let her in your room."

"No you didn't. Why did you do that? You guys know better than that. What the fuck Lonna? Ok, I'm sorry for saying that but you guys need to do me a favor?" I need another room on another floor. In the center of the hallway if you can."

Lonna the receptionist doesn't say a word and hands me a key.

"I will give you the money later. I have to go back in town to the bank."

She doesn't respond.

I run up to my room and Alice opens the door with a big "HI".

I then just realize I don't want this weirdo around me.

"Hey baby, when did you get back in town?" I say with a smile.

"I told you I would be back today. See I even wrote it down for you." She pulls out a sheet of paper from under some clothes.

"Oh.Oh yeah I must of forgot." We hug.

'Are those really bottles filled with urine?"

"No" I say and then walk out of the room. Alice follows me to the Patio.

"Is there something wrong Wolfgang?"

"Alice I have to be honest with you, I did forget. I really thought you were coming back tomorrow and I was planning a nice night on the town with you and Johnny takes off tomorrow morning and I was going to meet him with his brother Nick tonight."

She has a bitchy look on her pissed off face.

Listen I will be back at 1am. We'll sleep together and spend the whole day just you and me." I really have to go and meet them."

"Can I go with you guys?"

Fuck I don't know what to say so I blurt out "Nick doesn't like you."

"What? I don't even know him. Why would he say something like that?"

"I don't know baby but I really have to go."

"Just take a nap and I will be back in a few hours and me and you will grab a late drink and snack I promise."

I don't know why I have to put up with this shit I can easily tell her to fuck off but I guess I'm a nice guy and I want to see the squirter in action again.

Things I do just to get off.

I hug her and walk out the door as soon as the door shuts I take off running to the stairwell and up 4 flights of stairs to my new room. The receptionist hooked me up with a room dead in the center of the hallway. The bathrooms are at both ends. I start at my door and start counting my footsteps. 1,2,3,4,5,6, all the way to 42 then I open the bathroom door and I could hear it squeak which echoed down the hallway.
Perfect.
I meet the Irish in the bar I ask Nick to spot me some cash until later and he does. We drink and we notice a whole new group of female backpackers are checking in, this puts a smile on all of our faces. I break the moment when I tell them I have to split and I'm going to chapparouse. "Are you nuts you have a girl in your room and this bar is about to be packed with young fresh newbies man Cmon!" I sense Johnny's getting pissed only because he hasn't gotten laid and I could be ruining his last chance, fuck him. "Ok dude you guys stay here and I will be back in 45min,"
"What are you up too dude don't tell me you're going to meet that pig?"
I swallow my beer. Smile and stand up. "Guys I will be back in 45 minutes." I leave and jump into a cab. I can't believe what I am about to do and in front of all my new found friends, the bartenders and waitresses at chapparouse. Fuck it I will never see these people again. I walk up to the bar and I'm a little sketched out because I think that Nigerian can be lurking around, it is his corner. I walk into the joint and I am greeted by all the staff, I say my hellos and out of the corner of my eye I can see the beast sitting at the corner of the bar.
Oh FUCK.
The bar is packed and I squeeze my way thru all the hot looking people and end up next to the beast. "Hi remember me." She looks at me and smiles. "Hi Wolfgang" Fuck. I hate myself "Hi Sharon, what are you drinking?' "Bourbon." She responds. Of course what else would this beast drink. I can feel the staff is eyeing me. "Hey, Sharon do you want to play a game?" She looks at me. I grab the bartender and ask for twelve shots of Jack Daniels. He looks at me like are you O.K.? And pours them. "O.K. here's the game whomever can drink the most shots doesn't have to pay the bill."

"That's not a game." Sure it is. Where I come from this is very popular and it gets you good and fucked up." I just made that shit up hoping it will work because I have no more money. I can't believe I am sitting next to this beast. So I immediately throw down 2 shots. "I'm winning." She doesn't care. I drink one more and I could feel it come up the back of my throat. Uh oh what did I get myself into? The beast pounds 3 back in a row and doesn't even blink. "What do you think of that tough guy?" People are blatantly staring at this little fiasco that's about to unfold.

I clear my throat and ask for water. The bartender turns on me and says there is none. I down 1.2.3 just like that." Don't fuck with me Sharon. I am the king." I say as I am grinning. That pig summons the bartender and orders 4 more. I watch that animal drink slowly five shots in a row. Fuck. I have no money and I've been fucked up for weeks. "Sharon if you get me to drunk you're going to have to take me to my hostel." I say this as I lean over and touch her huge leg. "Oh really." She says with a smile. Good my plan is working. "One more shot" I scream and do it.

I start to become buddy buddy with the beast and now we are toasting together and every chic in the place is in disgust over my antics. Sharon gets off the stool to go to the ladies room and leaves her purse underneath the bar. People are all around so I bend down and act like I am tying my shoe which has only buckles, I unzip the purse and see a stuffed wallet. " Hey! What are you doing there!" the bartender sees me. "She kicked her purse over when she got up and I'm putting her shit back in there." The bartender just stares at me. He knows. Fuck him too.

The beast comes back "Hey Sharon I did 3 shots while you were in the can, your turn." "Bullshit If I didn't see it doesn't count." Fuck. She orders 3 more and the bartender fills them to the rim and the glasses are fucking warm. "Do it tough guy." The bartender wants to see this too. I have an audience. I smell it and almost vomit. Fuck. I say a little prayer out loud. "God if you didn't want this night to unfold the way it's about to happen you would not have put me in this position. Amen" No one gets it. I slam all 3, boom, boom, boom. My stomach is tossing and contorting. "I win." I could barely speak. "You gonna match that?" "No Way"
"What do you mean you pussy?'
"I don't drink moonshine."
"Moonshine?"

The next thing I remember is being helped into the bathroom stall and I could barely stand up. My vision is blurry but I can make out the chic next to me. Its Elky the waitress, a local Czech chic who is so damn beautiful, I was always too intimidated to chat with her. Anyway she puts a pen cap full of speed under my nose and I hit it by accident and it ends up all over my shirt. I take the bag away from her and pour out most of it on my palm. Elky is just staring at me. I stick my nose into my palm and sniff as much as I can, I now have white powder from my eyebrows down to my chin. I can finally stand up straight enough to piss.

"Wolfgang is true you're leaving tomorrow?" I try to adjust myself. "Who sayin' that? I ain't leavin for nuthin."

"Who are you with?"Elky says as she is cleaning my face and shirt.

"I don't know? Who is she?

"Wolfgang, you're all cleaned up. Stop drinking and go home. Alone".

"Elky I always liked you and you were never even kind to me.You always look mad and pissed when you waited on me and my friends."

"I've seen you for weeks here and you're very polite and generous. You're a nice guy but just to wild for me."

"Thank you Elky" I kiss her on the cheek and leave the restroom.

I'm somewhat normal now, not really but at least I can stand and talk. I make my way to the couch and plop myself in between 2 Goth chics. I can barely keep my head up and the floor is spinning. I lean forward and puke off the arm rest and this freaks people out and they clear the area. I look up and I see the beast, she lifts me off the couch with one hand. "Come on Wolfgang I have to take you home before you get your ass beat."

Everyone sees me leave with the beast and once I get outside and some fresh air in my system I am back to crazy again. My thoughts are back on track, I need to sneak this whale into the hostel without ANYONE seeing me. It would ruin my reputation.

I bring her down thru the basement, where the bus drivers enter and at that hour I knew none of them would be up. Here comes the big task. How am I going to get this whale to jog up 6 flights of stairs?

"Sharon I will race you to the 6th floor."

"Fuck you." she says

"You will if you meet me in room 609." I say as I trot up the stairs, I'm in my new room for 5 minutes before she comes in. I'm lying on the bed fully naked when she opens the door.

"Oh God." She says

"Oh God what baby?"

"I thought this is what you got me drunk for…so you can take advantage of me."

She laughs and kneels down next to the bed and starts jerking me off.

"Ouch…Ouch… what are you doing? Why are you pulling my pubs?"

"You need a shave down there your way over grown."

"I'm a man baby I don't shave my cock."

"I won't suck it unless I can clean it up for you."

"Well I don't have any scissors.

She looks around the room and says "You don't have anything."

"I travel light."

"Hold on." The beast goes rummaging thru her purse and pulls out a semi used bic razor. "Here we go." She says.

"What are you going to do with that?"

"I'm going to trim you up."

"Fuck. Ok try it."

I scream as she takes the dry razor and starts gauging at the top of my pubic line. "Wait Wait Wait. We need some sort of lube or soap, please. Go to the bathroom and grab a cup of hot water and a bar of soap please."

I can see little specks of blood below my belly button.

"Where's the bathroom?" She says

This is my chance. It's now or never.

"Walk out the door and take a right and or left and it's at the end of the hallway."

She leaves and I could hear here foots steps echoing in the hallway and I start counting as I am getting dressed...7, 8, 9, 10, I already have my shoes on and my hand in her purse. 14, 15, 16, 17 She has so much shit in here I can't find her wallet I'm opening every zipper inside and nothing. 27, 28, 29. I have to find it now. Its forty two steps to the bathroom and then a few seconds while she is in there and forty two steps back.

I have to get out of here before she walks out of the bathroom door. I take the purse and empty all the shit out on the bed, I see her day planner and I grab it and open it to the back flap because that's where everyone keeps cash. Bingo. I was right $300 hundred American dollars. I take the wallet and put it back in her purse along with everything else. What I took was probably emergency money and she won't notice it for a while.

I hear the pipes shake when she turns off the water and I leave the room with the door open a crack and run top speed to the stairwell at the other end of the hall way. She never saw me. I make it down 6 flights of stairs and back to my room without any one seeing me. Alice hears me enter "You're back early."

"Am I" I say as I plunk down in the bed.

I DON'T FEEL RIGHT TO MUCH TOO MUCH.

I need water and lots of it. I need vitamins. I need bananas. My body is starting to shut down and a fever is approaching me.

I wake up in pools of sweat freezing cold, Alice is up and reading. I feel like shit and now my mental state of mind is about to lose it I can feel the poison taking over as my body withdrawals.

"Alice I am very sick, look at me I am so fucking pale. I think you should leave I don't want you to catch anything."

"Don't be silly, I will take care of you, I'm going to the store what would you like me to buy you."

"A gun."

She laughs. And I think that's weird. "Lots of water and sugar and bananas. Please"

"Alright babe I will be back in a while I'm going to take the key so I can let myself in incase your sleeping."

"Whatever."

She leaves and I'm starting to get paranoid. What happens if people come looking for me? What if that beast figures out what I did and she calls the cops? What if the drug dealers and pimps find me? I freak myself out. All the piss bottles are full so I open the window and stand on the table and piss out of it. I have exhausted all my options and I have to leave before something bad happens. I am not normal. My stomach is making noises I've never heard before I can't stop shaking and I can barely keep anything in my system. I feel like death.

I am not having fun anymore and this chic is bugging me out, she won't shut the fuck up and the more I look at her face and her expressions the more I think she is really crazy. Fucking weirdo.

I am naked so I make her get naked and cuddle with me, it's not long before my bed is soaked and this chic is making animal noises. God get me out of here.

I wake up the next afternoon and my fever broke. I feel a lot better and Alice is nowhere to be seen and bags gone. Good. I run down and pay the receptionist and she gives me a bunch of notes.

1. Wolfgang. When you wake up if you wake up and go to New York call me Alice.
2. Dude, where are you no answer on door we saw the beast, come meet us in the bar.
3. Katy called to leave new number.
4. Outstanding bar tab must be paid today.

I must have really slept because these memos are marked from 2 days ago. I shower and brush my teeth. I try to comb my hair but it's like dreads now, useless. I have nothing to pack. I feel so good right now that I go into the bar and order a pint and pay my tab.

The bartender asks if I'm leaving and I tell him "No" just in case I need to start another tab. I have got to get out of here but I'm still tempted to stay with all these daily new backpackers pouring in. I have another pint and tell the bartender I want to start another tab. "I will pay it tonight when I get back from town." Lie. I see Nick pop in the bar. "Dude."

"Mate, we thought you died, you look better now you crazy fuck. I don't even want to know what kind of shit you were pulling the other night. Are you staying?"

"For what?"

"Do you see an unusual amount of people here? Do you see all the girls?"

"Yeah so"

"It's the U2 concert playing across the street in the stadium. This place will be slammed. How do you not remember there have been posters up everywhere?"

"I haven't been right since I got here. How the hell am I going to remember a U2 concert dude?"

I was planning on just jumping in a cab and going to the airport and wait for the next flight I can get on but this sounds better so I go back to the receptionist and try to get a room for the night.

"Sorry. We are sold out for the concert."

"I've been here for 7 weeks and your telling me you don't have a room for me?'

"Yes. You never booked the days. And you usually pay for five days in a row. You didn't this time and you never answered your door yesterday. So no rooms left."

"That's just great. How about your room? Can I sleep there for tonight? We could cuddle."

She didn't even smile that cold eastern European fuck.

Nick says I could crash on his floor and that was fine with me. The tickets to the concert are $96 bucks and that was way out my budget so I was going to scale the wall instead. We take a bus to the countryside because I don't want to run into anybody I might have fucked over. We find a cheap pub and plant ourselves there for 5 hours. Nick writes down his parent's bed and breakfast address and number in Dublin. "I will be there working and you can always get in touch somehow with that number." I write down my parents' home number and hand it to him. "You don't look so good Mate." I start sweating. "I don't know what's wrong with me maybe I'm not over being sick."

"You don't look sick man you look distressed." I have this pain on the left side of my groin I'm trying to ignore,

"Don't worry about it. I am going to poison whatever virus is attacking me buy drinking that bottle of Jack Daniels."

I point to the bottle and ask the bartender if I could buy it and before he says anything I put down $33 dollars on the bar. He takes it, puts it in his pocket and hands me the bottle. When I turn around to walk back to the table I collapse to one knee, it feels like I just got stabbed in the lower abdomen. "Holy shit, what was that all about?"

"Dude, open the bottle for me this will pass."

I sit down take a deep breath and drink one quarter of the quart. It's warm and I could puke at any moment but the pain in my side is distracting me from that.

"Nick I feel like I've got to take a piss. Will you wait and if I don't come out come find me."

He nods. I walk fine in to the restroom pull out my cock and try to piss. I have to but it doesn't really want to come out. Then I piss a drop and stop. I feel a little burning. OWW. I piss a little more and feels like someone cut my dick hole with a razor blade and I'm pissing salt. FUUUUCCK. NNOOOO. OWWWWW. NICK.

I am grabbing hold of the toilet paper dispenser and squeezing the fuck out of it with all my might and my other hand is choking my cock so no more piss comes out.

Nick is there.

"Nick, I can't let go it hurts too much I can't let it come out. Tell me you've had this before."

"Shit Mate no way. What is it?"

"The fuck do I know I feel like something is living inside me and trying to get out by way of my cock hole. WHAT THE FUCK DO I DO?" I can't let go man.

Nick says listen to me and leans over in my ear. I say "Yeah" and at that moment he puts he in a full nelson and my cock shoots off like a wild fire hose. Piss is going everywhere considering the bathroom is one toilet and a sink. I have tears rolling down my eyes and it hurts so bad I can't even talk. When I'm finished pissing Nick lets my arms down.

"Thanks dude."

"You got piss all over me."

"Sorry but what did you think was going to happen?"

I see piss dripping from the ceiling and my pants are soaking wet. We walk out of the bathroom together and we don't even acknowledge the bartender, we sit down and each take a huge gulp from the bottle. I see the bartender walk towards the bathroom and that's when Nick and I split with the bottle. We easily walk down a side street and into a park where I lay down.

"Dude, do you think that could be some sort of STD?"

"Probably, just go get some penicillin and hope it's not aids."

"You're a dick. Shut- up with that talk, man. Where the fuck do I get penicillin now, at this hour in the middle of fucking nowhere?"

"Get up I see a taxi"

I limp down into the cab and we continue to pass the bottle.

"As long as I don't piss I'll be fine. I will make myself throw up instead"

"That's the most fucked up thing I've ever heard. You're really losin it aren't you?"

"Do you want to have the cab take you to the hospital?"

"Fuck that. I know you have to grease the doctors before they see you and I barely have enough cash to get back home. Just let me chill in your room for awhile."

I keep chugging it and the pain is still there.

I need pain killers.

Back at the Hostel and people are everywhere getting ready for the concert across the street. I should be able to score some sort of opiate to ease my wound but first I go to Nick's room and then I grab some ice from the hostel kitchen then I wrap it in a towel and try to numb my cock. After a good five minutes I have no feeling and I try to piss again. It doesn't work and I'm screaming at the top of my lungs for 45 seconds.

"Fuck"

"Dude you pissed everywhere again."

As far as I can see there are people everywhere. U2 is blaring in the background. I'm to beat up to jump the wall so I just hang outside on the campus with thousands of others. I have to sit down because I can feel the pain starting to build up. I find a group of people with beach chairs and I take a seat. They can see I'm in pain. Nick follows behind and hands me 2 pills

"Here take this." I do.

"What was it?"

"Some sort of muscle relaxer the girl told me. So I just bought it."

"I hope so." We kick back and listen to the music, I get out of the chair and lay on the ground to stare at the stars and that's when it kicked in. I'm rolling, that fucker gave me ecstasy.

"Dude." I say.

"Yeah I know man. Just relax."

"Thanks dude. What a way to end a perfect trip." Then I hug him.

The pain is there but I feel so good I ignore it. I drift on and off into another world. Having dreams with my eyes open.

The sun is hot on my back and I wake up in the fetal position among other crashed out travelers. I check to see if I still have my passport and money belt. I do. Nick is nowhere to be found and I can't really walk back to the hostel. I have to piss bad and I can't hold it any longer I hop over to a tree in the middle of the park and just let loose pushing it out as fast as I can. I am getting looks from everyone around because I'm yelping like a wounded animal then I fall into a puddle of my own urine. I make my way to a parked cab, my white v neck is stained and tattered and my black slacks are muddy and wet with piss again. "Take me to the airport"

I am lying down in the back seat crying and whimpering for the 60 minute ride. What the fuck kind of STD is this? Who gave it to me? What do I tell my folks?

Am I going to die? Is this what aids feels like? Was I such a bad man that this is my payback, GOD? My mind is not thinking straight. I have to kill myself. How the fuck am I going to sit on a plane for 10 hours.

"My name is M.Wolfgang Klein and I'm trying to get a flight back to the U.S"

I hand her my itinerary and she tells me I have to pay an extra hundred dollars because of the open ticket. "Miss I don't have a hundred dollars I was attacked and robbed last night in Prague, look at me."
She does and then picks up the phone and starts speaking Czech.
Two women dressed as airport security approach me. "Mr. Klein are you ok?" Do you want us to call the police for you?" They put me into a wheel chair and wheel me into an office. "Really I'm fine I just need to get home." They hand me a wet towel to clean off my face and arms. I lift up my shirt and I hear one of the women Sigh so I look down to see a deep bruise on my lower abdomen. Now I'm freaked out.
"Mr. Klein we are going to waive your fee and put you on the next flight to New York, That flight leaves in 2 hours. Stay here and rest we will come get you when it's time to board."
I wheel myself out after 20 minutes and I find a pay phone.
"I would like to make a collect call....my name is Wolfgang."
"Mom."
"Wolfgang?"
"Mom." I start to break down and whimper " Mom I ..."
"Wolfgang is everything alright."

"Mom, I'm pissing sand and it hurts so bad, please call a doctor. I will be home by dawn, I will get in early tomorrow morning and I will call you guys from JFK. "

Then I hang up the phone because I don't know how expensive a collect call is and I don't want to have them pay for it. Then I roll myself back into the office and pass out. When the flight arrives I am woken up and they ask me if I can walk or do I want to be wheeled. I stand up and walk the best I can which isn't very well and when I reach the cabin of the plane I feel like I'm going to puke. I can see all these people staring at me with the look of fear that I would be placed next to them.

I make my way to the back of the plane where I am assigned and there is an empty seat next to mine and I pray to God no one sits there and no one does. I sit in agony for the first five hours, I am literally crying in my hands every time there is turbulence I want to puke and I am so dehydrated, I need some water but will not drink any because I'm afraid I will have to piss. I fall asleep. I wake with my head against the window and the sun beating down on me. I'm so fucking thirsty.

I can hear over the loud speaker that we will be landing shortly and fasten your seat belt. Fuck that. I can't even bend down to pick it up. I hold my breath as we touch down and then wait until everyone exits before I slowly limp out. I see the sympathy on the stewardess face as I walk past her and I think shit I really look fucked up. Since I have no luggage I go straight to customs and the let me straight thru, when I walk up to the concourse to use a pay phone I see my Dad. I'm in shock.

"What are you doing here?"

"Your Mother was worried and had me come all the way down here to get some information on you and your flight and pick your ass up."

I can see he is in a pissy mood.

"Now what's wrong with you? You told your mother you're pissing sand? Why would you say something like that to her, you know she worries. Now you tell me not her, now you're not pissing sand your probably passing stones."

My father then gives me a quick hug.

"Where are your bags?"

"I didn't bring any."

We get into his car and my father tells me I have an appointment with his doctor as soon as we arrive in Bridgeport.

"Did you spend alll3 your money?" He asks.

"All what money?" I reply.

He yea, Sharon. WAVING TOTTLES, LOVE YOU OK, senses the sarcasm and doesn't ask any more questions.

When I arrive at the doctor's office they put me right into a room with a pretty attractive young nurse and she helps me take off my clothes. "Okay Wolfgang. I am just going to take your blood pressure." She does. "So you just arrived from Prague what were you doing there?" She asks.

I look at her without an answer because I don't have one then I mumble "Partying."

What an asshole I am why would I say that, I could of said anything.

"Oh really, well Wolfgang it looks to me that you accomplished that." She doesn't look impressed. She then takes blood samples and tells me to wait for the doctor.

When Doctor Pontonio walks in I try to sit up. "No no, Wolfgang lay down. Your father told me you might me passing stones." He walks over and puts his knuckle in to my bruise. "Doc what the fuck."

"Sit still. Does this hurt?"

"You can't tell. Yes it hurts. Bad."

"Can you urinate in this cup?"

I haven't pissed in twelve hours and I'm so dehydrated I'm afraid, it hurts so bad. Could we just assume that they are stones and take care of with some pills and also can I get something for STD's…just in case you know?" The doctor doesn't seem amused and tells me to hold on and leaves the room. He come back a second later with this huge needle and a cotton swab on the end. I've seen this before.

"Doc you don't have to do that, please"

The Doctor grabs my cock and looks at me and says" Did you hear the new Billy Joel song?"

"WHAT????" at that moment he jams the needle up my cock hole and swipes back and forth.

"AWWWWW. NONONO."

He stops and I immediately have to piss, I grab the cup and fill it then I walk over to waste basket and continue on pissing. I have no control. I am taking short deep breaths.

"Was that so bad" He says with a grin. "I will be back shortly."

I start to cry not with pain but with disgust. How could I act in such a manner that I need to go thru this? What was this payback for. He returns and tells me that I have an infection in my epididymitis and in fact I am passing kidney stones. "The other test won't come back for a couple of days we will call you."

I spend five days recovering at my Parents house and I don't call any of my friends. I sleep and eat.

When I get in touch with Bud he tells me we have to re shoot a scene this coming weekend at his Parents' house. I am no longer interested. This project has been going on too long to hold my ADD personality. I really don't care anymore. But I show up.

I really want to kill the lead actor because he sucks so bad and I feel like he fucked us. Bud shares the same opinion but unlike me he will not quit and finishes what he starts.

He tells me that after the summer his Parents will let him use their beach house in Old Saybrook to edit the film. Bud leases a Steenbeck.

Shoot For The Stars

It's Labor Day weekend and I sneak into Newport, Rhode Island. I'm trying to not be seen by any police and everything is going smooth. I'm staying at my boy's pad and we have plenty of drugs. We leave the pad at 5pm to avoid lines at the bars because by 6 lines form around the corners.

We get right in to The West Deck, an outdoor bar on the bay. Our crew consists of 12 dudes, all Trumbull guys. I am good and fucked up and I'm not feeling any pain. This redhead starts chatting with me, she's ok and real nice and I am enjoying her company when she tells me she works in the Clerk's office at the Newport courthouse.

My light bulb just popped on.

I spend the whole night being a gentleman. Act like I care. Then I hit her with my DUI story. She feels bad. Then she tells me, "I can get you all of your documents, I can take your whole file if I wanted to."
"Really, Mara? if you do that I will give you four hundred bucks."
"Wolfgang, make it $800 dollars and you have yourself a deal."
She knew what she was doing.

I knew she was a bit shady which turned me on more. "Ok, Mara, let's do a shot to honor this deal." I order 2 Jack Daniels and we do them. I then try to kiss her neck and she stops me. "Hold on."
"What?" I say as she is pushing me away.

"When we first met I would've hooked up with you, but now we have this deal and I know you're the type of guy that sleeps with a girl and never talks to them again, which is cool. I don't really care. But I don't want that to happen in this case because I'd really rather have your money than your cock." And then she gives me a fuck you grin.
"I'm sure you're 100% right. Let me get your number and I will call you during the week."
We exchange napkins and I go back to the house and do a bunch of cocaine with my friends.

2 weeks later I meet Mara at the courthouse in Newport. She hands me a manila folder with all my arrest documents in them. I hand her the money. She tells me that she couldn't get to my traffic violations because that is a department of motor vehicles issue.

At this point I really didn't care; I had the most important charges in my possession.

The summer is over and I have no money. The autumn air always reminds me of college for some reason and this makes me depressed because it also reminds me that I didn't go to college. I have no degree. I have nothing. I have a friend's movie that I could put my name on. I am lonely.

I spend 4 months at Bud's parents' beach house watching Bud edit this movie. I drink all the alcohol in the house. I miss Elizabeth.

When I was a senior in high school I got myself a job at the Trumbull Marriott. The hotel had a fine dining restaurant that I worked at, first as a bus boy and then I became a waiter. I worked on Mondays, Tuesdays, and Thursdays. It was a corporate hotel so I made cash during the week as opposed to weekends like most joints. I worked with an older group of people I thought but they were really only 25 or so. It was a good job. I made on average $400 a week. I got to party late night in bars with this older crowd and I always had a weed connection. The black side chef's name was Irving. He was a year older than me and he lived in the projects in Bridgeport. He was a nice dude but he just grew up on the wrong side of the tracks, he was my main weed dealer.

One night I was driving him into the ghetto in my mom's brand new Acura Legend. I was a stupid kid.
I asked Irving where can I buy a pistol. He asked me if I had $200. I told him, "Shit yeah."

In a matter of 20 minutes I had a .38 snub nose in my hands. I never saw anything go so easy, he told me what building to drive up to, I gave him the cash and he walked off. I thought no way is this motherfucker going to rob me - because I work with him.
Right?

Two minutes later he emerges from the dark shadow on the side of the building, jumps in my mom's car and we take off. Easy. I see him at work the following week and we never discuss it.

The gun is beat up, it looks like it was thrown from a car and bounced around on the highway. The handle is taped. I wash the thing down with rubbing alcohol for some reason, I don't know. I call my buddy Sean and we go and purchase bullets for the gun. The owner of the gun shop seems suspicious until I tell him that they are a present for my dads birthday, He put a bow on the box.

At first we were shooting at street signs while driving and then realized it probably wasn't a good idea. I thought about robbing drug dealers but I was too much of a pussy back then. I decided to play Russian Roulette. I wanted to see what kind of balls my friend Sean had.

So we are drinking beers in my parents' basement one day after school and I pull out the gun and I put one bullet in the chamber and spin it. "Go ahead," I tell Sean. "Fuck you. Are you nuts, get that thing away from me."

"Come on. You saw *Deer Hunter*? Be a man," I say.
Sean is now nervously pacing around the basement. When he isn't looking I take the bullet out.
"Well if you're gonna be such a pussy let me show you how it's done. WATCH!" I yell at him. I put the gun in my mouth and pull the trigger. CLICK!

Nothing happens.

"You're an asshole, Wolfgang, I should kick your ass"
"Sean, dude, I was fucking around, look, I took out the bullets when you weren't looking. LOOK!"

I take the gun and fire it repeatedly at the concrete wall.
CLICK.
CLICK.
BOOM!

The gun goes off and a bullet ricochets off the wall and floor before it lodges into the ceiling. Sean goes running out and my mom's on her way home and the basement smells like someone just fired a gun. Holy shit. I grab all the bullets and the gun, run up into the attic, far end, lift up the fiberglass insulation and hide the gun and bullets under it, swearing I will never touch it again.

Until now, nine years later.

"Goin' to Make Me Some Rent"

The holidays are over which is good because I really can't stand them. I am staying at my parents' house now. Bud finished editing the movie and sent it off for post-production work, the sound mixing, the color correction, the transfer. The movie wouldn't be ready for a few more months and I was losing my mind.

January 3rd is a Saturday in 1998.

I'm with Bud and we're having drinks down on the strip in Norwalk when he tells me the news. "I spoke to Lance yesterday and he is done living in Nantucket." Lance is a Trumbull guy, a high school buddy.
"Yeah?"
"He got a job on The Domestic Diva Television show in Westport."
"Wait. What?"
"Yeah I spoke to him yesterday and he told me Margaret Steward is hiring for her new studio, she got her own television show and it's going to be shot in Westport. He gave me a contact number and I'm going to call on Monday," Bud says.
"Dude, how do I get in?" I ask.
"First let ME get in then I will give you the contact. Let me see how Monday goes."
"How did Lance find out?
"His buddy on Nantucket had the info. Someone he knew."

We continue to drink and I can't stop thinking about MS Studio. I need to get in there. I will do whatever it takes to land a job there, I need this. It would so make my year.
I drop Bud off at his parents and take off in high speed because I'm so pumped up. I have *Jane's Addiction* blaring on the stereo, I am feeling numb and I never see the tree as I'm approaching a turn in the back country, I'm going so fast I never see the road veer to the left and I hit a large oak tree. I never slow down and hit this fucker at about 50 mph. No skid marks. The 1985 Volkswagen Jetta I bought for a thousand bucks months before saves my life. When I realize what's happened I try to start the car and leave but no chance, the dashboard is on my lap and the front end of the car is almost nonexistent.

I'm in a posh neighborhood where the houses are set way back from the road but the loud noise from the impact has woken a few neighbors because I see lights go on and people coming out their homes.
I bail.

I fucked up my hip but could still jog a little. I am wearing black as usual. I am hiding along people's property when I hear the police sirens and the fire trucks.
Fuck ME.

I make my way to Bud's parents' house and to no surprise I see Bud standing outside.
"We heard the crash from here and I wanted to see how quick you would make it back," he goes.
"Fuck you, Bud."
"I knew you were going to bite it when you peeled the fuck outta here, you asshole."
"I think I fucked up my side."
"Do you want me to call the police?"
"Don't be a cocksucker, let me just sleep it off."
Bud lets me in and I pass out.

My parents tell me that they were woken up by the state police at 3 in the morning. They parked outside my parents' house and left the blue and red flashing lights on so everyone on the street was able to see.
"Mr. Klein, your son has been in a car accident and we can't find a body."
(That's exactly what every parent wants to hear.)

"The car is totaled, he hit head on into a tree and he is nowhere to be found. It happened off of Merwins lane. Do you know if he knows anyone in that vicinity he might have gone to?"
My parents tell them, "No, we have no idea what he was doing there."
They lied, they knew I was at Bud's.

I wake up in the morning almost forgetting about what happened the night before, until I look out the window and don't see my car.
I call the police and report it stolen.
"Yes my name is Wolfgang Klein and I want to report my car stolen."
"O.K. Klein, can I have the make and model and where it was stolen from?"
"It's a Volkswagen Jetta, burgundy, 1985 four door. And it was stolen from the side of the road on Merwins Lane."
"Can you hold, Mr. Klein?"
"Sure."

Longest wait ever. Then:

"Mr. Klein this is Detective D'elia, I will be handling your case. Can you come down to the station now?"

"Detective I would love to but I'm on a movie set in New York City and I'll be here for a week."

"So tell me how your car got stolen from the side of the road.""Well I was driving home from this girl's house I work with and I don't really know the roads around there and out of nowhere four or five deer jump right in front of my car and I tried to avoid them but I ended up hitting a tree. So then I pushed my car out of the way of traffic onto the side of the road and walked back to my coworker's house."

"Why didn't you call police then?"

"It was late and I didn't want to bother anyone."

"Mr. Klein, we have your car. We retrieved it last night after you decided to run from the scene.""I didn't run."

"Family Towing has your car. Mr. Klein, when will you be able to come in and fill out a report?"

"Not until next week at the earliest. I'm on set in the city and who knows how long it could last."

"O.K. Mr. Klein when you come back to Connecticut, come down to the station and ask for me. And Mr. Klein were you injured in the accident?"

"Not a scratch."

I hang up the phone and have Bud drive me to my parents' house.

No one says a word because they are used to this shit by now. I never show up at the police station. Two days later I realize not having a car really sucks and I can't take living at my folks anymore. I need money. All I do is sleep and I am so depressed I start thinking about killing myself.

I go up to my parents' attic and retrieve the gun I put here while in high school. My folks are at work and I'm stuck without a car.

I bring the gun into my room, sit it on my bed and start cleaning it, looking it over.

I make sure the gun isn't loaded. I spin the barrel and cock it a few times.

Then I grab the box of bullets and slide one in. I'm not thinking of anything at this point because I didn't think I would die today. I spin the barrel and flick it shut. I walk up to the mirror in my bedroom smile and pull the trigger.

Nothing.

I knew I wasn't going to die that day.

A couple of weeks into January I finally get a call back from the Steward Studio in Westport. (I spent the last couple of weeks calling every day, trying to get an interview and now finally.)

It's snowing out and I have to make this appointment and I have no car so I take my mother's Mercedes. I roll up to the studio and park in front, it's snowing like a bitch and I make a dash for the front doors. Once I get inside I'm amazed at how hot the receptionist is. She is warm and friendly and guides me thru the studio to the commissary. "You can wait here, the studio manager is running a little late," she says with a smile.

I can't believe all the hot, stylish women coming and going out of this commissary and I still haven't seen any men yet.
I need to work here.

I get introduced to Jill, the studio manager, and she takes me to her office where she introduces me to Pang, the facilities manager, AKA studio dick face. They both ask me a bunch off bullshit questions and I decide to tell them the truth because it ain't so bad.

I just finished producing a 16mm feature film.
I went to NYU but didn't graduate.
I've worked on 5 student films.
I've worked as an extra on movies.
I worked for a casting director in Hollywood.

I didn't lie and I think they knew it.

The interview goes well and then we discuss the job details. I would have to arrive at the studio at 6:45 am and jump into the 15 passenger van and pick up the New Yorkers at the train station. Do this from 7am til 9am, shuttle the people. Then go around and fill all copiers and water dispensers. Run errands. Help out in the commissary during lunch. Do odd jobs. And at the end of the day do the shuttle runs again.

I tell them I can handle anything and I explain to them I would be 100% committed, they couldn't find a better person for the job. No way. Three days later I get the call that I was hired on a 2 week trial basis.

The first day I'm given a tour of the facilities. I have never seen anything like it. The place housed 2 sets and it had a post-production wing and a producer's wing, a state of the art gym, 3 kitchens, a cook for the staff. Beautiful grounds. The place was also dog friendly. It was a pretty classy atmosphere, a nice place to work and beautiful women coming and going all day long.

Over the 2 weeks I got the swing of things, it was pretty simple. I was a gofer. I was a gofer for everyone and everything. If MS's driver was sick, I would drive. If a celebrity had to be picked up in a snow storm in New York and be driven to Westport for a taping, I was that guy. If something on the property had to be painted, I did it. If holes had to be dug to run power under the driveway, me. If asked to drive a 36ft rental truck 10 hours to Maine so I could drop off some of MS personal items to her castle, I did with joy and was able to spend the weekend up there.

The short days were always twelve hour days but I enjoyed it. After the 2 weeks they kept me on and gave me a variety of odd jobs. I was the studio manager's right hand. I worked for the studio and then slowly worked on production for the television show as a production assistant. The days they weren't shooting I was working for the studio and on shoot days and travel days I was with production. It was a real exciting job. I was never bored and the depression was gone. I was making $750 a week, every week.
And blowing it in 3 days.

I convince my parents to let me keep the Mercedes and I will lease my mother a car. They agree and I'm paying them $400 a month. I was a punk. I was a 25yr old punk rolling around in a 3 yr. old Benz as a production assistant at best.

When it was time to leave for the day, Bud and I would head over to the local Westport bars and always forget to take off our studio tags (that's what we said). This little bit of information really helps out in bars.

While in line at happy hour a woman sees the studio pass hanging out of my shirt pocket or around my neck or placed on the bar alongside my keys.
"Oh you work for MS?"
"Yes I do".
The next thing I know she's asking all the bullshit questions and I'm giving her truthful answers.
Now other people in the bar are chiming in, someone always has a Steward experience from living in Westport.
I don't give much of a fuck.
I just want to fuck this woman and I do.

The MS studio tags always work (even in Martha's Vineyard) then it just gets to be known that I work for MS because of all the errands I run for the studio. They use a lot of local mom and pop stores in the area.

Life is going really well for me, I have a weekly pay check, I work with beautiful women. I have a nice car and I was banging hot girls. And now the movie is just about finished and is accepted at the Brooklyn Film Festival in October. This gives us plenty of time to touch it up.

It is May.

Work is good. The weather is getting warmer, we spend every single night at the Seagrape with our Trumbull friends, we drink and hunt and drink and take drugs and fuck.
Every single night.
I always make it to my parents' house by 3am and I'm back up at 6am and I am never late for work. Never.

I shop at Goodwill and always dress in style. My shoes are always $250 Kenneth Cole Boots. I look good. I hardly sleep and run on adrenaline and drugs for weeks on end. I'm always excited. I'm always ready. I'm always on the go. I never say no.

It's the beginning of May and Steward is having a huge fundraiser for some woman running in Connecticut for senate or something. The 42nd President of the United States is going to be there and I'm able to work it, helping out the studio manager. Bud is with me.

For days the Secret Service is combing the neighborhood. Doing background checks on everyone. I see sharp shooters in trees. They close down the highway and surrounding roads. It's pretty cool. We get to hang with this guy Gus, he works for the White House, I forget what position but I remember it's was kick ass. He's a stud and the chicks at MS drool over him. He wears Giorgio Armani sunglasses.

Celebrities and politicians are everywhere, everyone trying to get a picture with the President.

I am on the sidelines watching all this nonsense. Then my manager asks me if Bud and I will run to the grocery store because they need more plastic cups and plastic forks.
Really?

We jump into my car and have the Secret Service check us out before we leave the grounds. The store is about 4miles away on country roads. I pull out a joint from under the matt.
"Come on guy, really? You think that's a good idea?"
"I think it's the best idea."
I light up the joint and speed to the grocery store.

I realize as I'm walking through the store this was in fact a really bad idea. I am fucked up. And now I have to deal with the Secret Service.

I leave Bud in the store and walk back to my car to get rid of all the hidden weed. In the glove box, in the armrest, under the seats, under the matts. The ashtray I just throw out. I drive next door to the gas station and vacuum out everything in it.

I return and pick up Bud and he just looks at me says, "The best idea huh?"

"Fuck off" I say.

I can't let him see that I'm really whacked so I keep my shades on. I speed back to the studio.

Now Secret Service is all over the car. They have dogs and mirrors. They make us pop the hood and pop the trunk.

Metal detectors everywhere.

They take Bud and I out and frisk us and check out the contents of the bags. My heart is racing and I won't take off the shades. After 2 minutes we're cool to proceed. As we walk to the studio we get hurried in by an employee, "Do you want to meet him!?" she says. We start running and make it on to the set just in time. I am the 3rd person in line to shake hands with the President as he is approaching me I realize I have a pencil in my left hand. I start thinking about how close I am to him and that I could actually stab him in the neck with this pencil.

I should not have smoked that pot.

"Nice to meet you Mr. President," I say and extend my arm, he grabs it with two hands and says, "Hi y'all doin' today," with a big smile.

He's my favorite President.

It's the 3rd week in May, right before Memorial Day weekend. I get a phone call from this chick Allison who I know from Newport summers. She's a bit older and works for a magazine called POV in Manhattan.

"Hey Wolfgang, it's Allison Flemming... from Newport.""Oh yeah, hey, what's up?""Well I was thinking about you and how you make independent movies..."

"Yeah?"

"Our magazine is having a short film festival with only 12 filmmakers and I thought you would be interested in being one of the 12."

"Really."

"Yes it's called The Dog Run Film Festival. The movie has to be no longer than 15 minutes and it has to be under a budget of 200 dollars. You can use your old footage or shoot something new. It doesn't matter, but the basis has

to be on how you incorporate Dog Run into your film. We will have a panel of judges and the winner will get a write up in our magazine. It will take place at the bar called the Library on the lower east side. They have a movie screen they pull from the ceiling, and it should hold close to 300 people."
"Ok. Ok! When does this have to be finished and can we use video instead of film?"

The festival is on the 21st of June, so you guys have a good month to put something together - and you can use film or video. But I need a 100 percent guarantee from you that you are taking this spot, you can't call me up in two weeks and tell me you quit. So are you sure?"
"You have my word Allison, and thank you for looking out for me."
"I will call you next week to get some info on your production team. Take care and don't get too crazy this weekend?"
"Crazy? Me?"
"Byyye Wolfgang."
I hang up the phone and jump into Bud's truck and tell him the news. I will be the writer and director on this one and he will be producer and camera man.

Cool.

WHORES LIKE ME

We pick up our friend Tommy who also is a Trumbull guy and freelances for MS as a sound guy. We head for Montreal for the weekend.

I have a few hundred dollars and a credit card I take in case of emergency from my parents. They know I get paid every week so it's no problem. I have a half ounce of killer bud in my pocket along with a big glass bowl. I am sitting in the back seat and I see signs that the border is approaching. I take the weed and pipe and stuff them into my boot. It's a tight fit and the glass bowl is pressing into my ankle. I have been over this border probably 20 times and never been stopped.

Until now.

"Gentlemen, will please pull the car over there and walk inside that building."

"Sure." Bud says.

I'm freaking out.

I can smell the weed thru my boot.

Bud gets out and Tommy follows, then Bud takes off his shoes and throws his socks over his shoulders. What the fuck is he doing!

This piece of glass is digging into me. I walk with a little limp. We walk inside and we are all standing in line waiting to be interviewed. I notice to my left, about 30 feet away, the door to the men's room. Should I just walk over there and dump it? Should I? Should I?

"Sir? Sir."

I turn my head, she's talking to me. "Yes?"

"Sir, do you have any identification on you and can you state your purpose here?"

"Yes," I hand her my license. "I'm here on holiday with my friends."

She doesn't look too pleased and I'm pale white.

"How long have you known these friends and where do you work?"

"Oh these guys I grew up with, and we all work together for the MS Studio in Connecticut."

"How long will you be staying here?"

"We will be here until Memorial Day. We decided to take advantage of the long weekend."

"Do you know that here in Canada we do not celebrate your Memorial Day?"

"No."

"No." She says and hands me back my license.

"Is that it?"

"Have a good holiday, Mr. Klein." I walk back to the car where Bud and Tommy are waiting.

"What was that all about?" I say.

"They just wanted to see if our stories matched up." "I was freaking out, I thought for sure I was going to get detained."

"Oh yeah. How would you feel if you had *this*?" Tommy reaches into the front top pocket of his overalls and pulls out a golf ball sized clump of cocaine.

"Are you fucking crazy?"

"You didn't tell us you had that, what the fuck were you thinking? All along I thought you were cool as shit. I was the one sweating it out. Well good for you, you crazy fuck, now bust it open." "Guys we should probably leave the parking lot first, and put that shit away now!" Bud says, pissed.

An hour later we are at the Marriott on St Katherine's street in Montreal. We take showers and smoke some pot and start doing little key bumps of the blow. Just to test it out.

As we walk down the avenue everything is going off. People, girls, bars and clubs. We are amped up. We've all been to Montreal many times before, so we know what to expect. It's easier than the States. These French Canadians chicks are loose when it comes to fucking and they're hot. Even better now that we have cocaine.

We come across a bar that has a special 2 dollar Jack and Cokes. Well it's a no brainer and we walk in. Bud and I walk to the bar (which is loaded with women), Tom walks to the bathroom. I order 6 Jacks. 2 each. Bud and I are enjoying the view for about a minute when we see Tom being pushed across the bar and towards the door. He looks at us and says, "Gotta go, guys, meet you outside."

Bud and I drink our drinks.

"What do you think he did?' I ask.

"I bet you a hundred bucks he got caught with the blow."

"He was only in there for a minute. Shit man we just left the hotel 15 minutes ago and I'm still whacked out from it. I thought we agreed on not bringing it out?"

"Tell that to Tom."

We are back on the street and decide to go to another bar, but I have to hold on to the bag of blow. I convince Tom that's the only way I would hang out with him. I have to be the responsible one. He gives me the bag and we walk into another packed bar filled with chicks. We all stand at the corner of the bar with our backs up against the wall.

"Can I get 3 Jack and Cokes with big straws, please" I ask politely.
I tip her well.

I'm thinking that the coke might be wearing off a bit so I decide it would be a good idea to do a quick blast, just to get the night going. I take the straw from the drink and I pull out the bag of blow from my pocket and put it in my left hand. I open the bag and cup it inside of my fist. You can't see it. I take the straw, put it inside the bag and do a big quick toot. Way too much.
I start coughing.

Bud and Tommy look over and take it out of my hands and put their own straws in it. I order 3 more drinks and tip the bartender very well.
I have a feeling she knows what's going on when she wipes powder off my nose.

We come to the conclusion it would be best to finish all the blow tonight so it doesn't ruin our weekend.

So 3 guys in the corner chewing their jaws, smoking cigarette after cigarette and turning their bodies toward the wall so we don't look obvious when we take huge blasts. No way would any chick come near us.

The bartender gets in on it after a while and she begins to pour huge glasses of Jack Daniels.
We drink them.

We stay in that corner til the lights come on at 4am and we are nowhere near finishing this bag of blow, never mind the big one back at the hotel. Tom wraps some up in a napkin and gives it to the bartender and tells her we're taking off.

I could see as the night goes on that the bartender is off her rocker and the more blow she does the more trashy she becomes. Tom did a good thing, otherwise that freak would be following us and wanting all our cocaine.

We return to the hotel room on the 11th floor. We immediately bust out all the cocaine from everywhere and lay on top the table.
It's a big pile.

Tommy cuts 12 huge lines. 4 each. They are the size of my arm.
I really don't want this coke lingering around all weekend, it will ruin our vacation. I take the first baby leg and almost throw up. Tommy takes all 4 four at once, only stopping to breathe. Bud tells us to fuck off. I am pinned. I am talking a mile a minute, my jaw swinging east to west. Bud is in bed and Tommy busts out a bottle of Jack and gin. No mixers. We are too paranoid to go to the lobby and get juice or call room service.

The sun is up at this point.
I'm cutting apart straws to find any last crumb of blow.

I keep scraping the wood table for anything left over and I end up snorting wood dust. I pick the carpets for anything that might have dropped. I do this about 15 times.

Those guys are sleeping or pretending. I fill up the bath tub and decide to swim in it. I finally get up the nerve and go down to the lobby, it's about 10am and I'm still gone.
I'm not fooling anybody.

I get freaked out when I see all the natural sunlight. I don't know what to do. Should I run upstairs and get my new Giorgio Armani sunglasses and come back down? I'm in a daze, staring out the window in the middle of the lobby when this hot concierge says, "Bon jour." I say it back and she starts speaking English. "Do you need a taxi, Sir?"

I draw a blank, I have nothing to say. I don't want a taxi. I can't stop staring at her.

"Um…. do you have a phone book?"
"Your room should have one in the desk drawer."
"Oh I didn't even think of that, Thank you."
I turn and walk straight to the elevators. I should not be out in public. I am so fucked up on blow it's noticeable, at least I think so.

I get back to the room where it's dark and find the phone book. I turn right to the escort section.
"Are you going to go to bed yet?" I hear in Tom's pissy voice.
"For what? I'm getting escorts. It's fucking Saturday already and I'm not wasting a day trying to sleep like you guys. And I bet you haven't slept shit anyway."
 "Didn't you run out of cash?" Tom Says.
"Do you mean paper," I snap back.
"Don't be an asshole. Do you have cash?"
"I have a credit card with permission to use. So fuck you, get up, get a drink and I will get the ladies."
I turn to the page: Cosmopolitan Models on call 24/7.
The ad says they had the hottest girls in Montreal, They all say that. I call and talk to Jack;

"Jack, my name is Wolfgang and I was wondering if you got any girls available now. Today now, yes. And I want to see if your ad is telling the truth when you print you have the hottest girls in town. Jack I am from New York City and I am a film producer for Jack in the Box Productions. I came to Montreal based on the fact that your city breeds beautiful, fashionable women. Now Jack, can you prove me right?"

"Mr. Wolfgang. What kind of girls do you want? You say it we have it."

"Come on. Really. I want 3 skinny women with big tits and round asses. I want one red head, a blonde, and a brunette. And they must be good to look at Jack."

"Listen my friend you will not be disappointed, all my girls are models."

"If I don't think any of them are up to my standards I'm tossing them out."

"Ok sir, but you won't be needing to do such a thing."

"How much is per woman?"

"125 American dollars, up to four hours and no tipping at all." "Jack, you're telling me its 125 American dollars each?"

"Yes."

"And they stay up to four hours."

"If they want to stay longer, up to them."

"Jack, Don't bullshit me, they better be hot. And absolutely no tipping Jack? Come on."

"Nothing. You pay once with a credit card and that's it."

"OK Jack, let's do this. Listen the credit card has a different first name than mine, is that ok?"

"Is it *your* card, sir?"

"Yes it's my card! The E on the card stands for Edward and I go by Wolfgang that's all."

"As long as the card goes thru we don't have a problem."

I give him the number over the phone and it works and in 45 minutes a few whores will be showing up.

Bud and Tommy are lying in bed just staring at me. Bud leans off the bed picks up the bottle of Jack and starts chugging it before he passes it to me. We smoke some more pot but it has no effect because I am so wired on blow. I take another quick shower to kill time.

I am so high I need to drink more. I order room service. 12 pack of Corona, 75dollars, one 750ml of Jack, 124.99 dollars. One quart of vodka, 68 dollars. Fuck it. I tell them to put this on the room tab and don't forget the mixers, juice, and soda.

I'm showered and dressed, Bud and Tommy are in their boxers, drinking and smoking. Knock. Knock. Knock. It's the toots. I open the door and let them in. I am ecstatic; these women are beautiful…just beautiful. They don't look like your average prostitutes. They have true beauty. I would make any one of them my girlfriend in a second. Just to be seen with this kind of beauty by other women is worth it. This is the real deal. In New York City these girls could get $800 an hour.

Bud and Tommy are in their beds. They don't say a word and the blonde and the brunette pair off with them. I'm with the redhead and I couldn't be happier. I take her into the changing room /bathroom. I take this instead of the beds because I want privacy. I have a bunch of pillows and blankets on the rug.

These girls speak French. I am in a jacuzzi with Isabella. So hot, and I'm drinking beer after beer, I get out of the tub and lay on top of the pillows and pass out.

One hour later Bud is banging on the door. I wake up with this hot naked chick sleeping in my arms. We are in the spoon position. "Yo, I will be out in two minutes" I yell back.

I am erect and I decide to slide into her from behind. She starts moving up and down, getting real wet. This goes on for 3 minutes then she pushes herself off me and starts screaming in French. I get up and unlock the door. She points at my cock and says, "Why no condom?"
Shit.
"I forgot. It was just for a second. I was still kind of sleeping. Should I be worried?"
"I have a boyfriend and everyone wears condom with me!"
"You have nothing to worry about. I have never had any sort of disease. I am .0008 percent of the population that can't contract those viruses. Really you have nothing to worry about."

I walk out of the room, let her get dressed. I see Bud and Tommie's girls lying on the bed. Clothed, smoking cigarettes.
They smile at me.

When Isabella comes out of the bathroom, the girls stand up and walk over to me and hand me their card with a hand written phone number on it. Isabella walks up to me and gives me a real nice kiss and hug and writes her number down on my hand.
I guess she wasn't mad after all.

The girls leave. Bud and Tommy look shot.

"Let's get out of this room for a while, its 3 in the afternoon. I want to go somewhere nice and eat. Let's get the maid in here to change the sheets," Bud says.

"Alright let me grab a beer and smoke a bowl and I'm right behind you."

Fifteen minutes later in the elevator and I'm not feeling so good, it's not a physical feeling it's more of a mind fuck. I just sink into a deep depression. I feel it come over me as each floor passes. I want to kill myself for that second. The doors open and we walk into the now crowded lobby.

"Bud, look at me Bud, I don't feel so right."

"I have seen you look better."

"I'm going back to the room, you guys do whatever, but I'm losin' it and I'm going back. I need time alone."

Bud and Tommy don't say a word and walk out of the lobby.

I get back to the room quick. I'm about to have a nervous breakdown. I can't believe how disgusted I am of myself. I curl up naked in the bed and turn on the air conditioner. My mind is racing with all sorts of bad and negative thoughts. It's a battlefield between justifying my actions or accepting them.

My mind is a circus.

I feel bad. I feel sad.

Then I remember.

The movie, the movie for the Dog Run Film Festival. My mind fills with creative thoughts again, I can no longer dwell on the past when I have to make this short film.

That's what I tell myself.

I get out of bed, smoke some pot, and think about how I am going to create this film. I take a shower. I feel good again. The demons have left my body so I make myself a drink.

"Cosmopolitan Models, hello."

"Hey, is Jack there? This is Wolfgang."

"Sure, hang on one second."

One second.

Two seconds.

"Hello, yes?"

"Jack, it's Wolfgang"

"Oh hello, Mr. Klein."

"Jack, I was just calling to let you know that you absolutely have the best models around and I really like doing business with you. You're my kind of guy."

"That's really nice to hear. The girls said you were very accommodating and they had a very good time."

"Likewise, Jack. Now Jack, do you have any black girls with British accents."

"What did I tell you the first time you called? We have whatever you want."

"Cool - and can she have long legs and a nice rack?"

"Are we using the same card as last time, Mr. Klein?"

"Yes, Jack put it on the card and tell me how long."

"Thank you, Mr. Klein. I really think you'll like this one and Oleaf should be there within the hour."

"Oleaf?"

45 minutes later she arrives.

She is tall and slender, the boobs are ok. Her face is stunning and she has short-short hair. "Oleaf," I say. She smiles and walks in. "You must be Wolfgang," she says in her British accent.

I am pumped. I offer her a drink and she goes for the bottle of Jack and takes a swig.

She takes off all her clothes, lays on the bed and lights up a smoke. Thank God I'm in a No Smoking room.

She's an animal.

Then she grabs my pot and I oblige. She asks me if I have any coke and I tell her we ran out. That's when she goes in her purse and pulls out 80 dollar grams.

"I would love to but I have no cash on me, do you take credit cards?" I say jokingly.

"I can have Jack charge it to your account, darling…"

"Shit. Really? Well in that case I will take 3 grams."

As soon as I do one little key shot I'm off the wall again. I take a jacuzzi with her, we talk, we drink, we do more blow.

I drink.

I can't get hard. No matter what she does to it, it is dead. I have dead dick. I don't care because I'm so wrapped up in our bullshit coked out conversation. We exchange numbers and promise all this crap to each other. Coke talk.

Bud and Tommy arrive and see Oleaf siting naked at the table. They look at me and turn right around and exit the room without saying a word.

The coke is wearing off eand I'm able to get semi erect. I tell Oleaf to watch me jerkoff. She does. I finish and ask her to leave. We hug and kiss and she tells me to call her later.

I order room service but can't eat.

Bud and Tommy return. They tell me they are too tired to go out and fall down on the beds. I tell them I have a little coke and they tell me to fuck off. I make a drink and listen to these guys tell me I have a problem. I pick up the phone and dial.

"Jack, its Wolfgang. I need two more girls and the redhead from this morning."

"Should I put on the same card, Mr. Klein?"

"Of course and in the future don't ask me that again, just put it on the card."

"Mr. Klein what type of models do you prefer this time, besides the redhead of course."

I look at Bud and we say nothing it's just a staring contest.

"Two blondes, Jack. Two blondes and the redhead .""Ok, give them about 45 min…" I hang up the phone and throw the coke down on the table. Tommy goes right after it. Bud is making the beds. I decide to steal blankets and towels and pillows from the laundry department. I take another shower before they arrive. Bud has gotten ice and clean glasses. Tommy can't speak and is pacing the fucking room.

When I see the redhead I instantly remember her name. Isabella. I really like this chick. We all sit around the table drinking and smoking, playing some Canadian card game. It was like a couple of guys and their girlfriends spending a night in.

Not even close.

As soon as the coke comes out these girls become professionals. Clothes off and girl on girl action. The two blondes are going at it. Isabella is naked and on my lap. I tell her to grab some blow and meet me in the changing room. She does. We end up sniffing blow off of each other's body and fucking like animals. She's so loud they hear her in the other room for the next 90 minutes.

When we're done I walk out and see everybody bored and watching TV. The two blondes are smiling at me. They both slip me their number and give me a kiss goodbye. Isabella thinks I'm staying one more night so she tells me she will be back tomorrow night with a surprise for me then she French kisses me in front everyone. They leave.

"Dude what were you doing to that girl? At one point we all thought you were murdering her, the way she was screaming. The blondes couldn't stop laughing."

"Look at my back and shoulders. I'm bleeding and I have her teeth marks in my skin."

I like her.

Whores like me.

It's midnight and I can't go to sleep in this filthy fucking brothel so I call down to the lobby and ask for another room. I tell the guys they can come with me and leave this semen stained room, but we are splitting the cost. They tell me I'm on my own.

Fuck them.

I leave and go down to a room on the 7th floor. It smells clean. Clean sheets. Clean Air. I open the mini bar and attack the bourbon first. I need to put myself down. I need sleep. I'm starting to get the heebie jeebies. Alcohol is the only thing.

Now it's 2:30 am and I haven't slept a wink. Everything I could drink in the mini bar is gone.

"Is Jack there please?"

"Oh he's gone for the evening."

"Well this is Wolfgang Klein and I have been using your services all weekend and..." She cuts me off. "Yes Mr. Klein, we know who you are."

"Good, can you send over a girl but this time I'm on the 7th floor. room714. I don't care what type of girl as long as she is skinny. I trust your judgment."

I wake up to someone kicking the door. Boom. Boom. Boom! It's Bud. I let him in and when I walk back to the bed that's when I notice the chick in the sheets. I totally forgot. I must have blacked out because I remember the phone call but that's it.

"You don't stop." Bud says. "We will be eating in the restaurant in the lobby, then I'm out of here. I'm leaving in 30 minutes. Get your shit together and get down there. I'm not waiting and I will leave your ass in Canada."

Bud shakes his head and leaves.

I wake the girl aup nd she tells me we drank til sunrise and passed out. I take her in the shower and try to fuck her but she won't let me unless I put on a rubber. I don't even know where the condoms are so I tell her fine and jerkoff. We both get dressed and meet Bud downstairs. She joins us for brunch and Tom and Bud are getting into heavy conversation with this prostitute who barely speaks English. I could tell they are making her uncomfortable but I don't give a fuck, I could feel the withdrawals coming on so I order a Bloody Mary. The prostitute gets the hint and leaves. I can barely pick my head up from the table.

I'm lying down in the back seat.

I keep on replaying my actions from the weekend in my head. It's making me uncomfortable. Why do I act this way, I keep asking myself? Why do I always have to go that far? What am I doing fucking call girls without condoms?

"Bud pull over. Now. Pull over!" I have the door half open as he's pulling onto the grass. We are in the middle of farm country.

"What's wrong with you?" Tommy says.

I leap out and start puking.

I have no control.

I have one hand on the bumper and everything is coming out.

I have no control.

I have nothing left in my stomach but it is still contorting. I break out in a sweat and walk back to the truck.

"Holy shit, dude."

"I freaked myself out so much I made myself puke and now I don't feel so bad."

"You're fucked up," Tommy says and reclines his seat.

I lie back down and quickly fall asleep.

I awake in Trumbull feeling pretty good.

None of that shit that happened in Montreal really matters, I convince myself. I justify it. Now how do I explain $1,475 For Cosmopolitan Models on my mother's credit card?

Back at work on Tuesday and everybody is asking, "How was your weekend?"

I say "nothing special"…

Bud and I agree to meet after work at the Seagrape to discuss this film contest. After a few pints we agree to purchase a $5000 digital camera, a Canon XII. We will split the price. Only thing is I have no money and I need to figure out this credit card thing before my mother finds out. I tell Bud to give me three days and I'll have the cash.

The next morning I call the credit company and explain to them that I think I have been robbed. I'm posing as my father. "I went to use my credit card this morning and it was simply not in my wallet and I haven't used it in months."

"Mr Klein, can you give me your social security number and your mother's maiden name?"

I know this information and give it to her without hesitation.

"Hold on, Mr. Klein, we have some transactions posted over this past weekend. In Montreal, Canada."

"Canada? I've never been to Canada in all my life."

"Yes sir, it shows here 3 nights at The Marriott and nine purchases from Cosmopolitan Models."

"How could that be Ma'am? I never left the States."

"Well sir, it sounds like your card was in fact stolen."

"How? When I still have my wallet with me? "

"If you placed it down somewhere, in a gym locker for instance, thieves will usually take one card so it's not noticeable for a while." "I was at the gym last week, but I have a locker."

"Well sir, you might want to go and speak with the manager there and tell him what you think, but in the mean time I am closing this account."

"Will I be responsible for the payment?"

"No, Mr. Klein, your card is insured and you have protection, you're o.k."

"Are you guys going to investigate?" "Most likely no, we already put a stop on the card and if anyone tries to use it the authorities will be called."

"Well hopefully you catch whoever did it. Now can you put a rush delivery on a new card?"

"Mr. Klein, we can have one to you within 36 hours, just call us when you receive it and we will activate it for you."

"Thank you very, very much. I was a little shocked at first but you guys did an excellent job on helping me out. Thank you again."

"Thank you for your business, Mr. Klein, and have a good day."

Five days later we purchase the camera.

I put half on the credit card and tell my mother I will pay it off in a month.

I have to make a movie.

I have a camera and no plot.

Bud and I decide to hold a meeting at the Seagrape with a crew of friends to see if they can help. It turns into a booze and drug fest but Kotch says I can use him as the star.

The next day is Saturday and we are about to shoot our first scene. We occupy this chick Nina's house on the beach. We set up lights. I try to story board it, but don't. We have a group of people there doing I don't know what. We drink. We smoke pot.

"Ok Kotch. I'm going to film you through the bathroom mirror while you're pissing in the morning. We won't see your cock, just your face in the mirror. Then you pullout a spoon and baggie with what appears to be blow. You do this last blast in the mirror. All in one take. Then you look at the empty bag and then at yourself in the mirror and say, 'Goin' to make me some rent.' And walk out of frame. That's the first scene."
"Did you just come up with that shit now?" Bud whispers.
"Oh yeah, Kotch, you're shirtless and shoeless. Now go! I mean action!"

We do 3 takes of the first scene just to make sure.
Nina is disgusted.
"Ok, second scene is you running out of the house and walking to.....let's go ask Billy at the deli if we can film a scene there."

I shoot Kotch bursting out the front door and walking down the street without shoes and a shirt and he has this little baggie filled with flour hanging out his back pocket. He is wearing bright green pants. People are outside watching, this is a very busy beach community.

At lunch we review the morning's work and have a few pints at the Seagrape. We need to discuss the script," Kotch says.
"What script?"
"That's what I thought and that's what I like about you," he says.
"I just need to see if Billy will let us use his deli for ten minutes," I remember.

I walk over to the deli and tell Billy what's going, I give him the low down on the film festival. He's also a Trumbull guy I know from childhood. He says yes but I have to be quick.
Cool.

Scene Three.
"Kotch, go into the deli and we will put Dave behind the register. Walk up to him like he is your regular blow dealer and say, 'Yo man give me a taste of that stuff.' Then he is going to pull out a tablespoon and put it up to your nose.

That's when you raise your right arm, which is covered in a brown hoagie bag and point it at him and say, 'Give me all the mother fuckin' money.' Then he is going to hand you a pillowcase filled with money.

I pull out a stuffed pillowcase with a money sign painted in black. You grab it and bolt out the door. Ok got it? We do this all one on take. "

It goes off perfect and the waiting customers have no idea what's going on so it looks pretty real. Billy was pissed about all the flour on his floor and the customers that ran out on him. I told him I'd make it up to him and left. We walked across the street back to the bar and began to celebrate our first successful shoot day. We drink and before you know it, its 4am.

Sunday, we start at noon we meet again at the Seagrape. This time the waitress wants to be in a scene in the film. I tell them I need to discuss it with my lead actor and the producer. I walk over to Bud and Kotch and say "Boys we are going to be drinking free all day. See those two waitresses right there? They want to be in the film."

I spend the better part of Sunday chatting up these girls with Bud and Kotch. We are drinking and smoking pot with these chicks and then before I know it the sun is down.

"Ladies look. The sun went down and it's too dark to shoot today. How about you guys give me your numbers and I will call you tomorrow so we can set something up for this week."

"Where are you guys going? It's only eight o'clock. We get off in an hour and we should hang out," the head waitress says this as she hands me her number. I end up leaving with them and the boys and we go to a house party on the beach.

It's 2am. I'm fucked up. I have to be in work in five hours. I'm lying on a gravel driveway while this waitress is jerking me off. I try to film it. She freaks out and I leave.

Monday morning and I'm back at th MS Studio. Bright and early, life is good. I am working my usual 14 hour days but I don't mind, I'm still running on pure adrenaline and marijuana. It's summer time and the livin' is easy.

I get up enough confidence to ask out one of the night editors, her name is Gina and she is a looker with a kick ass body. She turns me down. I tell her I feel stupid. Then she says, "Only because I'm in a relationship with someone else."

O.K. that's not so bad.

I planted the seed.

The 2nd weekend of filming is more exciting than the first. A lot more people are now showing up and giving us support. We abuse their kindness.

These two college freshman boys are walking down the street. I convince them to hold hands and skip down the sidewalk and when they approach the camera, stop and kiss each other on the lips. They do it, Scene Four done.

I tell my friend Tomas to dress as a security guard with a 2 inch rubber dildo duct taped around his junk. And for a baton he uses a 14inch rubber cock. "Now go and stand in front of that bar doorway and swing your cock."

No one is laughing. But he does it. Then I have him chase Kotch all over town waving a dildo and dressed as a kinky gay security guard.
This is the chase scene, I'm thinking.
We finish for the day and we're all fucked up.

The rest of the night is a drunken drugged out blur, I just remember Sunday morning at the diner;

What the fuck am I doing, I think while eating Sunnyside up eggs. I feel the chill of Fear going down my back, I starting sinking slowly into a pit of guilt and depression. I kept asking myself what kind of shit am I putting together. The people that are hosting this are taking it damn serious. Maybe it's not too late to quit.

I order a Bloody Mary to take the edge off. I look at all these crazy souls in front of me and realize I can't let these poor fools down.

Scene 5 or 6.

"Ok, Mudman, I need you to tie your hair into two pigtails." (He has long curly brown hair.) Make them look like dog ears" I say. "Alright, now can I get a dog leash and collar."

I put the leash and collar around Mudman's neck and tie the other end to a cable between two trees.
Hence dog run.

Mudman takes off all his clothes because he tells me, "Dogs don't wear clothes." Then he neatly places piles of mud from the ground around his genitals.
We fill up his dog bowl with flour that looks like cocaine.
"Now, when I yell action, you'll be on all fours with your head buried in that dog bowl. Make sure you get coke all over your face. Then you look up

because you hear something. Its Kotch running thru the woods onto your property, you start barking and acting like an attack dog. Kotch is going to jump over that stream with the pillow case filled with money and land next to you. That's when you attack him. Go for his throat. Just like a dog, you know. Now Kotch is going to roll out of it and start running away. You give chase and about 6 yards; your collar is going to yank you back to the dog run. Cut scene. Do you think you can do it?" I ask him.
"I want to do it! This is great. Can I get twenty minutes to get prepped up?"
"Sure." I say.
"Everybody, 30 minute break."

The scene was shot 3 or 4 times from different angles, everybody was into it, each take was better than the last. We clean up for the day and start our partying. Same bullshit. I have no idea how I am going to edit this piece of shit. I don't even know what it's about. If I show this in the festival, I will be laughed at.
Fuck it.
I drink more.
Bud, Kotch and I stay up the whole night at our friend Nina's house. We are taking Quaaludes and listening to a dance track called "Cindy Lauper Likes Green Drugs, Green Drugs," or that's what I think I hear,
I decide to pull out the camera and start writing scenes beside it. It's 5:30am and the sun is up.
First Kotch convinces me to film him fucking his own ass. I do. I watch this grown man drugged out of his gourd pull down his pants, sit on the floor and bend his cock until it goes up his ass. I wouldn't believe it but I have seen the video too many times. I still can't figure out how he did it with such a small wanky.

"Okay here is the scene: Bud you are on the couch in Nina's silk robe and wearing this shower cap. I am sitting next to you in a G-string and red winter snow gloves, plus I have the 14 inch fake cock hanging out of my string. I am wearing glasses without the lenses. This scene will be shot from underneath the glass coffee table looking directly up at Bud and I smoking out of a glass bowl. Then we hear a knock at the door. We cut to the door from the couch and we see Kotch standing behind the screen door.

He is holding a green pillow case with a huge $ symbol on it."

Knock. Knock.
Bud: Who's dat?

Kotch: Yo it's me.

Bud: You got my rent?

The camera cuts to Kotch holding up the bag of money.

Bud: Good.

Kotch: You got any of that white stuff?

Bud: Yup.

Bud gets up from the couch and walks up the staircase and returns with what appears to be 45 pounds of white powder in a clear plastic garbage bag.

They make the exchange at the door but first Kotch has to stick his head in the bag and whiff it. He does. It's all over his face and hair. He walks away down the street with no shoes, no shirt, bright green slacks and a huge bag of white substance draped over his shoulder.

It is 7:30 a.m. Sunday morning.

We start drinking.

I have no more ideas left and I have no idea how I am going to make a movie out of this footage. I am starting to have thoughts about showing this piece of off base material to strangers judging me.

It's noontime and we are at the bar again and all our friends are there. I decide to drink vodka so I can get some brain activity going. I am sitting next to Bud.

"I'm starting to have second thoughts on this festival. I don't know what I'm doing. I'm going to make an asshole out of myself in front of all those people. I mean who the fuck does this? This is no short film; it's a bunch of nonsense. I don't know what to do."

"Have the cop fuck the thief."

"What?"

"Have the cop fuck the thief."

"That's my advice to you. Make it a love story and have the cop fuck the thief. The gays will love it." Bud says.

"Gay sex?"

"Yeah, dude. Now think about and we will shoot it in a couple of hours while everyone is still here. Do you think you can convince Tomas to simulate anal sex on Kotch with that strap on he is wearing?"

I order two drinks of vodka and OJ and I call Kotch and Tomas over to the bar.

I hand them the drinks.

"Guys I just want to say thank you, you guys really helped me out when I needed it." "Cheers"

"Now we have one more scene to film later on and then we are done with the movie and time for celebration." "What's the scene?" Tomas asks.

"Another chase scene and then you catch him and.... something like that."

"Ok, no problem as long as I'm home by 7pm. My wife wants to have dinner with me and I have to teach tomorrow so no more drinking after this". Tomas says.

"Sure guy,"

Tomas walks back over to the group of people he was chatting with before. I tell Kotch, "It's your job today to get Tomas fucked up." I hand Kotch 20 bucks and two shots of tequila and send him off.

I can feel my body getting exhausted and all I am thinking about is work the next morning. I need sleep or cocaine. After a second of thinking about it I go up to Chase, this blow head from Fairfield. He is always on it and always holding. He is a dick, always was, always will be. But I'm in no mood. "Chase, come here." He walks over closer to me. I lean in his ear and say, "Dude, I'm not fuckin around. I need some whiff now. Don't tell anyone and here is 30 bucks."

He doesn't take it.

"Just go in the bathroom and give me a little in this" I hand him the plastic from a cigarette box.

"I don't know what you're talking about," Chase whispers back to me.

"Chase, let's not make this a problem, we all know you're a blowhead. Just hook me up a little, man. I need to start filming and I'm running out of energy."

"I don't do blow" he tells me.

"Asshole. I have done coke with you all the time and so has everybody in this bar at one point. So why are you fucking with me now?"

"Listen Klein, I don't care about your little neighborhood movie project or how you're feeling. If I do happen to have some, I'm saving it for that girl later on." He points over to this chick Sam I know.

"Dickhead," I say. "That's my friend Sam and I know for a fact she doesn't party. Don't even mention it to her, she will get disgusted. She's not into drugs, dude. Just give me the bag."

"I don't believe you. You're just talkin' shit again."

"Guy, I'm sitting next to you, she sees that I know you, now if you go up to her and offer her blow, she is going to think I associate with scumbags like you. And if that happens I'm going to sick Kotch on your ass."

"You're an asshole."

"Yeah I know, give me the bag."

Chase still refuses.

"Listen I am going to call Kotch over and tell him that you owe me money. Then he is going to go into your pockets and take out everything and when he finds that little baggie filled with white powder, he is going to keep it. You know this and I know this."

Chase turns his head and looks at Kotch in the corner, then turns his head back to me.

"Hurry up," he says as he hands me the bag.

I go into the bathroom pour some into a bill and fold it up for later and do huge blasts out of his bag. I never gave him the money.

"Thanks, dude," I shake his hand and sneak the coke back, then I walk over to Sam and Kotch.

Sam says, "Who is that guy? I always see him here"

"Chase, the town asshole his nickname is Dick."

Chase turns around in his chair and looks at all of us staring at him. We all smile and wave. He turns back around. Fuck him.

I tell Kotch to throw some more shots down Tomas' throat. Tomas is loving all the attention. He's walking around in his security uniform with this 3 inch rubber cock duct taped to his crotch. He is a High School English teacher in Westport. I don't think his wife would appreciate this.

O.K. Time to start shooting.

I bring the crowd from the bar out on the street. I have Tomas chasing Kotch thru traffic, then we cut to Kotch running in between houses. He loses Tomas.

Cut to Kotch stealing clothes from a close line. Then he changes behind Nina's neighbor's garage and comes out in women's lingerie.

Cut to Tomas running thru backyards yelling and waving the rubber cock. As he comes around the corner of the house they literally bump into each other and fall. The big bag of blow spills on them.

It's 10 at night and I shot all those scenes quick, but I still need the sex scene to happen.

I have heart burn.

I grab a bottle of Jack Daniels that I keep around in my car. I tell Nina to go inside and grab me three shot glasses, she does. I pour 3 shots and pull the cocaine out of my pocket. No one is near me or paying attention. I throw in about a half of gram into one of the glasses. I stir it around with my sunglasses arm until it dissolves.

"Tomas. Kotch. Come here," I wave them over. "Here is to the last scene." I give the coke shot to Tomas. He slams it back before I could say anything else. He is fucked up. His wife is going to be pissed at him. He is going to reek of booze tomorrow while teaching. He doesn't take drugs and now he is on a fair amount of cocaine. Tomas is going to be pissed with me when this is over.

"Ok here is the scene. Tomas you start wiping the spilled coke off yourself but you try a little, this makes you very happy. So Kotch then hands you a spoonful of it and you whiff that. Then you guys shake hands and then hold hands walking out of frame. Then Kotch is going to fuck you. Cool. Let's go."

"What?"

"What. What?"

"'Kotch is going to fuck me?"

"Yeah, well simulated with the fake cock, just get in the doggie position."

"No way."

"Tomas don't do this to me now we are just about done."

"Why do I have to get fucked?" He says while chewing his lip. "Why can't I be the one who does the fucking?"

"You want to fuck the prisoner, I get it. You win,"

Tomas is now smiling and started smoking cigarettes for the first time.

"Kotch you're going to be the bitch in this scene. Get on all fours. Tomas get behind him and lift up the nightie and take the 3 inch strap on and act like you're fucking your hostage."

"You guys discuss it while I go to the bathroom." I walk into Nina's house and do the rest of the blow.

I immediately feel like my heart beat in my neck.

"Guys let's get this done," I say as I walk into the backyard.

Tomas really gets into it, he's moaning and grinding. Kotch is on all fours with a joint in his mouth.

This is ridiculous.

The neighbors start gathering around and they don't look happy. A bunch of people are hanging around drinking and being rowdy. It's only a matter of time before the cops are called.

The scene is finished and Tomas is so fucked up I have to get Kotch to drive him home. Tomas is still wearing the 3 inch strap on and guzzling beers. His wife will not be happy.

Another day at work. Monday.

I'm happy to be there but I'm exhausted.

I enjoy working, I like the environment. I like all the beautiful women that come and go out of the place, I like the away shoots and the celebrity guests. I like my weekly paycheck but I'm still hoping there is a chance I can move into a position where I can work as a producer's assistant or associate. I need to get some sort of credit on the show titles. I need to learn as much as possible. But so far no one has offered me anything in the six months I've been there. I will keep waiting.

My supervisor Pang is breaking my balls because he is a no good piece of shit. He rides me like the prick that he is.
He doesn't like me.
Jealous.

Pissed off Asian. A social retard. Pissed off because he is a closet homo. Pissed off that I don't kiss his ass. Pissed off that he's not in my clique. Pissed that he can't fire me.

If I didn't do my job or Margaret didn't like me I would have been gone in the first two weeks. I am a gofer, an errand boy. A production assistant. I am well liked by the staff and do whatever I am told without question. My supervisor doesn't like me because he senses that I have no respect for him. And I don't. He is a lying, back stabbing Asian who is pissed off all the time. Pang has no interest in television work. He doesn't want to be there and it shows, he's always disappearing 3 times a week to finish his massage schooling. Everything else is cool. I try to avoid him as much as possible.

Been sober for four days.

I'm trying to figure out how I am going to edit this video, I don't have a computer. I put it off for a few more days and then I get a call from Allison. "Hey hun, I just want to know how things were coming along on your end?"
"Hey you, I was just going to call you. I was just going to start the editing process."

"Wolfgang where do you want to be placed in the line-up, do you want to be first, second?"

"I want to be last."

"Yeah, are you sure?"

"Oh I'm sure"

"And also I need the name of the film and a synopsis, and the names of the Director and Producer. It's for the program."

"Ok. The name is *Goin' To Make Me Some Rent*. The synopsis is, "It's wrong." I'm the Writer and Director and Bud Redcoat is the Producer."

"And what's the running time?"

"15 minutes."

"Thank you Wolfgang, I'm so excited. It's going to be a great evening. Also how many people do you think you'll be bringing"

"30."

"30? The venue isn't that big and we have 11 other groups to accommodate. How about 10?"

"Sure."

"Ok I will call you in the beginning of next week and send you out a copy of the program. If anything else pops up just call me."

"Bye."

I hang up the phone and start to get depressed.

These people are adults, highbrow people, and educated people.

Artistic people.

I am an Animal.

I don't know what Allison was thinking calling me up and inviting me to enter this thing. Why did I say yes?

I sit in on the weekend. We're at Bud's parents house, I think they're in Italy for the month. We drink beers and try to figure out this editing thing. It never happens so we call over some girls from work and go out for sushi. We act like normal gentleman. No drugs or out control drinking. The night is uneventful.

Sunday nothing gets accomplished, sit around the pool and drink beers, then at 3pm we go to the waterside bar at the Westport Country Club. Sunday afternoons they have a Reggae band and the place is packed with upscale chicks in their Sunday best. I order vodka.

As the sun is setting and the place is rockin' this chick Sandy walks up to me and my friends. She is alright looking. Brunette, a few years younger than me. But she has this 80's thing going on with her hair and clothes. I don't care. It sort of turns me on.

"Do you live in Westport?" She says.

"No, Trumbull. Why?"

"I always see you around town. You go to The Bean coffee shop in the morning."

"I do. That's where you must have seen me."

"I'm Sandy.""Great." I smile.

"Do you work near there?"

"I work for '*Margaret Steward*'. So I usually have to pick her up in the mornings and that's when I stop to grab her coffee."

"Really, what do you do for her?"

"Producer of her television show."

"Then why do you pick her up in the mornings?"

"Since I live in Trumbull and I like to have alone time with her to discuss the daily activities - without being interrupted - we ride together and then, I don't need to see her for the rest of the day."

"That's a smart idea. Can you hold my drink while I run to the ladies room?" She hands me her drink and my friends shake their heads.

"What are you doin? She looks like she's in high school."

"I don't care. Get away from me."

Sandy walks back to us.

"I think I'm going to leave, I'm parked all the way in the south lot. It's so far past the golf course and dark. Would you walk me to my car? What's your name again?"

"You never asked me. I'm Wolfgang. Nice to me you. Your car is kinda far and I'm chillin' here with my friends and I'm supposed to meet someone in five minutes.""Please, please!" She grabs my hand.

"Fine." I say as I turn and smile at the boys.

Sandy and I are now walking thru the golf course; she thought it would be a short cut to her car. That's when she grabs me and we start making out. I immediately try to fuck her right there but she repeatedly says no. Fuck this.

I really want to get back to my friends so I hurried her along towards her car. I can see she's pissed but I don't give a fuck. "If I had let you fuck me you wouldn't be in such a hurry to get back would you?"

"Yes I would," I say

"Do you want my phone number so you can take me out?"

"No, you're nuts. Where the fuck is your car?"

She points over to the second lot.

"Are you good now?"

She grabs my hand again and starts running to her car.

"Come on, Mandy. What are you doin? I gotta get back."

She pushes me up against her car and starts kissing me and this time she goes for my cock. I hear people talking and walking but I block it out as she starts going down on me.

"You really want to fuck me?" She whispers.

"Yes."

Mandy stands up and bends over the hood and lifts up her sun dress. No panties. As I'm banging her she tells me not to pull out so I don't. I have sweat dripping into my eyes and now more people are walking past. She stands up and turns around and kisses me on the lips.

"I'm sure I will see you at the coffee shop some time."

She gets into her little BMW and drives away.

I'm standing in a dark parking lot with my black slacks down at my ankles and my junk hanging out. I wipe the sweat from my forehead.

I pull up my pants. I wipe my face and jog back to the bar.

People are looking at me, more than usual. My friends look a bit shocked.

"What's up?"

"What did you do?' Bud says as he takes a step back.

People are starting to stand further away from me now.

"What do you think I did? I fucked her."

"Are you sure you didn't *murder* her?" Bud points to the bottom of my powder blue vintage button up polyester short sleeve shirt.

"Look."

"Holy Shhhhhh……..hit."

It takes me a second after I rubbed my hand on it.

"It's blood. What the fuck?"

"Dude, you got it on your face."

I run inside the well-lit country club, thru the restaurant, straight to the men's room.

"FUCK ME."

I say this not noticing the old men standing at the urinals.

It looks like I was shot in the lower abdomen.

That pig had her period and now it's on me, I throw the shirt out and wash my face. Thank god I always wear a white v-neck. I don't tell anyone.

I just leave.

I think about poisoning my boss.

I think about going in the studio basement and collecting the rat poison. grind it up into a powder and put it into one of his daily fancy smoothies. I have these thoughts every time I see this cunt. He is such a weak man he makes me hate people. I see through this insecure asshole.

He doesn't like me because he knows I think he is a joke.
He harasses me at work. We both have radios, so we can communicate to each other from around the compound. People are around me at all times and they can hear him over the speaker giving me tasks to do.
Fine.
Every 2 seconds, Pang is on the radio. Where Are You? What Are You Doing?!!.
"Pang, I' m putting paper in the copier like you asked me to do 30 seconds ago."
"What?! When did I tell you that! Hurry Up then come to my office."

Employees in an earshot look at me with a WHAT THE FUCK kind of expression. This happens 10 times a day every day. I go to his office and we have the same conversation. I hold back from wanting to choke him and I swallow my tongue.
"Ok Pang, I will try to be on top of things better. You're right. I'm wrong. Thanks for the advice." I leave his office defeated. He likes throwing his power in my face. The guy rides me. Other employees that I'm barely friends with told me that.
Pang is trying to make me quit.
I won't quit.

I put in my 13 hour days, then go straight to the bar.

I have five days to finish and present this piece of crap I made. I still have to edit it.

On Thursday night I go old school, I grab 2 VCRs and the camera. Bud and I drink Jack Daniels after work and cut the movie. We feed the camera into one VCR and cut from that copy and then lay it together on the 2nd tape. It's sort of raw but it fits well for the film. We write title cards on index cards with BB King playing in the background. I try to make some sort of story with this footage and all I could come up with is focused on gay men on coke. I do my best to edit the scenes together and it comes out perfect. I have one final copy on a VCR tape. No back ups.

Friday morning at work and I'm itching to get out of here. I have to be in New York City at 7pm and my dick boss still won't give me an answer if I can leave an hour early. He is well aware of this film festival and the date because I told him a month ago and every week since. He is just a dick.

Gina asks me if I can drive her to the store in one of the company vans. I grab the keys and meet her in the parking lot.

"I need to pick up something for my allergies, I can't stop tearing up." She says.

"It's the pollen. I get it too this time of year. I will take you to the pharmacy."

"Thanks, so I hear tonight is your guy's film contest. I wish you the best of luck."

"Oh Thanks."

"What's it about?"

I pretend I don't hear her.

"What's it about?"

"Oh."

I don't have a clue what to tell her so I blurt out, "It's about a guy losing his girlfriend in a car crash."

"Oh my. Really."

"Yeah, it's only a fifteen minute short, so we get straight to the point."

"What's the point?"

"One minute you're in love and the next minute she's dead."

"That's kinda morbid. Don't ya think?"

"It's about love really. Maybe sometime I can show it to you, if your boyfriend lets you…"

She just stares at me with a fuck you asshole look on her face.

Thank god we are at the pharmacy now and she just gets out of the van and I park.

I am an asshole.

When Gina returns to the van I apologize.

"That came out the wrong way."

"No it didn't. You're a sarcastic asshole."

"Now that's not nice, I was not being sarcastic. I simply thought your boyfriend would not like you coming over to my house to watch it. I actually thought about inviting you tonight, but I didn't know how your boyfriend would react. Gina you took it the wrong way."

"Yeah well me and him, we're at the beginning of the end. I don't see us together much longer. All we do is fight. He can't find a job, which makes things worse, and he is jealous of me working here. Every day it's something else with him."

"Man. I'm sorry to hear that Gina." I say with a huge smile on my face.

"I wish I knew. I would have saved you an invite."

I pull back into the studio and up to the front door to let her out.

"Next time," she says then leans over and gives me a kiss on my cheek.

"Thank you," she whispers as she gets out.

It's going to be a good night.

I'm getting calls at work from all my friends wanting to know when I'm getting out. I tell I everyone to meet me at the train station at 5:30. If my dick boss doesn't let me leave,
I'm quitting.

Its four o'clock and Pang comes out from his office to look for me. We meet up in the commissary and this dick has to give me a 20 minute speech on how he could get in serious trouble by letting me leave early. He's lying, but I go with it. Finally he says I can take off and I don't say a word I just get up and leave.

I rush home to change my ,clothes. Black slacks with pinstripes and another polyester baby blue vintage short sleeve button down shirt. I grab the movie and a wad of cash and jump into my car and fly to the Westport train station. I see all the boys hanging out in the parking lot drinking beer waiting for me. I do a head count and we have 14. Allision said I only have a guest list of 10 and I still have 7 friends meeting me in the city. She might be a little pissed. I start guzzling beer and smoking pot. Kotch pulls out a bag of 200 Ecstasy pills.

"Dude, are you fucking crazy, what are you going to do with all that shit?"

"I'm going to sell it."

He puts five pills in the palm of my hand.

"Here take these for good luck."

I put them in my shirt pocket

"You're nuts, get away from me."

Then everyone that can jump into Bud's car does and they immediately start doing coke.

"The trains going to be here any moment. Guys..? "

I hear the train hor0n blow and start walking to the tracks and I see everyone start to scramble. We all make it on the train and everyone is checking their pockets making sure they all have their stash. A bottle of Jack Daniels is being passed around and I can see some of the passengers getting uncomfortable. We all make into the bar car and take it over.

My friends Edfuckin' G and Ritchie are doing blow right out in the open. Kotch is erarranging his pill collection on the table and Cheen and Bud are getting high in the bathroom. I'm sipping on a beer, preparing for the police to be waiting for us on the platform at Grand Central.

Rounding up all these animals together, it's never a good idea. It's a zoo. We make it downtown in 3 separate cabs and thank god no one got arrested so far. I meet up with the other part of our crew in front of the bar. It's a hot June night, the humidity in the city is crazy, everything smells like piss.

Allison comes from outside the bar and looks around.

"All these people with you?"

"I guess so."

"I don't know if we will have enough room."

"I will sit in the front row if I have to."

"Well get in there before the crowd shows up…and come here I want to introduce you to my friend Collin. He is one of the judges that works for the magazine."

Allison grabs my hand and walks me inside.

"Hello, Collin. My name is Wolfgang Klein." I extend my hand.

"He goes by Wolfgang," Allison says.

"Hey Wolfgang. Glad to meet you." He keeps shaking my hand.

Collin is about 45 and feminine. I can't tell if he is gay. Probably. He is wearing a bow tie with black rimmed glasses and plaid shorts.

"I'm looking forward to seeing your film." He says.

"I bet you are."

"Can I get a drink here or do I need to go downstairs?" I say this so I can leave this stale dude.

"Right here" he says, then yells for the bartender. "Trevor, Trevor! This is one of the filmmakers. Wolfgang."

"Hello," he says.

"Whatever Wolfgang is drinking, put on my tab, please."

"A dirty Kettle One martini." I smile.

Now I *know* this guy is gay.

"Why thank you, Collin. You didn't have to do that."

"Oh, it's nothing. Allison told me you're a pretty wild guy. She says you guys have a blast in Newport."

"Oh did she?"

"Yeah she said you were...."

"Excuse me, Collin, I have to grab this guy before he leaves." I point to Kotch outside the bar window. I grab my drink and get up and walk outside.
That guy is beat.

My friends are on the sidewalk swigging from a bottle and smoking bowls. I pop one pill. I am getting a little nervous as more people show up.

Allison calls us in and my friends make room up in front of the screen so we can all sit together. The place is packed wall to wall. It is hot as hell in here. My friend Ritchie takes off his pants and is chillin' in his boxers. No one notices. My friend Rhett sits next to me and hands me a little baggie with brown powder in it.

"What is that?"

"Molly."

"What?"

"MDMA."

"Oh," I sniff a bit. "That shit burns!"

"You're supposed to eat it, swallow it."

Rhett grabs the bag from me and pours it into my vodka.

"There you go. Drink your gay martini and you'll be fine."

I chug what's left of it and go back up to the bar.

"Trevor. Hey. What's up dude? Can I get a Kettle ssando Easy on the soda and ice."

He laughs and over pours.

"Here ya go."

'Trevor can you put this on Collins tab?"

I yell to Collin at the other end of the bar, finally I get his attention and I raise my class. "Good luck, Buddy."

He raises his glass.

There is no reason I should be wishing him luck, he's not in the competition.

"See, Trevor - everything is cool." I smile and head back to my seat.

I see Kotch pissing in the corner.

Each short film is good in its own right but they suck and we are getting restless by the 8th short film. There are a lot of actors here trying to show their craft. I didn't use actors. I look around and everyone except my group of friends are sitting quietly and taking this whole event serious. I'm getting a few dirty looks for being so boisterous. The drugs are starting to take effect.

When my film starts the animals settle down and I can here Rhett laughing.
"Dude what are you laughing at? It's just the beginning credits."
"I know," he says.

I slowly shrink in my seat. I don't feel so bad considering. I don't pay attention to the film, I look around at people and their reactions. It's good. My friends and the whole bar are roaring with laughter. I feel good. When Allison announces the winner, I don't hear her. I'm too busy getting a drink and the place is loud as shit. Then I get lifted up and carried to the stage.

Holy shit I won.

I won.

People liked it.
Or the judges were afraid of my group's rambunctious behavior and thought it would be in their best interest to vote for me. Anyway it felt good for a little bit of time. My friends and I make it down to the Lakeside Lounge on Ave B. It smells like piss. It always smells like piss.

I eat more. Ecstasy and sweat. I can see everyone is their prime forms and it's way past three in the morning. I'm too fucked up at this point to even talk so I park myself on a bar stool and bury my chin into my chest. I can hear things, I just can't move. Someone grabs my shirt at the collar.
"I'm taking him home" she says.

I open my eyes and I see Bud right in front of me with this Puerto Rican chick. I turn to my left and see this white chick with piercings all over her face, she's not bad, she's thin.
"What..?"
"Come on, buddy, we're leaving," Bud says as he puts his hand on the back of my neck and guides me off the stool. The girl has her arm wrapped in mine and is walking with me on my left.
"Where are we going? I say.
"I'm taking you home."
"My home?"
"No. I live right down here."
I look at Bud and he's smiling, walking beside me with the Puerto Rican chick.
"Just go with it," he mouths to me.
"What's your name?" I ask her.
"Veronica."

"Veronica, I never met a Veronica before. Where do you live, Veronica?"
"One more block. Ave C and 5th. "
"Were you guys at the movie?"
"What movie?"
"We were at a movie premiere. Forget it."

We walk up five flights of stairs in this old pre war building when we enter the apartment we are all crowded in this little room. Real little, smaller than a jail cell. It has three doors; one for the bathroom and the other two are bedrooms. She shuffles me into the dark small bedroom and onto an air mattress on the floor. There is a proper bed on my right but I don't make any sense of it. I am going in and out of consciousness and mumbling shit from a dream state. I'm fucking her and falling asleep at the same time.

BOOM…?

The door swings open and in the shadow of the doorway I see this big jacked up black bald man in his tighty whiteys. Now I am completely awake and I jump to the back of the room, naked. Veronica gets up and attacks him. She is hitting him with her fists and screaming.
"Get out. Get out..!"
The black guy, breaks down and starts crying, whining.
"Veronicaaa!!!How many times have I told you stop bringing home strange men..?"
This dude is gay. Fuck it.
For a second I thought I was going to get raped and murdered. Veronica pulls me up. I know I'm going there tonight and I grab all my clothes and go into the bathroom. I fuck her in the shower. BOOM. BOOM. BOOM ..!
The brother is now banging on the wall. Then the neighbor starts banging from across the hall.
"Come with me!" Veronica says.

We get out of the shower and she darts back into the bedroom and starts fighting, again… "I Poppi, I poppi.I poppi..!" and then comes out with a blanket wrapped around her.

She grabs my hand and we walk out the door and up 6 flights of steps to the roof. I am buck naked.

We walk out to the center of the black tar roof and she lies down on her back with the blanket underneath her. I immediately start fucking her. I lose track of time but the sun is totally up.

It's like 530 am and I'm getting sober.

When I look at this chick in the daylight, I'm not impressed. I remember that she didn't seem too concerned about rubbers. I can't cum and the sun is beating down on my back. I decide to get this over with and I begin to jack hammer the shit out of her. Veronica is now clawing my back and won't let go of me. I am hate-fucking her at this point. Finally she finishes and I break loose from her grip, then when I stand up I see people in the windows of taller neighboring buildings looking down at us. One guy is drinking a cup of coffee and waves to me. When I walked downstairs to grab my clothes I bump into Bud, leaving.

What a coincidence.

I grab my shit from the apartment and meet him on the street.
"I've never seen anything like that before," he says.
"What?"

"Last night, with that chick I was chatting up, the Puerto Rican and Veronica, and you looked so fucked up passed out on the stool. Sitting up. The girls felt bad for you and that's when Veronica grabbed you. I saw you wake up and just follow her."
"Yeah I was out of it."
"I need sleep man. The Puerto Rican wouldn't let me sleep for shit. You know what? That's the 'fifth Latin girls I've fucked and all of the sudden they're screamin', 'I poppi. I poppi.' Is that a Latin thing? Do they think I don't know? The more I think about it, weirds me out. Oh Daddy. Oh Daddy. I am going to see if I can bang a Latin chic that doesn't say it..'

"That's what you came up with? I can't believe I'm hanging out in the bowels of New York and I end up banging this chick from Bridgeport. We take a cab to Grand Central and I see Kotch sleeping on the sidewalk next to the entrance. He is barefoot and his wallet and bowl are right next to his head. I see a NYPD officer tab him with his baton to wake him up. He doesn't say anything about the pot pipe lying next to his head and walks away.

"Where are your shoes?"
Kotch not looking right. "I took them off in some bar for some reason."
He checks his pockets. "Don't tell me I ate all those pills."
"Did you?" I say.
"I saw you last night throwing them around. You were MAKING people eat them. Everyone, strangers, the bartenders. Yourself." Bud says laughing.

We jump on the train back to Connecticut. I sleep on a lawn chair by Bud's parents' pool. I swim and put on the same clothes and Bud and I jump back on the train back to the City.

A couple of editors from M.Steward Studio are throwing party on the Upper East Side. We were fortunate to get invited, but I could care less this meant we had to be on our best behavior. I'm pretty sure they invited us just to be nice and hoping we wouldn't show. Because honestly if Bud and I show up, these stale assholes would have no chance with the any of the girls. Plus they didn't like us. We first stop at a bar and suck back some beers and then show up at the party around midnight. A bunch of girls get excited and I see Gina in the back room.

After mingling with a few of the girls I overhear that Gina and her boyfriend broke up and Sean the host is plotting his move. I hear them say that he's had a crush on her for the longest time. I walk right in the back room of the apartment where Gina is.
I walk up to her.

"Hey, funny to see you here'."

"Hey Wolfgang I could say the same thing about you."
"Why?"
"I didn't think you and Sean cared for each other."
"Why. Who said that? I have nothing against the guy. I don't even know him, He probably doesn't like me because I asked you out the first week I was hired and then I heard he was into you."
"Well he's not my type."
"Why he is a nice guy." I say smiling.
She hits me in the arm.
"So Gina I heard you and your man broke up."
"My man? You're funny. Yes we did a couple of days ago, it just got to the point neither of us were happy. So, wait didn't you have your film contest last night. How'd it go?"

"It was good I came in first place."

"Really! That's awesome I would love to see it."

"Any time Gina, listen Bud and I are going to take off.."

"You guys just got here,"

"Yeah. This ain't my scene. I just came here to see if you're here and say hi."

"Hi."

"So Gina can I call you this week and take you out somewhere."

"Somewhere?"

"Yeah, anywhere just as long as we can hang out together I don't care what we do."

She smiles.

"I'm taking off I will see you at work on Monday. Have fun at this party." I say sarcasticly.

She kisses me on the cheek and I notice people were watching me. I smile and wave and say "goodbye" then I grab a beer and leave with Bud. We make our way back downtown stopping at a few bars along the way. We come across the Lakeside lounge and go in. I order a couple of beers for Bud and myself. Then a couple more and then a few shots of warm house tequila. The pain melts away.

These two fat chics sit next to us at the bar. Bud and I know what each other are thinking and smile at each other.. One chic is about 6'1 230 pounds of packed fat. The other chic was a slob. Just sloppy. I order two more shots of the piss warm tequila. And when I throw them back I can feel the vomit rise in my throat. I don't make a pretty face.

"Are you alright?" The big fat chic says.

"He's fine he does this all the time." Bud chimes in.

We do the usual meet and greet and I see the bartender raise her eyebrows at me in a what are you doing Asshole kinda way?

"I'm leaving I got to go." I just came to my senses.

"Bud meet me outside I gotta get some air." I get off the stool and walk outside.

I end up walking to Bud's truck a couple of blocks away and lay down on the bench next to it. After a few moments of clarity, I hear Buds voice coming down the block. I look up and see this bastard running.

"Why did you leave me in there I thought I was going to get eaten. You alright?"

It's now Sunday and the best day to get fucked up. After a few hours of sleep I pick up Bud and we go to the Westport Country club. We drink vodka and meet up with some of our friends. I see some work people there and avoid them. I drink and mingle and Bud comes up to me with two nannies from New Zealand. They're not bad. Not bad at all especially for New Zealand. One of the chics has a snaggle tooth but I like it.

We chat and drink. I drink more. Bud suggests that we go back to his place and go swimming. They agree. They follow us in their own car and when we get there they immediately jump in the pool naked. I am fucked up. **Bud takes his chic inside and I start making out with snaggletooth in the water. I am so tired. I fuck her on the pool chair. Pass out. Wake up at sunrise** naked in the same spot as last night and no chic. I put on the same clothes I have been wearing since Friday and go to work.

Assault with a Mango

Later that day I run into Gina in the commissary.

"Hey you," She says smiling.

"Hi Gina." I reply as I'm getting a coffee.

"How was the rest of your weekend?" She says.

"Mello. Just chilled out after I saw you on Saturday."

"Let me show you something," I pull out a folded piece of paper." I got Barbra Streisand's phone number along with the president of NBC"

"Where did you get this?"

"I was driving Steward's car and she had a list of numbers next to her car phone so I jotted down a few."

"What are you going to do with them?"

"Maybe I'll get drunk and call her."

Gina laughs

"What are you doing for the 4th of July?" she asks.

"It's this Sunday isn't it? I don't know, hopefully hanging out with you."

"I don't have any plans, just maybe go to my sister's house on Sunday for a picnic," she goes.

"Do you want to come with me to see my Lance's band in New York on Thursday night?'

"Don't you have to work Friday?"

"Yes. These guys go on at nine. Finish by eleven and I could have you home by midnight."

"I don't know Mr. Klein. Should I trust you?"

"Have you ever seen me miss a day? No. Have I ever been late? No. I play by the book. You have nothing to worry about." I say.

"I'll think about it." she says as she walks out.

I'm in.

I meet Bud at his sisters apartment on east 33rd St . I am with Gina and her friend Nancy. Bud is making vodka drinks the girls decline and I accept. It's about 103 degrees in this apartment and I can't stop sweating. My hair is always damp looking. Bud makes me another drink and when I sip it my eyes almost roll to the back of my head.

I suddenly got a boost of confidence and ask Gina to come see me in the kitchen. When she walks in from around the corner I grab her in close to me and start kissing her neck. She doesn't pull away, she drapes her arms around my shoulders and starts giggling.

"I'm happy you decided to go out with me," I say, and I'm sincere.

"Would you call this our first date?" She says laughing.

"You can call it whatever you like, I'm just saying I'm happy,"

"Do you want to go out with me tomorrow night, we will just go for dinner or something?"

"Let's get thru tonight first and I'll think about it." She says.

I need to stop drinking and act cool, the more she sees me drink the less she is going to want to hang out with me. I walk in the bathroom to take a piss and I hear Gina calling me. "Wolfgang, we'll be outside Bud said to lock the door behind you,"

I take this opportunity to scan the medicine cabinet (as per usual) and I find nothing. I walk into the bedroom and start opening drawers. Nothing. Oh well. I grab a beer and shut the door behind me.

The bar is packed and I see a few of my co-workers up by the stage and I stay away.

"Do you want anything from the bar?" I say to Nancy and Gina.

"Diet coke and a water"

I meet Bud at the bar and he already has two shots of tequila waiting for me.

"I don't want that. I gotta act on my best behavior I got to impress Gina."

"Let me tell you something, Buddy." Bud says as he leans into me.

"You're already fucked up. You're slurring your words. Gina knows you're an animal now just do the shot."

He hands me the glass.

I catch myself staring at the band but not really looking. I'm in a trance.

I'm inside my own head.

I don't speak to anyone I just stare off into the distance. I have no intentions on speaking to anyone.

I don't even hear the music after a while.

I escape my body.

I'm not really here.

"Are you coming with us" I hear over and over,

"Are you talking to me?"

"Yes we are going to the diner before we jump on the train. Why don't you come with us?" Gina says.

I look around and I see Bud at the bar with a couple of ladies.

"I'm not that hungry I'm gonna grab Bud and we will meet you guys on the train."

Gina leans into me and kisses me on the cheek.

I'm in shock and take a step back.

It becomes awkward and I just walk away.

I can see Bud is liquored up and chatting with a couple Goth chics. I walk over and order a vodka soda.

"If you're going to ask me if I'm going to leave the answer is no. All I need to worry about is getting back to Westport for nine in the morning are you with me or not?" Bud says.

I raise my glass and we smash them together and they break. The chics were not impressed neither was the bartender.

"What? It's not my fault you guys have shitty glassware." Bud says to the bartender.

Ten seconds later we were asked nicely to leave by two big brothers.

We walk outside hoping no one from work saw and then the Goth chicks follow right behind us.

"Where are you guys going? " Bud says.

"Save the Robots"

"We are coming with you." Bud says and hails a cab.

Once in the cab the girls break out a vile of blow or that's what I thought it was. It was passed around and I'm starting to remember this feeling before. I was on Special K.

My vision is always the first to go, I get blurred instantly depending what type of drug I take. Special K is one of them. We all sit at a booth. I can't talk, I'm so fucked up I order drink after drink trying to kill this feeling. I should have left with Gina.

The next train is at 5:07, we have an hour to kill. The lights in the bar are turned on and I finally feel comfortable with all these toxins in my body.

"What do you mean 'we're going'?" I say.

"You have to be in work in two hours. You better make that train."

We walk outside and I'm walking behind Bud with the Goth chic to my left. Bud has a girl on both sides of him. I can barely walk and lose my balance on the 8 inch curb and fall into the front end of a 25 year old Lincoln continental.

I cut myself on the top of my right eye.

I get up and walk down the street holding my eye. Bud and the girls are around me. Half way down Avenue B. This wiry Puerto Rican guy gets in my face.

"Ey man you just broke my tail light."

I turn around to look at his car. I don't see any red plastic glass on the ground.

"Man I tripped and hit the corner end of your fender in the front."

"No man I was sleeping in the car and I saw you kick the tail light…"

"Get out of my face."

"Pay me or I'm calling the cops.."

"Fuck you. Where's the broken glass then asshole?"

This guy is two inches from my face. We stop in front of a bodega with a fruit stand. This guy is still yelling in my face, so I pick up a Mango and threaten him with it.

The little Puerto Rican walks away back to his shitty car.

"You gonna let that guy get away with that?" Bud says to me.

I take the Mango and I throw it perfectly. It smashes dead center of the guys back windshield. He throws the car in reverse and chases me down the avenue. At the corner of Tompkins Square Park he jumps out and it becomes a foot chase. I see a van of cops at the entrance. I run right past them and they don't even look. I run all the way thru the park with this guy ten yards behind me. I jog another two blocks before we both stop to take a breather.

"Fuck you" I say huffing and puffing.

"Fuck *you*." He says back as his hands are on his knees and he is trying to catch his breath.

I take off running again and he follows.

I have a big enough lead on him I jump into a cab and take off.

Three blocks later.

Three NYPD cars cut the cab off and drag me out of it.

I get driven back to the scene.

I see Bud and the girls talking to one cop.

They let me out of the back seat. Bud walks over to me.

"Dude I was just pointing out to the cop that there is no broken glass anywhere. I told them that this guy was trying to scam you. I think they might let you go."

The cop comes over laughing. "The guy in the bodega wants to press charges".

"For what?"

"You stole the mango."

"Come on officer I'll pay for it."

"And then you assaulted this gentleman with it."

"Are you kidding me? Look. I'm bleeding I tripped and fell and hit my head on the corner bumper and then he tried to get money out me, Sir. So I threw the Mango at him."

Bud looks at me and shakes his head.

"You're going to be charged with larceny in the 6th degree and assault with a mango."

They put the handcuffs on me and put me back into the police car. I have to be at work in one hour.

They drive me to the 23rd precinct and put me in a cell and handcuffs me to the wall. I fall asleep for 20 minutes.

I am woken up by prostitutes filing in from the evening. They remove me from the cell and handcuff me to a desk right in front of it. The sun is shining thru the windows and I think I'm going to be released soon. One of the prostitutes is spreading her legs while sitting on the bench across from me. I catch a glimpse and she isn't wearing any underwear. We make eye contact and I smile.

These two Latin women come into the room. They are cops and they are thick and they are hot.

"You need to give us your belt and shoe laces."

"Will I get the belt back, I just bought it and look I don't have shoe laces." I raise up my boot. "Wait. Why are you taking my shit? Aren't I getting out?"

The two cops look at each other. The sun is in my eyes.

"You're going to central booking downtown."

"What's this then?"

"Holding."

"Miss, are you sure there is nothing I can do to not go downtown?"

"Hopefully you'll get out before noon. They are going to process you and then release you."

"What time is it?

" 6:30"

"I have to be a work in a half an hour, Fuck,"

"Do you need to make a phone call because now is your chance."

I think about it is and there is no one I want to call. No thanks."

"What time do you guys get off?" I'm trying to make small talk.

"As soon as we drop you off, our shift is over."

"Do you guys want to get breakfast first? My treat."

They laugh.

"Come on Wolfgang. Time to drop you off."

They put me back in the cop car and drive thru the city. It's a beautiful morning.

When we get to Central Booking I no longer feel safe. I am put in one holding cell before anyone asks my name. The two cops come up to me and say.

"O.K. Wolfgang wait for them to call your name and the process shouldn't take that long, it doesn't look that busy. Also remember no one in here is your friend. So keep to yourself."

She shakes my hand thru the bars. I turn around and see four thugs creeping about. I sit in the corner with my arms crossed. I'm nodding in and out.

"Klein. Klein."

"Right here." I stand up and walk over to the door.
"Come this way."
I follow.
"Am I getting processed?"
"No."

I walk down the corridor and notice that holding cell after holding cell after holding cell filled with animals. They bring me down a few set of stairs and its freezing. We get to another corridor and again holding cell after holding cell. Packed. No windows. They open a door to a room with about 70 men inside. I walk in and scan the place. I am in hell.

I am the only white guy. Every seat on the bench is filled, the toilet has shit in it and the water fountain has a dribble of water coming out. I see motherfuckers literally putting their mouth on the thing try to suck a sip of water out of it.
Fuck this.

I find a spot on the filthy concrete floor and lie down. When I lean back a bunch of change falls out of my pocket and four brothers tried to jump on it like a seagull on a fench fry. I grabbed the change real quick and realized I don't need it. I have no one to call. So I throw in in the corner and lay back down. I am dehydrated and I haven't pissed in 9 hours. In the middle of the cell, carved in the floor is a circle. 10 feet in diameter and inside the circle it reads FUCK GIULIANI. I am lying next to the fuck part. I have my arms inside my shirt and shivering. I try to sleep.

But no chance. Every second I think someone is going to kick me in the head. If I move from my spot someone will take it and its standing room only.

At this point. I listen to story after story. After 12 hours in that shit hole they call my name and then move me to another cell. Again packed. What the fuck is going on when the fuck am I getting out of here, I walk into this shithole and this black crackhead says, "Welcome to the tombs. You're four stories underground on an island and no one can hear you."

I don't say anything and walk past him to this white dude in a suit. I have no idea what time it is and I'm starving.

"How long have you been here?" I say to the guy in the suit.

He looks at his watch and says, "26 hours and I haven't been processed yet."

"Fuck I think I got arrested at 4:30 Friday morning what time do you think it is?"

"It's 7 o'clock Friday night."

"Fuck. What's taking so long?"

"Systems down." He says.

"What?"

"It's been down since I got here why do you think no one has been processed? It's fuckin' Friday night and 4th of July week end. They are just going to keep stuffing this place all weekend and sort it out next week,"

"Why are you in a suit?"

"I was walking to my girlfriend's apartment on Thursday night. I just got out of work and I was going to take her to dinner. I cut thru Washington Square park and this fucking black dude keeps yelling at me, "Kind bud, kind bud". I make eye contact with him and began to follow me. I tell him I'm not interested and he pulls out dime bags and tells me to smell it's soon as he pulled it out I can smell it from ten feet away. It was good looking bud. I say "Fine just give me one. I'm sort of in a hurry."

"Yeah."

"Yeah. The motherfucker was an undercover cop. I wasn't even looking for pot and the guy entrapped me. Giuliani and his fucking drug task force are trying to clean up the city for the weekend. He's a piece of shit and my girlfriend has no idea where I am."

"Shit."

"That's nothing. You better hope they get this shit fixed because by Monday morning they empty the tombs and if you're still here you're going to Rikers. And Rikers, end of game, you won't come out." He says this with such authority you can tell it's been on his mind.

I still haven't pissed. I keep my mouth shut and listen to all the bullshit these criminals have to say.

Hours go by and the lights are still on and no one's name has been called. This Hispanic drug addict is telling me the last time he went to Rikers he wasn't let out for three years. He tells me, "Man they see you walk in there and they know you're a fish, and by the way you look man, someone will want to make you their bitch. And you're gonna have to fight for your life and that's when they slap extra charges on you."

"Not me guy. I'm not going to fucking Rikers."

"Give it time my friend."

"I ain't your friend," I am getting agitated. This guy is trying to get me going. I don't know how exactly. He's intelligent and smoky.

I walk to the other end of the cell and lay down. I am so thirsty. The door opens up and they pass out one slice of ham on white bread in a plastic bag. I use this for a pillow. Then they pass out a little cup of UN sweetened ice tea. I drink it in one gulp.

My insides are drying out.

I don't know if I've slept or not. My hands are filthy, my clothes are filthy. I can feel my stomach contorting.

I am getting more irritable each hour. I will bite someone in their throat if they fuck with me. My adrenaline is constantly pumping. I have no worries in the outside world. I could give a fuck about work, girlfriend, money, family, cars, and pussy. Nothing matters to me anymore and it is sort of a freeing feeling.

I stare at the florescent light from the ground. I wait and close my eyes but keep my ears open. I send out vibes and positive pictures of me getting released. I picture myself leaving this building out the front door. I keep this picture flowing thru my mind. I feel confident I will be released. I pushed away all the negativity. I feel safe. I stay inside my own head for a long period of time and transcend myself to Prague again.

I hear my name called.

I wasn't sure.

"Klein. Klein!"

"Yo, right here." I get up and walk out.

"Am I being released?"

The C.O's laugh

"Boy, you're going to get finger printed and your photo taken. Then put back in until the prosecutor calls for you and if she don't, you're going to Rikers."

"How long before that?"

"We'll, see, the system just got up and running. You could be out of here by tomorrow. If not they clear the place Sunday night and you'll be going to the island."
"No I won't, I'm getting out of here." I say with certainty.

Shit is not a joke anymore. I am afraid.

After they book me they put me into another cell with about 60 men. Enough already. It's freezing and this group of fellas don't look so mello. One dude is constantly screaming "Man Child" thru the bars down the hallway.

Man-child Man-child.

Then a bunch of brothers start screaming and threatening this guy. The guy keeps it up. Man-child Man-child. One brother walks up to him and grabs him by the back of his neck and slammed his face so hard into the bars it knocked the guy out. I thought that was pretty cool since I've never seen that shit before.
I need water.
Everyone is curled up in a ball trying to keep warm. The light is still on and I have no idea what time it is. I reflect on my Karma to see if this is some sort of payback for some shit I did in the past. I rack my brain and just settle on the fact that I deserve this one way or another. But besides...
The fact I'm in fucking jail, nothing really matters now.
Jail sucks and I can't imagine going to Rikers. I don't even want to think about it or put that thought in my mind. The filth and grime of this place is getting to me. I'm wondering what disease I caught from lying on the floor of New York City's jail.
I hope Bud straightens things out with Gina and worked it out and called my folks. What if I don't get the fuck out of here? I'm starting to sweat and go thru alcohol widthdrawls. I would pray to god but then that would make me a hypocrite.
I'm lying still as a board on the concrete with my arms inside my shirt and down my pants. I don't know if I'm going in and out of a dream state. I'm semi awake.
"MichaelWolfgang Klein," I hear someone say but not sure, don't know if I'm dreaming.
I get a slight kick and hear my name again "Michael Wolfgang Klein".
I get up and pull my arms thru the sleeves.

"Yes."

     The door opens and I get put in cuffs. They walk me down the corridor to a courtroom and tell me to wait next to the Prosecutor's office. It's not so cold in here. They call my name and I walk into the office, the woman prosecutor tells me to have a seat.

"Hi"

"Mr. Klein I'm Nancy Pellegrino I work for the D.A office. It says here you're charged with assault with a mango? Assault with a mango? I don't even want to know and larceny in the sixth degree because I'm sure you stole the mango."

"Miss Pellegrino it was a foolish mistake, and I regret it but I'm going to lose my job if I can't get to work Monday."

"What do you do Mr. Klein?"

"I just got a job working for Margaret Steward. I'm her personal assistant and if I'm not there Monday morning to pick her up, I'm done."

"You mean Tuesday. Monday is the holiday celebrated."

"Huh?"

"O.K. Mr. Klein I don't think you're going to skip court so I am recommending you to be released on a promise to appear. That will give you plenty of time to get a lawyer and get these charges taken care of. Now go into the courtroom and wait for your name to be called. Take this." She hands me a business card with the name of a New York Attorney. "Oh. Mr. Klein you are the last one on the docket for this evening, you just made it." She smiles.

     Night court ended and I was released 12:45 Monday morning. I can't make the train station on time so I get a room at The Hotel Pennsylvania. I buy a bag of peaches and plums and a pack of smokes. I shower and fall right to sleep.

     It's 9am Monday morning and I'm on the next train to Fairfield. I call Bud from the train station and ask him to pick me up. He hangs up the phone before I tell him where I'm at. I sit and wait and I see him pull in.

"Did you get raped?" was the first question he asks.

"No, asshole... If I was to stay any longer they were going to ship my ass to Rikers and there for sure I would've been raped. I can't believe it's Monday."

"I told them at work you got an emergency call in the middle of the night that your uncle died in Rhode Island and you drove your family up there."

"Great."

"They were all sympathetic. I don't think you have anything to worry about."

"What about Gina?"

"I told her you were locked up."

"Really? Asshole. I'm trying to date her."

"Don't worry, I told her you got arrested for fighting. I said we saw some guy slap his girlfriend in the bar and then you walk up to him to see what was going on and he cracked you with a bottle. I added that because you have the scar from the bumper. I told her after you got up you man handled the guy and at that point the cops walked in and arrested everyone involved."

"You said what?"

"Dude, don't worry, she thinks you're a hero. I told you I would straighten things out."

"Take me home."

At work I get sympathy cards and my boss is off my ass for a few days. I end up paying the New York attorney 1500 Dollars and he gets it dismissed in one court appearance.

Gina and I are now dating for a few weeks. She lives with her divorced sister and little kids I sleep there during most of the week and on the weekends I usually disappear to work on a project.

Bud and I are working with a couple of fellow employees on an independent documentary. One of the guys we worked with is B.J Cole he is a young associate producer for Steward. His stepfather is a Correctional Officer at a prison in upstate Massachusetts. He had gotten us permission from the warden to film there. We told them we're from Such and Such T.V and they let us interview everyone in there, from the guards to the gangs to the guys in solitary confinement.

We go up every weekend and film for 3 months. Bud and I had the camera and we funded it. Donald was the cameraman. BJ had the idea and got us into the prison. He was a shit producer and we fought with him for creative control and we argued every weekend. Bud and I had too much time and money invested with this DICK not to see it through. So we gave in and let him pretend he knew what he was doing.

It was funny I would be spending my weekends in a prison filming and they had no idea the truck I came up in always had at least a half ounce of bud and some sort of collection of pills. By the third month of filming I was burnt out with these people. So was Bud. I couldn't take B.J and told him to call me when he was ready to edit the piece together. We had way too many hours of interviews and this dick didn't know when to stop. Bud said the same thing. "Call us when you are ready to edit."

I go back to the usual grind. Work is still interesting, the women still hot. My girlfriend is cool. I am a bit tamer but not content. I want more. I want to be a producer.

We enter the movie *Jimmy's Story* in the Brooklyn Film Festival and it's premiering the week after Thanksgiving.

My asshole boss was busting my balls about leaving early that Friday. There was no real work to be done. They weren't shooting that day and Margaret was in Los Angeles anyway. He was being a cocksucker. I let it go and didn't ask him again.

Bud was packing up his things at his desk and Gina walks over. "Hey, guys are you getting ready to take off? I should be done in 15 minutes." "Cool, Jessica should be here by then and are we all jumping in one car," Bud says.

"I didn't get released yet, and I don't know when I will be. That chinky fuck is getting on my nerves."

"Wolfgang."

"I'm sorry baby, but this asshole is keeping me here out of spite. Everyone leaves early on Fridays when we're not shooting. He knows I'm sweating him. He wants me to beg."

"You two fucking guys have a fucked up working relationship, go tell that dick you're leaving." Bud says.

"You don't think I want to? That asshole wants any excuse to fire me. Jessica's here, you guys go without me and I will meet up with you there." Pang walks in.

"Wolfgang come here, I got a job for you I just got a phone call that an employee here has gotten a flat tire on her way home and she thinks she ran over a nail in the parking lot. I need you to go outside and scan every inch of the parking lot for that nail."

I see the look on Gina's face and all I can do is smile. She is in shock. Pang it's almost dark outside…""Here." He pulls out a flashlight that he had tucked in the back of pants. I grab it. I give Gina a kiss on the cheek and tell Bud I will see him there.

As they pull off they can see me walking up and down the parking lot with the flashlight waving back and forth. They beep.
It's cold out.

This stupid fuck is going to pay for this; all he is doing is giving me time to plot my revenge. It takes me thirty minutes and I return to the building. I walk into the commissary and I see Pang.

"I checked the whole parking lot. Didn't find one nail."
Pang is putting on his coat and scarf, his thermos is sitting on the counter.
"Alright Wolfgang. The week is over you can leave, just give me a second I got to hit the head and I will be right back then I will put on the alarm." He walks out of the commissary.

I don't think for a second I act on instinct. I grab the thermos and twist off the cap I pour out half of it and pull my cock out and piss to the top. I put the cap back on and shake it up and then I walk by the exit doors.

"It's about time Pang what were you doing taking a shit?"

I see him grab his thermos and hit the alarm. We walk outside.

"Shit it's raining. It's going to be a shit show driving into Brooklyn." Pang says

"Yeah, if you're driving into Brooklyn."

"Aren't you going to your film festival?"

"No. I was never planning on going, the big party is tomorrow." I lie.

The look on his face was priceless. I smile.

I am getting into my car and I see Pang take a drink from his thermos while he is letting his truck warm up. Then he takes another sip. Stupid motherfucker.

I don't bother going to Brooklyn. I go home and go to bed.

I find out from Gina the next morning that the film won best feature. The only thing I can think of is they didn't get that many applicants because the acting in our movie sucked. Wow we won. I call Bud and he tells me the same thing.

"I don't know how we won." He says with disbelief.

"Maybe it was the whole package. It was a good production. Good editing and score. The story was alright just the lead actor sucked balls. So maybe they over looked it." I say.

"Whatever the case. Now you're recognized as a producer on a feature independent film. That won an award. You could put that on top of your resume."

"Great. Can you sell it?"

"I don't know. I'll wait and see if any one calls I guess."

"Should we go out and celebrate? "It's ten in the morning…. Yeah pick me up." I hang up the phone and jump in the shower.

Dirty Rotten Scoundrels

Its Christmas break and we are snowboarding at Buds Ski condo in Vermont. We left our girlfriends at home and told them we would be back for New Year's Eve. After a long day on the slopes we would hit the bar. Bud orders two beers and tells me he's got the next idea for a movie.

"See that dude over there?" Buds says as he points to the bar.

"Which dude the one with the shitty haircut?"

"Yup take a good look. It's called a mullet.

"That's what it was. While we were filming in the prison I couldn't figure out why all these white mother fuckers had the same hair style. Fuckin Billy Ray Cyrus. They picked up that look in the eighties and stayed with it. Rednecks."

"Mullet that's what it's called. A mother fucking Mullet. It was cool back when it came out. I guess. But why are these clowns wearing this style 15 years later? These are questions people want to know. I want to know what is going thru your head when you ask for a haircut. Hey. You brought the camera right? Let's interview that guy up in the condo. Let's tell him we are doing a hairstyle segment for mtv."

"If you can convince that guy to talk on camera I will buy all the drinks for the weekend."

I walk up to the bar and order three shots of tequila. I give one to Bud and pass the other one to the Mullet guy.

"Here you want this shot Tequila?"

The guy looks at me and smiles yeah I'll take that. You don't want it."

"Nah. I thought my buddy said he wanted two. Take it. Cheers"

We throw them back.

"Where you guys from?" He says.

"New York." I lie.

"New York? What are you guys skiing for the weekend?"

"No, well a little. Where you from?"

"Vermont, here."

He extends his hand and says his name Jerry.

"What's up Jerry? I'm Wolfgang and that's Bud. Another shot?"

Sure. You buyin?"

"Yeah, well Bud is. You work around here."

"About a mile down I work at the produce market."

"What do you guys do?"

"You ever hear of MTV?

"Duh."

"Yeah I know. Well we work as segment producers for a new show called States and Styles. That's why we're really up here. We supposed to be working but we are actually snowboarding a bit much. Maybe you could help us out. We just need to get interviews with people from different states and talk about their personal style. You would actually be perfect."

"3 more." Bud says to the bartender,

"Yeah Jerry I'll give you twenty bucks for 20 minutes if you come with us to the condo they rented so we can do an interview with you and possibly put you on T.V."

"Are you guys shittin me or what?"

"$50 bucks and we have a stocked bar. Come on Jerry. I'm just going to ask you what inspires your style. You know what I'm talkin about. Just look at your hair. That tells me you take good care of yourself and you like to look good. I'm just gonna ask you questions like that. You can handle it. Plus if you do make it on the program, think about all the women around here that are going to want you."

We get the interview. This guy has no clue. Everything that comes out of his mouth is wrong for him and right for us. He is the definition of a Mullet. He told me he was offered a job for ten bucks hour roofing. But he had to cut his hair. He told the guy to "Screw off I aint cuttin' my hair for nobody."

This is when Bud and I knew we were on to something.

We made a plan to do a short documentary on the Mullet hairstyle.

We spend our weekends going to places we think Mullets would hang out at, this includes every white trash bar, bowling alleys, trailer parks, Wal-Mart and wrestling events.

Gina was supportive of me, just pissed all the time. I was never around. We would see each other for an hour at night before we fell asleep and at work. The weekends I am always gone, she did not like this.

Its spring time and I have been working for MS Studio for over a year now. No promotion, no raise. I hate my bosses. I have no respect for them. How could I. After spending a year with these two assholes I saw them for who they really are. Self-absorbed, lying back stabbing trolls. I saw Jill Sherwood purposely leave her husband at the MS Christmas party. He was too fat for her to be seen with. It would ruin her image. Her ego had run wild. The way I know this is because I rode up on the train with them, she didn't even introduce her husband… to anyone. I made friends with him on the train. He was a cool guy just overweight for his wife's image. She took a different cab then him to the party and walked in with a bunch of other coworkers. Never waiting for her husband. I hung with him throughout the night when I wasn't making pit stops to the bathroom to fill my nose. He told me that his wife was embarrassed by his weight. And that he had just recently gained it in the last year due to a thyroid problem. That cunt. The guy didn't look bad at all.

And Fuck Pang that guy blatantly stole from the company. Every time he went to Home Depot he was buying shit for himself on the studio's account. How do I know? Because I saw it every week with this guy, Shit, we even helped him load his truck up with brand new tools. He told us he was bringing them to MS house. At first I used to believe him, then I realized that's my job. I'm errand boy. I run shit back and forth to MS's house all the time except when Pang has to drop off tools, Funny. At MS property she has no tools, she doesn't need them. She isn't a carpenter. Anything she wants done she makes a phone call. Pang was stealing.

The only thing keeping me sane is making this documentary. I think we are on to something; everyone seems interested in it when we talk about it. Jimmy story is sitting on a shelf somewhere. Bud told me "No one has called about it so fuck it. I'm not putting any more money in to it". (It needed some minor color correcting and sound issues which could be fixed for a couple thousand dollars.) Besides The Mullet movie is ours, we don't need to rely on shitty actors, or dickhead producers. We are making it the way we want." "I just want to hurry up and finish it so I can enter it into film festivals before the fall dead line."

We drive from Vermont to New Jersey to New Orleans filming Mullets. I have Fake press passes that say HBO. MTV. ABC. We wear these when we want to approach people and then give them the bullshit line on the Styles and States series. It worked every time. I'm either a good bullshitter or an excellent producer, it depends who you ask.

I am feeling the effects of burning the candle at both ends. All I do is work 60 plus hours a week at the studio, any spare time is spent making the Mullet doc. My girlfriend hates me and I am always broke. I am again bored with everything and my job is starting to make me sour. BJ has the footage from the prison doc and won't let Bud or I cut it or sell it as raw footage. The novelty of working in television is wearing off. Celebrities don't impress me anymore. I hate the egos in this industry. I am getting bored with Gina. She's cool and everything but she's looking for someone to marry. And I ain't that guy.

I feel stagnant, everyday becomes a fucking hassle. My chemical balance is shifting.

My head needs a rest. Little by little I become more sullen. I realize I'm not happy because I'm a fucking errand boy. I am an assistant and that sucks at my age.

I need to sell a movie. I need cash. I need to kill my boss. I feel like I am being taken advantage of.

I find out that I have been getting fucked. All the extra hours, overtime I work, I was never paid for. At first I had no idea, then one day while on location and we are already wrapped and now I'm loading up the production truck. I'm hustling because I know the quicker I can get this done I can go home. My friend Bill the cameraman tells me to slow down we are getting a meal penalty. Oh what's a meal penalty? I have no idea.

"Wolfgang. You work production right? Well we go by union rules even thou we are not union. Yes we are all in over time now plus a meal penalty because we have to get a meal break at least every five hours. You should know this. How long have you been working in television? Man, there are rules they have to obey by. Didn't you sign a piece paper? A contract with your day rate?

"Yeah it was $150 a day, a ten hour day."

"And how many hours do you work a day."

"12 to 14 sometimes 18."

"And you never spoke up about?"

"Bill I didn't know, you're the first person telling me this stuff. Pang and Jill treat me like I'm not grateful, like I owe them something. They let it be known I could be fired any day and it's been that way since I got hired."

"Wow man you're getting fucked. It's like this, you work for Pangs department, and Pang gets a budget every quarter. If he comes under that budget that's his incentive towards his bonus at the end of the year. He screwed you out of overtime and it basically goes into his pocket."

"What?"

"Wolfgang, when we go back to the studio go into accounting and ask to see your time cards then add up all your overtime and present it to Pang. What can he do then? He's got to pay you?"

"Bill are you sure? Am I going to look like an asshole?"

"Wolfgang, ask anyone. I wouldn't fuck with you about something like that kid."

The next day I get to work early and walk into the accounting department. I see Lori there and I ask her if I could see all my time cards from the past year. She doesn't think twice and retrieves them from the file cabinet.

187

I look over each one and I'm speechless. There is white out over my hours and written in pen are eight hour days. Someone changed my time sheet from the first day. Every week someone whited out all of my hours and put in a total of eight hours a day. So I had 40 hour weeks and never broke overtime. It was right in front of my face there was no ignoring it. I felt bad because I didn't know how I was going to react. How can I approach these people when I can't even look at them. How can I be so stupid?

I don't say anything to anyone for a while.

I let it stew. I let it boil. A couple of weeks go by and I'm on another location shoot. I end up working 17 ½ hours on this one particular day. When it's time to fill out my time card I ask Al the line producer if I can get a double day. He tells me no. I say "But Al I practically worked eighteen hours. Everyone else is getting over time except me.

He takes his eyes off his desk and looks at me. "Eighteen hours is a double day, but you didn't work eighteen, you worked 171/2."

"Come on Al you can't throw me a bone. I have bent over backwards for this company and never asked for a thing. Never got a raise. Never got promoted..

"Sorry Man there's nothing I can do about it." He says as he shrugs his shoulders.

"Really nothing you can do about it? It's not your money I don't think $150 dollars is going to break the fucking budget. You're the line producer I work in your department on shoot days and I get paid the same as being a P.A on non- shoot days for the studio and Pangs department. How's is that?" Everyone else makes overtime in production except me and I bust my balls for you people for over a year now and got nothing. Not even a thank you. You and I know damn well if I didn't do my job around here I would have been gone the first fucking week.."

"Shut the door." He says.

I don't.

"Fuck you Al you sorry bastard, you're a dick. You're a pissed off divorced middle aged overweight balding shit breath asshole. Are you purposely being dick to me because I fuck your little secret crush Gina or is it because I get blow jobs in the storage room from every receptionist that worked here."

"You better calm down Wolfgang. Go outside and smoke a cigarette."

Pang comes around the corner and is standing back from the open office door listening with about 18 other staff members.

"Al Fuck you. Fuck Pang And Fuck Jill. I should tell MS how you people are conniving sleaze bags. We all know Al you skip out on work early Tuesdays and Fridays for guitar lessons when you told MS you have physical therapy from a previous accident. You're a bullshitter. There is no reason you guys couldn't pay me overtime. It was your fucking greed. I'm not stupid asshole I know how the system works."

I pull out my time cards.

"Why are all my time cards whited out and replaced with different hours? "Who gave you those?" "I grabbed them myself. I know where everything is in this studio asshole. I also know you watch porn from your desk. You're too stupid to notice the thing casts a reflection on the picture behind you."

Al stands up and walks out from behind his desk and towards me. I walk backwards out of the office.

And he shuts the fucking door in my face and locks it. I am looking at the people looking at me. I am about to lose control. I take a deep breath. I calmly knock on the window next to his door and lean into and say. "Hey Al I have your number." I then walked out of the studio without saying goodbye to anyone and never returned.

I smash the benzo 3 days later at a high rate of speed in the rain on the highway. No collision insurance. I walk away fine but the car is totaled. A week later I go to a car auction with a car dealer friend of mine I give him a grand and he puts me in a 4 year old 5 series BMW with 200 dollar payments. Gina breaks up with me because she knows we don't have a future together.

I get a phone call from Bud.

"Guess who I just spoke to."

"Your mother? How the fuck do I know."

"Alan Weisberg.?"

"He called up the studio looking for and audio guy and I heard someone mention his name, so I grabbed the call." "Get the fuck out, He's in film and television?"

"He's in L.A working for some reality TV show and he is trying to put together a crew to shoot some b roll for their L.A office here in Connecticut. They want to use the old mental institution in Newtown." "Give me his number."

"Why you don't do Audio. " "I want to see how that fucker is doing. You know Weisberg. Nothing is straight with him. He probably blacked mailed someone. I can picture him being a big Jew producer. The last thing I heard of Weisberg was he split UConn before graduation because he owed so many thugs money. He thought his life was in danger, so he checked himself into rehab to hide out. All bets were off after that. His family moved to Albany and I haven't heard from him since. That was 9, 10 years ago."

Bud writes down the number and shakes his head.

"Alan Fuckin Weissberg."

"I know this voice and I see it's a Connecticut number. Klein. Wolfy Klein. You mother fucker. How you been? I figured it was you since I talked to Bud not too long ago. So what's up I hear you no longer work for MS Studio?"

"Yeah I moved on to better things. So what's up how long have you been in L.A?

"Dude I got hear a month ago I work for a production company that is shooting a new reality series in Belize. It starts in a few weeks, for now I'm helping a buddy at Mtv. You don't do audio do you?

"No. Producer. I was planning on heading out there and trying to sell the Mullet movie Bud and I made. I just needed a contact in L.A and now your it."

"Come out here. I'm in West Hollywood, I have a two bedroom and I was looking for a roommate anyway."

"Tell me how you got into television, I had no idea. I thought you were either in jail or running an accounting firm. Shit it's been 10 years."

"I know. I know. Well, I always wrote scripts and worked on low low budgeted independent movies up in Albany. Nothing great right? For money I drove an Ice cream truck…for ten fucking years. This girl on my route I became friends with and she knew I was into making movies. So every day I see her and we chat. One day she tells me that her older brother is a Hollywood producer, his name is Tommy.

So a few days go by and I tell this girl that I'm going to L.A for a week for a job interview at a production company. I'm lying and of course she is excited and then she says to me I should give you my brother's number. BINGO. So I get it. The next day I book a flight to L.A. I barely have any money but I say fuck it. A few days later I'm sitting in this piece of shit motel. I can't afford a rent-a-car.

So I sit and wait. I make the call to Tommy and tell him I'm good friends with his sister and she told me to give him a call if I was ever in Hollywood. Tommy is a nice guy but tells me he is busy all week. If he gets a chance he will call me for a coffee. I wait all fucking week. I figure this guy wasn't going to call and on the last day he did and told me to meet him at the coffee bean on Sunset. I do.

I bring my scripts. Tommy tells me he is working on a development deal at the moment and that he can't really help me out. He was a real nice guy about it and he told me if something came up he would give me a call. I left L.A and went back to the ice cream truck. Two weeks later Tommy calls me and says how soon can you get out here? I tell him to give me four days. I pack all my shit and come out here .Tommy got a production deal with a network and I became his assistant. After a week he made me segment producer.

Now we are in pre -production and in six weeks we leave to shoot in Belize. A month ago I was an Ice cream truck driver and now I got an agent and a producer title on a prime time network show. Get your ass out here? "Yeah, I was planning on heading out to L.A, I need to try to sell this movie Bud and I made and since your there, and all set up. I'm going to take you up on that."

"I've got a Phat two bed two bath apartment in West Hollywood. The rent is 800 each, it's well worth it. Way worth the money compared to New York. I live on Westbourne Between Melrose and Santa Monica and two blocks from Beverly Hills it's a good gay neighborhood. You should like that."

"Fuck you. What about the job situation? How soon before I could land a job?"

"Just get out here, it will work its self out. I will set you up with my Agent and tweak your resume. Don't worry about it. Take the step." "Alright man Give me fourteen days and I will be there. Call me at the end of the week with your address and Agents name. Cool."

"Cool Bro talk to you then."

All I got is $1600 bucks from painting jobs and two bags of clothes. John Jay and K Russel INVITE themselves along for the ride across country. I don't mind the company but I won't let these animals drive, too dangerous behind a wheel. Speed demons.

I drive straight to New Orleans only stopping to piss and gas up. The animals smoke themselves to sleep or were too pilled out to drive. I did it in 18 hours from Connecticut.

I am tired and realize it's the start of Mardi Gras, every hotel is booked. I am fucked.

We drive around for another hour and half and finally find a bed and breakfast that has a room located in the Garden District. The women tells me that there is a two night minimum at two hundred per. I only need one night. John Jay takes out his wallet and slaps down his credit card and says "we'll take it." K Russel says he will buy the drinks for the night.

Maybe this won't be so bad.

The first thing we encounter is a guy selling Nitrous balloons. "5 for 20." he says. We buy fifteen.

We suck them back before we hit the French Quarter. It's a big fucking Mob scene and it sucks. Real bad White trash. I know K Russel has no patience for Rednecks or anyone else for that matter. I'm wearing my new Kenneth Cole Shoes and pissed that they are getting trashed. We make our way to The Marriot bar. We sneak in without wrist bands and convince the receptionist. with money, for three blue bands. Now the security wont hassle us and we can come and go out here at will.

Scotch and Percocets were the cocktail of choice for all of us. I am wondering about how life will be in L.A. Not really paying any mind to anything. John Jay keeps kicking my leg to get my attention, When I come to I see K Russel entertaining three slutty looking girls. I would put money on it that they are working girls from Vegas and they are working the Marriott. They all have blue bands on. They have a room. Krussel is ordering drinks for everyone.

I can tell by his smirk and demeanor that he is up to no good.

"So Ladies are you enjoying mardi gras? " John Jay asks. 2 of them reply with a smiling yes.

The pills just kicked in and I feel like I'm going to puke.

"You girls have a room here?" I ask.

"Yes were on the 5th floor how 'bout you?" the skinny blonde says.

"I got the penthouse for the whole week." I lie.

"Really??" She says giggling.

She's on something.

"Yes really, what's wrong with you, do you wanna see it?"

"Sure. I guess."

"My name is Wolfgang, What's yours."

This chic starts giggling "Really?"

"Really what?' "That's your name, Wolfgang?"

"Yeah.And yours?"

"Cindy. I never met a Wolfgang before. Did your parents give you that name?"

I don't respond. I grab her hand and walk towards the elevator. The chic is still talking about my name as the doors open. I walk in and press five. She finally realizes that the penthouse is not on five. "Hey this is my floor." "I know I forgot the key downstairs…what room did you say you're in?"

She pulls out the card key "Its' room 524." I grab the card and take a left out of the elevators towards her room. "Wait what are we doing?"

"Cindy I need to use your bathroom."

"Oh .O.k." She takes the card out my hand and slides it into the door.

I walk into her bathroom and piss. When I come out Cindy is wearing a pink boa around her shoulders and posing in front of the mirror. "Whadda ya think?"

"It fits you. Come here."

I tell her as I lay on the bed. She walks over and sits on top of me and we start making out. I never heard the door open. K Russel is standing over me when I open my eyes he scares the shit out of me and Cindy.

"What are you doin here Dick?"

"Anna wanted to show me her room." He says with that devil look. I know he's up to no good because he is always up to no good.

"Hey Anna Nice to meet you" I say.

She rips off her shirt and jumps on the bed. She and Cindy start going at it.

"Holy Shit" I mumble to myself. I see K Russel taking off all his clothes.

"Dude what are you doing?"

He picks up Anna and carries her to the bathroom and locks the door. I peel off Cindy's Jeans and flip her over. "Wait, Wait Condom. Do you have a condom?"

"Um No."

She gets up and goes over to her bag and pulls out a strip of rubbers and throws them at me. I am going limp at this point and could only get the rubber half on. As soon as I slip it in her, the rubber falls off anyway. I don't say anything and keep pumping. I here grunts from the bathroom. I can only imagine what this animal is doing to her. Then I hear " stop. STOP! I said No. Stop!." Cindy pushes me off her to go see if Anna is alright.

"Anna. Anna everything O.K?"

The door comes flying open. "This Asshole doesn't know the meaning of NO. He kept putting it in my ass." Her hair is wet from the shower and her naked body was turning me on.

"I thought No means Yes and Yes means anal." K Russel says smiling.

"O.K guys times up." Cindy says.

"Time. What do you mean time?"

"Come on lets go. Cheryl is waiting for us downstairs."

K Russel is still naked and he is now tossing around Anna on the bed.

"Come on I gotta get dressed. I'm not playin' with you. Knock it off." Anna's tone said everything.

K Russel lets go of her and starts getting dressed.

"Ok Guys that will be $250 each." Cindy says.

"For what?" I say.

Both whores give me the evil eye.

KRussell doesn't say anything and walks toward the door.

"Hey where are you going? Anna yells at K Russel.

He doesn't say a word and opens the door, that's when Anna went bat shit. She grabbed his hair and pulled him back inside the room. "Where do you think you're going?" She says.

"I have to go to my room to get the money. I don't have all the cash on me. What the fuck is wrong with you." K Russel says in a reassuring voice.

"I need to go to the ATM." I say.

The girls shoot me a look. "I will go with you" Cindy says.

"I'm just going to the lobby I will meet you guys back in the bar." I say as I rush to the door. I open it and let it close behind me then I take off running. I take the stairs and when I get to the lobby I see K Russel.

"Your fucking nuts, we need to find John jay and get the fuck out of here."

"What are those girls going to do? They can't call the police. Fuck them. I'm going to the bar and waiting for John Jay"

"Usually working girls have pimps."

"Yeah so."

"What if these girls have a pimp? They definitely came here with someone."

"Who cares, what do you want to drink?"

K Russel is standing at the bar with his back facing the door he doesn't see the whores walk in.

"Are you guys all set?" Cindy says.

"Oh hey, we are waiting for our buddy he has the room key" KRussel says.

"Yeah I forgot that my wallet is in the room too."

Cindy grabs my back pocket "What's this."

"My Wallet, I meant to say I left my bank card in the room."

"I get the feeling you guys are fucking around with us. WE WANT OUR MONEY!"

Now she is making a scene.

KRussel turns around and says in a calm and quiet voice.

"Ladies calm down. I will make it very easy for you guys. You're not getting shit so get the fuck away from me." He smiles. "I'm going to get that cop from the lobby and tell them you're soliciting the guests and then the Marriott is going to boot your ass out. So shut your mouth and get the fuck away from me so I can enjoy my drink."

Amanda takes his drink out of his hand and throws it in his face and walks off. Cindy follows. K Russel laughs and wipes off his shirt.

The lobby cop comes walking up to us, "Everything alright here. Gentlemen?"

"Now it is. Those whores wouldn't leave us alone. I guess they don't understand the word no. That one chic was grabbing at my cock while I caught her friend trying to lift my wallet. I grabbed her hand and that's when the blonde thru the drink on me. Do you think the Marriot know they have thieving prostitutes staying here and preying on their guests?"

The cop pulls out his Billy club and points it in K Russel's chest. "Rip off your wristbands…"

"Officer we are just waiting for our friend…." The baton in one quick motion gets thrusted up in Krussel rib gage. He falls to one knee and that's when I realized this cop ain't fucking around.

"I saw you pieces of shit walk in here. We had our eye on you guys. You think you can pull that shit down here." The cop rips off K Russel band. I rip mine off and throw it on the floor.

"Officer we are leaving right now but do you know what happen to our friend we walk in with?" I ask. The cop doesn't respond and turns his back and walks into the lobby. I see K Russell pop back up and crack his neck; he is smiling ear to ear.

"Betcha anything they paid off the cop, the cops not stupid. This is fucking Mardi Gras and everyone in this town is looking to make a buck."

"Probably." I say as I'm holding the door open, That's when I see the girls running thru the parking lot toward us.

"Let's go." I say.

"Wait, wait I want to see what these whores want now."

K Russel can't let it go.

We walk to the end of the parking lot and one of the whores throws a glass bottle at us. It missed but broke right next to us. "Hey" I hear a man say, so we both turn around. The two whores are standing there with a nineteen year old red head red neck. This dude was wearing a mullet and a ball cap. He was big, 6'2 or 6'3. He looked retarded, "Hey you owe my girls something." he is yelling as he come towards us. I see people stopping around us. This doesn't look good.

Krussel lets this asshole come in an arm's length of him and then he strikes him right in the throat and the dude drops like dead weight. He is unresponsive on the ground. The Whores start screaming and I see the lobby cop at the door on his walkie.

"Let's get the fuck out her."

I grab KRussel and start walking. "Yo the cop is to your left at the door on his walkie." I watch KRussel turn toward the cop and give him the finger. I decide this is a good time to start running.

"What the fuck is wrong with you?"

He laughs then we both see a cop car with lights on pull up at the exit of the parking /Garage lot. I turn left and run thru the maze of parked cars. I get on my stomach and I'm sliding from one car to the next without being noticed. I see from underneath the cars that the lobby cop has one arm on K Russell. Then all I see is the lobby cop on his back and KRussel's legs go sprinting by me.

FUCK ME NOW.

If I get caught they are definitely putting me in jail tonight. I stand up and run to the back wall and just take a leap over it. I drop about eight feet to the alley and run into the crowed French Quarter. I take off my shirt and throw it on the ground. Now I am just wearing a white V-neck t shirt.

I need to get out of here, I need to get away from KRussel.

I make my way back to the Bed and breakfast in the Garden District. I see a light on in the room so I peek in to see John Jay banging the third whore. I tap on the door lightly, I wait and do it again. He opens the door. I pull him out.

"I'm outta here dude your boy KRussel flipped out, he beat up their Redneck pimp and laid out the lobby cop. You can't let this Whore know what happen, as soon as she is in touch with the other whores the cops will be here."

John Jay softly and slowly opens the door. We both see the prostitute on her phone. John jay walks right in grabs the phone out of her hand and throws it to me. I drop it on the floor and smash it with my boots. John jay gets dressed. The whore starts going after jay and she jumps on his back. He flips her on the bed and holds both of her hands down while sitting on her then he grabs the pillow and puts it over her face.

"Grab my bag and K Russels, check the bathroom for anything. Hurry I can't hold this bitch down. Take her top so she can't leave."

I grab the bags and my car keys and just run out towards my car. I throw everything in and now I'm waiting for John Jay. What the fuck.

Hurry.

He comes running out and jumps into the passenger side.

"What the fuck were you doing" I say as I speed away.

"I calmed her down and left her four hundred bucks. I figured she was being a good sport about it."

"I'm dropping you off at the airport unless you want to stay, but I'm getting the hell outa here now. And I need to drive the rest of the way alone, I need my head clear. K Russell is crazy, Fuck him."

"I'm cool with the airport. I need to show up to work anyway before someone notices I'm not there. KRussel should show up at some point, if he is not in jail. I would imagine."

We both look at each other and say nothing.

I get to Houston at 8 in the morning. I pull into a cheap motel off the 10. I sleep till midnight.

I get up and don't check out I can't eat I just drive west. I'm having too much alone time with my thoughts and the positive is battling the negative. I think about Gina. I think about Elizabeth. I think about all the rotten shit I put them through. I think about my family and how I should treat them better. I think about religion and politics which puts me in a horrible mood. I think about how man has been fucking man since the beginning of time. I think about ways of killing myself and overdosing on heroin seems like the best way to go. Or I could put a gun in my mouth too. I think about manipulation and why everyone feels the need to. I think why does man seek control? I think why are people hung up on material things? I think why have I become this way. I think why do I have to fit in? And then it hit's me. Pussy. Man does it all for pussy.

Man needs to impress. Feel important and wanted. Man seeks control because he is weak. Man made money and money is the root of all evil. Man made religion and fucked that thing up. Too many gods too many stories. A lot of contradictions and manipulation in those books that man wrote. Religion is violent and unforgiving. Religion separates man and casts them against each other. Politicians are no better; everything comes down to who you know not what you know. Everything is corrupt.

I start thinking about money and movies and fame and pussy. I am a walking contradiction because of our screwed up society. I smoke so much pot and my mind is racing with thoughts. Time goes by quickly.

Fun, cocaine. Fun Fun.

It's early morning L.A, the smog hasn't burned off yet. I pull into a Denny's and order a coffee. The waitress is a little trashy and looks like a meth user. I call Alan.

"Are you up?"

"Are you here?"

"I'm at Denny's havin' coffee, what's up with all this smog?"

"Welcome to L.A Animal. Don't eat yet. Get here and we'll go to the valley and eat. Theirs this chic I've been checkin'out. I'm going to jump in the shower when you get here ring the buzzer and I will throw down a parking permit so you can park on the street…"

"Wait what's the number?"

"How many times have I told you dude? Didn't you write it down? This the last time. 432 Westbourne. Apartment 4B. Get your ass here.."

I hang up the phone, I leave a five dollar bill on the table and I get up and walk towards the door.

It took me 15 minutes to get settled in I hung up my clothes and tossed my sleeping bag on a futon mattress. The apartment is mint, big windows. Well lit, hard wood floors, 2 full baths 2 bedrooms. Open living room with balcony and bar and huge kitchen. On the roof is a pool. Alan has the place set up. All I need to get is Kitchen Utensils and a real bed. Alan said he doesn't cook so he doesn't need plates.

"All set Animal? Let's go to Studio city. You drive."

"Dude I'm sort of beat why don't you drive?"

"I'll drive your car."

I hand him the keys.

"We need to get your resume out today. You'll take any job right now just to get in. Right?"

"Yeah Guy. I need money. Our pot dealin' days from UConn are long gone. Remember those days?

"I try to forget them." Alan Smirks.

"Pay attention to where I'm going. I'm going to take a huge loop. Up Laurel Canyon thru the valley to Burbank. But first we are stopping at the Coffee bean. I want you see this chic I'm trying to fuck.

My heart is racing. I'm in Hollywood. I made it. My adrenaline kicks in and doesn't slow down all day. Alan takes me from Coffee house to coffee house. I'm a bit star stuck at everyone. The women out here are unbelievably hot. All of them. My head doesn't stop moving. It's a good thing I'm wearing sunglasses otherwise I'd creep people out.

We are at our fourth coffee shop it's 12:30 in the afternoon. I'm jacked up on caffeine.

"Listen Animal, It's easy, if you listen to me and do what I say? O.K?
     First, you're going to take a job as a production Assistant for my friend Leola. Don't worry it's only for a month. She is a Casting Director and her department needs help. It's a pilot on Reunions. Family reunions, Work Reunions. High School Reunions. It's a fucking Reunion show. All she needs you to do is research over the phone. Basically talk to people and get info. Oh Yeah I told her we used to work for the same news network in Albany and you dealt with the guest segments. Don't worry just go with it. Now after the month is up. I will send you to see my Agent Zowie. On your resume you will have this Pilot listed and you're going to put down that you were a Casting Associate. If Zowie calls Leola, Leola will vouch for you. That's how shit works out here. It's all who you know."

"Are you serious? Are you sure?"

"Animal, I told you I would hook you up, I know you can do it, just start playing the game. These people don't know us, they don't know where were from. They don't know what we're cable of. Bunch of pussies out here. I will be in there a few times a week when I have time. Don't worry about a fuckin' thing. You're an Animal. Now I'm going to take you to Santa Monica to meet our drug dealer."

     I spend the rest of the weekend in awe. I'm meeting all of his friends and contacts. So many women. So much cocaine everywhere. It's so shallow and trendy, I can get used to this. I like L.A.

Monday morning comes quicker than I expected. I'm a little nervous. The drive to Burbank is a real real bitch. Traffic like I have never seen before. Now I know why people shoot each other on the freeways out here. I want to shoot someone.

     I pull up to the studio in Burbank; this is one of the biggest studios out here. The guard asks for my name and the make of my car and license number.

"Um Wolfgang Klein. It's a BMW tag number 623-K4ll, Connecticut is the state."

"O.K Mr. Klein. Let me just find your name on the list and here it is. O.K I'm instructed to tell you to go to lot #4 and park underneath then go to resources on the 2nd floor and then you will get your studio ID and parking pass. Have a good day. Mr. Klein."

I'm beside myself I'm actually going to work in Burbank California for a major studio. I don't care about the position. I'm happy that I get a pay check each week and that I'm not painting fucking Ghettos in Bridgeport Connecticut. When I walk into the office I am greeted by this sexy black chic, it's Leola. I should have known by the name.

"Wolfgang hi. I'm Leola. I just got off the phone with Alan and he says hi. So Alan had told me you just arrived from New York and you're ready to work." She scans over my resume

"Oh you worked for MS Television."

"I did up until I needed to focus all my time on completing The Mullet Uncut documentary. Which you can see right there, I was traveling to film festivals the last 7 months and now I'm just looking for distribution".

My resume is 85% true and definitely tweaked. I know she's not calling any references because I already have the bullshit P.A job.

"That's great Wolfgang. Let me tell you a little bit on what we're doing here. On this floor we are gathering information for a pilot called Reunions. Right now we are concentrating on High Schools. You will be sitting in this office with a stack of ten year old Yearbooks that we gathered from around the country. We need to find story lines on these people. For instances. The prom queen and quarterback. The school slut. The secret crush. The geek to sheik. The bully. Do you get where I'm coming from. What we are trying to do for the show is re unite these people after ten years. They are planning on shooting in Hawaii or Malibu. Anyway. We are looking for controversy. Unresolved high school B.S. So pick a School and Charity will get you the contact list. Introduce yourself as a Casting Associate for XX Television or Casting Assistant. Whichever. Then tell them the pitch. Everything should workout." Leola gets up from her desk. "Follow Me."

"Wolf gang this is Charity, David, Mindy, Idy, and Seth."

Holy shit. The girls are hot. Charity looks like a porn star with her big tits and low cut blouse. She is wearing black rim glasses and a white lab coat for some reason.

"Hi guys." I say with a smile and non-threatening tone.

"If you have any questions Wolfgang come and see me I will walk you through it." Idy says with a smile. I'm thinking I would fuck her second to Charity. Who am I kidding I'd fuck whomever.

Once a week I need to report to the Executive Producer with progress in the storylines and what High School has the best contestants. His name is Mik Wiess. The first time I met him, he never took off his sunglasses. Then I figure out he never takes off his shades. He wears shorts and dirty t-shirts to work. His huge office was papered with Grateful Dead Tapestry's. And it always smells like weed with lemon air freshener. It was rumored that his cousin was some big time Madam. How the fuck did this guy get a development deal. I wonder. It didn't take me long to realize everyone and I mean everyone is Jewish. I think they hired Leola as the token black chic so they wouldn't get in trouble I'm also pretty sure they think I'm Jewish because of the introduction from Alan Wiessberg and one of the girls in Accounting signed me up for Jdate the Jewish singles site. I will go with it if it gets me more work and women.

I like Hollywood and all its shadiness.

I live one block away from the oldest bar in W. Hollywood. Sloans. It's a joint. A hole in the wall. A good drinking establishment. My kind of place. It takes no time to befriend the bartenders and score some blow. I like the fact I can walk home and every night of the week the bar is jumpin'. I can tell this is going to be trouble.

Alan is getting ready to leave for Belize for 8 weeks, I have the apartment to myself and take full advantage of it. Back at work I spend my time on the phone all day trying to come up with story lines for the pilot. I have a slew of potential contestants that are sending me photos of themselves. As I gaze through them I stop on this chic Lexi I read that she was from Orange County but relocated to north Hollywood. I grab the phone number from her sheet and call her.

"Hello Lexi. This is Wolfgang Klein from XX Television, I'm pretty sure we have talked before about the reality show called Reunions…"

"Oh Yes. Hi. Wolfgang. I remember. Did you guys choose my High School for the Show?"

"Well all I can say is your school has the potential of being chosen for the series. I need to get a little more info and put together story lines for the executive and then he is going to decide sometime next week Also Lexi. I was wondering since you live in North Hollywood now, would you like to help me out with putting together some these mini story lines about your graduating class."

"Really?"

"Lexi it's totally up to you, I just need to have something complete by Monday afternoon to show my boss and I figured since you live in the area.

We could get together and you could help me hammer out some segments and scenarios."

"Wow. Wolfgang …I need to cancel my plans. You, you want to meet tonight?"

I can tell by the pitch and enthusiasm of her voice that she's excited.

"Yeah tonight, well since its 430 already how about I take you out for a bite to eat and we can start discussing the characters in your class."

"O.K. Wolfgang where do you want to meet, Should I come up your way?"

"Do you know Urth Café?"

"Yes I do

"Great let's meet there first. I live around the corner and many good restaurants are in the area."

"How's 7 o'clock sound?"

"Sound great Lexi see you then." I hang up the phone.

I am fucked. This is against the rules. I signed contracts stating that as an employee of XX Studio I cannot fraternize with any potential contestants. Basically I cannot fuck anyone or use my influence to score perks. Bullshit. I am taking full advantage of this opportunity. I need to get laid. She is good looking for 27 but you can tell she has been damaged. Easy prey.

I am a Monster. I meet Lexi. I bullshit, she talks. I could see in her eyes she was desperate. She is fooled by television…just like everyone else. She thinks I have the golden ticket to her "One Big Break." She is a nut bag. I listen to her family background and history but all I'm really thinking is if she is going to let me fuck her. At this point I talked her into walking to Sloans bar a half block away. I just want to get this over with I can't stand listening to this whack job any more. "I thought we were going to eat" She says as we enter the dark piss smelling joint.

"Oh yeah Lexi, I just want to grab a drink first I was supposed to meet the other Casting Director Carl, here at 8. As soon as he walks in I just need to get his pitch on another High school because he won't be in work on Monday so I said I'd take them in."

I order two vodkas and sodas and walk them over to the table.

"You know Lexi I shouldn't be telling you this, I could get fired."

"What. Telling me what?"

"Well the decision between the two schools that will be chosen for the network is between Carl and myself. I like your school and I'm really pulling for you guys. I want my executive Producer to see the quality I see in people like you. I want to show him true reality." I almost make myself crack up.

"I think it would do great things for you and your vintage clothing line if you were broadcasted to maybe 5 million 10 million people a week. Think about it Lexi."

I walk up to the bar and just nod at the bartender and motion to him to stiff up the already stiff as fuck drink. I walk back to the table and I can see Lexi's brain in motion.

"You know what Lexi? I lean into her across the table. "As soon as Carl leaves, you and I are going to read his pitch and the both of us will make sure the one I delivered is just a little more unique than his." I wink at her. She winks back, smiles and sucks her drink thru her little bar straw.
There is no Carl. There is No Pitch.
"Her hands swipes across my leg as she gets up from the table and from that signal I knew she wanted to get fucked."
Forget dinner I tell her I have a grill and we could cook out back on my balcony. She's almost clueless so I take that as a yes. When we get to my apartment she asks me is she can lie down and of course I say yes. She walks into my bedroom. I thought she was going to crash on the couch. I walk into the kitchen and pull out a bowl for cereal when I go to shut the cabinet I notice a Frisbee in the back. It's turned upside-down and I slowly take it out.

Well fuck me. There is at least 4 grams of blow on this and it's in a nice neat pile. I'm thinking someone left it here and forgotten about it. Who cares? I roll up a dollar bill and stick it straight into the pile and suck as much as I can up my nose in one shot.. I put the Frisbee back and walk over to the sink and I start protruding vomit on to the wall. Wow. That was a surprise. I clean up quickly and walk over to the bar and pour myself a glass of Lord Calvert.

Hollywood is about to bust. I can feel it. Hollywood is alive and well tonight. The city is sending off fuck me vibes; it's going to be a good night. Except I got this chic passed out in my room and it's too early in the night to call it quits.
I leave a note next to her on my bed:
Dear Lexi, I had to run out and Meet Carl

    Stay. I will be back shortly.
    -Wolfgang

I notice her phone keeps vibrating and I see the name Baby next to the missed calls. I shut her phone off. Sorry Baby.
As I walk back to Sloans I notice the moon is full. I actually felt it before I looked up to confirm it.

I can sense that the weekend is just about to begin.

I have never seen a bar so packed for karaoke. Then I remembered I'm in Hollywood and everyone wants to de discovered. I go upstairs where people still smoke. This chic catches my eye as I see her bend down over the pool table. I glance around and notice 3 more chics all tattooed with piercings and bad haircuts. They are hot. I walk in back of the girl about to shoot the stick, as she is pulling back she hits my arm.
"Excuse me, I'm sorry" I say.

She doesn't say shit. She gives me a fuck you kinda look. I take a step back and just stare at this girl. I am in a trance. This girl has such a beautiful face, you can't stop looking at it. Her head is shaved. She has   little black peach fuzz. Both arms are heavily tattooed. And she has hoop earrings on, very black eyebrows. Green eyes. She is wearing a wife beater. Ripped jeans. Motorcycle boots and a chain wallet. And she smokes the reds. I want this girl.

After her pool game is over I see her walk over to the 3 other girls and it clicks. It's the ----- chic punk band. I walk down stairs and grab tequila. I am mingling in the crowd havin a good time and then I get that cocaine urge. The Itch. I throw back my drink take a piss and literally run the entire block to my apartment.

I need to be real quiet because I don't want Lexi to wake up and ruin my evening. She is still sleeping only now she is under my covers and I can see her pants are crumbled on the floor. I hope she didn't piss the bed. I softly close the door and walk lightly on my feet into the kitchen. I pull out the Frisbee and dump a good amount of the blow in to a sandwich bag, I let it all fall in to the corner and twist off the excess plastic. I put it in the small pocket of my jeans and then I stick my nose into the rest of the pile on the Frisbee. No straw.

I take a deep breath. I don't why my heart is racing? From the full sprint over here or from the blow I just did. I put back the Frisbee and I go to sit on my couch. I think I might be having a heart attack. I take my pulse and the only thing I can determine is that my pulse is beating fast. I forgot how many beats the normal heart has per minute. But mine feels like it just might be going a little too fast. I need to get out here. I walk slowly to the door and gently open it and shut it. I take deep breaths in the elevator and when I get outside I lite up a cigarette. The adrenaline kicks in and I'm on a path of debaturey. I order a vodka soda and make my way towards the back of the room near the Tattooed chic. I'm watching her nonchalantly and when she walks into the girl's room. I wait 5 seconds and follow right behind her.

It's a one toilet bathroom and she didn't lock the door in time. I open and shut the door behind me. It startles her and she turns around.

"Hey what the, Get the fuck outta here!!"

"SSHHH." I motion to my pocket and pull out the bag of white and then I put a finger over my mouth. She doesn't say shit. She takes a step closer and I motion to her to make a fist then I gently pour a small pile on to her knuckles. She doesn't hesitate and goes right at it. I do a little myself, wrap it up and put it back into my pocket.

"Hey thanks a lot." I say in a soft voice. I wink, smile and exit out of bathroom.

I know it's a matter of time before she comes and looks for me, so I walk into the middle of the bar and order another Vodka. This time I motion to him with the turning of my wrist. When I get the drink I can barely sip it. It's pure gas.

The speakers are so loud and I can't hear shit. I'm in my own world. A few weeks ago I was in cold Connecticut. Now I'm in Hollywood. I got a good job. A nice pad. Great weather, beautiful women everywhere. And a huge partying problem that followed me from the east coast. I need to make movies. I need to sell my movie. I need money not a pay check. I need a distribution deal. I need a development deal. I need to stop thinking these thoughts right now and enjoy the moment.

I know when I sober up the demons are going to start showing up.

Time to poison those bastards once and for all.

I order a shot of Tequila and another Vodka. I chugged the first one.

Couldn't be any more perfect timing and the tattooed chic walks up to me.

"Hey let me buy that for you." She says.

I lean over and say "Thank you but I already paid for them." I smile.

"What's your name?"

"What?"

"WHATS YOU'RE NAME"

"Wolfgang." I say screaming in her ear. She drags me to the furthest point of the bar, away from the speakers.

"Amanda my name is…. Amanda."

"Hey nice to meet you." I just raise my glass.

"That shit was good, where did you get it?"

I just look at her. "Really. I don't know where it came from but I'm sure a Mexican delivered it." She smiles. "Let me know if you need another bump. Are you guys in a band?"

I see she gets taken back like I'm supposed to know her band, and their one hit they had on the charts for11 weeks 8 months ago.

I do know. I know exactly who she is.

"Yeah something like that.."

"Cool" I cut her off. "Follow me." I take her arm and lead her up the stairs. I go for the corner overlooking the bar. I turn my back towards her and pull out the bag and tap a bump on my thumb nail. I turn around and put my thumb to her nose. She does it and then puts my thumb in her mouth and sucking on it. This chic is nuts. I like it. My hands are gross I hardly ever wash them unless in the shower.

I pull her closer to me and bend over to kiss her neck. She lets me and I instantly get hard and like the animal I am I start rubbing it on her leg. "Let's go find my friends." She says in my ear. She takes my arm this time and we make our way thru the crowd. I softly pinch her ass. She turns half way around and smiles.

"Hey I'm splitting I will probably catch up with you guys later." I'm standing there like a dick with no introduction.. I crack a half smirk and get pulled away.

This chic looks trashy and dirty and she driving a Mercedes convertible. I don't open the door   I jump over it into the passenger seat.

"Come on really." She says.

"No Really. Where are we going and can you drop me back off here? I live a block away."

"How much coke do you have?"

"Why? Enough."

"We are going to Malibu."

"Now?"

"Don't worry when we get there I will replace your stash, I'm pulling into this gas station. Will you pump my gas while I use the ladies room..?" She says holding out her hand, palms up. I put the bag in her hand and get out to pump.

I am too amped up to think about anything other than fucking this girl. But I don't want to go to Malibu. I have no choice. When she gets back in the car I ask for my bag back, she hands it back to me with barely anything left. I don't care I take the rest of it and dump on my knuckle. I lean over and start kissing her neck as she driving fast and recklessly down the 101. All my worries are over I feel like a million bucks. I feel unstoppable. I feel like I can take on the world. I am on drugs.

Holy fuck me. I've never been to such a phat pad. At least I can't remember the last time. Everyone is on the beach off the back of the house. I take Amanda and walk into a bathroom.

"Hey how long are we staying here?"

"Why?"

"Why are you asking me why?"

"I 'm staying here."

"You live here?"

"Sometimes. Come on ." She says as she grabs my arm. I pull her into me and we start making out. She gets me hard and then walks away.

"Wait."

She leaves and I follow her outside. There are a bunch of people sitting around a fire pit. Amanda literally throws an unopened beer bottle at me and then introduces me to everyone.

I say hello and walk towards the ocean. I'm starting to have chest pains and I ignore them. I lite up a cigarette and think about Lexi at my house. I think about work. I think about how I shouldn't be doing so many drugs all the time. I think about Elizabeth and wonder how her life is.

The coke is starting to wear off.

"Wolfgang. Wolfgang, come back." I hear Amanda yelling.

I turn around and realize I walked a bit of a way. I walk back.

At this point everyone is inside. I need some sort of substance I think to myself. I walk over to the counter with all the booze on it and pour myself a Vodka and ice.

"Wolfgang come with me upstairs." Amanda says but I don't see her. I turn towards the staircase and walk upstairs.

Holy shit. As I turn the corner I see Amanda in bra and panties. Her bedroom is the size of the whole house with windows exposed on all three sides. She has this flat stone on her bed with a pile of coke on it and gestures it to me and I obliged.

I overdo it. Way over do it.

I stopped eating her pussy because all I wanted to do was more coke and talk. I just wanted to talk. Now the sun is about to come up and I can't stop doing blow. Amanda is sleeping and I'm pacing back and forth smoking cigarettes doing more coke. I have delusional thoughts. Twisted thoughts. My brain went into information overload. I'm starting to figure out everything is MATH. Numbers. Numbers. Everything is numbers.

I need to get the fuck out of here.

I never turn around. I see the stairs and walk down into the kitchen. I see Amanda's bag on the counter and I turn it upside down. The keys and a bunch of other shit falls on to the counter I grab them and walk out the sliding door on the left.

I can feel the sun and it's going to be a hot fucking day. I jump in her Mercedes and put on her cat eye sunglasses and rip out the drive way. My nose is a bit stuffed up.

I park the car in front of Sloans with the top down and keys in the ignition. I walk back home and hope Lexi isn't there. I can feel the heebie geebies settling in, should I make myself a strong cocktail and ride this out. Or should I scare the living hell out of myself with my horrific thoughts. I unlock my apartment door and walk over to the bar and immediately without hesitation I take off the cap to the Jim Beam bottle and suck back as much as I can before I gag. I walk into the kitchen to get a glass of water and when I open the cupboard I see the Frisbee.
This must be a sign. I think.
I take it out, place it on the counter and stick my nose directly into it and inhale.

For a second I forgot about the girl in the next room. I slowly creep open the door and there she is, clothes on the floor and sleeping under my sheets. I shut the door and go back into the kitchen. FUCK ME. I'm in a dilemma. I could be a good guy or a bad guy. I could take advantage of her or tell her she's got to go. Or I can lie next to her and just sleep. That's sounds good . That thought makes me feel warm. I bust open Alan's door and immediate start rummaging thru is drawers and medicine cabinet. I know he's got pills, some where there are pills. I need to sleep. For some reason something told me to look on the bottom of his laundry basket. I dig thru it and find an unmarked pill bottle. Bingo. I crack it open and see an assortment of different pills. I take two blue ones I think they are a Zanax. I hope they are. I quickly wash my hands and face and brush my teeth. I slide into the bed naked and slowly drape my arm around her. I can feel myself fading fast. I feel warm.
I beat the devil this time. Good night.

I get woken up from an elbow to the chin. I'm in a drug haze and this chic is screaming. I glance over at the clock and it reads 10:37. The sun is still out. Now I realize I'm pissing, apparently on this chic. I'm too much in a stupor to care and continue to finish I hear her screaming and the bathroom door slams and the shower goes on. That's the last I heard of Lexi. On Monday morning I sent an email to her and her classmates stating that production was at a halt until further notice. I threw out the complete file.

Weeks later I'm out of a job. So all I do is try to hustle the Mullet Doc. I have no money. No real money. I'm down to my last $400 and I'm waiting for a credit card in the Mail, 4 weeks ago I was sent a pre-approved credit application. If I filled it out and paid $35 they would sent me a credit card with a $2000 limit at 25% interest rate if I didn't pay off it each month.

When I get it. I go straight to the bank it's issued from and take out $1500 cash advanced and leave $500 on credit.

I take the master copy of The Mullet uncut and have 1000 copies made on DVD. I have the barcode in place. I had my buddy Damon do the artwork for the cover. I have a copyright, and the final product is shrink wrapped. All this cost me$1850.

I spend my days selling DVDs. I set up shop sometimes on Venice beach and the Flea market on Melrose. I quit most days after I make $200. I sell the DVDs for 10 or 20 bucks. Whatever I can get.

I call independent video and music stores and sell them a small quantity each month. I drive up and down the coast, from San Diego to San Francisco selling this DVD to anyone who would buy it. I did my best on college campuses. Whatever money I made was pretty much gone within a short period of time. I spent it as soon as I got it.

I'm living fast. I'm doing everything I shouldn't. I party 6 days a week for months. At this point I've been hustling and working P.A jobs on music videos. I am still waiting for Alan to give me his Agents number, I just keep forgetting to ask him. I drink way too much. I have conversations with people and then have no memory of meeting them. I don't know why I have become a full fledge animal. I live to fuck and get fucked up. Money is an added pressure I don't want. I get fucked up all the time to fill the void... except I don't know what the void is.

I want fame and glory and riches for all the wrong reasons. Or are they the right ones. I'm into instant gratification because I don't know if I'll live tomorrow. I am a mess. I need to get back on track. I need to make some real money. I need to clean up and sober up and wear condoms from now on. I am going to change my ways, I am tired living this hedonistic lifestyle. Tomorrow I am going to change. But tonight I am going to launch myself into the ring of fire.

12 days straight. The first two I couldn't get out of bed and close to suicide. Then I made myself get up and I started juicing Beets and Kale. Beets and Carrots. Beets and Celery. I drank a gallon of water a day and took long walks in Griffin Park daily to clear my head. I feel pretty healthy considering. It's time I clean up my act and try to find a girlfriend. I do want to get married at some point. But I forgot girls like guys that have a lot of money, so it's time I get a real job.

I'm sitting at the coffee bean with Alan we are back to our regular routine.
"It's time Dude." I say.
Alan looks at his watch and says" 8:30"
"No Guy, I said it's time. It's time you introduce me to your Agent. I need a real gig if I'm going to stay out here and try to make it happen."
"Are you ready for the big leagues?"
"Fuck you reality television isn't big league. Just give me her number and email and I will do the rest."
"I'm kidding. Listen I will set up the interview with Zowie. What you need to do is practice."
"Practice?" I say.

"Listen and don't speak for two minutes. You need to ace this interview with Zowie. You do this and this woman will get you high paying reality show gigs. Now make sure your resume is rock solid, I know it's tweaked, just make sure you have your contacts in place, if she calls them. Dress up for the part. You know what I mean east coast style. Not this flip flop and shorts thing they do out here. Get your monologue ready; make sure you can carry the conversation in your favor or direction. Ask her questions. Be ballsy and confident and smile and kiss her ass all at the same time. Can you do that?"
I nod.

"Good. I am going to call her and highly recommend she sets up an interview with you, I am going to tell her that you and I worked together on the east coast on the Albany news program and I will tell her about MS and how you were her" personal assistant". Then I am going to tell her that I worked with you in Casting on the Reunion pilot and you did an excellent job. I am going to tell her that you're a money maker and it would be a good idea if she represents you. Basically, I am going to lie so don't fuck this up and make me look bad. You're going to walk in there and kill it for me. Right?"
"Of course Dude. Say no more."
"Good that's what I want to hear. I will call her first thing tomorrow. You owe me one, Bitch" He says with a smile.

A week later I have the interview. Zowie is a no nonsense, 57 year old sharp looking Jew. I can tell right away she doesn't fuck around, she's all business. I put on my game face and the charm and we hit it off. She keeps inquiring about MS and I tell her it was a great experience but it was time for me to move on. Stella asks me what my former employer would say about me and without hesitating I blurt out "She will say she misses me." And I smile. Zowie smiles back.

She has no idea.

"I see you have worked with Alan and just recently with Mike Weiss on Reunions in the Casting Department. Okay" she says.

I don't say a word. I stare directly into her eyes without blinking. I am pushing all my positive energy towards her.

"Well Wolfgang, I will consider on representing you I just need to check on a few details and I or my Assistant will get back to you in two days." She's smiling with her arm extended.

"Zowie it was very nice meeting you and I look forward to your call." I shake her hand and exit the room. Now I need to call all my contacts and have them cover my ass for me.

Alan and I decide to hit the beach in Santa Monica, its hot as hell. 3 days have passed and no word from Zowie. Did she contact someone else from MS studio? Did that person bad mouth me? Alan assures me that she will call, "she's just a busy woman. Don't worry about it." He says.

So I don't.

I doze off. I wake up to see the lifeguard helping Alan to the blanket.

He is in pain clutching his arm and limping and moaning,

"Dude, I'm fucked." Alan says.

"He was body surfing and hit shallow ground. Hard." The lifeguard says.

I stand up. "Should we go to the hospital" I say.

The lifeguard nods and says" I would go just to get checked out, it looks like you could have fractured your arm."

Alan starts limping towards the parking lot. "Take me home." He says. So I gather the things and take off. Once I get him in the car I can see his wrist is blown up like a grapefruit.

"I think you should go to the hospital. That thing on your arm doesn't look right."

"Fuck that I don't have health insurance. Take me home I have some pain killers."

I help Alan into the elevator and into the apartment. He plops down on the couch wet bathing suit and all.

"Go in my bathroom and into the medicine cabinet. There is a bottle marked aspirin bring it to me."

"Aspirin?"

"When I grab the bottle and look inside I see a handful of Percocet. I take two on the spot and bring Alan the rest along with a glass of water.

"Thanks" he says.

"Hold on let me get you a bag of ice for your arm."

Ten minutes later we are both passed out on the couches. I wake up the next morning in the same position I fell asleep. My bathing suit is dry and I hear Alan in the shower. I try to fall back asleep."Yo do you wanna come to Mexico with me today?"

"For what?"

"I am going to buy more pills, I'm leaving for Bermuda next week and I need to fix this thing."

"I don't think pills are going to fix your arm."

"Yes they will." He says smiling.

"Why don't you just go to the Doctor?"

"I told you I don't have health insurance."

"Yeah but think about how much money you'll spend on pills and gas and I know once your down there your also going to drink and fuck prostitutes. So if you take that money and instead go see a doctor, I'm sure it would cost you much less."

Alan stops and stares into space. "Fuck that I'm leaving in five minutes. You commin'."

"Nope." I say and jump into the shower.

The urge came back. I sorta want to go out and get fucked up. I want to see women. I want to get back into that creative mind set I have when I'm whacked out.

Being straight sucks.

I want to make a cocktail I want to buy blow. I want to fuck porn stars. But then I remembered the promise I made to myself. I will not party until I get a job. I will NOT PARTY UNTILL I GET A JOB.

It takes me a moment to come to my senses. I don't want to fuck up this good energy thing I have going on. I feel healthy. I workout. I eat right. I sleep well.

I let the thought pass and I go for a walk down Melrose. I end up sitting at the café for hours, writing pitches for reality shows. At this point I have nine different shows. Everything is written out in detail, no more than one page each. It's all original. I have not seen or heard of anything like what

I have written. I need to copyright this. I need to get meetings. I need a development deal. I need big money.

I see Alan 2 days later.

"You're just getting back now?"

"Yup."

I turn around from off the couch and I see this huge pharmaceutical bottle. Huge, one liter in size filled with pills. Pain pills. Alan is holding it and smiling.

"You should have come to Mexico. You Mexican."

"What? Man you look fucked. You drove like that?"

"Like what?" Alan tries to straighten out his eyes.

"You're a whack job. How's the arm?"

Alan looks down at his arm and pauses for a moment. "Oh it's great. I forgot about it."

"How much money did you spend?"

"Total."

"Yeah dude.."

"I would say a little under $800."

"On Pills?"

"On pills, on whores, on weed, on booze on hotel rooms. I needed a little recuperation time from my accident. Ya know."

"You're fucked up." I say and Alan tosses me two soma pills. I eat them and within a half hour we are both comatose on the couch.

I was in a pilled out state for the next couple of days. It was just one big dream. And now Alan is leaving for Bermuda, he will be gone for 8 weeks on a shoot.

"Animal Wake Up. You got to drive me to the airport. The taxi service said they will be here in 45 minutes and that's too fuckin late I'm gonna miss my flight. FUCK. Wake up."

"Really Guy." I say half asleep.

"Get the fuck up now! If I miss this flight they will tell me to stay home. I can't believe I over slept. Now get your ass moving. You can drive my car."

When I get into the driver's seat I see Alan shoveling pills down his throat. Did you take the bottle with you?

"Hell no. I didn't feel like getting arrested I just took enough to get me thru the ride. Now hurry up before I start puking."

I'm thinking about that big ass bottle of pills and I start driving like a mad man to the airport. I get Alan to his flight on time and when I get back home I find the bottle sitting on Alan's desk I eat 4.

I take off all my clothes, turn on the air conditioning and lay down on the leather couch. The sun rays coming thru the windows keep me warm while the AC is cooling me off. It's a very comfortable feeling. I zone out.
My mind is in a state of suspension. I am constantly fixated on my future. I need to find stability. I haven't spoken to my family in 5 weeks. I just don't pick up the phone when they call, for no reason. I don't have anything to tell them. False hopes. Hollywood is micro cosmism of the world and everything wrong with it. I need to get a development deal. I want to create.

Day 5 and still no clothes or shower. I drift in and out of conscience only getting my head straight enough to eat more pills. My apartment is spotless and the hardwood floor is nice and cool as I lay on it. The A/C is constantly running, the sun is always shinning. Every time I walk outside on the balcony to smoke, I am reminded how blazing hot it is. I can't imagine anyone going out in this desert heat. I am more comfortable on the leather couch in front of the tube. I cook once a day and its ground meat with taco seasoning in it and sometimes Jell-O in the evening. Got to stay away from carbs.

I do sit ups and push ups and pop more pills. I have a notebook with half written ideas spread out on the table. I find old VHS tapes of porn under Alan's bed and this prompts me to find a VCR. Which I do, tucked away in a box in his walk in closet. I spend days watching old porn from start to finish. Day 9. No clothes. 2nd shower. Half of Alan's pills are gone. I will just deny it if he asks me. I haven't left the apartment. I've been writing more pitches and I think I have a winner. The pitch is this: Homeless to Home.

Find seven homeless people and put them in a house together. Each person has certain duties that they are responsible for. Cleaning, cooking. Laundry, etc. Plus they would be given jobs, anything from McDonalds to hotel cleaners to a doorman. Now each person will be ranked each week on how they perform these tasks and duties. Poor scores would result harder work, while high scores would be rewarded. The person with the highest average at the end of the season wins the house.
Million dollar show right there.

I watch honeymooner reruns, I eat more pills. I still haven't left the apartment, its day 15. I ran out of meat but I have two ten pound bags of edamme in the freezer. 3 boxes of Jell-O. A plastic container of tofu. Matzoh ball soup in a jar from months ago. Some spices and rotten bananas.
I have been sober for a while and it hasn't bothered me. I eat more pills. I do pushups and sit ups.

I write a short story based on a runaway from New Mexico. A sixteen year old runaway hitching the rails across America. She's looking for her real father while running from her mother's abusive boyfriend. When she comes across an unlikely character that is also at the pitfalls in life. Together they embark on an adventure of love and betrayal and when someone shows up dead. The girl's real father is the lead investigator hunting down the culprit....

Now I need to find a copyright and get things movin' along. Eat more pills and I lay back down on the couch.

Day 21. I take a shower and go back to sleep. I wake up when it's dark. I go outside to smoke a cigarette and the heat is still unbearable. I can hear the strip bustling with people and traffic. What day is it? I eat a can of soup and some crusty Jell-O. I decide now would be a great time to crush up these pills and snort them. I can't believe I didn't think of this before. The bathroom is too far away so I piss in the potted palm tree. My apartment is spotless. I don't have internet. I wake up and its light out I don't have a clock and my cell phone has been lost for days. I don't know what time it is but I know it's fucking hot outside. I stopped smoking cigarettes because I ran out. And I'm not leaving this apartment for anything. I do 75 pushups and 75 sit ups a day I do 3 sets of 25 and alternate. Sometimes I use a chair. I write a suicide note.

Dear friends and family.
Don't be shocked I told you all I was going to do it.
Blame it on Religion and the government that's what really killed me.
Your pal,
Wolfgang

I fold this up and leave it on top of the bar and go back to my nodding session in front of the couch.

Day 26. The phone rings. I think at first it's the Television. 30 Minutes go bye and it rings again. I think I'm dreaming. Maybe another 30 minutes go bye and I hear ringing from the kitchen. I get up to investigate and find the cell phone in my utensils drawer.
"Hello."
"Mr. Klein."
Yes
"Hi Mr. Klein. My name is Sharon Rothchild I work for - - - Television. I got your name from Zowie Silberman."
"Hi Sharon. Call me Wolfgang."

"Hi Wolfgang I work as a producer for Kathy Goodwyn. And we are starting production on a reality show entitled "The love Experiment." We are putting together the casting department and Zowie highly recommended you. I would like to know if you would come in for an interview. That is if you're interested..."

"Hey Sharon when is the start date?"

"If you can come in ASAP that would be great."

So it must be Monday today.

"Ok can I have Zowie get back to you, I will need to speak with her first, and she handles all my negotiations."

"Umm Ok WE will be waiting for her call. Thank you Wolfgang, It was nice talking to you and I hope we talk again."

I hang up the phone.

Fuck. I really don't want a job, I was having too much fun living in dream land all month. I sounded like an asshole on the phone. I ponder about this as I lay back down on the couch.

It takes me 2 days before I run out of the pill supply. I finally put on some clothes and go outside to buy smokes. I don't feel right my body aches and my eyes hurt from the sun. The heat is unbearable I think the withdrawals are settling in. I drop my clothes off at the dry cleaners and grab a coffee. I am visibly shaking as I watch myself trying to pour cream into my cup. I feel depressed and I start thinking of ways to kill myself. I could just run into traffic and end it all.

I need to get right in three days.

I show up to the office building in Santa Monica. I am wearing black Hugo Boss slacks and a black J crew polo shirt with Kenny Cole boots. I am 20 minutes early for the interview but I go in any way. I am greeted by a woman in her 40's, she used to be hot, stripper hot, but not anymore and it shows. She also has a dragon tattoo on her arm.

"Hi, I'm Wolfgang Klein. I have an appointment with Sharon Rothchild."

The woman smiles and puts her arm around my shoulders and guides me into her office.

"Hi Wolfgang, I'm Sam, I am the production manager, Have a seat. Sharon is on the phone. She'll be off in a minute. We have been waiting to meet you, Zowie had nothing but good things to say. What did you do to that woman? She's never that nice. So I see you worked for MS, So did I. This was way back when she got her first book deal before she exploded on network television."

"Oh Really"

"Yes, And you worked for Mik Wiess, I know him, very interesting gentleman. …"

My nose is starting to run and I'm getting the chills. My body aches. I pull out a faded green bandana and cover my mouth when I cough. This meeting better hurry the fuck up. I'm starting to break down.

Sharon walks into the room and has her arm extended and gives me a very enthusiastic "Hello."

"It's nice to meet you Sharon." I stand up and give her knuckles. "Germs." I say.

"So Wolfgang I spoke to Zowie again this morning she really has nice things to say about you, I told her you are going to be our lead casting director. What we're doing is putting two unlikely people that would never date together. The catch is they CAN NOT speak about their careers.

We will be shooting in Puerto Rico by the way. I need for you to find me a guy around 30 years old that makes over $100,000 a year. Good looking guy. The type of guy that would bang a stripper but wouldn't date her, wouldn't introduce her to his mother. Then I need for you to find me a stripper. Second I need a Girl about 25 years old with the *girl next door look.*

We have 2 more casting directors working on other characters for the show. You'll have your own office and two assistants working for you. I discussed your salary with Zowie and she said you would agree with $1850 a week. You would be under contract for three months with --- Television. Come with me I will show you your office."

I'm in shock. I can't stop thinking about strippers and $1850 a week. I enter my office and I see two young girls, early twenties. Aliza is Israeli and hot. Michelle is tall and dorky from Seattle. She just graduated from College and moved to Los Angeles they both turn around the same time and say "Hiii.."

"Hello" I wave back.

I walk back out and into Sharon's office. "Wolfgang We would like for you to join our team, would that be something you're interested in. So what do you think?" I did enjoy sitting around my apartment nude and pilled out for a month, but this seems like it could be a neat little adventure.

"Sharon, I want to say it was very nice meeting you and your associates and I think it would be very exciting working with you guys, I can feel the good vibes around here. The energy is great. But. I just need two days to finish up a project I was working on and I will be ready. Is that cool?"

Sharon looks at her calendar. "Well we really need you, like yesterday but I guess we will just wait for Friday."

"Thank you Sharon." I lean over and kiss her cheek. I don't know why. I just did. Sharon is startled and it shows. I take a good look at her and say "Was that inappropriate?"
She nods here head back and forth.
I need to get the fuck out of here I'm not thinking right.
"So then Sharon I will see you here at 9am on Friday?"
"Make it 10." She says.

I take all my clothes and bring them to the fluff and fold. I get my car washed. I still have the sniffles but considering. I weathered the storm pretty good. It's hot out and I decide to lie out at the pool. I was smoking pot when it hit me. I have a job. I have a fucking job. I get up and take the elevator to my floor and get out. As soon as I open the apartment door I bee line it to the bar and grab the Johnnie Walker black. I grab some ice from the freezer and make my way back to the pool. It has been a while and I feel no guilt. I landed a sweet job with a major network and I have two attractive assistants. I don't know how to work a computer, but Fuck it. $1850 a week times 12 weeks equals a little more than $22,000 grand. I could save about 15 grand at the end of the run. I take a sip of my cocktail. I let the sun hit me in the face and I smile. Life is good.
        After I bought a steak and cooked it, I walked over to Sloans. I made eye contact with the bartenders and smiled. I drank 7 beers and was doing little key shots of blow with Axl the bartender. I could feel myself about to go off.
About to lose control.
        I want to take it to the next level. I want a huge bag of blow. I want whores. Then something happened to me. I put down my drink and walked out and straight home. I took off my clothes and climbed in bed. Something had come over me.
        Friday is my first day of work. I am dressed like a New Yorker. All business. I enter my office and I'm greeted by Michelle and Aliza. I put down my bag which has nothing of importance in it. It goes well with the outfit. I don't have a clue what I'm supposed to do. They gave me a lap top and I can't open it.
"Hey Michelle do you want to catch me up to date?" I sit down.
"We have a meeting at Rogersons diner in 30 minutes and we will probably discuss some methods on casting calls."
"Who's going?'
"Aliza, Sharon Myself and you."
"Oh good, good ." I can handle this.

"Alright guys I guess I will see you there. Is there anything else I need to know?"

The girls look at each other and laugh and say "no." I put on my sunglasses and walk out to the parking garage. I get stoned and drive to the diner.

"Wolfgang you could have waited for us, jumped in my car. Save yourself the gas." Sharon says .

"Thanks but I had to make it to the post office."

"You made it to the post office and across town that quick?"

"No, I was going to go after the meeting." Sharon doesn't pay attention and we all order breakfast."

"Wolfgang do you have a plan of execution?"

SHIT

"Guys I want to cast this show properly, I don't want to waste your time or my time dicking around with people that we know will not make the cut. I need to set up cattle calls and take photos then I will interview only the TV worthy people. I need to have business cards made up. I will hit only the high class strip joints. If we are looking for a successful guy around 30, where do we go? Country clubs. The V.I.P. rooms at Vegas hotspots. *The girl next door* we can do by casting calls in bars and malls. Anywhere we go from now on, we are always scouting, we are always working, are eyes are always open. At the beach, at the supermarket, walking down Melrose. Be ready to approach anyone you think will make the cut."

"Wolfgang."

"Yes"

"The studio executives don't necessarily want people from southern California. If you find someone who really stands out. Great. But we want to focus on other parts of the country."

"Sharon, What about casting in New York City and or Connecticut? A lot of wealthy guys on the east coast."

"Yes we will be casting in NYC, Miami, Vegas and San Francisco."

Really

"You will need to find venues in each city and hold open casting calls. Get in touch with the radio stations and whatever print advertising you can get for almost free. Michelle will be traveling with you. Aliza will deal with the itinerary and such at the office. Michelle will be helping you with potential contestants. Gathering info and photos etc, etc. And I need video tape interviews with the top ten from each city. "

"No problem Sharon I will have the line up as quickly as possible. I'm looking forward to finding you guys with the best personality out there. I will find you the star you're looking for."

I don't have a clue. I'm just going to wing it. I'm going to let my assistants do most of the work. I get all of my paperwork done and Aliza already has the grand Hyatt booked for three nights in Manhattan.

"Hey Sharon. I was thinking since we are so close to Connecticut I should do some scouting there. I did grow up in Fairfield County. We can definitely find the girl next door there and I can hit all the posh country clubs on the gold coast for your guy."
"You would know where to go?"
"Exactly. A no brainer."
"Ok. Tell Aliza a good place to stay that's central. And start making appointments with the venues you want to hit."

ARE YOU KIDDING ME?

"Wolfgang I want you to start tonight. I need you to hit all the strip joints and take Polaroid's of the best looking dancers. We will give you petty cash, just bring back the receipts."
"How many girls do you think I should get? Do you know some of these places are real shit holes? And I don't know if you ever been to a strip joint usually there is a cover charge, about twenty dollar and then a two drink minimum. If I want to speak to the girls I have to pay for the time, be it a lap dance or a drink."
"Wolfgang we understand" She hands me a manila envelope with $600 cash in it.
HOLY SHIT.
"Sign here," She hands me a clipboard with a piece of paper.

It's Friday night and I have 600 bucks and a business card that reads Casting Director with my name underneath it and the network logo. I now have the golden ticket.
I ask the door man at "Girls,Girls,Girls" if he wants to be on T.V. and then I hand him a casting card.
"Yeah I'm here looking for dancers and bodyguards. It's for a reality show. I will only be ten minutes." I say. The guy takes the card and opens the door. No Cover. "Thanks Guy." I say and smile.

Once inside I order a Vodka and diet coke. Then another one. And then one more. I make my move to the table and the girls come right up to me. The bouncer leaked out I was a Casting Agent. Those cards work wonders. I order drinks and shots for numerous girls I'm getting lap dance after lap dance.

Fuck I forgot the Polaroid, I need pictures.

I order more drinks and I'm making out with one little blonde. I start asking for blow.

The next thing I remember I was in my bed fully clothed and soaked with piss. I have no memory. I check my pockets. I don't have the manila envelope. No money. My nose is clogged up. I walk down stairs to the parking garage and I see my car parked crooked, taking up 2 spaces. I get in to move it and I see a thong on the floor of the passenger seat and when I look in the back I see a bra and a blue punk wig. I have no Idea. I have no memory. I have no photos and no receipts.

 Great first day on the job.

It's Saturday night and I'm going to take it easy. I walk to Sloans and drink beer. I'm mello. It's mello. The band is ok. and it's not that crowded. I meet this little half Asain girl. Very, very sweet. Cute and thin. She told me she was Dick Brooks Assistant and I was interested. She was young. I went outside to piss and grabbed some flowers from the property next door. I walked inside and gave them to her.

"My name is Wolfgang. Here these are for you. Pretty flowers for a pretty girl."

She puts her hands over her mouth, she is clearly taken back. "WOW."

"I knew when I saw you something was missing." I say.

"My name is Jen, thank you I mean I am sort of embarrassed, I've never had that happen before..."

"You've never received flowers from a guy?" I say.

"Not a huge bouquet of flowers ripped out of someone's lawn."

 "Well I thought you deserved it."

"You make me laugh" she says.

I only had 3 beers and don't feel like partying much.

"Can I buy you a drink?" I ask Jen.

"No thank you. Can I buy you a drink?"

"No I'm done drinking for the night." I say.

"Good me too." She says. "Ya want to go for a walk down Melrose?"

"Yeah."

 Jen motions to her friend and this cute young blonde walks up with her boyfriend,

"We are going for a walk don't leave without me. Carrie this is Wolfgang."
"Hi"
"Hi"
Jen grabs my hand and leads me out the door she is carrying the flowers in the other.
"Where do you live?" She says.
"Why do you ask?" I say in a flirting manner.
"I didn't see you with any car keys, so I figured you live close by and walked here."
"Wow, Jen you're pretty observant. I actually live a half of a block down on the right. Do you want to check it out?"
Jen looks at me and I can tell she has a million thoughts racing around her little head. She smiles.
"I'm a little hungry." She says.
"All I have in my freezer are waffles from like 2 or 3 months ago I can toast them for you."
"No that's OK but I would like to see your apartment."
"Come on really." I say sarcastically laughing.
 We get up to my apartment and Jen is looking around before she walks into my room and plops down on my bed. I am 5 seconds behind her. We start making out
"I can't believe this?"
"What?"
"This. I just met you what 30 minutes ago. I am sober and it's not closing time."
Jen takes off her shirt and she reveals 2 long paper thin scars that go across her chest.
"I have cancer." She says. Just like that "I have cancer." No emotion.
I don't know what to say, so I say "No you don't." and continue kissing her.
Things get heated up quickly and we are both lying naked in my bed just softly touching each other.
        "I have had it all my life, I am in a support group for people with terminal cancer and I have seen 23 people die so far." She takes her hand and pulls the skin tight on her neck and 3 little bumps become visible.
"These are tumors; I've had tumors all over my body, that's what these are from". She points to her scars. "It's only a matter of time"
"Everything is just a matter of time." I hug her.
"I didn't mean to turn you off."
"You didn't, I was just lost in thought. You are a much braver person than me."

"Wolfgang I have learned to live in the moment and appreciate everything and take nothing for granted. So when I saw you I thought you were cute and then when we spoke I already knew I liked you. I just didn't want to waste any time. I could of given you my number and maybe you would of called or maybe not. I'm here now and that's what I wanted. Now do you want to fuck me?"

I instantly get hard.

"I don't have any condoms." I say.

Too late, she climbed on top of me and started grinding.

She moans real loud and I have to keep asking her if I am hurting her. She replies with a loud ."I'm cumming." This excites me and I can no longer hold my own.

"Are you on the pill?"

"What?"

"Birth control; are you on any birth control?"

"No."

"No?"

"Don't worry I can't get pregnant."

We cuddle for fifteen minutes and then Jen gets dressed.

"This has been one interesting evening already." I say.

"Do you want to sleep over?"

"No. I have to get back and meet my friends are you going to come with me."

"Do your friends have cancer?"

"No. just me." My heart sinks when she says that. I put my clothes on quickly and we walk back to the bar. "Do you think I will see you again?" I say.

"Do you want to?"

"Of course." I hold the door open for her as we walk back into the bar.

"Do you want a drink?"

"Yes now I do, Can you get me a Makers Mark."

"You drink that?" I say.

She laughs and goes to look for her friends.

It's around 12:30 and I'm sitting in a booth watching how fucked up Jen and her friends are.

The blonde can barely stand up and her boyfriend is sleeping in the booth next to me. Jen is in good spirits.

"Are you going to drive them home?"

"I don't drive, I never got a license. I was always driven around and Dick Brooks has a driver for me during the week"

"No way am I going to let you get in a car with those guys, your sleeping over."

"What about them?" She points to her drunk buddies.

"They can crash in my roommate's room if you can get their asses there."

We literally drag them to my apartment and put the two to bed. I'm in bed with this little girl curled up next to me sleeping. The clock reads 4:12. I can't stop thinking about this poor girl. She knows she is going to die and yet she doesn't really seem to let it bother her. It bothers me. This girl didn't deserve this. I deserve it. I am the bad man here. If I can take her cancer so she is free of it, I would. I keep thinking god works in mysterious ways. Then I think fuck god. Maybe I brought this on to myself. Maybe none of this is real. Everything is a dream. I'm fading fast.

I wake up three hours later and Jen is in the same position. I can't help but think. "Is she dead?" I shake her and she wakes up.

"Hey."

She turns over to face me and opens her eyes and smiles. "Good Morning."

"Are you hungry? I whisper.

"I could eat something why are you going to cook me breakfast?"

"No I was going to give you a few dollars and point you in the direction of McDonalds."

I smile and by the look on her face I can tell she is confused. "I'm kidding." She lightly punches me in the arm "Go wake up your friends and I will take you guys out for breakfast."

In the diner, in a sober state and with daylight. Jen and her friends look real young to me. I wonder if I look old to them. I can't stop thinking about this poor girl. I feel bad. Life isn't fair. This whole experience is making me see things in a different light. It makes me sad. Why did she come into my life I keep thinking? Maybe it's a dream. Maybe everything is one big fuckin' dream.

After Breakfast I drop them off at Sloans and give Jen my number. "Call me anytime you want Jen, I'm around after work." She leans over and kisses me on the cheek. "Thank you."

I go back to my apartment and start freaking out about work. I somehow need to cover my ass. Should I go back to the strip joint tonight and see if I can take some quick Polaroid's? I need to get receipts so I go to the office supply store and buy books of receipts and a rubber stamp that reads PAID. I go back to my apartment and have my neighbor write out cash receipts from three different places. I need nine girls so I go to Spearmint Rhino. It's a shitty Sunday evening, very hazy and hot. I walk in and walk right up to the doorman.

"What's up guy? Can you point out the manager for me?"

This shitty looking biker guy is just staring at me. I hand him my card and he walks over to this woman behind the bar. I see the two of them look over at me and I raise my eyebrows.

The woman approaches.

"HI. My name is Wolfgang Klein, I am a casting director for - - - Television and I'm here because we are producing a show on the world of dating and they wanted to get a dancers perspective on this. They want me to find nine girls and they will choose three for the show. All I need is some Polaroid's and their personal information. "

"Hello Wolfgang. I'm Julie the manager. And yes we would be delighted if one of our girls were picked. We have about 32 girls on tonight, are you looking for anything particular?

32 girls.

"Um. No. Well yes they have to be in shape and have all of their teeth." Julie just stares at me. "Come with me." she says as she pushes open the door to the stage. "Holy shit. I mean nice. You really have some nice talent here."

Julie brings me into the dressing room.

"Ok lady's. Listen up this young man here is Wolfgang Klein. He is a Casting Director for - - - television and he is looking for any dancers that want to participate in this new reality series if you're not interested go out to the stage. The rest of you line up to have your picture taken and you will need to fill out this information slip to go along with it. "

I have 23 girls line up and I take 23 pictures. I'm cool for work tomorrow.

I'm looking for pills. I'm looking for something to take the edge off. I can't focus on anything. Everything is closing in. I hate work. I hate people. I hate the game. I need to get out of this mood.

At work Kathy pulls me into her office.

"Good job. I like how you grabbed all these girls over the weekend but unfortunately we will probably not use them, "

"Why?"

"We don't want fake tits or if they are fake they have to look damn real. It's not your fault I should have told you that. On Wednesday you will be flying to New York with Michelle you have 8 days. Four in Manhattan and four in Connecticut. You decide which one you guys want to hit first. Aliza will be your contact here in L.A. if you have any problems call her. Go see Lionel in accounting he is going to give you your petty cash and receipt forms. Come back with our stars."

Shit. Lionel is the accountant.

I give him these bullshit receipts and he doesn't even flinch. He looks at them and puts them in one envelope then he hands me another envelope. I put it in my bag and walk out of the room .I don't think I said two words to that guy.

"Hey Michelle, you're coming with me right?
"I want to know if the petty cash I have is for both of us."
"They gave me my own account."
"What? They gave you your own cash."
"800 dollars cash and the company credit card." She says.
I rip open my envelope and I see a wad of cash. All hundreds. I count it right there $2000. Shit did they give me the wrong amount I'm thinking.
"Cool Michelle, Are you excited?"
"Oh yeah I've never been to New York before."
The night before the flight I go out, which was a big mistake. I blow 300 hundred dollars of the petty cash on booze and weed. I leave Sloan's bar heavily intoxicated with a quarter ounce of weed in my pocket. I am already packed so I pass out with my clothes on. I wake to the house phone ringing. It's the car service they have been waiting 15 minutes already. My head is killing me. I realized I pissed myself and I don't bother to change. I don't even brush my teeth. I grab my bag and take a shot of Jameson. I almost puke. I put my sunglasses on and I tell the driver I'm ready. I feel like shit. I ask the driver for a receipt and he tells me the car is paid for.
"Yeah I know, but can you just give me some blank receipts." I hand the guy a twenty and he gives me three blank receipts. I walk into the airport and check my bag and go to the bar. Its 730 in the morning and I see a bachelorette party waiting for their flight. I go up to the girl wearing the cheesy veil.
I don't care.
"Hey ladies, let me guess you guys are going to Vegas?"
"How did you know" she says.
"Um the veil and you're sitting in an airport bar at 730 in the morning."
"My name is Wolfgang Klein and I'm actually heading to New York for business." I pull out my casting card and hand it to her.
"What's your name?" I ask the chic sitting closest to me.
"Brandi."
Hi Brandi. Do you have any sort of pills I could take for this long flight?"
"Pills!" She yells.
"SSHH. You know something to take the edge off. Anything. Let me buy you guys around of bloodys."

The chic with her veil goes in her purse and pulls out two vicodent and hands them to me under the table. I wink and mouth a thank you. I get up and go to the bar and tell the bartender I need six bloodys. He gives me a $72 dollar bill. Fuck me.

I meet Michelle and we board the plane. I quickly pass out and sleep all the way to New York. We rent a car and drive to Stamford Connecticut where we have reservations at some corporate hotel. I immediately contact all my friends and Michelle is setting up casting calls at local bars and The Westport Country club on Sunday. I find a bag of weed in my luggage. I must have put it there the night before.

I put on my duds and start hitting the local bars in Stamford that night, I get real fucked up but I booked 8 interviews for the next morning. Michelle tells me we have a tight schedule and we need to hit these twelve venues and do interviews, everything is back to back.

We already have radio promotions going on and the venue tonight is a Martini Bar in Norwalk. When I arrive I see a line around the block. I see a huge banner with the network logo on it and I see a table set up for me. Holy Shit.

I'm wearing a Hugo Boss Suit with no tie; I am drinking Vodka and mingling with all the women. I get to pick and choose who I want to interview. The owner of the bar tells me that the local cable news is there and they would like to do a live interview with me for the eleven o'clock news. I said fine, that gave me an hour to get real fucked up. Michelle is taking names and setting up interviews. I hired my friend's girlfriend to help out for the night and she was snapping away on the Polaroid.

Things were good. I am the man. Free booze and girls are all over me. When the television crew shows up at eleven, they notice I'm slurring my words. "Hey Wolfgang we are going to give you a ten second spot , we are going to shoot the street and the bar and then JoAnne is going to ask you ONE question. So make it short."

The lights are on. The camera is rolling; the News woman is doing her spiel. "So Mr. Klein can you tells us the difference between this reality show and all the others that flood the television market these days," I look into the camera and smile and say "Yeah Joanne the difference between my show and the rest of them is this; my show is class and the rest is trash." I flash the peace sign and walk out of frame. No one was happy with me. I leave the bar and go across the street to another one less crowded. I run into old blow dealers and of course I buy 3 grams because I don't know what I'm doing. The next thing I know I wake up with this chic naked in my hotel. I don't have a clue who she is. I wake her and tell she's got to go. I call Michelle and tell her to come to my room.

"Wolfgang its 625 in the morning go back to sleep".

She hangs up. I start the shower and escort the girl to the door and tell her I will call her later. I have no idea who she is and she is not hot. I shut off the shower and climb back into bed.

At 10 am I am waken by banging on my door. Its Michelle, I let her in to the suite. I have two bedrooms, a kitchen and living area, it's just like an apartment. She sets up the video camera and lights. "We have interviews starting in 45 minutes, you should probably clean this place up and wipe all the coke off the coffee table."

I walk over to the table and I try to snort it.. Michelle is not amused. "I am going to call the cleaning service they will have this place in tip top in ten minutes."

"How do you know? How do you know there not busy right now?

I pick up the phone and call the front desk.

"Yes this is Wolfgang Klein In suite 203. Last night I made a request to have an early morning cleaning, well I just got back from my 6 mile run and the place is not clean, I have interviews that start in 20 minutes. Just tell them to walk in I will be in the shower." I hang up the phone.

I smile at Michelle and tell her to "Relax, I am going to jump in the shower." When I get out the place is clean and Michelle has everything ready. I put my clothes on.

"Do you want to do the interviews?" I ask her.

"You're the casting director and I'm your assistant."

"Yes Michelle I know. I was giving you a shot to see if you could hold down the fort. If you don't feel up to it no problem."

"Oh, no I want to, I just didn't prepare myself for this."

"It's ok.Listen I am going to give you the questions I prepared back at the office, their basic. We want to know a little history of their background, what they do now. Are they looking for a relationship? What's your perfect match? Shit like that. It's very basic. You'll get the hang of it."

"Where are you going?" she asks.

"I have to go find some strippers."

"I thought we were going to do that in New York?" She says.

"Yeah but I have a hunch about a place in Bridgeport, Look we are killing two birds with one stone. If we meet are quota before we have to leave we can take a few days off and not work so hard in New York. You get me Michelle?" I wink and smile at her.

"You'll be fine." I say and walk out the door.

I couldn't sit there, my ADD is attacking me. My fucking brain is wet, I can't think straight. I already hate this job, I'm over it. I need a drink to kill the depression. I meet my friends at the strip joint in Bridgeport at noon for the lunch buffet. The girls are ok, I would fuck them but I don't think they are television quality.

I pass out cards and talk shit. I can feel the effects of the alcohol kick in. I feel good again. I don't feel bad that it's one in the afternoon and I'm in a windowless strip joint getting fucked up, it is work after all. I continue this behavior into the night. I have my friend Derek drive me back to Stamford in my rental because I am too fucked up.

When Michelle sees me she is not happy and I have to remind her who is boss. I get blown out and brush my teeth and head off to another venue on the list. This time we are heading to Fairfield to an expensive Restaurant and lounge called Tommy's. It's not a normal casting call. It has not been announced to the public, Michelle and I will just approach people that we think fit the part. I don't eat. I am sitting with Michelle in a booth and she is eating a salad and I have vodka in front of me.

"Wolfgang, do you think you going to last in this business?"

"What are you talking about?" "Well you don't really follow any kind of instructions. You do what you want. You're on drugs."

"Yes, so."

"Don't you feel like you'll have repercussions? The shit you do and say to people isn't right."

"Michelle I am your boss. Right. I am going to go back to L.A and tell Kathy that you should be promoted, you did an excellent job and I am even going to recommend you to my Agent."

Michelle just looks at me and drops the subject.

I pay the bill and ask the waitress for any receipts that people left behind. I throw her a twenty and she gives me 8 or 9 receipts. Michelle is just staring at me.

We split and start conversing with people in the lounge. I am now onto Martini's and I'm getting the itch for some blow. I tell Michelle to take the keys and I will meet her back at the hotel. I leave and go to this private Greek social club down the road. I know them and they are quick to let me in and join their card game.

Something caught my eye, it was the sun peeking its head in the window. I am so blown out and I have been drinking for 6 hours down in that basement I forgot about daylight. I leave with 50 dollars in my pocket and take a cab from Fairfield to Stamford. I walk into my room 2 hours before my alarm goes off. I am shot.

I can't wait for this job to end. My body and mind can't take it anymore. When I'm not fucked up I am depressed. I'm in a pit and I can't get out. My thoughts are disturbing. I don't see the point to all of this. Why am I doing this? I keep asking myself. Do I really need money? And how much? Money is just a tool used to get laid. I get laid enough. Fame is another tool used to get laid. I don't want to be famous. I want peace of mind. I don't want the worries that every man has. I don't like the feeling that I have to rely on some mother fucker who's going to play boss with me to get paid. I hate this. I hate television. I hate the movies. I don't see the point for anything anymore. My body is starting to convulse on its own and I violently puke nonstop. I never heard Michelle walk into the room.

"Damn Wolfgang. Hit it a little hard last night?"

"Fuck You Michelle. It was something I ate at the Restaurant that's why I left early I didn't feel well."

"Riiight, I remember you ate nothing! You told the waitress you'll pass. Remember?"

I am naked lying on the bathroom floor. I am shaking.

"Michelle I'm sorry. I'm sorry." I start crying. Real cry.

"I don't know what I'm doing I'm slowly losing my mind." I cover my hands over my face.

"Wolfgang. Wolfgang." Michelle says as she bends down towards me. " It will be alright. I know you're under a lot of stress. It's normal for anyone to break under that amount of pressure. It's ok."

She cradles me in her arms and within in two seconds I'm getting erect. I try to place her hand down by my cock as I kiss her neck; she drops me on the floor.

"You're an asshole."

I start laughing." Why Michelle It was your fault, I thought you were giving me all the right signs."

"Like I said before you're fucked up Wolfgang, you've got issues."

"Come on Michelle I thought I made it clear that I was in to you." I say as I turn on the shower and I point down to my hard naked cock.

"You know you're sexually harassing me."

"Do you wanna jump in with me?" I point to the tub.

"Get your ass ready I'm leaving in twenty minutes and I'm taking the car. The Westport Country club is expecting us early to go over some guide lines." She slams the door.

It's a beautiful Sunday afternoon in September, The patio overlooking the water is packed with your average douchebags and women dressed to kill. Everyone is showing off.

I have the spot light. I have a table set off to the side and two well-dressed assistants taking photos and information. Michelle directs anyone with any questions towards me and lets them know I'm the Casting Director. I have my first drink at 3pm. I love the attention. I am playing it cool. I am wearing my Giorgio Armani shades. I hand out my business card with my cell phone number on the back to a shit load of woman.

My friends show up and they drink on my tab. Strangers are getting me high in the parking lot. I am doing my job and I'm doing it well. I leave with this chic Molly. She says she met me last summer, I don't remember. Michelle tells me that I can't drive. She is being a bitch for some reason and Molly takes me back to the suite.

I thought I was dreaming but I heard knocking at my door at 4am. At first I thought it was the wrong door. Then I heard it again, louder. I think it's the cops so I don't answer it. I go back to sleep.

My telephone rings and its Michelle,

"Open your door I'm coming downstairs we have work to do and interviews start at ten."

"Good Morning Michelle."

"Good Morning Wolfgang. Make sure the door is unlocked." She's pissed it sounds like.

I leave the door open and jump in the shower. I don't hear Michelle come in. When I get out and walk into my room I see Molly getting dressed. "Hold on." I say and I start undressing her. She says nothing and takes off her underwear I fuck her on the desk in my room. The pounding on the wall became louder and faster. And that's when Michelle walked in. Molly freaked. Michelle just turns around and slams the door.

"Who's that?"

"You don't remember her from last night that's my assistant."

"She looks different."

"Good." I say and start pounding like a jackhammer and the pictures on the wall are now shaking and I'm waiting for security to knock on my door. And then I came.

"When do you go back to California?" She says as she is putting on her clothes.

"In a week I think. Why? would you like to see each other again before I go?"

"Yes" she says and walks out I hear her say goodbye to Michelle and Michelle says nothing in return.

I turn on the T.V.

I walk out to the living room and I see Michelle glued to the set out there.

"There's a fire in the World Trade Towers."

"Shit that's going to tie up traffic. What time this afternoon do we have to head in?" I ask.

"Around One."

I am looking at the TV as I am tying my tie Michelle is sitting to my left. Then I see a plane enter the frame and strike the second building. I wasn't sure what I saw. Michelle looks at me and I can't speak. The news anchor says it was the second plane. In ten minutes we find out other planes have been hijacked. Holy Fuck.

We watch T.V together and call family members. I call my Executive producer and she is just waking up to the news. She tells me to sit tight and wait for her call. It's obvious now I'm not heading into New York. I change my clothes and Michelle and I go to the Seagrape in Fairfield. All my friends are there. No one is working. We drink and watch the reply of the events. It's a sad day.

After twelve hours of drinking I ask Michelle if she would like to drive, she declines. So I drive. When I get back to the suite I tell Michelle if she feels like it she could sleep over.

She does and I fuck her.

I wake up in the morning knowing this was a mistake. My head is pounding and I fuck her again.

"How long are we going to be held up in Connecticut? What did Kathy say? Should we just drive across the country?"

"Michelle, I don't know. I know what you know. I don't think they will have the airports closed for too long. How could they? Do we have enough photos and interviews if we pulled the plug now?"

"I think we will be alright considering what happened."

"Do we have the guy Michelle?"

"Well we have a selection to pick from but no one stands out. No stars."

"Fuck I have no receipts; I haven't been keeping a log either. My head is killing me, let's just go back to sleep."

I order room service and nurse my hangover. I can't think straight. Then at that moment it came to me. Ed fucking G. He's perfect. I can tell him exactly what to say to impress the executives. Also I will give Lance a call he's got that Montana rugged look and ladies love him.

Problem solved and I go back to sleep.

Two days later I have Ed fucking G giving me an interview. I tell him exactly what to say.

"Ed I'm going to ask you about seven questions on video. One of the questions is would you date a stripper/dancer? You're going to say this exactly the way I'm going to tell you." "I would of course date a stripper, I mean I don't know if I would take her home to my mother but yeah I would probably sleep with her a few times and if she was real hot I would take her out in public."

Well why Ed? I need a woman who has a career and this goes for waitress and bartenders too. I don't want to date someone who's in a transition in their lives, you know." I take a deep breath.

"That's it. The rest of the questions will be similar to that. You are not supposed to know the meaning behind the show. So act like you don't and if anyone asks we don't really know each other."

Ed does the interview like he was a trained actor. I put his video on top of the list and then I call Lance and go thru the same bullshit with him and put his video next to Ed's.

I remain sober for the rest of the week and after five days they open up the airports and we fly back to Los Angeles, my assistant blowing me all the way. I kept my sunglasses on so I didn't have to look at the other passengers.

Back at work and everyone is a little shook up about the attack but they tell me the show still has a green light and we can continue with casting. I tell Kathy that Michelle and I really broke our backs on this one but I think we found the Star."

I tell Kathy to watch Ed fucking G's tape first and then Lances. I tell her these are my top two picks and she shouldn't waste her time going thru the 41 other videos.

They ask me for my petty cash receipts and Michelle produces them to my surprise. She had my back. She liked me. Kathy is very impressed with Ed fucking G. "She told me he hit the mark he said everything she was looking for." She wanted to get him on a plane and interview him herself as soon as possible. She had other plans for me.

"Wolfgang I am very happy with your picks. You're doing one hell of a job considering the events that happened. I am also going to call Lance and see if he would fly out for an interview. I want to give the network a couple of choices. In the meantime I want you to fly to San Francisco and find us the stripper."

I am over this job. I need rest. I have only been back in California for 4 days and she is sending me out again.

"Is Michelle coming with…"

"No. it will be a short trip for the Weekend, you arrive Friday morning and leave Monday afternoon. We need you to pull this one off. It's very critical for the show. I think San Francisco will produce some great results if not you're going to Miami."

"What?"

"Start calling up the venues and get things in order you'll be leaving in 24 hours. You're on your own. Don't let us down. "

I walk right into the accountant's room to get my envelope of petty cash.

"Wolfgang .. Good I was just coming to see you. I have some questions on your last account. You gave us too many receipts."

"What do you mean? Too many?"

"You over spent... You used your own money and I have a check for you for the reimbursement of expenses."

"Oh yeah I almost forgot." I have no clue.

He hands me a check for $433. Michelle somehow hooked me up.

I grab what I need and leave the office. I head to the cleaners and then the bank. I pack my bag and call back my boy Brendan. He is from Connecticut, the Hartford area and he has a lot of Connecticut boys living in Hollywood.

"Brendan what's up? I saw that you called."

"Yo man what are you doing this weekend?"

"I am going to San Francisco I've got to Cast."

"Shit, I was calling to see if you wanted to come with us for the weekend, we're heading up there tomorrow for Luis Birthday."

"Dude I have an envelope filled with cash and I have appointments at strip joints all weekend. I am going to hire you as my assistant when we get out there. It's cool, you just bill the network $150 a day as a freelance production assistant."

"That's great I could use the cash. It's tough being an actor in this town." "Yeah. But you're no actor. Con man scam artist yes, actor no."

"My boys have a limo and our buddy owns this hip little sushi joint on Union let's meet there Friday at five. I will call and tell him that you're coming to town and casting at his bar. He knows tons of chics and all the strippers in town. Don't worry shit will be cool."

"Yeah but Brendan I'm not casting anyone. I just need strippers."

"Don't worry just bring your Casting Cards and I will take care of the rest."

I hang up and walk to Sloans. I order a pint and the fuck head bartender won't serve me unless I do the warm tequila shot he puts in front of me. "Really dude?"

"Really."

"This how you want to start the evening? Fucker."

"It's not evening yet Wolfgang. Get your shit straight."

"What's up your ass?"

I do the shot and it takes everything in me not to puke right there on the spot.

"Fuck you. What was that? That was not tequila."

"Moonshine." He says and walks away into the kitchen.

I chug my pint and he walks out with a mason jar of pure moonshine.

"We are going to drink this."

"We?"

"Yeah we. You and me and if you don't I am going to ban you from this bar forever."

"Right. I'm going to leave and I'm not paying for the beer."

"Wolfgang you know I don't fuck around I will ban your ass as soon as you step out of that door."

"For what."

"Drink." He pours two shots .

"Could you at least chill it."

"No. Drink."

It burns when it hits my stomach and I immediately need to chug another beer.

"I don't like this game. Got any coke?"

"Drink."

"Hold the fuck on, I'm going to puke. Can you give me a second you fucking maniac and I need blow if we are going to continue this nonsense."

He throws the little white baggie on the bar and when I go to grab it he slaps my hand and says "Drink."

I do and he pushes the baggie towards me.

The antics begin. Shot, beer, blow. That's how it went for the rest of what I remember. But somehow I woke up on a plane in my suit heading to San Francisco. I barely have any recollection other than hanging out in the bathroom at Sloans the night before. I am trying to put pieces of the evening together and all I'm getting is little fragments of memory. How fuck did I get to the airport.

Where's my car? Was I drugged? How come I can't remember? Fuck it. I reach in my pocket and I find my luggage ticket and the envelope with cash, I'm afraid to see how much I spent so I don't open it. I reach in to my jacket pocket and pull out 13 white pills. I have no clue to what they are. I pop one in my mouth and ask the stewardess for one of those small bottles of wine. I drink 3 of them and it stains my teeth.

When I get to the terminal I see that there is a car waiting for me. I don't remember any one mentioning a car at work. I ask the limo driver where I can score some coke and what a surprise he has some on him. I dig my hand into the envelope of cash and hand him 200 bucks for an 8 ball. He pulls up to the Hotel Monaco and I ask him if this is the right address. Then the bell hop opens my door and greets me with "Mr. Klein."
Sweet Jesus. This is the most expensive hotel I have been in. How can the network afford this?

I am treated like royalty. I am blown away by the suite its huge and it has a 4 person hot tub attached to the massive bathroom. The room goes for $700 a night. I am suspicious Michelle hooked me up with the arrangements. I hang up my clothes and go down to the lobby where a wine tasting is going on. I am in a black suit with a white short sleeve 1950's dress shirt. I look good but don't feel so right. I manage to drink three glasses of wine before leaving and heading to North Beach. I am getting a shoe shine on the sidewalk when I get a call from Brendan.
"Yo we're here. Meet us at Rock n Roll sushi on Union."
"I was thinking about hitting the strip joints first."
"No you don't want to do that. Come meet us. You won't find anything good at this time of day wait and we are all going to go together late night."
"I found blow."
"Then stop fucking around and meet me. We're here so hurry the fuck up."
"Nice talk. What's the address?"
"Just get in a cab and tell them the place they know it." He hangs up.

Madison

I hate work and I keep forgetting I have a job to do. I meet Brendan and the boys and it's almost five o'clock. I haven't had a crumb of food all day and my stomach begins to growl. This reminds me that I need to eat but I don't want to so I go into the bathroom and start shoveling huge amounts of cocaine up my nose. I walk out of the men's room and order another bottle of wine. After an hour of this I begin to feel good again, back to my likeable self.

The night couldn't be better. I own the night. I have the attention of beautiful women. I have the run of the bar because it's my boys boy and he thinks it's cool to have an L.A Casting Director there. He makes sure everyone knows this. I have a little bit of a runny nose but I don't let it ruin the evening.

I eat a pill someone gave me and in an hour and a half I feel the effects hit me. Its ecstasy. I'm rolling. I can barely keep my eyes open. Brendan grabs me and puts me in the back of the limo. That's when I meet her. Madison Carloni.

"Hi Wolfgang."

I turn my head to my left and I can barely see who said hello to me.

"Do I know you?"

"No, I'm Madison I'm good friends with Luis."

"Oh." I lean my head back. I'm so fucked up I just faded out for twenty minutes. When I wake I'm alone in the car everyone jumped out at the strip joint except Maddy.

"Were here?" I say confused.

"We just got here, come on." She grabs my hand and pulls me out of the limo. As soon as I get in the joint I go straight to the men's room and shovel more blow up my nose. I am back to my normal self.

I go up to the V.I.P. area where my boys are at. Maddy makes room for me and motions to me to sit next to her. The place is loud and I have Brendan coming up to me every five minutes with a different girl. "How about this one?" he says. I just hand them a card and tell them to write their name and number on the back. Maddy is organizing the strippers and actually doing all the work. I am guzzling booze just watching everything unfold.

Maddy is a petite dark complexion Italian from San Francisco. She is always dressed to the nines and has a very welcoming personality. She has long straight black hair. Like Pocahontas. She takes a liking to me and after 3 hours of knowing her I am fucking her back in my hotel suite. No condom.

She is hot. The next morning I go with her back to her apartment in North Beach and then we meet the guys for brunch. We all start drinking tequila shots and I forget about work. I have no receipts and no one on film. I fuck Maddy in the bathroom of this bar were at. She tells me she really likes me and that we should start seeing more of each other. I agree. Normally I don't date pigs I fuck in bars.

Well that's not true.

I call up the production office and tell them I'm extending my trip. No need to worry because I'm checking out of the hotel and staying with a friend. I need more time to cast I tell them and I will be back on Wednesday. It's Sunday now.

I am partying like an animal with Maddy. I had her score some ecstasy and told her to stick it up my ass. And she obliged as long as I did it to her. We fuck. Maddy is a Pharmaceutical rep. She makes great money and has her own schedule. We don't do anything but lie in bed on Monday. She can cook and cooks for me.

I am starting to get the heebie geebies again I feel guilty for some reason. I feel bad. My mind is starting to race with bad thoughts. Everything looks good on the outside but shit is not straight on the inside. My mind is my own worst enemy. I take out the numbers I collected from the strippers and call ten of them I ask them if they can meet me in North beach. Maddy is at work and said I could use her pad for interviewing. I interview 6 girls and you can hear on the video that my voice is shot. I have two of the girls strip for me on video, and one chic blew me on video. So now I can only use three of the videos. I will for sure get fired for my interviewing antics.

Maddy tells me she already told her four sisters about me. She wants me to fly to New York next weekend to meet her two sisters there. She buys me the ticket. I guess I have a girlfriend now.

When I arrive back to work on Thursday I sneak into the office and can't remember what tape is what so I have Michelle look thru them. She deliberately put all the bad ones on the top of the pile.

I don't have any receipts and I tell my executive I need to fly to New York for a memorial service for 911. I lie. She is pissed but that's nothing compared to her response when she sees the tapes. I am already in New York when I get the voicemail. "Are you kidding me Wolfgang, these are your interviewing skills. You can get us into serious trouble using your credibility with the network for your own personal satisfaction. You Asshole. Are you on drugs or just plain stupid? Why would you even want people to see that shit. I am going to try to clean this mess up before anyone catches wind of it. Your ass is mine Wolfgang Klein. Call me as soon as you get this. It's Kathy."

Oh fuck.

I don't call. I party hard for 48 hours in New York. I'm with friends and my hot girlfriend and her stylish sisters. I take too much of everything and can't sleep on the red eye back to L.A.

Monday morning and I look like shit. No one at work is happy to see me.

I am in trouble.

"Wolfgang?"

I peek my head in Kathy's office.

"Hey Kathy what's up?"

"Did you get my message?

"No I couldn't get service in New York for some reason."

"Shut the door and sit down."

"Yeah what's up?"

"Are you fucking kidding me!" She throws video tapes at me and I block them.

"Kathy. Hold on what's this about?" I'm playing dumb.

"You asshole don't you fuck with me Wolfgang I will bury you in this business."

"Ok, Ok So what now. Am I fired?"

"Unfortunately no. You're under contract, if we bring this to the attention of anyone it could shut down our whole production especially if the media gets hold of it."

"Get rid of the tapes. Destroy them. These girls I don't think want any trouble. I will deny everything. Fuck it Kathy. You worry too much."

"Wolfgang after this production is in the can I am going to ruin you."

"Are you threatening me Kathy?"

"Wolfgang that is not a threat that is a fact that is going to happen. I knew you were a piece of shit when I interviewed you and I went against my better judgment. It's my fault really. Now you better straighten your ass out the remainder of your time here. I need to know how well do you know Ed and Lance and did you taint their interviews."

"Now Kathy you're insulting me. I told you I would cast the show and I brought you two of the best candidates. This is my job and reputation and I'm not putting that on the line for anyone. I'm sorry about those tapes. They were supposed to be personal, not for business. These girls knew they weren't getting on the show. I was just havin' fun with it. If you didn't see it we wouldn't be having this conversation and everything would be cool. So pretend you didn't and forget about it."

"Wolfgang get out of my office." She points at the door.

I walk into my office and see Michelle sitting at her computer with a shit eating grin.

"Thanks a lot." I whisper in her ear.

"You're a piece of shit." She says softly with a smile.

"Maybe so but who the fuck are you? I'm thinking you sucked my dick on a public plane. What a classy chic you are?" I whisper back in her ear.

I keep my mouth shut and smile. I gather what little things I have on my desk and put them in my bag.

"Goodbye ladies."

"Where are you going? Are you fired? Michelle says.

"Michelle. They can't fire me I have a contract. I just feel like working from home. You know while I'm lying out by the pool." I grin and walk out the door.

"Wolfgang? Wolfgang? Wolfgang!" Kathy's voice raising a bit higher each time she says my name.

I don't respond and walk to my car. On the way is the trash container and everything I had taken from my desk is now thrown in it. As I drive out of the parking lot I can see my colleagues standing at the window 2 stories up staring at me. I am wearing sunglasses so fuck them.

My phone won't stop ringing. It's Kathy. This goes on for 3 hours before I pick up.

"What Kathy?" I say in a real pissed off voice.

"Hey Wolfgang is everything alright?" Her tone completely changed.

"Listen Kathy I don't mean to be a jerk. I'm sorry about the videos. I am so stressed out I think I need to see someone. I can't think. That memorial service fucked with my head, I know I haven't been acting normal Kathy. But I don't feel normal. I'm losing it."

"Wolfgang It's alright. We understand. You're just now feelings the effects of your friend's death. I know you have been working your fingers to the bone for me. Listen if you need to take some time off to clear your head I understand… But don't quit on us."

"Thank you Kathy. I won't quit. I wouldn't do that to you guys. I am just freaked out after seeing my friends new wife and his parents."

"Wolfgang takes as much time as you need and please check in with me so I can see how you're doing." I can hear her voice crack.

"Kathy I will call you guys tomorrow." I start to whimper on the phone. " I gotta go."

"Wolfgang, you take care and call me." I hang up the phone.

The whole thing was a big lie now I have the week to myself.

Acting classes finally are starting to pay off. I am going to hell.

I take off to San Francisco. Its 406 miles from my door in West Hollywood to Maddy's Door in North Beach. I drive on one tank of gas and it takes me just 4 hours and 30 minutes. I spend another ten days with her and all I do is eat and drink. I like San Francisco but it's too cold. We talk about me relocating up there and Maddy even goes to the extent of looking for jobs for me. Everything seems to be happening quickly. I'm in a different world every month.

My friends Ed fucking G and Lance are flown in from New York to start the interviewing process. They are both there for three days. Meeting and greeting doing all sorts of test, including submitting to a drug and std test. Ed Fucking G was sweating about the STD check more so than the drug testing. I have to show up for work during these days to follow up on my candidates. I don't speak to anyone. I've been sober and drug free for seven days and I'm still not happy. At the end of the interviewing sessions Ed Fucking G and I decide to go out and get fucked up on his last night. I take him up the road to a gay bar.

"What the fuck are we doing here?" He's not happy.

"Relax. I know as soon as you get a couple of vodkas in you you're going to be asking me to make the call. So me being smart I decided to pick up now before you get all antsy later."

"Fuck you."

"Relax guy, there's my boy tony right there. Should I ask him if he wants to suck your cock?"

"Get the fuck out of here."

I leave my drink on the table and walk up to tony, this crazy leather wearing mustache riding maniac. I give him a hug and he kisses me on the cheek. I slip him a hundred and he slips me the bag while we were hugging.. I walk back to Ed fucking G and motion to him lets go.

"You know some strange cats." He says as we walk down the street.

"Gays know how to party now let's go to Daddys and get fucked up."

We grab a booth near the window. The music is loud. People are swing dancing. We are high on blow.

"Ed, you got to promise me no matter what happens you cannot tell anyone that we are good friends or that I gave you guidance or help getting on the show. These people already hate me. I cannot have a scandal happen to the series. I pretty sure I am not going to be working for XX studios after this gig anyway. It ain't my thing. You know. I'm a man about movies, film. Not fucking bullshit reality television. I mean it's good for you. A guy who wants his big break, I understand that but man you know all I've talked about is movies. And when...."

"Hey, Hey. Wolfgang."

"What?"

"Stop doing cocaine, you're talking a mile a minute and I don't give a shit I'm trying to think if I'm having a heart attack."

We end up leaving and going back to my pad because we both didn't look good in public. Ed continues doing more cocaine until his flight leaves. I'm normal by then or at least I think I am.

"Remember what we talked about." I say and I get a weird and confused look from Ed and we both burst out laughing. I give him a hug and send him off in a cab.

I don't feel so right again. Something is really going on inside my head. The voices are back.

The last thing I want to do is work for any of these people. I have a problem with douche bags and this town is filled with them.

I don't return to work and still get a check every week. I call Zowie and tell her that I need to line up another show. By my surprise she is glad to hear from me, I'm guessing she hasn't spoken to anyone from the network.

"Wolfgang, I'm glad you called I was meaning to call you but you know how things are day in and day out around here? About a week ago Kathy Goodwyn called and said you are doing a wonderful job and they like your candidates. So keep it up. I do have a couple of interviews set up for you but people are waiting for the green light to start pre- production .As soon as I get the call you will know about it. "

"So how have you been Zowie?

"Busy, busy. I don't get a fuckin break. But hey I can't really complain. So enough of your bullshit Wolfgang I will call you ASAP any day. O.K Bye.."

I wonder how long before my name is really mud. Maybe Kathy is scared of my agent. Who knows? Who cares?

Maddy fly's in for the weekend and Alan has this chic from Sacramento also coming in. Alan has never met this chic in person he met her casting over the phone for "Reunions" and has had a phone sex relationship with her for the past few months. Her name is Kerrie Lipchitz.

Kerri arrives on a Thursday evening and she is blazing, fake tits, tall slender body, and big hair. Sacramento trash with money to buy expensive clothes.

Alan, me and Keri go out for light drinks on Thursday night then home early because he has to work in the morning. I hear him fuck her. In the morning Alan asks me to show her around town because he is taking his car and he works 12 hour days.
No problem.

I cook Kerri breakfast and tell her I need to go to the bank in Studio city, She says she wants to come.

I take her thru the valley and show her all the tourist attractions. We end up eating lunch in Santa Monica and the conversation turns to sex. I tell her how she is turning me on so much I can't stand up. She starts rubbing my crotch from underneath the table with her foot. I tell her how bad I want her but Alan's my friend and I won't go there. She tells me that's cool but if I jerkoff and she watches it's not really cheating. I agree and race back to my apartment... As I am lying in bed on top of the comforter the air conditioner is on high and the sun is so bright it's lighting up my bedroom.
"What time is your girlfriend coming?" She says as she is stroking my cock.
"Why are you bringing up my girlfriend? I'm trying to stay focused. I have to pick her up at LAX at 9 o'clock."
"Is she into girls" She says as she takes off her t shirt and lays back down on top of me with her big fake tits.
"'Umm. I don't know I never asked her. Why?"
"Just wondering, Does Alan ever come home from work early?"
"Noo Damn it. forget it I can't cum." I get up and pull my shorts up.
"Wait come here."
I walk back to the bed and this chic pulls out my cock and starts sucking it right there.
I am a bad roommate and a bad boyfriend.

I am drained I don't have the energy to go out tonight. Before I go and pick up Maddy I stop at the bank and hit the ATM. I check my balance and still can't believe I am getting direct deposits every Friday. I don't remember the last time I went to work.

She looks real good. She's excited when I see her get off the plane. She hugs me. I grab her luggage and we jump in my car.
"Have you touched it?" Maddy says smiling.
"What? Noo. I told you I wouldn't and I didn't."

She just looks at me.

"I swear. I didn't."

Maddy starts rubbing my crotch with her hand and I get instantly hard.

"See I told you." I say confidently

"Well see Mr. Wolfgang Klein." Maddy leans over and starts kissing my neck. I don't have an ounce of semen left in me. This girl is going to be disappointed.

When I get back I see Alan and Kerrie already dressed and blowing lines. Maddy says hello to everyone and Alan pours her a glass of wine before she even gets to the kitchen.

"We are going to be late if we don't get going." Alan says. "I didn't know we were going out?" Maddys snaps back.

"I didn't know either do you want too?" I say.

"Alan can you wait 20 minutes I want to decompress and freshen up."

"Of course we can wait sweetie. I don't even know what the big hurry is." Kerrie says.

I grab Maddy's bags and walk them into my room. She follows and shuts the door behind her and quickly takes off her jeans and boots.

"Hurry." She says.

I am really not interested I have nothing left. I have been jerking off a couple times a day for the last two weeks and I just got blown 5 hours ago. I don't want to fuck. I just want to get fucked up.

"I am only doing this for a minute. I really want to save myself for later when we have a long time together."

"Shut up and Fuck me."

I do for sixty seconds. I counted.

"Come on lets go I don't want to keep them waiting and I know you take forever to get ready."

"You're being mean," "No Baby. Don't take it that way. If you want to stay home and fuck all night. Fine. "

"You will..?"

"No. I'm kidding come on and get dressed. I promise I will drill you later."

"Promise.?"

"Yes baby now get your ass moving."

I walk out to the living room and join Alan and Kerrie for a drink. I tell Alan we are going to take separate cars because I don't feel like staying out late and Maddy's tired. Kerrie keeps eye fucking me behind Alan and Maddys back.

The party is way up in the hills and they have valet parking. Weird to me since this is someone house. The party is kickin' exactly what you'd expect of a Hollywood party. Drugs, Drugs and more drugs. Maddy and I indulge in everything I could get my hands on. I look good because I got this hot chick hanging all over me which makes other chicks want me and I can see Kerrie constantly doing blow. Alan is nowhere to be seen. Maddy is bullshitting with some loser reality star from a loser reality show. I am so fucked up but I feel my rage take hold.

"Come on Maddy." I say and she pretends she doesn't hear me. At least that's what I think. I walk up to her and I see her flirting and smiling she doesn't introduce me. The reality douche bag thinks he is going to get lucky with my woman

I am all animal.

I grab her by the arm and pull her into me. "Follow me to the bathroom." I turn to the douche bag and say "Yeah." I smile and take Maddy by the hand. "What are you doing?"

"Shut up and pull down your pants." I'm pissed off and trying not to show any aggression. But I can't help it. Maddy looks at me weird and pulls down her pants turns around and bends over the vanity.

"Oh my god, you're so turned on." She says

I grab her by the back of her hair and start nailing so hard the vanity is pulling away from the wall.

"Is this what you want Maddy." I whisper in her ear. "You're a bad girl Maddy." I push her face against the mirror. I hear knocking on the bathroom door I don't say anything.

"Oh my god. O.k o.k O.K. O.k O.K o.k…ok I came." She licks the sweat off her lip. I continue to bang away because I can't cum with all the drugs running thru my body.

"You're starting to hurt me. Hurry." She moans and I bang harder. I am thinking about killing this Gucci little piggy.

"I can't." I push away from her and pull up my pants. I sit on the toilet out of breath." I think I might be having a heart attack." I say.

"You want to go." Maddy says as she is re applying her lipstick in the mirror.

"Yeah, there is nothing here for me. I just got laid and I don't think I should put any more drugs in my body."

"Shut up, you just got laid. Can't you speak nicely to me Wolfgang?"

"Oh no Baby you know what I mean. Why do I want to stay here when I can be with you alone. Together, Just me and you and my bed. Why do I want to be with all these dick heads when I can be alone with you? Come on lets go."

We look around for a while and Maddy can barely walk that's when I see Alan.

"I'm outta here man."

"Have you guys seen Kerrie? Where the fuck is she I have been looking for her for 20 minutes now. I might leave too if I can't find her."

"I bet she is in the corner somewhere shoveling cocaine up her nose."

Maddy hits me. "Wolfgang!"

"Alright guys. Drive safe. I am only staying a little bit longer, so I will see you later or in the morning."

"Bye"

"Later."

I can hardly keep my vision straight and pull over.

"Maddy you got to drive. I'm seeing double." "I don't know L.A plus I don't drink and drive."

"Do you want to walk home, because I can't drive .I can't see fucking straight."

"Can you call a cab?"

"And leave my car WHERE? No cab company is coming all the fucking way out here anyway. Just drive."

"O.K. If you're going to be a jerk about it. Will you tell me directions back to your apartment?"

"Yes Maddy."

Maddy drives and we get home safely. "Something get into you tonight Wolfgang your not acting yourself."

"Yeah I don't like seeing my girl flirting with some cheesy reality ass fuck." I push the elevator button.

"I wasn't flirting."

"Yeah o.k."

She hugs me and we walk into my pad and go straight to the bedroom. I should have known. We have crazy sex all night and pass out. Around five in the morning I hear the door slam.

"Take your shit and get out you fucking whore piece of shit." Alan's screaming.

I hear the luggage being thrown around and then Alan slams his bedroom door.

The sun is up.

Maddy had turned over and was just staring at me. She heard the same thing.

"What are you going to do?"

"Me? I ain't going to do shit. Ain't my problem."

"Go out there and see what happened."

"No. You go."

"I'm going to the bathroom." Maddy gets out of bed and tip toes to the door and slowly opens it and walks out trying not to make a sound and she is naked.

"She is just sitting out on the balcony with a blanket on her. You should go talk to her."

I just stare at Maddy and now I am thinking did that crazy chic tell Alan she blew me. Oh Fuck. No. I know Alan he would have kicked in my bedroom door as soon as he got home.

"If you really want me too. I will do it for you baby." Maddy kisses me and snuggles under the comforter. I put on a pair of shorts and quietly walk out to the balcony.

"Yo what's going on? I heard you guys come in." I say in a soft voice.

"Your asshole roommate flipped out on me at the party. He accused me of cheating when all I did was pass out in a bedroom because I was drinking so much."

"wow."

"He fucking embarrassed me in front of everyone at the house and on the car ride back he threaten to kill me."

"Noooo he didn't. He was just mad. I should have probably told you he has an east coast temper. So what are you going to do now? Change your flight?

"No I am waiting to get picked up from this guy I know in Santa Monica. I will stay there the night and take off on my normal flight." "I thought you never been to L.A?"

"I haven't."

"Oh...You didn't mention to Alan anything about us did you?"

"Oh God No."

"When's your ride coming?" "He said 930 he would be here."

"Well you've got a few hours why don't you come and try to sleep in my room with Maddy and I. Don't worry I have a lock on my door and Alan will be sleeping till 2 in the afternoon.

I walk in my bedroom with Kerrie and her luggage. We try to be as quiet as possible. Maddy is naked under the covers. I take off my shorts and slide in next to her. Kerrie pulls off her one piece dress. No bra. Just a G-string. She climbs into my left. Maddy is leaning over me whispering to Kerrie about what happened and Kerrie is telling her. Maddy doesn't seem to care that this chic with fake tits is pretty much laying on top of me. I have one of each of their breast on my arm and chest. These girls are way too much into conversation and I doze off.

About an hour later I wake to see both girls sleeping beside me. The blanket half off the bed.

I decide to jerkoff and the constant movement of the bed woke Kerrie. She grabs my cock and starts jerking it for me. I close my eyes. I feel some one climbing on top of me and I open my eyes to see Maddy riding me. I look over at Kerrie and she smiles and puts her tits in my face. Maddy doesn't say a word then Kerrie starts sucking on her breasts and this drives Maddy wild and she is bucking and cumming on me. She is screaming and now I'm a little freaked out that Alan is going to wake up.
Maddy excuses herself to the bathroom and this time she takes the sheet to wrap herself

Kerrie takes this opportunity to start blowing me and she stops as soon as she hears Maddy open the bathroom door. "Wow what an interesting morning so far." Maddy whispers as she enters the room.
"Wolfgang will you help me with my luggage." Kerrie asks as she is getting dressed.
"Sure." I say as I am getting my shorts and flip flops on. I tell Maddy I will be right back and her and Kerrie exchange numbers. I carry two huge suitcases to the curb. Kerrie tells me her ride should be here any minute and writes down her telephone number for me. I put the piece of paper in my wallet.

"I had a good time Wolfgang. Despite meeting your roommate. You were very nice and it was great hanging out with you. You have a good girlfriend and tell her I said she is lucky to have you." She kisses me on the cheek. I turn my head to see this black bmw idling on the side of me.
"Is that your ride" I say.
"Oh yeah here he is." This dude gets out of the car and pops the trunk. He looks at me and shrugs his shoulders. It looks like he hasn't slept either.
"O.K Bye." I turn and walk back into my building then it dawned on me I remember that dude from the party. He asked me how often do I go to Sloans because he sees me there often and that's when I told him it's my neighborhood bar.
How the fuck does she know him from Santa Monica?
She doesn't.
I climb back into bed with Maddy and fall back asleep. A few hours later I hear Alan knocking on my door.
"Yo you guys awake?"
I look at Maddy and she's looking at me. I whisper to her "Don't say a thing."
"Al what's up.?" He opens the door and walks in.
"Hey if I woke you guys this morning I apologize. I kicked Kerri out."

"We heard something but didn't really know what you were saying" Maddy says and I pinch her side under the covers.

"What happened dude?" I say.

"We were all having a good time at the party, things were good. I was ready to leave a short while after you. I can't find Kerri anywhere. I don't pay much attention because there were so many fucking people. Another 30 minutes goes by and now I'm like what the fuck. I swear to god I hear these two guys talking about a chic who just suck one of them off in the bedroom. I know I was fucked up but I did not imagine this. I walk into the house and I finally see Kerri and her hair is all fucked up and she doesn't look all together. I ask her where she has been and she tells me that she passed out in the bedroom upstairs. I don't believe her and start freaking out at the party. I don't think I will be invited to anymore of Johnny Black's parties. Fuck it she was a whore I fucked her ass the first night I met her."

"Uhh dude my lady is in the room."

"Oh Wolfgang I don't care." I pinch her again.

"Oh yeah sorry. Anyway I'm pretty sure she was sucking cock at the party and she is lucky I didn't throw her out of my moving car."

"Alan, give us a minute and I'll meet you in the kitchen."

He shuts the door and I get dressed.

"Listen Maddy don't say a word that we saw Kerrie this Morning. The last time we saw her was at the party. Right?"

"I guess so."

"What do you mean you guess so? Say right."

"Sure"

"Sure what Maddy?"

"O.K." she says.

"Something wrong with you?" I say as I leave the room.

In the kitchen I see Alan cooking eggs and making Bloody Marys. I still not one hundred percent sure he doesn't know.

"I saw her leave in a BMW this morning." I say.

"I'm a bit freaked out what if I perceived the whole thing wrong, what if I accused her of all that shit and It's not true. What if I did imagine it?"

"Al, I am willing to bet money on it. That girl was a cock whore. Who the fuck is the guy in the BMW? And she just takes off with him? Come on dude your smarter than that. Don't be so hard on yourself."

"When is Maddy leaving?"

"I hope soon but I think tomorrow night. Why?"

"I have big plans, so I will go with you when you drop her off at the airport and then we will drive to Hermosa Beach I got to pay someone a visit."

"Who?"

"Oh don't worry about it. "

"Well then why do I want to drive to Fucking Hermosa Beach? "Do you want to make some cash?" "Yeah."

"Enough said."

Maddy walks into the room.

Hey guys what are you talking about?"

"When is your flight tomorrow?"

"8pm."

"Pm is no good you have to change it for around noon. Alan just told me Sonny Brooks invited him over for lunch tomorrow and I'm going with him. I want to see if I can get some networking done." "Well that sucks. I can't go with you guys?

"Maddy its work and you will be a distraction, come on babe, I will come see you next weekend."

"Fine but I'm not happy." She walks into the bathroom.

Alan smiles.

Maddy jumps on the 1:05 flight to San Francisco and I race down to Hermosa with Alan.

"Remember the old days." He says.

"What?

"The days when you were a pot dealing animal."

"Yeah and what were you ?" I say.

"We are driving to the beach to get 2000 ecstasy pills. When I make the call to him he is going to walk out of his apartment with a back pack and down the back alley. Its two blocks from his pad to the beach. I will be parked at the beach waiting for him to show up. "

"So why am I here, I really don't want to be involved in a fucking major drug transaction."

"Listen I met this dude at a bar like three months ago, he sells ecstasy. I have already been down here before buying 300, 400 pills at once from him. He trusts me. He has no idea where I live and every time I come up here I use a different car. He is selling me each pill for five dollars I turn around and sell all of them for 10 to a dude I work with. All in one transaction. So now I talked him down to 3.50 a pill but I have to buy a thousand or more. "

"You didn't bring the cash did you?"

"I brought you."

"I don't know dude. This sounds pretty fucking shady."

"Do you want to make ten grand by tonight? I got a guy back in the Hills waiting on them. He is paying me ten dollars a pill times 2000.."

"Holy shit, all in one deal. How do you know this fucking guy isn't going to set you up?"

"He's a Jew."

"Oh. O.K .That's supposed to make me feel better you asshole."

"I don't know Al we are getting old and this is a major felony. Multiple felonies. What if the guy is carrying a gun? "

"Good point. The dudes name is Chris he isn't much taller than you and you probably got a good 15 pounds on him. He's like 24 or 25 years old. He's a fucking punk drug dealer. You would be doing society a favor. Ten grand all yours."

"Fuck. Fuck. Fuck. I got a bad feeling."

"I have been setting this thing up since I met him. If I didn't think you couldn't handle it I wouldn't ask you."

"So I have two blocks from his pad to the open beach. It's fucking the middle of the day."

I think about it.

Alright I need to go and buy clothes and a hat. I need a loud big Hawaiian shirt and one of those cheesy straw hats."

"Take your next left and you'll see a strip mall, you can find that shit there."

Now Alan is in the driver's seat and he makes the call.

"Christopher I'm here in the parking lot, same one as last time. What color cap are you wearing? Cool when I see you I will get out the car and wave you over. See you then."

Alan hangs up. "He is wearing a red Chicago bulls cap and he should have a blue back pack on .Go now and I will meet you wherever you want when you call me."

I can't believe this shit.

I can't believe I am going to go thru with it.

Fuck it. My only worry is going to jail. I don't want to go to jail in L.A. No fucking way. I am not going to let myself get arrested.

I walk from the beach down the alley to Christopher's apartment. When I get a view of his building I immediately see him walking out. I take out my cell phone and act as if I'm looking for directions. A few people are walking by paying no attention. I cross the street so I am now on the same side as Chris. I see him approaching me.

"Excuse me do you know where Second Street is?"

"What?" he says as he pulls one of his earphones out of his ear.

"I said do you know where …

I saw the opportunity and took it

I put all my body weight into an 8 inch punch under his chin.

There was no sound.

I laid the fucker out cold I was in awe for a few seconds just standing over him. I slip off the back pack and put it on. I see people gathering around. "My friend just passed out. Does anyone have any water?" I yell and drag him onto the sidewalk and prop him against a postal box.

"He's diabetic I got to go get him some Orange juice."

I keep yelling as I walk into the circle K. I take off the straw hat and shades and shirt and throw them out and buy a box of cereal. I walk back outside and no one notices me. I take a sharp right and I can see beach police on their bikes racing by me. I stop and see all the commotion and pull out my cell phone and call Alan.

"Got it. The dude is still sleeping. I can see you in the parking lot, you need to exit and go to the north east corner. I will be standing at the crosswalk."

I keep the phone to my ear after Alan hangs up and I'm looking down the street at the two bike cops. Alan pulls up and the light is red, I open the door and get in.

"Holy shit. Go!!"

"The light is still red. Hold on man be calm."

I sit in silence and stare straight ahead. Two minutes later I'm on the 405.

"Did you look inside?"

"Are you kidding me? When did you think I was going to look inside?"

"Well open the fucking thing up."

"Just keep your eyes on the road."

I pull out exactly what Alan said was in there. Two clear plastic bags with 1000 white and yellow pills in each.

"You weren't kidding." I say smiling as I hold up the two bags.

"Will you put that shit down are you fucking crazy. That was phase 1 now we have to go and deal with the Jew. Phase two Kid. You need to drop one of those pills."

"Al I'm not droppin' shit. No way. No way dude."

"That was part of the deal."

"Fuck you Alan. Deal what deal. Your making this shit up as you go along. I will throw this shit out the window. Pull over I will drive and you drop it asshole."

"Alright chill out. I'm pulling off the freeway and we are both going to take one."

"Why? Do you think they could be bunk?"

"You never know. But if this Jew gives me 20 grand and the pills don't work he knows who I am."

"I don't give a fuck. I'll drive and you drop it. When we get to the Jews house in an hour you will be rollin and he can see for himself."
Alan pulls into Denny's parking lot. I get into the driver's seat and Alan walks in to get a Pepsi.

"Which house is it man? Stop fucking around and open your eyes." I'm getting fed up with this guy.
"I forget let me call him."
"Alan do me a favor and open your fucking eyes. How the hell are you going to dial the numbers?"
"21388 w crescent. I remember."
"Really then why did you tell me to drive up Mulholland? I'm going to take these pills and throw them in the river."
"River.?" Alan looks over at me.
"Relax I have the Address in my wallet let me grab it." Alan speaking in his mello voice.
"That pill fucked you up that bad huh? Thank god I didn't take one. You look like an asshole. You should put on your sunglasses and not take them off.
I can't see any house numbers but Alan tells me to take a quick right into this driveway.
"Are you sure?"
"Yeah dude I've been here before. Pull up and pull to the left and park."
"Am I going in with you?"
"Uhh yeah get out."
I walk up to this huge contemporary house and the Jew is waiting for us at the door, I can see the security camera out of the corner of my eye. An uneasy feeling comes over me.
"Wolfgang, the Jew. The Jew, Wolfgang." We shake hands and I don't say a word. I can see he is nervous.
"Come in Come in, he shuffles us in quickly. Alan takes the bag and hands it to him. The Jew puts it on the sofa.
"I am not waiting around for you to count 2000 pills. We are sort of on our way somewhere."
The Jew opens the bag and smiles. "Alan hold on I need to run upstairs and grab your cash."
I sit on the couch. I stick my hand in the plastic bag next to me and take a hand full when I am pulling my hand out Alan catches me.

"Animal I will kill you." All of a sudden Alan is straight and serious and shoots me a look. I drop the pills back in the bag.

"He weighs it asshole." Alan tells me in a low voice.

I stand up and walk over to the open wall extending his house to the pool and gardens. Who the fuck is this guy I am thinking and how did he get so much money. I just want the ten grand and I am happier than shit.

The car ride back Alan tells me the Jew is a serious producer and he might look like a pushover but he has connections on both sides of the law. Then he hands me a stack of money.

"What I tell ya kid. When I say something I make it happen don't I." Alan getting on his high horse.

"Yeah you made it happen alright. You crazy fuck. I appreciate this but this is the last time I'm getting involved in any sort of criminal activities with you or anyone else."

"O.K hot shot. Just never say Brother Alan never hooked you up."

I blow five grand in five days.

I spend 800 bucks on tires and a tune up for my BMW. I pay rent 800 bucks. I buy and ounce of weed 275 bucks. I spend a little over 400 hundred on food and household needs. I go out every night and drop 3 to 400 dollars on dinner and drinks. I don't see Maddy for a two weeks and I act like an Animal. Doing everything a responsible person wouldn't do.

I am still getting direct deposits in my bank account and no one calls me from work anymore.

Five days later another five grand is gone.

12 hours in Vegas. Blow, hookers, gas and gambling. Now I'm back to normal.

It's Tuesday and Sharon calls me.

"Wolfgang. How are you? I'm calling to let you know we have chosen Ed from Connecticut... He made the cut with all the executives and passed the test and we were thinking if you wanted to call him with the good news."

"Really?" I'm half asleep.

"Yes Wolfgang, We decided you can tell him after all you discovered him."

"Discovered him?" I think about it for a second and say "Do I need to come in to work to do this?"

"You're too funny Wolfgang. Are you going to call him or should I?"

"You call him. He won't believe me if I call."

"Ok. Are you coming to the party Friday?"

"Umm. What party?"

"Casting party. The show is casted and work is over. Well at least pre-production is. Have you got anything lined up for after this?"

"The show's over? I mean the job is over?" Now she has my full attention.

"Yes. Your department is done we start shooting in a month in Puerto Rico."

"Any chance I can get hired on the production, I will do anything. I will be a Production Assistant. I need to get to Puerto Rico."

"Wolfgang I don't think so. First we have Michelle coming as a P.A. And second you're out of your mind if you think for one second I would work with you again, let alone bring you to Puerto Rico. You're lucky I don't call Zowie and tell her what an Asshole you are and unprofessional your work ethic is. You ruined yourself among your colleagues here and don't forget this is a small town."

I inhale and exhale into the phone speaker

"Oh Sharon, You are so right. But guess what. I don't give a fuck. You and Kathy can go fuck each other for all I care. I casted your show in one week. You're putting my guy on national TV. I did my fucking job. I dare you to call Zowie and bad mouth me and then we will see how far you get in this town. Don't you threaten me with your reality show bullshit. Remember Sharon it's who you know not who you blow. Fuck you and your stale love connection show. I will be working in film, in the big leagues Sharon. So Fuck off and Good luck with that." I hang up.

I spend two weeks in San Francisco, hustling The Mullet doc. Maddy is happy I am here but I am getting bored with her. She's too flashy and always wants to go out. I am running out of money and she suggests to me that I come and live with her. Fuck that I hate the weather. I tell her. And that's when she breaks the news to me.

"Wolfgang I know how much you like New York."

"Do you?" I say sarcastically.

"Well you talk about it all the time and my sisters are there. Soooo my company told me that there is a sales position opening up in New York and they would like to offer it to me. If I did take it, the move won't happen for about three months. What do you think? Do you want to move together to Manhattan it would make me so happy."

"Maddy that's great news. You'll love New York. I think we need to see how the next three months are before I make any drastic moves. But I think you should take the job offer."

"I want to go only if you're coming with me. I thought we were going to get married. I will move to L.A if you want me too."

Holy shit this chic is nuts. I should tell her now. I should tell her to run far far away from me.

"Maddy No, I don't want you to move to Hollywood, I want you to do what makes you happy. I think you should go and move to the city, you will be with your sisters. I want to go too I just need some time here to clean up my loose ends. I think you should take the job and plan on moving to New York."

"Wolfgang your coming!!!."

"Yes, just don't mention it to Alan when you see him."

She jumps in my arms and I rip off her jeans.

I am back in West Hollywood. I never gave it a second thought about moving back east. Hopefully she will get sick of me by then and dump my ass.

I'm almost broke, so I apply for credit cards I see advertise on television. I need to pay $35 dollars to get a credit card worth $750 and if I don't pay it off in the first month the interest rate jumps up to25 percent. I end up receiving 3 cards with the total credit of $2,250. I have no intensions of paying them off. I feel like the credit company is preying on poor souls and taking advantage of their situation. Fuck them.

I rent an Isuzu trooper and drive to Utah for the Sundance Film Festival. The truck rental is $250 a day. I am loaded up with boxes of The Mullet uncut DVDs. I show up in town without reservations and all I have left is 600 bucks. I spent a night in Nevada and hotels, gas and booze add up. One of the Inns on Main Street in Park city has only two nights available before the big weekend. I took them. The first day I explore the area, I hit every bar in town and any showing that I could get into. It's snowing and it's cold. I get in touch with an old friend from Trumbull on the phone. He tells me one of his college boys works at the biggest bar in Park City. His name is P-train. When I show up, he is waiting for me.

"What's up dude I'm Wolfgang."

"Hey maan. P- Train. That's cool your Seddy's boy from Trumbull."

"Yeah Seddy told me you're the man to see when I'm in Park City. I should be here all week trying to make some movie deals."

"100 bucks a gram."

"100?"

"Look where you are."

"Fuck it just give me one gram." I say and hand him a fresh 100 dollar bill.

I call Maddy and tell her what a great time I'm having and I tell her all about the movie stars mingling down here. I know this strikes a chord with her.

"I'm going to jump on a plane and come see you for the weekend." She says with determination.

"Maddy, I don't know if that is a good idea. I'm running out of money and all the rooms are all booked up for Sundance. I'm only going to stay thru the weekend and start driving back on Monday. I met some locals and they said I could crash with them."

"Wolfgang I will be flying out tomorrow. Just pick me up in Salt Lake and I will make sure we have a hotel for the weekend."

"Maddy I think that would be great but that's a lot of traveling for a weekend. On the other hand I would love to see you."

"Ok Baby I will call you tonight with my plans I got to get back to work. Love you bye." She hangs up.

I knew there was no way she wasn't coming. She is a star fucker and this place is filled with stars. I continue drinking and doing blow all day, Meeting some real nice folk that are in the industry. I have the rented truck plastered with movie posters of the Mullet Uncut. I am handing out the movies for free because I was already warned by the police I cannot sell anything on the street without a permit.

I get so fucked up I forgot that I had one more night left in the Inn. I sleep or try to in the rented Isuzu. Its soo fucking cold I can't believe I survived. I have eighty bucks left to my name and I need gas money to get back to Hollywood. I start drinking at 10 am. I remember something about being at the airport for 1pm but I can't remember the flight number. I am pretty fucked up when I bump into Maddy. She walked right up to me and I didn't even notice.

"Wolfgang? Wolfgang, Hiiii." She hugs me and smells me. " You don't look so good. Wolfgang are you fucked up already? It's only 1 in the afternoon. You look like shit and what's with the beard? Can you drive?"

"Hey Baby, of course I can drive, let me grab your bags."

"I got us a room downtown so we can walk to everything." She said.

"How did you do that? I tried everywhere and everything is all booked up."

"My sister has connections." She smiles.

"Really, what does that mean she's in the mob?"

"Nooo.. These hotels have rooms put aside for the more exclusive crowd and my sister is a part of that."

"Maddy what the fuck does that mean? Whatever. I don't care, I think you might have to drive I'm too fucked up and I need sleep.
"Wolfgang again? Why do you keep doing this?"
I pull over and let Maddy drive after she punches me in the face and swelling up my left eye.

At the hotel and Maddy is showering and I'm trying not to sober up. I keep guzzling the little shot bottles in the fridge. I then decide to go thru Maddy's purse. I see that she has vicodent and I take 2. When she gets out of the shower she comments on my dirty clothes and scruffy beard. She tells me again she doesn't like it. This pisses me off and I decide not to shower or shave.

We end up at a high end restaurant that I can't afford. She is in awe with all the celebrities. I could give a fuck, I'm just trying to calm the raging demons inside. I don't eat and I act rude to the waiter that my girlfriend is flirting with.
"Have you made any contacts?" she says.
"Umm No."
"Well what have you been doing here the last three days? I thought you told me on the phone you were making connections and hitting private parties."
"Maddy when did I talk to you on the phone?"
"Wolfgang I swear to god. You better straighten your ass up or I'm outta here."
"Maddy. I was kidding. Of course I remember." I put my hand inside the jacket pocket and pull out a bunch of business cards. "Look at all these, when I get back to Hollywood I got to start making phone calls. Come on Maddy don't get pissy, I will straighten up. Look I will try to get us into the party across the street."

She smiles and continues eating and then picks up the tab. I'm fucked up and my Dr. Jekyll Mr. Hyde personality comes out.
It's snowing and we are waiting in line for twenty minutes. When we get to the door, I can see Ray Liotta and Matt Dillon from where I am standing.
"Private Party," the doorman says
I look around "Hey Guy. No its not. Why are people waiting in line for a private party? I don't see any signs anywhere stating its private."
"Have you been drinking sir?"
"No." I don't drink." I say but I know he can smell the alcohol on my breath.

"We refuse the right to let anyone enter this establishment if we feel they have consumed too much alcohol. But your girlfriend is welcome."

"Ehh What!" The rage is being sprinkled with gas.

Maddy walks in without me and yells "I will meet you back at the Hotel later."

I'm dumbfounded.

I pick up the trash can that's on the side walk and hurl it into the side of a truck. The cops were sitting across the street when they saw this happen. I avoided being arrested because the truck that I damaged happened to be the one I rented. The cops tell me to get back to my hotel or they will arrest me for public intoxication.

I do.

I go thru Maddys luggage and find her billfold of credit cards and I take 2 more of her vicodents. I take one visa card out and put it in my wallet, I put everything back. I order porn to the room and passout fully clothed on the bed.

I wake up in wet pants and my jacket is still on. Maddy is on the other side of the bed, I don't think the piss hit her yet. I go out to the rented Isuzu and see I huge gash on the back passenger side door. What a cheap piece of shit. I know I have half a joint hidden in here, somewhere. I lift up the floor matt and find a little baggie with a line a coke in it. I must have put it there in fucked up state of mind.

I do it.

I walk back to the hotel room and open up the mini bar. This awakens Maddy.

"Are you kidding me Wolfgang?" She says as my head is tilted all the way back as I am sucking back a shot of Jim beam.

"I don't kid around baby. What time did you get in last night?"

She just looks at me and at this moment I can tell she is contemplating our relationship.

"Wolfgang you don't remember?" she says calmly.

"I was sleeping babe."

Maddy gets up and opens the bathroom door "Look." she says.

"Holy Shit."

The vanity is pulled off the wall, the mirror has a huge crack in it. The toilet seat is missing and the shower curtain is in a ball in the tub.

"What the fuck happened?" I yell.

"Why don't you open the door and look down the hallway. You really have problems Wolfgang."

I open the door to the hallway and turn my head left. I see the toilet seat lodge in the ceiling about fifteen yards down.

"What the fuck were you doing last night?"

"ME. "She yells.

"You are an animal, First you accuse me of cheating on you because I went into the party. I only stayed an hour and when I came back you were sleeping then an hour later I wake up and you're trashing the bathroom, screaming at me calling me a whore and a slut"

"No. Really?"

"Yes Wolfgang, really. You were so out of control security came up here and warned you."

"What did I do?"

"You calmed down until they left and then five minutes later you ripped off the toilet seat and hurled down the hall. Then you quietly shut the door and laid back down to sleep."

"I guess I was pissed that my girlfriend leaves me out in the cold and walks into a party without me. I was so pissed I don't even remember. My sub conscience took over." "Wolfgang I didn't come all this way to watch you self-destruct. And in case you forgot I got the room. So if you want to continue to act like an animal I swear I will have you tossed out of here and I will never speak to you again,"

"I'm sorry baby." I lean towards her and she pushes me away. "I'm not touching you unless you shave that rat on your face and please take a shower and throw those clothes out."

"Maddy I don't know what happened to me over the last few days. I'm losing it for some reason. I am becoming angry. I want to kill someone Maddy. I swear that drive up here might have fucked with my head. I can't think straight"

"Wolfgang, maybe you should stop drinking and taking whatever you're taking. I don't like this side of you."

I shave and shower and Maddy bought me new clothes, ones that fit her taste. I could care less about a $200 shirt and $457 wool marc Jacobs coat, on sale. I looked good for a guy with no cash in his pocket and 31 dollars combined on 3 credit cards.

We spend the afternoon shopping and seeing movies and eating and mingling. Then we stop in the pub in the center of the strip. A fire is blazing and the place is toasty warm and filled with beautiful Hollywood people. I can't control myself and order a beer. Maddy grabs a seat next to the fireplace and immediately encages in conversation with the stylish women around her.

Maddy looks at me.

"Just one. Relax." I then motion to the bartender.

"Can I start a tab, I'm sitting right there with my girlfriend and she has my cards in her purse." "What do ya need?" She says. I figure she thinks no one is going to walk out on her, she is trusting.

"4 pints of the local Lager and put Maddy as the name on the tab." She puts down four pints and I take two and walk off in the crowd towards the bathroom.

"I will be right back." I yell. Before I reach the back of the room, I have already killed one pint. I take a leak and kill the second. I fight my way back to the bar and grab the other two.

"What's your name" I ask.

"Shawna."

"Thank you Shawna. I'm Wolfgang and I'll be right over there." I point with my elbows.

"If you want I can send someone over when you're done so you don't have to keep getting up." She says with a smile.

"Thanks Shawna." I sit down next to Maddy and hand her a pint and she shoots me this don't fuck around stare at me.

"Wolf gang I would like you to meet Allison and Julie and Kate and I'm sorry, what's your husband's name?" she says. I pay no attention. I smile and wave my hand.

"Hi, I'm Wolfgang Klein." The chic Julie is so stunning I can't speak or stop staring at her.

Maddy whispers in my ear." Baby pleeaase don't drink anymore I like you now, when you're sober. You look good too, so don't ruin it." I kiss her on the cheek and I'm grinning and I whisper back. "I'm just going to drink beer. I'm done with hard alcohol and drugs, it turns me into a beast and baby I like you too much to lose you." This makes her happy for some reason. I do not know why. She is nuts.

The pub is getting more and more crowded and now we have table service. This is good and bad. Good I don't have to fight the mob at the bar to get a drink. Bad because I have to piss like a dog and I can't see myself leaving the spot I'm in, next to the warm and toasty fire place. I can see Maddy is feeling better and she has a buzz on and she is disappearing in the crowd for 15 minutes at a time. I don't give a fuck. I see my chance and take it. I pull my cock out of the zipper so just the head is barely peeking thru. I take my empty pint glass and casually hold it in front of my cock. Everything looks pretty normal.

I turn toward the fireplace so my back is facing the crowd and I fill up that pint glass so fast. I had to put it down. So I wasn't thinking and forgot where I was and I poured the pint of piss on the fire. It didn't put the fire out. It made piss steam. By the time the staff came over I was all cleaned up and explained to them that the guy wearing the denim coat knocked his beer into the fire. The guy was already loud and fucked up so I figured it was easy to blame him. They tossed his ass out and I walk off into the crowd to find Maddy.

"I had enough. I'm going back to the hotel." I whisper in her ear.
"Really Wolfgang? Whyy? I'm having sooo much fun."
"You can stay, I don't feel right I need to lie down and I can see you having too much fun being the center of attention with these dick heads." I slap her on her ass and kiss her cheek and walk out of the pub.

I'm starting to lose my mind slowly. I know this girl is bad news and my rage is always ignited when near her. I have moments of clarity which throw me into a deep depression.

I am curled up under the covers in the hotel in the dark. I can't relieve the pain. My head is going to explode. I get up and rummage thru Maddy's toiletries and find sleep aids, I eat 4 of them.

"What time did you get in last night?"
"I came in an hour and a half after you maybe and you were sleeping I couldn't wake you up.Sooo I went back out with some friends." I turn my head toward her.
"Are you fucking kidding me? Friends? What friend's Maddy? Those slobs you were talking to at the bar. Really? Let me see your phone?" I get out of bed and grab it.
"Wolfgang, give me that phone now or I swear to god I will call hotel security and have your ass thrown in jail. I know you have no money. So be nice."
"Fuck you Maddy. Don't turn this shit around. What friends? Maddy guys just want to fuck you because you have fucking whore written all over your face." I throw the phone at her.
"I'm done with you, I'm leaving, fuck you. You whore." I already have my clothes so I just go to brush my teeth and as I walk to the bathroom she throws her phone at my face and splits the corner of my other eye. I

over react. I fall on the ground covering my face and I don't say a word I'm just groaning and letting the blood cup in my hands and I smear on my face to make it look worse than it is. I get up on one knee and stumble into the bathroom.

"Wolfgang, I'm sorry." I hear this but I'm not sure if I'm imaging it. I'm brushing my teeth as the blood is trickling down my face. "Wolfgang I'm sorry." I see Maddy in the mirror.

"I'm sorry Baby your right I shouldn't have gone back out." She says.

I turn towards her. "What do you mean I'm right? Did you fuck somebody?"

"Nooo."

"Did you suck someone's dick?"

"Wolfgang." I can see I'm pushing it now.

"Well what do you mean I'm right, what happened last night?" I can feel the rage brewing.

"Calm down, I'm just saying I should of stayed in with you because I'm your my boyfriend and your right those guys were all over me last night buying me drinks and I'm really hung over now.."

"Maddy did you touch any one last night with any part of your body."

"Noo. Now stop it." I can see she is pissed. "I'm sorry too." I grab her into me and I just hold on.

I need some sort of stability. I need Elizabeth to be here. I walk her back into bed and some reason we are both turned on and we have make up sex. Later on that afternoon I dropped her off at the airport and I convinced her to give me five hundred bucks. I told her I will drive to San Francisco in a week and I will have her cash. She trusted me. I make it to Las Vegas without sleeping and I'm beat to shit. I get a room at the hard rock for real cheap and start to gamble.

I don't drink; I'm too fucked in the head because the car ride mentally killed me. I make $1150 in three hours and go to bed. The next day I take off bright and early to L.A. I drop off the SUV in the parking lot of the rental place. I leave the keys inside and walk away. I don't want to deal with problems that will arise if I stick around with this damaged truck and bunk credit cards.

Alan picks me up walking down Melrose.

The wrap party started at 8pm. I'm still in my apartment waiting for this make-up artist chic to show up. I walk over to the bar and decide to make myself a drink. Vodka and soda with 3 ice cubes. I promise myself I will not get overly fucked up in front of work people. I don't have much money in my pocket or the bank for that matter. The party has free alcohol and finger foods.

Great.

Kristen is the Make-up artist for the T.V show I worked on. She has jet black hair with bangs, small boobs and a big butt. Taller than me and a huge nose. She's perfect. I like watching her do coke with that huge shnoz. I fucked her once and afterwards told her I feel real bad because I have a girlfriend in San Francisco. She actually felt bad for me and we became just work friends. But tonight I'm going to try to fuck her again. If she lets me. I see her pull up to my apartment building in her Mercedes from my balcony I walk inside to buzz her in.

"Finally" I say as I open the door.

She kisses me on the cheek and walks in and throws her shit down on my couch and walks over to the bar.

"I can't believe the traffic. Every day any time of day the 101 is a nightmare." She pulls out a baggie of blow and starts chopping it on the bar.

"Do you want one?"
"Hell No. I don't want to be around work people when I'm all geeked out. Keep that shit away from me."
"I'm work people" she says." "You're different."

"Why"
"Because I fucked you. Now hurry up with that crap and let's get going." I grab my wallet and keys.

I let her drive just in case I decide to get whacked.
"Are you really leaving in six weeks to New York?" "Who told you that?"
"I overheard you talking to Fernando you asked him if he had any New York contacts or connections he could help you out with."
"I don't know if I'm going, my girlfriend is moving there for her job and she is begging me to go. I haven't made up my mind yet."
"Are you going to marry this girl?"
"Uh I think she thinks so."
Kristen looks at me and I smile.
"Really Kristen I don't know what I'm going to do. I like L.A and I like New York it's a tough decision."
"If you weren't with your girlfriend would you be considering moving back?"
"No."

"I guess the question is how much do you like or love this girl." "Shut-up." I snap back.

"The question is I need to get another job very very soon or I am fucked. I have only about a month left before I kill my account. I need work if I am going to stay here. I know you have some contacts Kristen. Hook me up. "
"I will keep my ears open for ya." She says.

We pull into The Firm and up to the valet. I don't wait for Kristen, I walk in alone. I don't want to be seen with her. People will get the wrong idea. I get lost in the crowd and start mingling with some co- workers.
I am Bored.
I hate all these people deep down inside.
Pretentious, shallow, reality TV, egotistical jerk offs. Uncreative people.
I make my way to the bar and grab the only empty seat in the corner. I order a drink and sit back.
I'm thinking about getting nice and juiced and have Kristen find me at the end of the night.
I am going to Drink my problems away tonight.
"Excuse me" she says when I notice her.
"Can I just squeeze in here to order a drink?" "Yeah. Sure". I move my chair over.

This girl looks young, she has short brown hair, cut like a boy. She is wearing a black mini skirt and a men's white V-neck t shirt. Her tits are huge. She has olive skin. I think she might be part Mexican but she's not fat. She is petite and has a huge smile. She smells good. If her diamond earrings are real they look very expensive. She is put together well. I like her.
She orders her drink turns and smiles at me.
"Hi." I say
She doesn't respond. She turns back around.
I tap her on her shoulder.
"Hey what's your name?"
She grabs her drink from the bartender and turns towards me.
"Suzzana."
"Hello Suzzana. I'm Wolfgang"
"Hello."
"How come I don't remember seeing on any of the shoots Suzzana?"
"I don't work in television, my cousin Fernando invited me."
"Fernando's your cousin?"
"Yessss."
"How nice. Fernando is a good guy."

"What do you do?"

"I am a school teacher in Glendale, the 4th grade."

"Cool. What are ya drinking?"

"Gin."

"GIN. Are you fucking nuts? I can't even smell gin nevermind drink it. I used to drink tons of it in my youth."

"Your youth? How old are you now?"

"30. And you. How old are you?"

"I will be 26 in July."

"Really because you look younger than 26."

She smiles.

"Do you have a boyfriend?"

"That was quick.."

"Well depending on your answer will determine the rest of my night. If you say that Yes you are seeing someone and you're not interested in me. Then I'm going to leave this shitty party and go to bed, because these people here disgust me. If you say NO that you don't have a boyfriend then I'm gonna try to convince you to give me your number."

"You're Nuts." She says.

"So what is it? Boyfriend, no boyfriend. Lover, partner. What?"

"I'm still standing here listening to you." "Ok that's a good sign. Do you live in Glendale? "Yes."

"That's a drive from West Hollywood. Are you going to be alright driving back tonight?"

"I should be."

"Not if you keep drinking those glasses of Gin you won't."

"You have nothing to worry about Wolfgang."

Fernando walks up and kisses his cousin." Are you hitting on my cousin?" he says to me.

"I'm trying but she won't budge."

"Good stay away from this guy. You can see in his eyes he is the devil."

The two of them start laughing and speaking Spanish.

Fernando than hugs me and kisses me on the cheek and walks off.

"Fernando said you were a good guy and too bad you're straight."

"Ha Ha. Are you from Mexico?"

"No. Why?"

"Where did you learn your Spanish?"

"People learn Spanish in school.."

"Yes I know but you and your cousin I thought were part Mexican."

"We're Cuban."

"Cuban?"

"Yes my Parents and relatives came over in the Seventies I am the first generation born here."

"Holy Shit that's pretty cool. Do ya wanna get drunk?"

Suzzana laughs and I order two shots of Jaeger.

" No. No,No. I don't do shots."

"Me neither."

The bartender lines up 2 shots and I give her one.

"Don't worry tomorrow is Saturday. School is OUT."

"Cheers" she says and throws it back.

I stand up from my chair and take her hand and guide her into the seat.

"I don't me to be rude I should have offered the seat to you sooner."

I can see she is impressed.

"Bartender 2 more."

"Wolfgang, No. I have to be responsible. I can't. Really I won't."

"No problem, you don't have to." I throw back both of them.

"So what did you do for Fernando, on the show?"

"I was a production coordinator."

"I know nothing about television. I'm just proud to see my cousin succeeding."

"Yeah Fernando is a good guy but reality TV isn't my thing. I came out to L.A to sell a movie I made and in the mean time I need to work. Fernando isn't a bad guy to work for."

I ask her if she will watch my seat while I run to the men's room. She says yes. I walk into the crowd searching for Kristen.

Then I get my ass grabbed.

"Where have you been? You left me at the entrance." Kristen says.

"I was just looking for you. I turned around at the door and you were gone. I'm on my way to the men's room, can I see that thing?"

"What thing?" she yells.

I lean over to her ear and yell "cocaine."

Kristen jumps back "You're an asshole you know that"

"I do."

Kristen goes into her handbag and non-discreetly pulls out a vile and hands it to me.

"Wolfgang just do a little. It's not mine, its someone else's."

I pretend I don't hear her as I already walked away.

I do a few key shots in the stall and sneak back to the bar without Kristen seeing me.

Suzzana is onto another drink.

"Is that water?" I ask her.

She laughs. I pull the drink towards me and smell it.

"Holy Shit. What is that? Smells like rubbing alcohol."

"Gin." She giggles.

"Gin? Are you sure.? You must be drinking the cheap shit. Good luck with that."

Suzzana puts her hand in mine and asks me if I would like to dance.

"I don't dance .I'm white"

"Come on Dance with me."

When she gets off the chair she stumbles

"Suzzana you look a little drunk. I don't think you should be driving back to Glendale. I'm going to get Fernando."

"I'm fine. My heel got caught on the chair."

"Bullshit. I'll let Fernando decide."

"Ok so maybe I'm a little buzzed. But don't ruin Fernando's night with some bullshit like this Wolfgang"

"I wouldn't I'm just fuckin with you. But I still don't think you should drive. If you want I will drive you home."

I just remembered I don't have my car with me. I order a vodka soda and kill it.

I walk back to Suzzana and she is dancing by herself in the corner, she looks good. I hand her a proper Gin and Tonic.

"Drink this."

I'm getting fucked up and ballsy so I take my arm and put it around her waist and pull her in close to me. We start making out.

She pulls me deeper into the corner and we are going at it. I'm positive my co-workers all saw what was happening. Fuck them.

"Where are your car keys?"

Suzzana pulls out a key from her pocket and starts dangling it in front me. I swipe it and grab her hand all in one motion. "Come on."

I walk her outside.

"Where is your car?"

She points across the street at an old Jeep.

"Let's go"

I drive. I pull into my parking garage and take my roommates spot.

"Crash for a little while on my couch and when you feel better you can take off."

I walk to her side of the jeep and lift her out of the seat. She starts kissing me again. I carry her to the elevator and all the way to my door. I unlock the door and throw the keys on the bar.

"Suzzana walks over to the couch and plops down.

"Do you have any pot?"

I don't say a word I go behind the bar and pull out the bong and tray of weed. I pack it for her and go into the kitchen. She pulls a few tubes and comes back to life for a moment.

"You live here by yourself?

"I have a roommate but he is never around. Are you hungry?"

"No but can I have a glass of water." she says

"Yeah, I'm going to cut up some fruit. Are you sure?"

She doesn't say anything.

I walk out of the kitchen and I see her passed out sitting up.

Poor Girl.

I lay her down and throw a blanket on her and go to bed.

I'm woken up around 5am by Suzzana climbing into my bed and putting her arm around me. I can feel her bare tits against my back. I turn around and we start going at it. She's rubbing and stroking me but won't let me take off her g string. I keep trying every three minutes figuring she is going to give in. She doesn't. We fall back to sleep.

I'm at the diner at noon. Suzzana is sitting across from me. We don't talk for a period of time. No big deal we just don't say anything until our food comes out.

"What are you going to do the rest of the day Wolfgang?"

"I don't know. I was thinking on going to Venice for a while. But traffic is already a bitch."

"Do you want to see where I live, in Glendale?"

Without hesitating I say "Yes,. Yes I do."

"Good then I don't have to drive you back to your apartment. You can come with me now and I will drop you off later"

"What are we going to do?"

"I have a big backyard with a grill and fire pit, we can go shopping for Food and Wine and I will cook for you."

"I'm in Baby." I give her a kiss.

It takes about an hour to get to her house. She lives in a cul-de-sac, Surrounded by a wooded area. Lots of privacy and trees. Her house is small and quaint she decorates well, like a gypsy.

"I like being out here it reminds me of back East. It's so quiet and smells better than the city."

"I like living out here. My school is close by and the area is generally safe. It's nice."

I bring in the bags of groceries and when I get to the kitchen she attacks me and we go at it again. I can feel how wet she is but she won't let me in. Damn her. I need to release.

I walk into her bathroom and immediately go for the medicine cabinet. Nothing there. I open up her closet and riffle thru some first aid kits Nothing. Fuck. I flush the toilet and walk out into her living room. Suzzanna has a bong out with a pile of weed next to it. I'm happy and I crack open a bottle of cabaret sauvignon. "Try these I made them 3 days ago" She hands me a brownie. I take one bite and I know they are laced with pot. I'm in heaven.

I wake up from a weed nap and Suzzana is on her phone speaking Spanish. I don't understand so I pack the bong again and walk outside. There is a fire going. I fall asleep on the lawn chair.

"Wolfgang, Wolfgang?"

"I'm outside."

"Hey you how was your nap? I have a few relatives coming by. I hope you don't mind."

"What? Is Fernando coming over?"

"No not Fernando but his sisters and my brother and his wife."

"Really that's great."

Bullshit I am stuck here. What the fuck.

"How are you going to introduce me? As a friend? and if so where did we meet and when? You know they are going to ask me. Or should I say I met you last night in a bar."

"No, No I will tell them I met you on Fernando's set a few weeks ago and we have been hanging out since."

"Cool. I'm really having a good time being with you Suzzana. I'm glad you invited me along. I was just thinking we never exchanged numbers?"

She laughs.

The Sun sets and everyone is having a goodtime, drinks are flowing and joints are flying. More and more people showed up at her house, mostly family. Her aunts and cousins, mother and uncle and I can feel myself slowly crossing over to the dark side. I should slow down on the drinking. Suzzanas hot slutty 21 year old cousin Maria has been giving me fuck me eyes all night. Every time I sit down some where she joins me. As she talks to me her hand is on my knee or on my shoulder or touching my hair. I can feel the vibe. Suzzana can sense what's going on and grabs my hand and we walk into the front yard. She pulls out a joint and lights it up.

My cell phone is vibrating again. I don't want to look at it because I know it's Maddy.

"Wolfgang let me ask you a question."

"Shoot."

"Do you have a girlfriend?

"I already told you No."

"Do you think I'm stupid?"

'Come on now Suzzana, where are you going with this?

"You don't think I noticed your phone has been buzzing all day and you don't answer it..."

"Well Suzzana because the time I spend with you is special and I don't want to waste a minute dealing with business when I'm with you." I smile "Aw is this our first fight.."

WHACK

She slaps me hard on the cheek.

"BULLSHIT. You're lying to me already."

"Suzzana, calm the fuck down. What's wrong with you?"

I need to be cool before this chic blows her Cuban lid. And her crazy Cuban family comes after me.

"I looked at your phone while you were sleeping before. I didn't mean to it just kept vibrating and I didn't know how to shut it off. The name Madison kept calling you. Who is Madison?"

"Suzzana .Relax. That's my Agent; she's probably got an interview lined up for me."

"So why don't you answer the phone?

"I just told you I don't want to waste any time with anything but you."

We start making out and she grabs my hand and leads me into the house thru the front door, people are scattered and not paying attention. She brings me into her bedroom and shuts the door. There is no lock so she presses her back against the door and unbuckles my pants. She starts blowing me. Right there.

I can hear people in the hallway and kitchen.

Suzzana stands up and pulls off her shorts to reveal a shaved box. She puts one leg on my shoulder and inserts me into her. I can't believe this is happening.

"It turns me on to fuck this close to people and public places." She whispers in my ear as she digs her nails into my neck. I am banging away and the door is taking the beating. Suzzana is moaning and I can hear the people in the kitchen clearly so I'm positive they can hear her.

KNOCK. KNOCK.

I hear a male voice in Spanish.

KNOCK. KNOCK.

"Who is that" I say softly.

Suzzana starts yelling in Spanish and her cousin goes away. She starts biting my neck and that makes me cum instantly. Inside. I pump as hard as I can, making as much noise as possible until I hear her scream and scratch the fuck out of my back. I give her a minute and wipe the sweat from her lip and my forehead.

I leave and walk into the back yard. She disappears into the bathroom. I shut my phone off and take out the battery. Madison is going to flip if she isn't flipping already, I told her I might drive up the coast this week and meet up with her in San Francisco. But I get the idea the Cuban isn't going to leave my side.

I sit in a lawn chair by the fire I don't understand a word these people are saying. I take the cork out of a bottle of wine that was sitting next to me. It's more than half way filled. I put it up to my lips and don't put it down until it's empty. What few people that are left are abit taken back. I don't give a shit and smile and light up a smoke. My mind is racing with thoughts of money. How can I get my hands on some and soon? What am I doing sitting in a backyard filed with Cubans at 1 am in the morning. Where is Suzzana?   I move on to some cheap rum and start swigging that out of the bottle. The rest of the Cubans leave after this. I piss on the fire and shut off all the lights. Suzzana is fast asleep in her bed.

"Baby. You awake?"

She rolls over and pulls me into bed.

"I just wanted to say thank you for staying tonight and I'm sorry about that slap."

"No worries Baby." I kiss her.

"I need to get back to Hollywood early tomorrow. Is that cool?"

She puts her arm around me and mumbles "Sure."

I lay awake in bed. I'm all alone with my conscience. My mind won't shut down. The same question keeps repeating itself over and over in my head. What are you going to do? What are you going to do about EVERYTHING? Am I ever gonna sell this movie?

I hate Reality Television and everyone involved in it.

Should I stay in California and dump Maddy. Let her go to New York alone? If I could get a job in the next five days, I still won't get a check for at least 3 weeks.

I owe Alan rent.

Will my antics from my last job prevent me from landing another gig?
I hope not.

Maddy does make a lot of cash and she WILL set us up in a nice pad in Manhattan. My friends and family are there. Do I even like this crazy chic or is it because she's hot and horny and looks good and makes a lot of loot. She likes sex more than I do but she is too much of a control freak and I can't trust her.

This Cuban chic I lay next to is pretty damn hot. So is Maddy. But Maddy ain't Cuban. Fuck Maddy for now, she's a superficial name dropping slut.
But So am I.
This day I am going to let the cards fall as they may.
I don't remember sleeping. Suzzana wakes up and in a second and starts riding me. I like this girl.

We get back to my apartment in West Hollywood and Alan is there. It's around 5pm.
"Alan what's up man? This is Suzzana. I met her at the MTV wrap party.
"Hello Alan." She says.
Alan shakes her hand. "Nice to meet ya Suzzana."
"I haven't seen you in a long time bro, I heard Zowie hooked you up with a job."
"Yeah. We'll talk about it later. What's going on tonight?" I say as I sit on the couch.
"Well if you and the lovely Suzzana want to accompany me to a party in the hills you guys are welcome. It should be pretty big, it starts now. Tons of food and drink. It's a catered cookout. You know industry people."
I ask Suzzana if she will walk to Urth Café on the corner and crab me a coffee. I hand her money and walk her to the door before she says anything.
Alan waves me into the Kitchen.
Look what I smuggled in from Bermuda.
He pulls out 3 grams of yellow rock/powder. I know what it is.
"You took this on the plane?"
"Yeah, I packed it in my checked luggage and forgot about it and now its here."
"You're fucked up." I pour myself a drink.
"What's with Madison calling me looking for you? How did she even get my number?" He says squinting.

"She what?? That bitch went thru my phone. I knew she was crazy but what the fuck. I wonder who else she called. FUCK. Give me your phone."
I dial her number and it fucking rings forever and goes into voicemail.
"FUCK"
I press redial. and it goes straight back into voicemail. Good I will leave a message and not have to deal.
"Hey Baabbyy. I just wanted to let you know I lost my phone and wallet two days ago. I would have called you sooner but I didn't have your phone number memorized. Thank god you called Alan and he saved the number. He just got back from Bermuda and gave me the message. I will straighten out my banking and lost credit cards when the banks open tomorrow and I will buy a new phone and give you a call in the afternoon. OK BABY miss you." I hang up.
"I am going to take a shower. If she calls back, you tell her you're out and you won't see me till tomorrow. "Got it Einstein?"
"Yeah. Yeah. I'll be right here grinding the fuck out this shit."
"I don't know if Suzzana is cool with that."
"Don't worry about it."
I take off my clothes and I hear Alan's phone ring. I turn on the shower and jump in under the hot water. I am mentally beat.
I don't want to drink.
I don't want to smoke.
I don't want to fuck.
I don't want to eat.
I don't want to talk to anyone.
Thoughts of killing myself won't escape me.
I need money. How the fuck am I going to get it?
I need to press my Agent harder. I will tell her I will take any job for any price. I just need to work.
As I walk out of the bathroom and cross over into my bed room I glance to my left and I see Suzzana bend over the bar doing a line. Alan catches my eye and smiles. I get dressed. I'm wearing 1973 polyester bright red golf shirt, a white V-neck t-shirt and black slacks.
"Alan I need you to call everyone you know for me tomorrow. I need a job by the end of the week or I'm busted. Busted. Busted..Suzzana I didn't know school teachers did blow..." I say sarcastically.
"I'm Cuban."
"Oh. OK that makes perfect sense."
"Alan thanks but no thanks. I'm not going to the cookout. I don't feel up to it."

"Here."

Alan hands me the plate of blow. I push it back.

"No dude. I'm beat. I need to get my head together. I want to be productive tomorrow."

"Good. I'm glad. I do have to teach in the morning." Suzzana says.

"Then why the fuck are you sniffing cocaine?"

"I told you baby, I'm Cuban."

Alan laughs and Suzzana smiles as she bends over the plate with the straw up her nose.

"I'm going up the road to the Saddle Ranch. I'm going to have one drink and maybe a burger then I'm coming straight home and going to bed."

"Yeah right one drink. I heard all your bullshit before. Just shut up and do this." Alan puts the plate under my nose. I take it and throw it on the table.

"Watch me dude. No drinking for me tonight. I will be home by 10."

"Right. I won't be here anyway. I will talk to you tomorrow."

Alan leaves. Suzzana goes behind the bar and pulls out two shot glasses and the bottle of Jack.

She pours.

"Suzzana you just heard me tell Alan I'm not drinking." "This is from me Baby; did you think three days ago you would be spending all weekend with me?"

"No."

"Then this is to us." She raises the shot and kisses me on the lips before she throws it down her throat.

I throw it back. Suzzana comes around the bar and hugs me.

"You make me really happy Baby."

"When did we start calling each other Baby? Baby,"

She laughs "You started it. I was shocked the first night when you called me baby and after only 2 hours of knowing each other."

"You're right. It has been a great weekend"

"Let's go grab a bite to eat and come back early and get into bed."

Suzzana freshens up in the bathroom. I pour one more shot. Turn out the lights and grab my keys.

"I can't believe you're from California. You live in the Valley and you've never been to the Saddle Ranch?"

I press the elevator buttons.

"I've seen it before, just never went in. Always too crowded and I never go out in Hollywood or on the strip for that matter."

"I like it. It's close by. It's touristy but I don't care. The place is always packed."

The elevator opens up in the parking garage.

"I thought we were going to walk." She says.

"Nope, Get in." I open her door for her.

The strip is unusually lively for a Sunday night. I don't valet. I park on Havenhurst. The walk from my car to the bar is almost as far as my apartment. The 2 shots I did back at my pad took the edge off and made me get my appetite back for drinking.

Suzzana takes hold of my hand as we are walking down Sunset.

"Do you think we will see each other again after tonight?"

I look at her and smile.

"Why would you say that?"

"I'm afraid once I leave for work in the morning. I won't see you again. We haven't left each other's side since we met. And I hate to think this but I get the feeling that you have these little 2, 3 day romances all the time."

Traffic is very loud and the sidewalks are crowded.

"Are you kidding me, now you bring this up. On the street. In public. Those drugs fuck you up?"

"No. I was just thinking." She says quietly as we are waiting for the light to change.

"Suzzana everything is cool don't worry. If you want to sleep over tomorrow night too, you can or if you want me to sleep at your place, I will. Whatever you want me to do. I will. I just want to make you happy." She puts her arms around my shoulders and gives me a strong hug. I kiss her on the cheek, grab her hand and walk across the street into the parking lot of the Saddle Ranch.

The line out the door is filled with a bunch of tourists, actor/model wannabees, and Orange County cheese heads.

"No way am I waiting in this fucking line." I mumble to myself.

"What was that?" Suzzana says.

"Stay right here I will be right back." I walk up to the big black brother at the door.

"What up man? Do you recognize me? I live right down the road on Westbourne. I'm here a few times a month with my boys. Is Julie here?'

"She's waiting tables tonight."

"Good I came to eat with my lady and I'm starving, can you put me in Julie's section."

I extend my hand as to shake his and he does the same. When I make contact I slide a folded up twenty in his huge palm. He glances at it and lets me in the door. I motion over Suzzana. The brother tells the hostess to sit us in Julie's section.

I don't know any Julie.

I don't know anyone that works here.

I grab Suzanna's hand and walk thru the main room with the mechanical bull and straight outside onto the deck facing Sunset Blvd. The hostess seats us at a round table for twelve.

I don't know why.

We sit side by side each other at this huge circular table, while people are jammed in every standing space available. Our Waitress Julie shows up and looks a little confused.

"Hey Julie. How are ya?

"Hi Guys" she says back.

I wink at her.

"Do you guys want to order drinks first?"

"Yes we do. I would like a Cadillac. And the young lady would like.." Suzanna looks up and holds up two fingers.

"I guess we'll take two Cadillacs

Julie looks at me.

"I want to start a tab but I will tip you in cash". I hand her a twenty, she smiles and walks off to get our drinks.

"What's a Cadillac?" Suzzana asks.

"Why did you order it if you didn't know what it was."

"It's a Huge Margarita served in a half carafe topped off with… I don't know. It comes with oranges and lemons".

"I love Margaritas." Suzzana says as she cuddles into my shoulder.

Julie comes back with the drinks. "Are you guys ready to order?"

"Not yet let me enjoy this drink and keep looking at the menu for a bit."

"OK but I'm going to have to hold on to a credit card if you're drinking and running a tab."

"No problem." I hand her a credit card. The credit card I gave her is bunk it hasn't worked in a year, but the expiration date is still valid.

"Julie. When I get the bill later on, let me see it before you run it. I might want to pay cash, depending on the total."

"Oh sure" She says politely. "I'll come back and check on you guys in a few minutes."

Suzzana is rubbing my thigh under the table. I could see she is getting fucked up. We both split some appetizers and drank 3 or 4 Cadillacs each. The table is littered with empty plates and glasses. People passing by are putting their empties on my table. It's sort of pissing me off.

"Will you wake me in the morning?"

"You don't have an alarm? I wake up at the crack of dawn, just to let you know."

"No you don't. You haven't since I've been sleeping next to you."

"That's because we stay up late and I'm drinking. When I don't drink or party, I'm up when the sun rises."

"Yeah whens that?" Suzzana says laughing.

Out of nowhere this drunk dick sits down at my table and right next to Suzzana. He's fucked up.

I was going to kick him out when Suzzana says "Just let him sit, he's not bothering anyone."

"Yeah he looks pretty fucked up, I got to go to the Men's room. It might take a moment getting thru this mob scene. Make sure Drunk boy here doesn't do anything stupid." She kisses me on the cheek and I get up from the table and fight my way inside to the other end of the bar and wait in line to use the Men's room.

As I'm going thru my pockets I find a little vile half filled. I never gave it back to Kristen from The wrap party. I make my way into the stall and shut the door. I don't know why but I start shoveling Cocaine up my nose in a very quick manner. I spilled enough on my shirt where dudes noticed in the men's room and motioned to me to wipe it off. I'm fighting my way back to the table and my heart is racing. I can see Suzzana from afar and another dick just sat down at the table on the other side of Suzzana. I can't make it over there fast enough and my mind is turning into poison. I feel the rage instantly appear.

"You know this guy." I say directly to Suzzana.

"No he just sat down."

"Hey Buddy, you're in my seat talking to my lady."

I put my arm on the back of his chair as to help him out of it but he got the hint and left.

Suzzana smiles.

"You called me your lady."

"Yeah Yeah."

The other drunk dick keeps smoking my cigarettes I left on the table. Suzzana sees this. "Oh he's fine. I think his friends are over there." She points.

I never took a piss in the bathroom. I forgot and now I am ready to explode. Suzzana is leaning over the opposite way talking to the drunk jerkoff. I grab an empty carafe and hold it under the table while I fill it up with piss. I slowly put it back on the table without anyone noticing. I am pinching my cock to hold back the rest, and then I can't anymore and say fuck it and piss all over the floor. No one knows shit. I zip up my pants and push the drink towards the drunk. It looks perfect, fruit floating on top and there is even an old straw in it.

"Hey Buddy." The drunk dick looks at me and I motion at the drink I just put in front of him.

"The waitress brought one too many, so take it. On me." Suzzana looks confused. The drunk is staring at it. "Cheers Buddy" I tap his drink with mine. "Come on Buddy the least you can do is take a sip and act appreciative. After all, I let you sit at my table, you smoked my cigarettes, and I saw you touching my lady. Just take a sip. Cheers."

I don't take my eyes off him while I kill my drink. I see Suzzana out of the corner of my eye and wink at her. The drunk takes a sip. "Don't be a pussy." I say. He looks at me and licks his lips, "Don't be rude friend, drink it." He stands up. I stand up. I have a huge piss stain all the way down my leg. The drunk leaves the table with the Carafe of piss and I see him walk towards a group of Big Fucking Dudes.

"Did you just do what I think you did?" Suzzana says with a confused tone. I see the big dude smells it and this makes me smile and chuckle inside. Then all at once they look over at me while the drunk dick is pointing.

"Get up! Now!"

Suzzana can't see the Hurricane that's about to hit the table.

"What…"

WHACK. I crack the biggest dude in the head with an empty carafe. It does nothing. People are now pushing and scrambling.

I grab Suzzana underneath her armpit and help her out of the chair. I literally throw her over the railing onto the street. I see the bouncers going at with everyone. Mayhem breaks out for a minute. I go to jump over the railing to escape onto the street and this bigfucker tags me in the back of my head with something hard. Too hard to be his fists. I fall over the railing and Suzzana drags me onto the sidewalk.

I am trying to blend into the sidewalk traffic but I have a shit load of blood on the back of my shirt. I hear people scream in the background and when I turn around I see that big dude and his roided out friends running down Sunset. I grab Suzzana and throw her over my shoulder. I dart across the BLVD without looking and run into The Standard. I walk right in and head for the bathroom. Suzzana comes with me.

"SSHH. Ya think they saw us come in here."

"I barely saw anything. You were throwing me around so fast and everybody screaming, and you're bleeding and now we're in the bathroom at The

Standard. Do you make that guy drink your pee? That's disgusting." Suzzana whispers as she is cleaning the blood from my neck.

My heart is beating so fast and this reminds me I have narcotics in my pocket. I have visions of the door being kick in by the cops or the muscle bound meathead and his cronies. Either way it's not going to be good. I pull out the coke and I'm ready to flush it when Suzzana just looks at me. I can tell by her face she wants it. I take her hand and put it into a fist and then I pour out a huge mound in between her knuckles. She Does it 1, 2, 3. I pour out the rest on my knuckle and falls all over the place. I don't care. I do one huge bump and coke is all over my face. I take off my red golf shirt, wipe my face and neck. Suzzana flushes the toilet and I drop in the vile. We check each other's noses and leave the stall. I throw my shirt in the trash can and walk out into the lobby. Suzzana tells me to stay right here and walks away. I am trying to see if there are any cops outside and Suzzana grabs my hand and leads me out on to the street. She puts a cowboy hat on my head.
"Thanks. I don't even want to ask."
We walk towards my car and I can see all the sirens up the road in front of the Saddle Ranch.
"Fuck. We are going to walk to my apartment and fuck my car. I will get in the morning."
"Didn't you give the waitress your credit card?"
"Shit.Shit. Ah. Don't worry about. They will just run it and I will grab it tomorrow."

I'm thinking the police are definitely going to get involved once they realize my card is bunk. They have my name. They could be waiting for me in front my pad.
"Suzzana let's walk down Sunset to Mel's and grab some food."
I need my car. I figure I will wait for everything to calm down and walk back to my car.
"Good I'm hungry."
"How can you be hungry?"
"I'm just hungry."
"Wow I can't eat shit."
Suzzana orders chicken noodle soup. Go figure. My leg stars tapping endlessly on the diner floor. My mind is again going a million miles a minute. My heart is beating heavy.
"I'm going to leave for a while and clear my head.."
"Leave where?"
"Here, no .L.A. California. I have to get away for a while it's too corrupt for me."

"You're too corrupt for you" Suzzana says smiling.

Fuck you I'm thinking. But I just laugh "HA HA."

"I'm not hungry anymore."

"You just told the waitress you wanted soup 3minutes ago."

"I know but now I have cramps and I don't feel well. Can we just go home?"

"Home?" Really. "Alright stay here and eat your soup or don't. I am going to get the car and pull up in front." I stand up and throw eight bucks on the table and give Suzzana a kiss on the forehead and leave.

I had enough. I had enough of this chic. I had enough of this lifestyle. I had enough of L.A. I get to my car with no problem. I sit there and think should I pick her up? How much money do I have? Should I go to New York and live with Madison? I don't really like her either. Fuck.

I'm losing my mind.

I need money. I need sanity in my life.

I pull up and I see Suzzana waiting on the curb. She gets in.

"Everything O.K?"

"No problems Baby."

I pull down Westbourne ave and immediately stop and pull into a parking space on the right and shut off my lights.

"What's going on?"

"Look all the way at the end of the street."

"What? I don't see anything."

"You don't see the Sheriffs car parked in front of my building?"

"Is it?"

"Yeah, here." I take my apartment key off my key chain and give it to her.

"What are you going to do?"

"I don't know. Let me think about it."

I already thought about it and FUCK IT I'm outta here. Later to California.

"Wait for me in my apartment. I'm going to drive around the block and see if I can park and then sneak into the building."

"I don't believe you."

"Suzanna come on. Where do you think I'm going? You have my key. I just don't feel like getting arrested tonight. Please come on. I will see you in my bed in 15 minutes."

Suzanna kisses me and it starts to get passionate. I start getting turned on and now I'm contemplating if I should stay.

I'm fucking losing it.

"Give me your phone number." She says
"What?"
"You never gave me your phone number. We never exchanged numbers. What's your number?"

Suzzana is staring at me with her cell phone in hand. She knows. She knows she might never see me again. How the fuck does she know? I rattle off my number and I can see her starting to sniffle and tear up. "Come on Suzzana. I will see you in 15 minutes. Keep the bed warm for me."
We hug and she kisses me on the cheek and gets out of the car and walks up the road towards my apartment.

I take my cell phone out and turn it on. I call Alan and it goes right into voicemail.
"Al. What's up Dude? I'm leaving California, NOW. The sheriff's department is looking for me. And you know the deal. Suzzana is sleeping in my bed. Tell her the bad news for me and sell all my shit and keep the money for rent. Thanks for the ride it, was an experience. I will see you on the next run at it.Talk to you later bro."
I hang up.
I have $793 dollars, one pair of clothes and 800 DVDS of the Mullet uncut in my trunk.
I need weed.

I swing by my friend Nate's house, his lights are still on. I spend 100 dollars on a bag of the chronic and then jump on the interstate heading east. I drive for the night and pull of the road somewhere in Nevada to sleep for a few hours. When I wake up I plug in my phone and see all the messages from Madison and one from a new number. I am guessing its Suzanna's.
I don't even listen to Maddy's messages. I just call her.
"Your Alive" Is the way she answers the phone.
"Hey Baby. What a crazy weekend I had. How was yours? I feel like I haven't talked to you in weeks."
"Wolfgang. Are you alright? Where are you? I wasn't sure if you were bullshitting me about your phone. Then I tried to call Alan on his phone, and that constantly went into voicemail. I didn't know what to think."
"Alan was on a plane and I told you I lost my phone and wallet. Actually I'm pretty sure it was stolen at the wrap party. I had my shit in my jacket on the back of a chair that I wasn't attending to it. I should have known better."
"Are you home?" Why would she ask me that I'm wondering?
"I I'm in my car in Nevada."
I wait for it to register

"WHAT ARE YOU DOING IN NEVADA? Are you in VEGAS? I had a feeling you were up to something."

"Madison. Chill out."

I left this morning. I'm heading to New York. I had all weekend to think about it, since I had no money or phone. All I did was sit around my apartment trying to make these decisions. Should I go to New York with Maddy? Should I stay in L.A? Do I want to start a life with you? Do you really want me going with you? I had all these ideas going thru my head and I didn't know which one to go with. So, on the spur of the moment I made up my mind and jumped in my car and started heading east. It feels right. Ya know Maddy?

"You're going to New York for me??"

"Yes Baby. I want us to live together. I want us to take this to the next step."

"Oh Wolfgang you just made me so happy. So you WILL be in New York before me. Are you staying at your parents or do you want me to call my sisters and see if you can stay with them? I want us to pick out an apartment together. I am so excited. I going to call my sisters now and tell them the good news."

GREAT.

Whore.

We had gotten an apartment on MacDougall St. above a Mexican restaurant. It was a small one bedroom and it was littered with cockroaches. This irked Madison, she was not happy about the situation since she just signed a year lease. The cockroaches didn't show their face for the first month so we thought we had a clean pad. I could live with the roaches I just couldn't live with this douche bag of a women. The only thing she could talk about was high end pocket books and what movie stars her and her sisters fucked. I couldn't find work because I was fucked up all the time because I hated my girlfriend and my UN productive life. I was in a vicious cycle.

It's Wednesday evening and we are both spooning on the couch its 9:45 at night.

Her cell phone rings.

"Hello oh hii."

"Yes really. Is Peg going too?"

"Really, that's wonderful. O.K."

"I will call you when I'm leaving."

She hangs up the phone and gets up off the couch. I hear the water for the shower go on.

"Are you going somewhere?" I raise my voice.

She doesn't answer. My blood is beginning to boil. I am still lying on the couch.

"Maddy? Are you going somewhere? I say a little louder. I get off the couch and walk over to the bathroom and push the door open a little more than it was. I see Madison on her cell phone with her back towards me. I walk back out and take deep breaths. I am going to kill this fucking girl.

I kick the door open and it swings back into the wall and this startles Maddy.

"Did I get your attention now?" I scream.

"Why are you ignoring me?"

"I'm not."

"You're not. This apartment isn't that big Maddy. You're telling me you can't hear me."

"Get out of here." She pushes me back in to the kitchen.

"What are you doing that's so secretive?" I say.

She doesn't answer and I can hear the shower running. I take this opportunity to go thru her things. I rip apart her purse and leave everything on the floor. I see random business cards with hand written numbers on the back. I am pissed. She still won't answer me. I kick open the bathroom door again and she is getting out of the shower.

"Maddy just tell me who called you and why are you taking a shower at ten o'clock at night?"

"Fuck you. I'm not talking to you."

"Where are you going? Answer me."

She walks into the bedroom.

"You fucking asshole. What are you doing?"

"Well you won't fuckin answer me so I had to go and see what you're hiding."

"Why do have so many random business cards with cell numbers written on the back, Maddy?"

"Since when do Pharmaceutical reps deal with lawyers and graphic artists and this fucking actor guy?"

I throw the cards in her face.

"Maddy just tell me where you're going."

"I'm going out." "No shit."

"Peg is going to a party for the promotion for this movie her friend directed." "What?"

"Peg invited me."

"You're sisters a whore."

"Tell me again why you would leave your boyfriend, whom you were just snuggling with on the couch. Take a shower, blow dry your hair to go to a party where you have nothing in common with these people. You don't work in that industry. Who's at this party you want to see? Tell me what the fuck is going on before I kill you."

"My sisters a whore"... she says as she attacks me with a closed fist.

"Yup." I say as I grab her arms and toss her on the bed.

"Tell me why you are going to this party, who do you need to meet when your god damn boyfriend is here."

"Get out." She says and grabs a butter knife off the counter and points it two inches from my throat.

"Get out or I'm calling the cops."

"I already called them." I hear a voice say coming from the hallway. It's my half gay neighbor.

"You guys have been going at it for over 30 minutes and I'm trying to sleep. I look at Maddy." Really this is what it's come down to. Have fun at your fucking party. I grab my jacket and head out the door.

I kick my neighbor's door in and leave. I jump on the metro north train towards Connecticut.

It's not going as I planned. My life sucks I have no Money and I have no Job. I have no home, I'm sleeping on my cousin Gino's couch.
Every month I spend less time with Madison, It might be a week or a couple days. We have sex and then I get into this jealous rage when she insists on telling me about all her affairs. I was attracted to the rage she set off in me.

I'm at some nuvo Italian restaurant on the lower east side.
I'm meeting Madison there.
"Wow you look good" she says as she greets me at the table.
"I started working out." I lie. I give her a kiss on the cheek and sit down.
"You must try the gnocchi; it's the best in the city." "Oh you've been here before." I say but now I'm thinking who did YOU fuck from here.
"Me and my sisters come here a few times a month. Peg is friends with the owner."
"I took a Viagra." I smile.
"Why Wolfgang? .. I didn't call you into the city for that."
My heart drops.
"Well Madison than why did you call me here" I'm looking around for cops and hidden cameras.
"Wolfgang we need to talk about the rent situation."
The waiter comes over and takes our drink order.
"Can I have a Dirty Martini straight up?"
"You're drinking? I thought you stopped. I'll have a glass of pinot. Thank you" She says and smiles at the waiter. My blood is beginning to heat up.
"Did you fuck that guy too?"
"What's wrong with you? Knock it off. Let's try to have a pleasant evening once."
The waiter puts down the drinks and whispers something in her ear; she looks at me and laughs. "Maddy why did you call me here if you don't want to fuck me?"
"Wolfgang I told you no. I need you to take responsibility for your end of the bargain."
"Are you high? Are you taking different pills? I stayed with you for maybe two months before you started fucking everyone. Fuck you, do you take me for an asshole. Have one of your boy toys pay you for your services."
"When we moved to New York you said you would pay half the rent if you can choose the apartment. You chose that shitty roach infested place,"

"Fuck you Maddy. I'm fucking living on a couch in Bridgeport Connecticut. A far cry from Hollywood."

"You were the big shot with the big mouth, where's all your movie contacts now where's the movie deals you bullshitted everyone about. You're a fucking loser with a drug problem."

The waiter comes back to take our order.

"Hold on buddy, I need a couple of minutes to let my girlfriend decide whose cock she is going to suck tonight."

"Huh..Wha..??"

"Come back in ten minutes."

"Wolfgang my family comes here all the time. Don't embarrass me. Be a fucking man for a change."

"What did you say? Be a man. Be a man. You wouldn't know what a man is if he came up and pissed on you. Try being a self-respecting woman. I fucked you after two hours of feeding you bullshit and coke. You whore. You didn't even ask about condoms. I fucked you in the toilet in dirty bars you filthy pig."

"Waiter. Check." She says.

"Truth hurts. Now you're leaving because you can't take the truth."

"I feel sorry for you Wolfgang. You have all this anger in you."

"Maddy you put it there. You UN loyal cunt."

This behavior happens all the time when I see her. But I can't seem to pull myself away from the chaos.
I do this for months.

I flip out as usual. I punch walls and break my hand. Cops are still tracking me down from the first domestic call. I can't catch a break. I am confused once again on how my life went from sunny California to miserable New York. I spend most of my time in the Black Rock section of Bridgeport. I can walk from my neighborhood bar Tabby's to the couch I'm sleeping on. I drink and take drugs and contemplate suicide more now than ever. I had what looked like the perfect life 7 months ago. Now I'm in a pit of depression.

I'm always down and sad and have this weight of guilt on my mind. This feeling of being unworthy eats at me and consumes me and all my ambition. I sleep all day. I don't want to talk to anyone. I lose 12 pounds from no appetite. I stop talking to my family. This girl is toxic and I am addicted to the fumes. Time slowly drifts by and I self- medicate in the local dive coke bars.

One morning I wake up and the pain is no longer there. I don't even think about her. I stay clean one day at a time and I start meditating. I focus all my energy on finding a distributor for the Mullet doc. and after three months of working the phone and internet I find a European Distributor that buys it. I make a deal and all I get is seven thousand dollars and ten percent of royalties for 5 years.

I move off my cousin's couch and split to Nantucket for a month. I live in a dilapidated house with this alcoholic from Montana. I call him Brother Dave. I drink for a month straight. I fuck this deaf girl from Iran and this paralyzed girl that lives on the island. I didn't want to but I felt bad for her and I thought I was doing god's work. When I get sober I want to kill myself. I leave Nantucket and rent a house in Black Rock a block from Long Island Sound. It's a nice two family house, I have the first floor and these two girls from Brooklyn live on the second they are young and good looking. I buy furniture and Televisions and kitchen utensils. I buy towels and drapes. I live like a normal person. I live alone and I am lonely.

I am single.

I'm 34 years old.

ME CRAZY YOU CRAZY.

Life is going on, I work as a location scout for production companies that want to film in Connecticut. I hate it. I hate the people. I make O.K. money but can't save any of it. I sign up for internet dating and things get out of control. I am out of control. I drink at the neighborhood bar five nights a week and fuck not so nice girls. I do a lot of drugs to kill my loneliness. I think about suicide daily. I think about Elizabeth often and that makes me sad. I need more to life than this.

I lie awake at night thinking about killing people. My mind keeps racing around this thought and won't let it go. I mean bad people. The scum of the earth people. Pure evil. I want to be the judge, jury and the executioner. I want to make someone pay for this pain we all feel. I have no problem justifying killing someone that hurts women and children. This thought stays with me and every time I drink I convince myself I have to do this in order to release the pain I carry. It's a fucked up world we live in.

I go on the internet and look up all the registered sex offenders in Bridgeport. I see 33 of them in a two mile radius of where I live.
What the fuck.

I am going to kill one of these mother fuckers. This is my goal. This is my destiny. I now know my purpose.

I retrieve my gun from my Parents attic and I leave it unloaded in my kitchen drawer. The more I drink the more I can't get the thought out of my mind. I am going to kill this Puerto Rican Felipe Sanchez. He was paroled a year ago, he did seven years for raping a 9 year old. This is the fucker that is going to pay. I don't sleep nights so I drive around Felipe's apartment building with a loaded gun under my seat. I know I'm out of my mind but I don't give a fuck. I am bored with life. I need to have a purpose and I think I found it.

I leave Tubby's bar and walk towards my car. I'm fucked up and ready to hunt down this piece of shit. Before I reach the door I see two Bridgeport cops parked across the street. Something tells me not to get in my car. I walk pass it and cross the main avenue and head home on foot. I learn the next day that they pinched a shit load of people for drinking and driving and thank god I didn't drive because I would be in jail right now for carrying a loaded stolen gun in my car. I abandon the idea of killing Felipe. But I still got his number.
I should stop putting drugs in my body.

I use the internet for dating, mostly just scanning photos of chics and looking for that vulnerable fish. I don't want to date anyone I just want to get laid.

One Sunday morning I'm checking my inbox and I see a message from this pig and she says the normal crap and leaves a phone number, I call her as I'm sitting on the toilet.

"Hello Marsha."

"Yes."

"Hi this is Trevor from singles r us, you left me a message and your phone number."

"Oh Hi.'

"Yes Marsha I was flattered by the message BUT I'm not really looking for any kind of relationship."

"Oh."

"But if you want to come over this afternoon around 530 I could show you a good time."

I don't hear anything I think she hung up. Then.

"What's your Address?"

"I live in Black Rock where are you?

She tells me she's coming from Norwalk and she will be at my house on time, I give her the street name and number. Now I have 6 hours to kill. I look at porn and try not to jerkoff for two hours. I clean my house not that it was dirty I just like clean hardwood floors. I dust off my brown leather couches and open the windows. Once I start cleaning I don't stop, two more hours go by. I take a shower and endless bong hits until I see her car pull up.

I can't believe I am going to do this. Do I really want too? I see her get out of her car and she is a little chunky not bad but definitely not good, I see she has a bottle of wine under her arm. Her car is a piece of shit. I'm judgmental. I open the door before she rings the bell. I hope my neighbors don't see this pig walking into my house. I hurry her in.

"Hi Marsha I'm Trevor. Come on in."

She walks into the living room. "This is a nice place." She says. She must be poor if she thinks that.

"Yeah it's not bad I like the fact the beach is a block away."

She walks around the living room and dining room checking out my art work.

"Would you like a glass of wine." she says as she waves the bottle at me.

"No, I don't drink... But you can. Hold on I will get you a glass." I walk into the kitchen and grab a glass then I walk into the bathroom to take a piss, I'm staring at myself in the mirror I smirk and then I spit on the mirror and chuckle and walk back into the living room. This pig is sitting on the couch with her legs crossed.

"Here you go."

I hand her the glass and she pours herself a drink. I sit down on the same couch on the left of her. She is talking non -stop and I wasn't one bit paying attention to whatever it was she was saying. I look at the clock on the cable box and realize 25 minutes have gone by and she is almost done with the bottle. I stand up and stretch.

"Well Marsha I do only have a certain amount of time before I have to jump on a train to New York." I unbutton my button fly and pull out my cock. "Yum." she says and starts blowing me as I'm standing in my living room looking out the window. I'm disgusted but I get hard. I sit back down on the couch and now Marsha kneeling on the floor between my legs blowing me.

I take my right hand and slowly slide it behind the pillow on the couch and pull out my 38. I tilt my head and put the barrel underneath my chin. She is sucking my dick and has no idea until I cock the hammer and the noise triggered her eyes to look up at me.

AUGHHHHHHHHHHHH, OOOOOOOWWWWWWWWW.

She bit it!?

STOP. STOP. STOP.

I throw the gun on the chair across from me and then I grab her face and try to unlock her jaw from my cock.

"What the fuck is wrong with you." She screams.

"I'm bleeding you cunt, I have your fucking teeth marks on my cock"

"You're lucky I didn't bite it off you sick freak. I should call the police."

"For what? You assaulted me. I'm the one whose bleeding" I put my bloody cock back into my pants and grab the gun from the chair and put in the back of my belt. She doesn't see this.

"Where's the gun?" She snaps.

"What gun? There was no gun. It was my fingers. I'm pushing her towards my front door and every step I take I can feel blood trickling down my leg.

"You just got to go. I got to jump on a train in ten minutes and I have to get ready." I shut the door in her face and turn the lock. I walk into the bathroom and that's when I hear the window break.

That bitch threw a rock thru the glass pane on the front door. I don't fix it. I have little pieces of tissue all over my dick. It looks like I cut myself shaving except it's on my cock. I get cleaned up and walk to Tubbys and don't speak a word of the situation that just happened.

I need change.

I need to grow up.

I need a girlfriend to keep me on the straight and narrow. I scare myself.

I need a handler.

My mind doesn't stop, it never rests. The wheel of my thoughts are spinning in tornado fashion now. Suicide still fascinates me and I like living in a drug haze.

Nothing seems worth it anymore. I don't have fun. Most of my friends are married now and a few of them already have children. I am not even close. Time goes by and I don't know what to do.

The movie business is insane and I can barely get a grasp around it. I just want to make my movies in my head. I am so far from Hollywood and I don't have the cash to get back there. Then I remember I don't have the patience for all that bullshit again. Ass kissing shit talking mother fuckers. I am better than that. I can't work on other people's movies I realize and quit being a location scout.

The drip and the Eastern European chic.

I'm in the local stagehand union and I work also as an interior painter, I make a living and that's it. I sort of make my own schedule and I don't really have a boss, so things are good on that end. I calmed down on the drinking and drug taking. Well I sort of switched from alcohol and blow to weed and opiates. I occasionally hit it hard in the bars but not like I used to.

I work as much as I can and always have a grand or two in the bank and always one month away from being homeless. If I hurt or break my hands I can't work. I don't have health insurance. I don't have a savings account. My parents are old and broke. My sisters are married off and taken care of. I rarely speak to any of them, for no reason at all. I dis associated myself from the fairy tale they live.

I am fucking poor. I am a working blue collar man that never makes enough money.
I can barely keep my head above water but I manage. I never made a lot of money so it didn't matter anyway. I wake up to the grind every day.

I want answers.

I decide to write pitches I write 2 game shows and a reality show and a play called "Blackie don't die. Blackie don't die." The play was about a boy and his black lab .On how Blackie saved the boy's life when he was an infant and now Blackie was facing certain death and his owner needs five grand to pay the vet so he can take care of Blackies cancer. The owner turns to his criminal roots to raise the cash and Blackie is saved. It's a beautiful story about a boy and his dog.

I don't show anyone and I lose interest after I wrote them. They are sitting in a folder somewhere with the rest of my film shit. More friends get married. More children are born.

I start warming up to my family and seeing my parents more often. I try to be good. The voices have settled at the moment and I am starting to have peace within myself.

The neighborhood drug dealer got his hands on a shipment of liquid Oxycodone 600milagrams for $150. The bottle came sealed and a measuring syringe was included, it was like an eyedropper. The dropper could hold anywhere from 5 milligram to 40 when it was full.

At first I could take 12 and a half mil. If I took any more I would be stationed in front of the toilet for 10 hours. Then I worked my way up to

15 milligrams at one shot then I could maintain it with increments of 5 every couple hours. All my friends had bottles. The thing never left my shirt pocket. The first bottle lasted me a month. The second bottle two weeks. I would do everything on it. I was attached to it like a baby to a nipple. It was a delicate drug and had to be treated with respect.

For 3 months I have been emailing this Romanian girl I met on" Singles R us", She responds with short little "Hello's" and" How are you's" I can tell by her writing she speaks broken English. She tells me she lives in Port Chester and only has a computer when she is at work and sometimes she can't respond immediately. I have my doubts. Oana is her name. We exchange pictures and write about our families and work. I gave her my number and told her when she is ready to meet me she can call me.

I'm watching spring training at my friend Todd's house. Not really watching the television just doped up on a Sunday afternoon. My phone rings and I don't recognize the area code. I think it's a debt collector and I decide to pick up to fuck with whoever is on the other end.

"Helllo." I say

"Ello Volfgang."

I get off the couch and walk out the front door and on to the stoop. The phone is breaking up.

"Hello, Hello.."

"Ello Volfgang its Oana."

It takes me a second.

"Oana."

"Yes."

"Hi. I wasn't sure you were real." I say.

"I don't understand."

"I don't trust these dating sites you're the first person I had contact with. I get all these emails from Russian women asking for money."

"Oh no, I'm not Russian. I'm Romanian," she says.

"Oana, I know. Wow. It's so nice to hear your voice and I am happy that you called. So can I take you out for coffee or if you like you can bring your dog up to where I live because there is a beach here and he can run around, remember I wrote you?"

"Yes .O.K. Volfgang I will give you my work number and you call me tomorrow and we see where we can meet."

"Sure."

I walk back into Todd's house and my heart drops. I can't believe she called. I tell him I got to split and I run home and check out her photos again online. I spend what seems like hours staring at her. I barely sleep and the next day I count down the hours until I call.

"Hello Oana its Wolfgang."

"Ello Vofgang how are you?"

"Good Oana I was wondering if you want me to pick you up from work and I could drive you home and we could grab coffee in your neighborhood."

"I vork in Stamford and the train takes about 20 minutes to get me to Port Chester station."

"No.No I will pick you up at your work just tell me the address and what time."

"Oh, O.K. My vork address is 4368 vest ave in Stamford and I go to 9112 king street in Port Chester."

"O.k. Oana what time shall I pick you up?"

"I get out at four o'clock today."

"Oana, I have a black Tahoe truck I will be waiting outside of it."

"Tank you Volfgang, see you then."

I jump in the shower and primp myself. I only take enough drip not to get me sick. I clean my truck and head on down to Stamford. I have butterflies in my stomach for the first time since High School.

I pull into the parking lot of the address it looks more like a factory than a corporate office. I hear a bell ring and 3 minutes later I see her walk out the door with 9 or 10 other people.

You know when you get that feeling?

I got that feeling. She was the one I will spend the rest of my life with and I haven't even fucked her yet. I just knew.

"Hello Oana. I'm Wolfgang." She kisses me on both cheeks.

"Oh come on I recognize you from your photos Volfgang. It's nice to finally meet you." She says as I open the truck door for her.

"Volfgang you don't mind driving me to Porch ester to get my dog?"

"No I told you Oana I would. Look this gives us perfect time to talk to each other. By the time I drive to your house if you don't feel like you want to go out with me all you have to do is say no and your already home." I smile and pull on to the parkway.

"O.K Volfgang."

In the 30 minutes it takes me to drive to her house she tells me a few things about herself. Like she was married before to her Romanian boyfriend that she came here with 10 years ago. She left him because he was violent 6 years ago. She tells me how she ran out of the house one night with nothing and never returned. She tells me she used to live in Brooklyn before she got this job in a jewelry wholesale factory in Stamford. She is some sort of floor manager. She tells me her father died when she was 17 and she had to wait a day for the ambulance to come and take him away. She tells me he had a heart attack and died in her arms, her mother was not home. She was visiting people in the United States. She tells me she learned her English in this country and she gets her citizenship in 3 months.

Her English isn't bad, it's very heavy. She uses the wrong words sometimes, but so do I.
She tells me she lives in a house with roommates and they are all Romanian.
She does not like to drive and doesn't have a license.
She is very direct and forward. She is a strong woman.
She is only 30 years old.
When I pull into her driveway she tells me she will be right back and walks into her house and comes out with her cute springer spaniel and a big bag.
"Ok ready Say ello Cosmo." She says when she gets back in my truck.
"Oh O.K. Oana. Hiii, Cosmo. This beautiful well behaved dog gets in and lies right at her feet. So do you want to go back to my house and go to the beach and park?"
"Yes and if you like could you stop at grocery store I buy some food and I cook for you."
"Really. You want to cook for me?" I 'm almost embarrassed for some reason.
"No. No Oana I can take you out. I have money. I was planning on taking you out. You don't have to cook for me."
I can see she feels uncomfortable for some reason. "How about this Oana, You can cook if I can buy the food you need?"
"O.k. Volfgang that's sounds good." She turns to me and smiles."
45 minutes later I'm at the grocery store in Black Rock. Oana has Cosmo in the cart and acting as if it's normal. I'm playing along. Then I realize that I hate food shopping and tell her I will wait outside and help her with the bags. I hand her a 100 dollar bill.
We just clicked. At first I thought this was too good to be true and I was being set up for something. But her face looked too innocent and her vibe was welcoming.
We walk around my neighborhood and ask each other questions about our lives and what we want out of the future. She told me she would see me again, so far.

She is impressed with my pad and how clean it is. I show her where all the cooking utensils are and she takes control of the Kitchen. She smokes and drinks beer as she cooks. I'm sneaking bowl hits on the front porch.
 We sit and eat.
"This is the best first date I've ever had." I say as we cheer.
"Oh Volfgang it is our first date but we talk so long on internet before we meet I feel like I know you very good."

I am amazed by her beauty. Her porcelain doll face that doesn't show her age despite the fact she smokes Marlboros and drinks a lot of beer.. Her flat chest and perfect ass are fine by me. Her hair is black with blonde streaks and bangs, sort of Euro trashy but hot. Her accent turns me on. I don't want to lose this girl. I will change. I will become a new man.

It's funny how life changes without expecting it. Oana moves in with me after a week. I told her I could not make the drive back and forth to Port Chester everyday it was killing me. She was cool with it and didn't pay rent because she still had a rent she was paying on her pad. She had 4 more months to pay off. I fenced in the yard for her dog and I painted the kitchen for her. I drove her to and from the train station every work day. I did anything she asked. We were in love.

I work as grip and I'm in the New York local. My money situation is always a problem. I either have a couple grand in the bank or nothing at all. I don't pay the electric bill or the gas bill until they threaten to shut it off every three months. I like that system better than paying bills. I have boxes of unopened mail. I only open checks. Oana works five days a week and she makes $500. She has no idea about my credit or my bad bill paying techniques. She doesn't like the fact that I'm constantly smoking pot but I told her I don't like her beer drinking every single night. So we agree to disagree. I rescue a little tea-cup yorkie from the shelter and call her Bella. Bella and Cosmo become friends. Oana cooks and cleans all the time. She is not afraid to get her hands dirty. She is always talking on the phone to her mom in Romania.

I have been on the drip now for eight months. No one knows. When I run out every 4 to 5 weeks I go thru withdrawals and Oana is starting to think something is up. I'm laid out for 5 days, on the second day I start puking and cold sweats set in. I can deal with that. I can't deal with the mind games and horror thoughts that dance around in my head, I'm afraid to sleep. Oana doesn't say anything about my episodes …Yet.

I take the drip and pour it into a vitamin B bottle so it doesn't look suspicious every time I'm sucking on the nipple.
I nod out at stop signs.

I'm living the perfect life. I play house with this beautiful Romanian and I curbed my drinking. I am always building shit in the garage and acting like a responsible adult. I stay away from the bars and cocaine.

My family fell in love with her just as I did. I play the roll pretty well. I get invited now to all my married friend's parties, we dine with other couples. People are always stopping by to eat, the house is always full. Oana asks me if I want to go to the Catskills to visit her Romanian friends. She tells me that there is a big community of Romanians that settled up there. I agree of course and drive 4 ½ hours there on a random weekend in January. Snow everywhere. Everything seems cool for a moment.

I don't speak Romanian and I don't understand a fucking word of it. The Romanian Church Community I'm in is very tight. I'm the only American to enter the group. Her friends are this couple, Pete and Kasia they are in their fifties and very very nice and accommodating. They just don't speak English that well. They have a house up here in the middle of nowhere, on the out skirts of a rundown blue collar, steel manufacturing city. It's peaceful and corrupt at the same time. These Romanians are gypsies, they are involved in the church and friends with this Priest they call Mike. Mike is a guy in his fifties also he is Married with two kids. He is a landlord to an apartment building I saw in town. But there is something shady about this guy I wasn't able to pin point it yet.

I travel up to the Catskills 3 more times before Oana asks me if I would like to buy a house with her up here. I say yes on the spot and I don't give it much thought. I know I have bad credit, Oana does not. We spend a month looking at property. I'm driving back and forth every weekend now and I'm getting sick of it plus I don't want to live in this shit town. I tell Oana that we should look for a two family house and rent one floor and use the other one as a vacation home. I told her I wouldn't be able to find work up here and she agreed. She wouldn't be able to find work either.

I'm poor and the houses are cheap .We come across this house 3 doors down from Pete and Kasia, it's a two family and needs some renovations. The price is fifty thousand dollars. I tell Oana that my credit score is low and we should put the house in her name so we can save on the financing. She didn't flinch, she agreed. We had to come up with7 grand for the down payment. $3500 each. She had it. I had to scrape and borrow but I came up with it in two weeks.

Life goes by quicker now. The weeks and months just fly by. I'm still caught up inside my own head. I don't have right thoughts. I don't trust anyone and that scares me, because I actually feel it. physically.

I'm having second thoughts and I'm starting to manifest a way to escape. I don't know why I have these fucked up thoughts. The drip has become second nature. I don't crave it and when I'm out and about to withdrawal. I go with it and suck it up, I'm used to it. As fucked up as my mind gets I know in a certain amount of days I will feel better. I can take it or leave it I have no addiction problems. I have problems living a bored life. I have   problems with people. I have problems trying to fit in to a certain way of life. I work and I work. The money always disappears. I hate this cycle. I just want to grow pot, hunt and make moonshine and be left alone with the voices in my head.

I don't care how hot your girlfriend is or how cool she is at a certain point you get sick of fucking them, or at least I do. I'm sure she felt the same because she never approached me.

Oana's company moved out of state and she lost her job. It was no big deal because she made the same amount of money collecting unemployment. I freelance so I am able to take time off as I want. We both spend time renovating the apartments. I was amazed to see this hot Romanian chic work a wet saw and cut and lay tile. We would spend weeks at a time up there; our place was gutted so we would sleep at Pete and Kasias.
It was a Thursday and I was beat to shit. I have been working non -stop and my chic can only do so much. I needed a break.
I just get out of the shower at Pete and Kasia's.
"Oana do you want to go down the road and grab a few beers?"
"Not tonight .You vant to go out?"
"Babe I need to decompress. I want to talk to people. I sit here every night and listen to you guys speak Romanian. I have already watched all the DVDs, I'm just going to go out and get a beer I shouldn't be too long."
"Volfgang you going to vork tomorrow right?"
"Yeaaah, Baby what else am I going to do up here." I say sarcastically.

She shoots me a look and it pisses me off. I give her a kiss on the forehead and tell her I'll be back in two hours. It's a shit bar and I had no idea there was a brewery in this town. The chic behind the bar is cute and young and I can see the nipple ring popping thru her black tank top. I say excuse me to this older gay gentleman who is sitting at the bar and he lets me scoot in between he and some bull dike.

"Hi. What's your name and what can I get you?"

"Are you talking to me" I say kiddingly. "Can I get one of those house beers?"

"Your name what's your name"

"Really, Wolfgang what's yours?"

"Kathy"

"Well Kathy nice to meet you and what do I owe you?"

"Two dollars."

"Two bucks. That's it. Are you kidding me? I can see myself being a regular here." I say with a smile on my face. The gay guy turns toward me and says "Where are you from?" I'm from Brooklyn." I lie. I don't want anyone to know where I'm from, "My girlfriend and I bought a house up the road so I will be spending some time up here."

I can see that makes Kathy more interested in me.

"Yeah we are renting one floor out and we will keep the other for our vacation getaway, I've been renovating the shit out of it and now I'm almost done."

The gay guy introduces himself and so does the bull dike. I'm Samuel and that's Lori.

"Nice to meet you guys, Let me get you guys a beer and Kathy do you have any smokes behind the bar?

"What kind?"

"Reds and what kind of shot do you want."

She throws the pack at me and pulls out the Jack Daniels and pours herself a shot. The bar starts to get crowded and I found a seat with the gay dude and the bull dike. We bullshit for a while before the topic of drugs come up in the conversation. I tell them I have some serious kind bud and Samuel tells me he has a shit load of Zanax. I let him smell the pot and it makes his dick hard, he wants to trade. I tell him to give me one now and I will give him some weed when we leave. Kathy the bartender asks me if I want to join her for a smoke outside and I do.

I'm buzzed up.

"Kathy, I really dig those nipple rings, I love piercings…

Before I could finish my sentence she flashes me.

"Whoa. Whoa. Let me see that again."

She flashes me one more time.

"I can see that I will be spending a lot of time in your bar now."

She kisses me on the cheek." I have other piercings I want to show you"

Are you kidding me…

I walked into this bar two hours ago and now I have a pill connection and a hot 22 year old bartender I'm going to fuck. I order round of shots and beers and the gay dude keeps throwing me more Zanax. I keep eating them. I give the bartender my phone and she is taking pictures of her bald pussy with it behind the bar. I like this redneck town. Now I am blatantly smoking pot outside the front door with half the people from the bar, I'm getting to know everyone in this shit town. I eat more Zanax. I forget what time it is. Samuel asks me if I want to take a ride to his house. He left a script there and says he will give it to me.

"How much is that going to cost me?" I say.

"I thought you want to trade?" He says..

"I do but this bud is worth its weight in gold I will give you three grams for the bottle. How many come in a bottle?

"60."

"Perfect. I think that sounds about fair."

We jump into his car and the bull dike is with us. She hands me a huge yellow pill and I take it before I ask what it is.

"What is it?" I ask.

"Methadone."

"Shit I never took Methadone before, how bad is it going to fuck me up?"

"It's 20 milligrams. It's a low dose so it might not even affect you."

"Will I puke?

"Maybe."

"Good that's exactly how I want to spend the rest of my night." She catches my sarcasm.

Back at the bar and I'm throwing Zanax down Kathy's mouth and taking shots of Jack Daniels. I'm starting to fade.

"Wolfgang do you want to join me for a smoke?"

"Yeah let's go."

She walks out from behind the bar and the bull dike follows.

We are outside smoking and she says "I really want to kiss you."

"Come on really?" I say. This shit is getting crazier by the minute. I'm trying to focus my vision because I'm getting blurried. We start making out and the bull dike says I want to suck your cock. Both Kathy and I look at her. "I thought you're gay." I say.

"I am but still like cock."

I don't know if I feel comfortable letting this shaved headed tattooed work boot wearing acid jean frumby beast sucking on my cock. Plus I have girlfriend at home.

"Come on it will be fun." Kathy says.

"What?"

"Yeah it will turn me on come on we can go in the back inside the old phone booth."

"You guys are nuts I don't know about this. The bar is packed."

"I will go in with you." Kathy says.

"Really, you guys seem real eager about this. What's up?"

"You're hot Wolfgang. Come on." Kathy grabs my hand and we walk back inside.

"First I need another beer and shot. You guys are crazy." I say.

The bull dike starts rubbing her hand on my cock underneath the bar and to my drugged out surprise I'm getting hard. I look around and no one in the bar is paying attention, I throw back two more shots of J.D.

"Are you ready?" Kathy says.

"For what? Oh yeah you guys are for real. This is nuts."

Kathy walks from behind the bar to where I'm standing and starts rubbing my hard cock under the bar with the dike. I look around again and no one see's this crazy shit happening. Sam the gay is nowhere in sight.

"Let's go." She says and grabs my hand.

"I'm fading fast. My eyes are getting real heavy."

"Relax." Kathy says and shoves her tongue in my mouth.

I feel my pants being pulled down and my cock being sucked. The phone booth is old and musty, we are like packed sardines. Kathy and I are standing up going at it the bull dike was on her knees. She pulls up her tank top and I go right for the nipple ring, I open my eyes for some reason and glance down, it takes me a minute to realize that this isn't the bull dike knobbing on my cock.

I put the palm of my hand on his forward. Like I'm trying to palm his head like a basketball and I remove him from my dick. Kathy grabs my cheek and is kissing my neck. I'm a bit confused for a second.

"Whoa. Hey, what the fuck man." I start pulling up my pants.

"It's ok Wolfgang we're just havin' fun." I slide open the door and walk out.

The fag Samuel and Kathy were still in there. I never looked back I walked straight out the door and walked home. When I got there Oana had locked me out so I end up sleeping in my truck and using paint tarps to keep me warm. My whole body was covered so I never saw the sun come up. I heard Oana and the dogs walk beside the truck.

The look on her face said it all. I was in deep shit.

"Hey Baby..." That's all I got out before she clocked me in the mouth. I step back and catch the blood in my hand.

"Oana what the fuck is wrong with you?" She swings again and I move.

"Baby please what the fuck."

"Why you not come home last night?"

"Wait. I did and the door was locked and I didn't want to wake you or Kasia and Pete. Look I slept in the fucking truck."

She takes another swing at me. "What the hell is that on your neck."

Without thinking I say. "Baby look at me I was in a fight. Some fuckin' guy started strangling me over keno. It took the whole bar to pull him off me. Look…"

She walks passed me with the dogs and I look at my reflection in my truck window. I see marks on my neck and when I look in the rearview mirror my worst thoughts came true. That bitch gave me hickeys. I look like a piece of white trash and I feel like shit. I climb back into the back seat and pull the tarps over my head, I feel the bottle of zanax in my pocket and I think it's a good idea to take two.

Bang, Bang, Bang, I rip the tarps off my body and notice right away that its dark out then I see Oana banging on the door with a metal spoon. "Hey what the fuck are you doing?" I scream in a panic and get out of the truck.

"You slept all day Volfgang. You embarrass me in front of my friends. We are wasting money up here." I can see she's holding back tears,

"Oana listen I will talk to Pete and Kasia. Everything will be alright we are right on schedule. Oana I wouldn't of went out if I knew we had a lot of shit to do. But we don't. I will come up in the middle of the week with Bud and he will help me hang the doors."

"You disappoint me Volfgang."

"Hey Oana, that's not fair. I've been busting my ass up here for you. Do you think I want to live in this shit hole town with these fucked up gypsies. I am doing it for you"

"Shit hole. That's what you say. My friends are gypsies. Volfgang.."

"Listen your taking it the wrong way. It's not what I meant. You know what I mean, just cut me some slack. I was in a fight last night."

"Vhy Volfgang You always get in these problems."

"Oana are you nuts? When have I gotten into any problems since I've been with you?"

"I don't vant to talk to you any more go take a shower and let's go."

I walk inside and I see Pete and Kasia at the kitchen table.

"Hey guys thanks for letting us stay here while we work on our house. Sorry about last night I drank too much beer." I motion with my hand as if I'm drinking a bottle.

"Next time we come up we will be moved into the house and shortly after I will be throwing a party." They laugh because I don't think they understand me, I grab a towel and walk into the bathroom.

The whole ride I couldn't help my flashbacks. I would have freeze frame thoughts of this old gay motherfucker taking my dick out of his mouth. I look over at Oana and growl."Ggrrrrrrrrrrr."
"Those look like hickeys on your neck." she says as she turns her head towards me.
"What. Enough, Oana I told you what happened. I don't feel good about it, in fact I feel pretty shitty. I was drugged and beat and all you can do is give me shit as I drive your ass back and forth from that shithole."
I pull the car off the highway and put it in park.
"Drive. I want to take a four hour nap. Come on, get out and drive."
She just looks at me with terror.
"Yeah I thought so Oana."

I put it back in drive and take off. I know I'm being an asshole and it's all that fags fault.
We drive the rest of the way home in silence. The radio was on NPR. Oana fell asleep. The dogs were sleeping. I couldn't escape my thoughts, everything was a puzzle and I didn't have the right pieces to begin to put it together. I have no clue what I am doing, I don't think I want this anymore. I am losing it more rapidly now and I want to kill that fag for molesting me. My mind doesn't rest at all.
The rage calmed itself down once I arrived in Connecticut. I pull into our driveway and I quietly carry Oana up to the door before she wakes up.
"I'm sorry baby if I hurt your feelings."
"You didn't Volfgang." She kisses me and puts the key in the lock.
Just like that back to normal.
A few weeks go by and things seem to be going well. The weather is getting warmer. I haven't been up to the Catskills in 5 weeks. Oana has gone up by train a few times to do some minor work. I stay in Connecticut and work as much as I can, I hate it. Oana's mother is coming to visit in 3 days for 6 weeks. I cleaned up the guest room for Oana and I so her Mother can sleep in our room. The house is immaculate, the refrigerator is stocked, dogs are groomed. Then Oana asks me if I can go up to the house and finish hanging the door before her mother gets here. I tell her "fine but I have to leave now if you want me back on Thursday to pick up your mom from the airport."

The price of the drip just went up to $200 a bottle. I'm a two bottle a month kind of guy.

I call up Bud and ask him if he would come up with me and he does. I have this weird feeling as I'm driving that this just might be the last time I'm in the Catskills. I don't tell Bud about the situation that happened up here. But I can feel that he senses something's up with me. I drop 18 milligrams as soon as I get off the exit. I pull up to the house and I see that Oana has put up a little fence in the front yard and the front door is painted. Why didn't she tell me? Bud and I carry in the bedroom door and start working, it's five at night. I notice that Oana has cases of beer stocked next to the refrigerator. 8 cases. Maybe she got a good deal on them. Who knows? Bud and I start drinking. Bud tells me he is impressed with the place and can't believe it was only fifty grand. I remind him that we are four hours from New York City in the middle of bumble fuck.

"Dude I met people up here that have never been to NYC in their life and I also met this chic and she told me she has never seen the ocean."

"Then you should fit in fine with these fucking rednecks. Do you call them rednecks up here or is it Hillbilly or Cousin Lovin. Or just plain WT."

"Fuck you Guy…. What's WT?"

"Think about it you white trash motherfucker."

"You're an asshole. Should I clean this place up and head out for a drink?"

"Yeah, I want to see the kind of people you associate with in this town."

I clean up the tools and we guzzle another can. We start walking down my street towards the bar.

"I gotta say Wolfgang your fucking crazy."

"What now dick?"

"Your nuts if you're going live up here. I bet sooner or later Oana is going to want to move. Look how she decorated the place man. Her friends live two houses down. Her mother is flying in from Romania."

"What the hell does that have to do with it?"

"Oana has lived with you what 6, 7months and now her mother decides to visit, she wanted you to hang the door because her and her Mother will be staying up here."

"You are fucking nuts Dude, Oana and her Mother will be up here for a couple of days, so what. Shut your mouth anyway, you just want to see my blood boil."

"I want see what kind of inbred people you been hanging out with up here."

Bud opens up the bar door and we walk in to a not so crowded place. I look around and I don't notice anyone from the last time I was here. We plant ourselves on the stools.

"Is Kathy working tonight?" I ask the man behind the bar.

"She's off tonight. Do you want me to give her a message?"

"No thanks just 2 house beers."

"Who's Kathy?" Bud asks.

"It's a long story. She was the bartender last time I was here."

"Wait that is the chic you have on your phone? Wow she's a good looking girl. I didn't know she worked in such a shithole."

"Be nice." I take a look over my shoulder and I see Gay Samuel in the corner. He doesn't see me yet. I need to get to him before he comes up here and starts talking shit in front of Bud.

"I got to take a piss." I get up and walk towards gay Sam. We make eye contact and I don't let my eyes off him until I'm in front of his face. "What's up Buddy?" I say as I extend my arm. He looks at me at first and I can tell he doesn't recognize me, it takes a second. "Wolfgang?"

"Yeah Buddy how you been?" I let go of his hand and walk right into the men's room. I know he is going to follow and he does.

I am standing at the urinal and Sam takes to the one on my left.

"Soooo. How you been? We thought we'd see you much sooner. Kathy's off tonight but I can call her up."

I turn and look at him. I put the fear of god into him with just a stare.

"Hey Wolfgang you weren't upset about last time. You looked so fucked up. You took a piss in the barrel of peanuts and then watched as people stuck their hands in it."

"What???"

"Yeah you're a funny guy we got a kick out of you. Kathy liked you."

"Sam, I have a guy I work with out there and is good friends with my girlfriend, so do NOT bring up any of the antics from last time."

"Sure, sure I wouldn't do that. We are glad you're cool with everything."

I just look at him as I zip up my pants "I never said I was cool with it."

I walk out of the Men's room and back to Bud at the bar. Bud has two shots of tequila waiting.

"It's going to be one of those evenings already." I say as I throw it back.

"Don't start your whining now, how soon before you decide we should score some cocaine."

"I'm not doing blow, I haven't done blow in almost a year I think. I'll give you the drip if you want."

Bud takes it out of my hands and squirts it in his mouth. "Thanks, but I still would like to do some cheese. I know you must know someone up here. Come on the girls aren't with us."

"Alright let me see." I look around the bar and I see Sam. I wave him over,

"Sam this is my friend Tom." They shake hands. "Sam We want blow. Plain and simple and I know you know somebody."

"Maybe I do. But how do I know your friend here isn't a cop. I have only met you once before Wolfgang we really don't know each other that well." Then the motherfucker winks at me.

I get up from the stool and place Sam on it from the back of his neck. "I'm not here to play games with you. You know I'm not a cop and I don't associate with police. Now find someone before I go through your pockets."

"Ok. Ok Geez Get so touchy, is he always this tense, no wonder you eat so many downers. Ok I do know someone its fifty a gram."

"If it's not real I'm going to shove up your ass" Sam looks at me and smiles "Fuck you, you know what I mean and I'm not paying you until I taste it."

"Ok, O'k. Is he always this angry? I will go get you your drugs just order me a drink. Scotch for when I return." Sam gets up and leaves the bar.

"How do you know that guy?" Bud says. "Forget it I don't want to know." I order Sam's drink and I pour in 40 mil. of the drip.

He had told me before that he doesn't like opiates his body can't take it that's why he is strung out on anti-anxiety pills. I have been on the drip for 8 or 9 months. I think. I can't remember but I still can't take 40 milg.at once. This drink should put him in a state of hell.

I watch Bud's eyelids fight to stay open, He's awake and talking, his eyelids just decide to shut. He is fucked up and I can see he needs the boost of blow to come out of the drip haze.

I watch the ice melt in the scotch. I'm picturing this homo bent over his toilet for the next 14 hours throwing up is organs and that puts a smile on my face. I feel a hand on my shoulder "Are you thinking of me?" I turn around and the fag is whispering in my ear.

"Get the fuck away from me. Did you get it? Let me see it." I grab it out of his hands and open it up and stick two fingers in it then right up to my nose.

"Be discreet why don't you? They do have cameras in here." I hand the bag to Bud and he walks into the bathroom.

"They have cameras here?"

"Yeah look." He points over the bar and in the corner. "And usually some ones in the office watching."

"Really. So someone was watching you suck my dick.?" I can see this makes him uncomfortable.

"Noo. No. You're not mad about that are you? We were just joking around Kathy thought it would be fun. You know, she's been asking about you. I'm sure she likes you. Really, No hard feeling Wolfgang. Lemme buy you a drink"

"I already got you one Sam." I slide it over to him and raised my beer. "I'm not thrilled about what you guys did to me but I'll get over it. " We cheers and I watch him drink the glass of scotch, the whole glass.

"Sam you can make it up to me and I will forget everything if you pay for the blow and buy Bud and I around of beers,"

Bud is back to normal now and shooting pool I can see Sam starting to bump into things. He's having problems walking straight. I order around of tequila and put it on Sam's tab. I pull out the drip and drop another 40 in his shot. I walk over to the pool table and pass one to Bud and the other one to Sam. I raise my glass. "Sam it was good seeing you and thanks for that thing." I watch him throw it back and almost throw up in his mouth. I motion to Bud and we head for the door. I don't want to stick around when this dude crashes his car I'm thinking or chokes on his vomit or just drops dead from an over dose.

We exit and start high tailing it back to the house, we pass out till morning.

I feel better about myself now. It was like a burden lifted off my shoulders. I couldn't let this guy walk around after he molested me thinking he got away with it. I justify everything and he deserves whatever happens to him.

I'm not feeling right when I'm at the airport. Oana's mother's plane is late and I'm turning yellow. I hate the smell of this airport. I hate waiting.
"Volfgang, are you OK? You look pale and you have sweat on you."
Oana takes out her bandana and pats my forehead.
"Thank you baby. I don't know what happen I just got ill. Maybe something I ate."
"I cooked for you Volfgang, what you say about my cooking?"
"Nothing Oana, don't get excited. I don't know what it could be from."

I know exactly what's happening I'm starting to widthdrawl and I'm going to be sick in an hour or so if I don't get my lip to the drip. I left it home and I never leave it home.
"I'm going to wait in the car. I think I'm going to puke."

I walk out of the airport and into the garage I am sweating and laid out on the seat of my truck. I hear the door open and that's when I wake. I meet Oana's mother for the first time and I look like hell I get out and put her luggage in the back. I am soaking wet with sweat.
"Volfgang are you ok to drive?"
"Yes baby, Hold on, I'm going to make it back in record time."
I drive like a junkie looking for a fix.

Oana's mother doesn't look happy being tossed around in the back seat as I swerve in and out of traffic. I'm not right in the head and I'm starting to fall apart. When I screech into my driveway I don't bother helping anybody out.

I run inside and straight to my room and open my dresser drawer and grab it. I drop it under my tongue and go into the bathroom and lay down on the rug in front of the toilet. By the time I get back to normal and remove myself from the bathroom. Oana has brought in all the bags from the truck and she is starting to cook in the kitchen, her mother is sitting at the table with a cup tea.

"Hello Ms. Nowak. I'm sorry about before." I extend my hand. "I don't know what happened to me."

She smiles and shakes my hand she is this little foreign lady with gray hair. She looks like my Grandmother.

"Volfgang she don't understand English."

"Well tell her that it is very nice to meet her and I'm happy she came to visit and that I'm in love with your daughter.... Come on tell her baby."

Oana speaks to her mother in Romanian; they both look at me and smile and chuckle. I smile back and walk out of the room.

The drip is starting to take its toll. The voices are starting back up again but this time I hear echoing whispers in my head. People are chatting in my head.

One day after Oana's mother arrives they ask me if I can drive them up to the Catskills.

"Baby I thought you were going to wait for me to finish this job in 9 more days and we were going to go up together."

"Volfgang I know but we have nothing to do here. I want to show my momma the house I was thinking tomorrow is Saturday and maybe you can drive us."

If I say no the two of them will be pissed here for the next 2 weeks.

"Oana I was just there. Then the airport. I need a day to relax before I start this job."

"You can relax on Sunday." She says with that determined European accent.

I change my attitude and say "Sure baby."

I pack the truck up again and I don't speak to anyone.

"Why are you packing the dogs things I thought they stay here?"

"They are coming with momma and me."

"So you're going to leave me alone. Thanks."

"Oh, Volfgang you'll be fine I made enough food to last you all veek."

"Whatever Oana, get in the truck I will be out in a second."

I run inside and pop a zanax and eat a pot brownie I had made for this occasion. I make sure The Drip is in my jacket pocket.

My Girlfriend is a Gypsy and so is her Mother.

When I arrive I don't even get out of the car they unload their crap and I get a kiss on my cheek from Oana. I drive back to Connecticut. Something's not right I can feel it.

The first week goes by and my job got extended for another few days. When I speak to Oana she's cool with it. So two weeks go by now and when I speak to Oana she tells me she will be staying another week. I don't bother driving up there if I am going to drive back home alone plus I don't want anyone to recognize me, I'm not sure what happen to Gay Sam.

I start drinking at Tubbys again and I speak to Oana every other day. We are going on week number four.

"Oana I forgot I had a girlfriend what a surprise you called."

"Volfgang are you drinking."

"Maybe, what's it to ya anyway? Let me guess you're going to spend another week up there?"

"Volfgang I don't like it when you drink you know this. Now listen to me. Momma and I want to come back next Wednesday. She has some friends in Brooklyn she wants to see."

"Oana what's going on? I don't feel right"

"Stop drinking Volfgang."

"No Oana I don't feel right about you. Us. Something's up."

"Volfgang not now I will talk to you when my momma leaves. So you come on Wednesday?"

"I guess I will take off work then, you can't come back the weekend before or catch the train and I will pick you up at the station."

"No Volfgang that's too much for momma."

"Oana I'm going to lose work if I keep taking days off."

"Volfgang come on I have the dogs."

"Fine baby I will be there on Wednesday am I spending the night or am I going to turn around and drive back?"

"Oh Volfgang I forgot maybe you come Tuesday and we leave on Wednesday?"

"Fine if I'm not there Tuesday I will be there Wednesday morning."

"Thank you Volfgang."

This is the end I can feel it and my instincts are never wrong. Oana is up to something I just can't figure it out. This will be the last time I ever go back to the Catskills. I leave Connecticut at 4 am on Wednesday and I arrive at the house around 8:30 am. I want to get in and out. I don't trust the situation. I load up my truck with the dogs and Oana's things. Then I take a good look at her.

"Oana what happened?"

"Vhat you mean?"

" Oana look how skinny you are. You're skin and bones. Shit baby you didn't need to lose any weight. What's wrong, are you sick?"

"I told you I will talk to you when momma leaves."

"Oana if you think I'm going to wait a week for you to tell me you're breaking up with me. Your outta your mind you know me better than that."

"Nothing is wrong Volfgang . I'm not breaking up with you, I have just been depressed lately."

"Oana if depression hits you like this maybe you should talk to someone. What do you have to be depressed about? Look your mom is here. You just bought a house and fixed it up in a matter of months. Which is pretty amazing. You don't have to worry about money; I have things covered for a while. Baby, don't be sad. Things will work out." I give her a hug and she doesn't hug me back.

The drive back is silent. I can't help to think that she doesn't love me, maybe she never did. Maybe I was set up. I can feel the rage start to build. When we get back to Connecticut I'm exhausted. I am mentally drained from the fucked up thoughts I had on the ride back. I just want to lie down. I want things to be normal.

I hear Oana laughing from the living room. It goes on for a while so I get up to see. When I walk in she stops. I see my laptop opened up in front of her and she is typing. I go back to bed. I wake up in the middle of the night and I see she is not in bed when I walk out into the living room I see her asleep on the couch, under a blanket with the dogs around her. I tap her on the shoulder.

"Baby come let's go to bed."

"It's o.k. I'm o.k. here."

"Oana I want to know what's going on with you." I say in a whisper.

I grab her on the shoulder and put a little force in my grip. Now she turns around to look at me.

"Don't touch me Volfgang."

"Oana I'm not playing fucking games I will wake up the whole god damn neighborhood at this point." My voice is raising.

"Volfgang, please momma is sleeping."

"Tell me. Tell me what's going on with you. Are you alright? I'm worried about you. Why won't you talk to me?"

She turns back over and ignores me. I calmly walk back into the bedroom and shut the door. I lie down. I'm going thru every bad thing I did. What could she possibly know. No way she found out about Kathy and the bar. No way. I think she is playing me. She has a house in her name and completely functional now. She doesn't need me. I paid her way since I met her and now this. I don't get it.

I get out of bed and stomp into the living room. The dogs perk up because they can sense the rage but Oana is sleeping hard. I open up the lap top next to her on the coffee table. She forgot that all her passwords are logged in my computer. When I open a few screens I find her Facebook page. She has photos of the dogs and of the beach and of the new house and the renovations. No photos of me, Then I see a long conversation between her and some Romanian dude. I can't read fucking Romanian. I can't be this stupid. I slam down the computer on the table.

"Wake your ass up Oana. I'm done with your bullshit games. I will throw your ass out the house and I don't give a fuck if your seventy year old mother is in the other room. I spent the summer alone. I thought I had a girlfriend. What the fuck is going on that you can't tell me."

"Don't you talk to me that vay."

She slaps me in the face.

I turn around and leave. I leave the house with the clothes on my back. I drive a block away and sleep in my truck. In the morning I wake at dawn. I can't figure out what is going on with her. Shit is not right. I don't bother going back I drive to my friend Kotch's house and wait a few hours before I call.

"Hey I'm sorry for losing my cool. But I haven't seen you in weeks and you're not talking to me. I just want to know what I did or didn't do. I want to know you're ok and not sick or anything"

"Volhgang that's it. I told you not to explode when my mommas here. You woke her up last night with your yelling."

"Oana I'm sorry but you got to understand why I'm mad. What the fuck is wrong with you... I read your Facebook page you cunt. Who is that greasy fuck that you're writing two pages of shit too. You haven't talk that much to me in two months. And Oana how come you don't have any pictures of US on Facebook? I think I get the picture now. I'm done being nice, you better start telling me what's going on now."

"Oana?... Oana?" She hung up on me.

I jump into my truck and fly back to Black Rock. When I arrive I see Oana's mother sitting in a car with the dogs. I go inside and she has all her shit gathered in black trash bags. "Wait. What are you doing? What did I do? I'm sorry Oana... I'm sorry. Don't do this. Why can't you just talk to me? What are you doing this for? I have been more than generous to you haven't I. Done everything you said? Give me some respect." She's grabbing random shit and putting it in the bags. She lifts one up and it's too heavy for her so she starts to drag it towards the door.

I just lost it.

I take 3 huge steps and punt the trash bag thru the door and all over the lawn. Her Mother and friend just stare at me.

"Oana get the fuck outta here." She starts picking her shit up.

"Bella is mine get her out of the car."

"She's coming with me. I'm not separating the dogs."

"What about my money? What about the house Oana?"

"Oana what about the house!?"

She ignores me and grabs what she can off the lawn and jumps into the waiting car. My neighbors are watching me explode but they don't dare say anything. I trash the place. My urge to break things has become priority number 1. I don't understand what happened am I in shock. If she found out anything about me she would have told me right? Did she play me all along? What the fuck is happening.

I drink I buy cocaine. I suck on the drip till my body is numb. My picture perfect life just went to shit. My woman is gone. Just like that back to the state of sadness and depression. I replay the situation over and over in my head and I can't come up with an answer. I drain my bank account in two weeks and don't take on any new work. Oana's phone number is changed. She probably got sick of me leaving vile and threatening messages whenever I was fucked up. I have to restrain myself mentally from driving up to the Catskills, because I'm afraid of myself and what I am capable of. She doesn't know this but I'm letting her live. I'm letting her breathe.

Fuck You Peru.

I stopped taking drugs, all types of drugs, even pot. I had a month to sulk and be pissed off and pity myself. Then I woke up one day and decided I wanted a clear head and I stopped. Everything. I worked out during my withdrawals to minimize the angst. It was mind over matter so I thought. I have no cravings for that shit any more. I always fancied myself like the character "sick boy" from Trainspotting. I could quit drugs at any time. I moved on.

I like living healthy except I have no money left and my landlord is raising my rent an additional $375. The reason being so much is that he hasn't raised my rent since I moved in four years ago. I tell him I need sixty days to move out and he's cool with it. His intentions were to have me move out any way so he can remodel it. I can't pay $1500 a month in rent and then the gas bill and the electric and cable and phone and internet. It adds up to over two grand a month just to live and I'm already living paycheck to paycheck. I'm not worried, I have some time to think about it. Now that my head has been clear for some time now I am starting to get real creative. I write another synopsis for an action movie.

Big Fucking Action. The working title is called *Time is Money*. It's a cops and robbers type of movie, a heist. The two main characters are down and out independent filmmakers living in New York. Broke. They unhatch a plan to steal the clock in Grand Central Terminal. It's been noted that it's worth between 10 and 20 million dollars. The two filmmakers pull all their resources to set up a fake movie shoot in Grand Central. They jump thru all the hoops they have too, they get all the permits they need, they borrow money from some shady characters. But they get their chance to shoot in the terminal in the early hours of the morning. They hire a scaffolding company to cover the ticket booth that supports the clock with a green screen. So during the meal break these two guys sneak off and try to steal the clock..
Fill in the rest with chase scenes add a hot girl to the mix and a crazy Arab that wants to pay for the famous clock.

I type it up and put it in the folder with the rest of them. I try not to think about anything. I keep busy working out and working as a stagehand for the union. I don't bother looking for another place and I sell off my furniture. I ask my folks if I can spend a week at their house because I'm in between moves. They are glad to have me. I show up with only a backpack filled of clothes. Everything else I sold or put in the garbage. I want nothing. I want no material objects. I am 37 years old and I am back under my Parents roof.

Thoughts of suicide enter my mind on a daily basis. But I can't do it. I'm still a pussy. I can't hurt my parents like that. I hide the gun back in their attic underneath the fiberglass insulation. I have nowhere to go. No body I want to see. Nothing I want to do. I go thru my old emails and I come across Nick Welsh from Prague. I write 3 words to him in the past 12 years. *Where you at?* I get a response *Peru.*

Peru huh? You married? What's up with your brother Johnny? Thinkin about taking a little trip you?

I get the reply. *Johnny's married. Come to Peru I live in Lima my chic is a Stewardess. Give me dates.*

-Nick.

I go online and purchase a ticket to Lima for $534 round trip. I now have $3367 to my name.

Nick what up man I booked my ticket for Lima I leave on Saturday. I arrive at Lima airport at 530 at night. Should I call you when I get off the plane?

He writes back. *This Saturday?*

Yes in two days. I write back.

O.k I will be at the airport at that time. You're coming from New York?

Yes sir. Thanks and see you there Nick.

I tell my folks I'm going to Peru for six weeks and they are not happy.

"We thought you had gotten another apartment and needed to stay here before your move in date."

"I don't think I ever said that."

"Well what were you planning on doing after your week was up?"

"I just figured it out now, I'm goin to Peru. And when I get back I will get my own pad."

"You're a grown man, I can't tell you what to do. But six weeks. Who goes on vacation for six weeks?"

"Alright, I can see where this is going and I'm taking off now if I'm going to have to hear about my decision making. You have nothing to worry about. I know where I'm going and what I'm doing. When I get back I will probably move in the city and get a real job. So everything's cool right mom?"

She just looks at me. I know she knows I know that we have all heard this bullshit before.

"Just tell me you're going to be careful and use your head."

"Yes Mamma of course." I smile at her and she shakes her head.

I don't give a shit about anything, I'm going to Peru and that's all that matters. I have my carry on and that's all that I'm bringing, one little backpack.

I sit in the bar at JFK airport. I'm so excited I can hardly contain myself. I start drinking and never looked back. Fuck my health regime for now I'm going to concentrate on getting whacked. I have 3 hours before my flight and I pound beers. I become friendly with the Indian chic bartender and I keep tipping her like I'm a big shot. I have already blown 127 dollars in t his joint.

"Are you going to cut me off?" I ask.

"No. Why? You seem fine." She says.

"Just askin'. I need to get really fucked up so I can pass out on the plane." I say.

"I'm terrified of flying and I forgot my Zanax at home." I lie.

"Oh" she says then ten minutes later she walks over to me from behind the bar as if she is acting to clean it and slides me two blue pills. I know exactly what they are.

"Wow. Really. For me? Thank you."

I pop one in my mouth and the other in my pocket. 30 minutes go by and I'm starting to see double, time for me to board the plane. After lift off I buy 3 beers. I pull out a pen and pop a hole in the side of the can and shot gun the beer. It sprays a little bit and the stewardess is not amused. Thank god I have no one sitting next to me. I finally pass out and when I wake 3 1/2 hours later I have to piss so bad my dick is hard. I get up to go to the restroom and the stewardess stops me and tells me to sit down and buckle up we are about to land.

I can't wait ten minutes. I can't wait one minute. I grab the empty beer that's on the seat next to me and I grab the blanket I was sleeping in. I cover my whole body with it. Head to toe. And then I quickly fill up the can not realizing I have to empty it out and fill it up again. Fuck. I have a can of piss between my legs and I have one hand pinching my cock to cut the flow off. I look like I'm wearing a red berka without the eyes lit. I could only image what I look like to the other passengers.

I don't know what to do. Will they arrest me if just piss on the floor. I'm in Peru. I take my head out of the blanket and with one hand I bunch it up into my lap. With my other hand I slowly let the pinch off my cock and I shoot jet streams of piss into the blanket then I quickly throw the pinch back on so I don't overdue it all at once. My free hand grabs the flimsy pillow and I throw it on top of the now wet blanket. My bladder is empty enough where I can put my cock away. I take the soaked blanket and put it on the empty seat next to me. No one notices or at least I think no one does. I can't believe I don't have a wet stain on my pants. I take the full can of piss and put under the seat next to me and we hit a little turbulence and the can spills and starts rolling around. I hit the stewardess button and she comes running over at this moment I throw the piss blanket on the floor and try to soak it up.

"Me cerveza...uh, uh fuck. The beer fell on the floor and it was open."

I show her the piss blanket and she comes back with a plastic bag and discards it. It takes me a minute to realize that I'm in Peru. This shit is different. The military or the police or whatever they are, give me the creeps. The airport is pack full of guys with guns and the taxi drivers hound the shit out of you. I go and finish my piss in the restroom and that's where I bump into Nick.

"What's up Mate?" I turn around and I see this tall pale Irish Fuck.

"Yo Man, what's goin on dude." I put my dick away and extend my hand. Nick pushes me back. "Go wash your hands you crazy fuck."

I follow him to the parking lot outside and its getting dark. All I can smell is gas fumes. We get into his 1992 Toyota Corolla.

"You cut your hair."

"Yeah, right after Prague, 12 years ago. You look the same. I can't believe I'm here."

"Well, you're here mate. You haven't traveled since Prague?'

"No not outside of Canada and Mexico, mostly in the States. What have you been doing?"

"Mate I traveled to every continent. Moved my Parents to Spain and bought real estate and built high end luxury condos that we rent out. I ended up in Peru last year where I met my girlfriend Lisa and stayed."

"It's too dark out to see anything so tomorrow I will take you about."

"Man I smell gas. You don't smell that? I can taste it in the back of my throat."

"I don't smell anything Mate. We will be arriving at my flat in ten minutes. My girlfriend is there but tomorrow she leaves for work for 3 days, she's a flight attendant for Taca Airlines. Oh yeah she doesn't speak any English."

Nick lives in Mira Flores an upscale section of Lima, it sort of looks like Beverly hills if Beverly hills had twelve foot walls with cattle wire in front of every building. There are armed guards in front of places like Starbucks and McDonalds and the Calvin Klein store. Every corner there was some sort of military or police just standing with M16 rifles. Nick tells me I have to watch out for the police and taxi drivers these are the ones that will fuck with you.

I walk into his apartment and its sweet, 3 bedrooms 3 bathrooms with a balcony overlooking a park, great furniture and a flat screen T.V. with armed guards in the lobby. When I meet his Girlfriend Lisa I'm beside myself, this woman is stunning. I can't take my eyes off of her. She's tall and slender with tits and an ass and has a mane of brown hair flowing off her shoulders. Piercing green eyes.

She greets me with a hug. She smells like flowers." Hola Wolfgang."

"Hola Lisa."

Her presence immediately makes me warm and happy.

"Mate here is your room and this is your shower." He points to the left of the kitchen." Do you know that in South America you don't put paper in the toilet? Throw it in that little can next to the toilet. If you flush it will totally fuck up the system and flood. Don't flush the paper!"

"That's gross dude."

"Welcome to south America. We are going to grab some dinner in 30 minutes mate. Do you want to take a shower first?"

"Yeah give me five minutes." I strip off my clothes and jump in the hot shower.

I finally feel free. Not one hint of depression. I already do not want to go back to the states and I've only been here an hour.

Nick takes us to an upscale restaurant and we are meeting Lisa's friend Jackie. I'm impressed but not really it looks like any other restaurant in New York except everyone is Peruvian. Nick assures me that he will tour me around Peru as soon as his girlfriend takes off.

I order the guinea pig.

The rest of the evening was uneventful. Uneventful meaning I didn't get laid or find any coke. I actually sat at the table and had intellectual conversations with Nick and Jackie. Jackie speaks well and was educated in Miami, Nick interprets back and forth for Lisa. Uneventful.

The next day when I wake up I smell gas fumes. Again. I hear Lisa and Nick in the next room and she's getting ready to walk out the door for work. I wait until I hear the door shut before I leave the bedroom. Nick is making breakfast when he tells that we are going to drive south for a couple days and staying at the beach El Punta Hermosa.

I still smell gas and the smog doesn't burn off until noon he says. We go to the modern supermarket to buy food for tour trip. I go to the bank machine at the bank directly across from the store. I take out 4 one hundred soles bills and walk into the store. We buy mostly fruit and yogurt and beer. I hand the cashier one of my bills and she holds it up in the air to examine it. She shakes her head and gives it back to me. I'm confused and I look at Nick. He just looks at me. I hand her another one and she does the same thing. I give her the other bill and she takes a closer look at them and calls over an English speaking manager.

"Sir these bills are counterfeit." The English speaking Peruvian says.

"You're kidding me right? I just went over to that bank machine." I point at it from across the street.. "And came over here. Nick you believe this shit?"

"Yes I actually do Mate."

"Well you take credit cards, visa?"

"Yes we do." She points to the visa logo on the register.

I give her my credit card and ask for the counterfeit money back and to my surprise she hands it over to me. I don't understand. Nick tells me it's a good chance the mafia runs the bank and they are filling up the ATM's fake notes He says they launder money that way. Welcome to Peru. We get on the highway and head south. The most chaotic scene so far. No rules on the road. No lanes. I see a donkey pulling a cart in one lane. I see a family of four riding on a scooter. We pass pueblos or what I think they are. People living on the side of a mountain. Burrowed in the mountain.

Shacks inside theses barrios with no trees to be seen.

Poor living conditions, 3rd world.

Every one begging. Dirt.

We get to El Punta Hermosa and it's totally a different world. We have to drive a quarter mile down to sea level on a steep steep paved road. It's almost at a 45 degree angle. This is where all the wealthy Peruvians own houses and vacation. The little village is built into the side of the rock.

Huge waves, the biggest I've seen. I 'm not even going to attempt to surf it. Nick checks us into a little cabina at the end of the beach. The night life and discos are up that steep hill to the main drag. This is where everyone parks their car and Taxi's it down to the village. There is no room for cars at this seaside resort. We have a room on the water with two twin beds, a toilet, a table and two chairs and no T.V.

It's around one in the afternoon, the sun is blaring and the beach is packed with families and girls in bikinis and surfers and it's fucking great. I notice all the different types of Peruvians. The lighter your skin, the higher up the food chain you are, the wealthy are all pretty white. While I see the help is much darker and indigenous looking.

This place is just as corrupt as the rest of the world if not more. It takes 90 minutes on the beach before the subject of blow comes up.

"How's the cocaine in this part of the world, Nick."

He looks at me and smiles. "The best in the world, fucking pure mate. Rocket fuel."

"Interesting, does your lady party?"

"No. No way she's against it because everyone she knows is so fucked up on it. And she doesn't need to know anything about our behavior."

"What do you mean Nicky? Are you saying we going to get fucked up."
I can't stop grinning.
"Listen Mate I told you to come out here so I can get away too. My chic is
cool but she is the only one I know in Peru. It gets kind of old hangin with
your lady all the time. Plus she doesn't do drugs and barely drinks. So Mate I
am just as amped up as you are for being here Cheers."
 We tap beer bottles." Now watch how easy it is to get the cheese."
Nick summons over a server to our chairs on the beach.
"Do you want another beer?" he asks me.
"Of course." I say then he starts to speak to the black Peruvian in Spanish. I
don't understand shit. The dude goes away.
"It will be like fifteen minutes."
"That was it, just like that."
"Yeah Mate you just have to be careful who to ask because the dealers work
with the police."
"Well how do you know that guy?"
"I don't but he works for the resort and he works on tips and every bloke here
is trying to make ends meat. Look they don't live here they probably live in a
mud hut 20 miles away. They want the money."
"So then why are you telling me about the police?"
"Sometimes they will sell you out to the police to get there drugs back and
then you have to pay to stay out of jail. It's a Racket man."
"So, it's corrupt as anywhere else."
"I would say a little more than The Eu or the States."
The waiter comes back with two beers and a Styrofoam container. The one
they would use for a hamburger. Nick pays the guy 10 American dollars and
tells him to keep the change.
"What did you order?" I ask him.
"Nothing."
"Then what's in that. I point to the container. And Nick passes it to me. "Open
it up."
I open slowly because the wind is blowing and I see a half golf ball size
pink rock.
"I'm not sure what it is dude?' I pass it to Nick.
"I've never seen it pink like this before. We have to start chopping and
grinding right away." Nick gets up and walks directly in the cabina." Go get
two more beers and bring the chairs back in." He yells and I do.
        When I get back I see nick smashing up the blow. He covers the pink
rock with some Peruvian magazine and then repeatedly hit the magazine with
a beach rock. Cocaine starts to fly around the room.

"Shut the drapes." I just noticed the huge windows facing the people and beach.

"How much did you pay for that?"

"You saw me give the guy ten dollars."

"That's it and we got two beers and this pile of blow. For ten bucks? Unreal, there is like 12 grams of pure cocaine here."

"Welcome to Peru Mate." Nick hands me his open knife blade and I take the smallest little bit on the tip.

It hits me so quick I don't even know if it's affecting me. I'm blindsided and instantly high. I drain my beer and tell Nick I need to get outside because I am so amped up this room isn't big enough to pace in. We walk the length of the beach a couple times before we jumped in the freezing Pacific Ocean.

"Mate you're going to spend the whole six weeks in Peru? You should hit Argentina. My Girlfriend can get you round trip for around 300 American Dollars."

"My cousins husbands Family lives there." I say.

"You have plenty of time to decide or if you just want to hang in Peru that's cool too. Let's go get a drink."

We walk up to the little shack bar and order two Pina Coladas. I had a passion fruit one, it went well with the blow so I drank six of them.

First big mistake coming to South America, not learning any Spanish.

Two beautiful Latin women in bikinis join us at the bar shack. Thank god Nick speaks Spanish because I don't and these girls do not speak English. I buy them drinks and use Nick as a translator. I tell them to meet us back here at eight o'clock and we will share a taxi to the discoteca.

The cocaine is strong and we can't stop doing it. We sit on our little porch overlooking the sea. I can actually hear my heart beating.

"What are we going to do with all that fucking cocaine?" I say with a little panic in my voice."

"Relax mate. We can throw it out when we leave. Maybe you should slow down."

"I'm going to jump in the shower and get ready". I grab two cans and drain them while showering. I make a mental note to myself; do not take any more blow today.

It's a beautiful night, The sun is already set but the moon is bright, shinning off the water. We walk to the taxi stand and wait. I notice that Nick and I are the only white people around. No other tourists or Europeans or Australians. The two chicas come walking up and greet us.

"Hola"

Nick engages in conversation with both of them while I stand there like an idiot.

"Come on lets go." Nick yells at me as he is jumping in a car the girls flagged down.

"This is a taxi?" I say.

Nick replies in English. "All you need to be a taxi driver here is the taxi logo on your car, and you can buy them on any corner."

He then smiles at me while he is sitting between the two chicas in the back seat. I'm in the front seat I look at the taxi driver and he doesn't look like anything to me. He drops us off in front of the discoteca and I see police on motorbikes hanging out in front of the club. I give the cab driver a dollar. We walk in holding the girls hands and that's when they grab us and use a metal detection device and scan it over my body and arms. I'm not carrying a gun so I'm not worried, but I do have a couple of grams in my pocket.

We grab a table and a bunch of cocktails. The two chicas won't leave our side and I'm getting approached by every chic in here.

I'm the only mother fucker in the place with blue eyes.

I get up to go to the bathroom and chics follow me. This is great. I do blow while I piss and when I get back every one is dancing. The dance floor is huge and I see nick because he is the tallest fuck in the place and pale white in the middle of the dance floor. I don't even attempt to make it out there so I hang back.

I have barely any food in my system and a lot of vodka and cocaine at this point. I am really enjoying myself being numb in Peru. This older well-dressed good looking Latin women walks up to me and starts to speak Spanish and I cut her off. "No hablo Espanola." I smile and sip on my drink. She grabs my hand and pulls me onto the dance floor. I move and grind a little bit before I pull out the baggie of blow and pour a little on my knuckle. I offer some to her and she takes it. Now I start dancing like a fool on cocaine. Five minutes goes by and I had enough and walk off the floor and up to the bar. She follows.

"Do you want to come back to my place?" She says.

"You speak English?" I say surprised.

"Yes."

That was the end of it. I left with her and went to her pad on the beach I did too much blow and my dick wouldn't work so I watched the sunrise and walked back to my cabina on the beach. No sleep. I ate a spoonful of scrambled eggs and a Bloody Mary. My nose is running and I feel great. Its 10 in the morning and Nick and I are playing paddle ball on the beach. My heart is racing with all this running I'm doing so we decide to take a break and walk back to the bar. I can't believe I'm not tired or hungry. I keep partying until it's time to go back to the discoteca.

I totally forgot about the states, Maybe I won't go back.

Repeat of last night. Except now more women recognize me from the night before and I am getting approached like I'm in a whore house.

I drink more.

I do more cocaine.

I make out with different women.

Nick and I are the only gringos and I'm starting to get stares from these unhappy Peruvian men. I can feel the vibe change.

Or maybe I've been doing too much cocaine and I'm just paranoid.

I'm starting to have thoughts of my high school girlfriend, Elizabeth. This freaks me out. My brain is going into overload. I approach Nick at the table with the girls.

"Yo man I gotta go. I'm not feeling so well. My fucking mind is playing tricks on me."

"What Mate I can barely hear you with this fuckin music and all."

"Nevermind."

"Hey do you want to leave? I'm about ready to get some sleep I want to get up and go fishing in the morning." Nick yells.

I'm happy to hear this.

"Yeah. I'm beat myself. What about these chics?" I yell and point.

"Ditch them."

"Good idea." Nick just gets up from the table and no one is paying attention. Two seconds later I get up and walk outside to the parking lot.

Nick lights up a smoke and calls over one of the many cabs parked in front.

"What time do you think it is?" He says .

"Dude I have no idea."

"It's 1am. I can't believe it time just flew by today."

Nick says this has he is getting into the cab and then he speaks Spanish and the cabbie pulls off. I have my head leaned back and my mind is drifting. I can hear the tires on the dirt road.

My eyes are closed but I can still see the red flashing lights. I turn to my left and open my eyes and I see Nick staring at me. We don't need to speak we already know what's going on. How do we get pulled over on a quarter mile road?

"They are going to shake us down. You don't have your passport on you do you?"

"No." I whisper for some reason.

"Good, these fuckers want money."

"The cops? From us?" I'm confused. The cab driver won't turn around and look at us, in fact he is not moving at all he's not even shuffling to get his license and papers and shit. I don't hear my door open and I'm being pulled out my by two cops. They put me up against the car and frisk me. I look at Nick who is directly across from me. Same thing is happening to him. They turn me around and start speaking Spanish. I turn and motion to Nick. "Me no Spanish."

There are five cops all together, they look military and they are on enduro motorbikes. One of them turns me around and tries to put his hand in my front pockets. I knock him with my shoulder while the other officer has my hands behind my back.

"Be cool Wolfgang." I hear nick say.

The cop pulls out of my pocket the counterfeit bills and an American 100 dollar bill, he lays them on the back seat of the car. Nick and I catch each other's eyes. We didn't have to speak. He knew what I knew. I put the baggie of cocaine in the crack of the back seat and now they're running their hands thru that crack. How the fuck did he know? This was planned, they must of saw me in the bar or those fucking whores did something.

"Nick,Nick.. He's putting me in cuffs. Say something?"

"Look over here." He raises his hands as far as they can go behind his back. "Fuck." he's cuffed too. This short fat older cop walks over to us and he speaks a little English. "Where's your passport?" he asks me. I immediately say "Lima." "Tourists have to carry passport with them at all times."

"It's in my hotel safe. In Lima" I'm not stupid, no way am I going to let these fucks into my bungalow with all my shit and the huge pile of cocaine sitting right out in the open on the table. They place Nick and I on the side of the road while they converse.

"SShhh." Nick says. "I'm trying to catch what they're saying."

"Mate if they bring us both in who the fuck are we going to call to pay for our release? I can't call Lisa, She's not even there and if she was she would break up with me over this shit. She'd leave us here."

"What are you saying?"

"I'm saying you need to take the blame and I'll go back to Lima and get the cash out of my bank."

"That sounds pretty fuckin shady Nick. What's another option?"

"Mate I don't think there is one. This is Peru. We better hurry up with a plan. Look there coming over now."

"Nick I got money, fuck it, pay them."

The short fat cop walks over and tells us that the fine is 10,000 soles. And do we have the money? I could barely cover it, it was 3 grand. Nick looks at me. I nod. Nick starts speaking Spanish real fast and keeps pointing to me with his cuffed hands. Nick walks up to me and we are staring at each other, the cop is behind him taking off the cuffs.

"Mate I told them it was yours and that you're a stupid American. I made them realize that if we are both locked up No one is getting any money. The bank opens at 9 I could be back here at 11am the earliest."

"11am? It's not even 2 now. Really dude. You know if you don't come back I'm going to die here. I can't take being locked up for any period of time. This whole thing is making me sketched out."

"Mate don't worry I'll put up the cash and we'll take care of it when you get back to the States." Nick says as he slowly descends down the hill.

"I don't speak Spanish Amigo." The cop just looks at and motions for me to jump on the back of his bike.

"My hands are cuffed behind my back how am I going to jump up?"

The cop is already on the bike and standing it up right all the other cops are waiting revving their engines.

"Vaminous!"

I throw one leg over the seat and steadily get up my hands are holding on to the back of the seat near the brake light. The cop guns it and I fly back almost falling off then I trust forward into his back. I can't see what's going on but I have this feeling the cop could care less if I fall off at a high rate of speed. I keep my eyes almost closed because of the dirt and wind and smoke. The whining of the engines is so loud I can't think.

I'm trying to hold on for dear life as he is whipping around corners and jerking each gear. Now I don't see any lights except the headlamps of the other four bikes. And the roads became dirt. Fuck.

In the middle of nowhere is this dilapidated building, one level. Nothing else is around. It's a square building that reminded me of my elementary school. In the middle of that square building was a square courtyard with a huge round hole dug 7 feet into the ground. It looked as if someone dug out a perfect circle for an in ground pool. I was being escorted through the halls I see other cops but with different uniforms. The florescent light bothered me. They bring me into a side office and uncuff me. Then they push me into the courtyard where two other uniform whatever's grab me and march me down seven steps to this clay pit. They walk back up to the ground level. I can see that the moon is full, big and bright. If it wasn't out I would be standing in total darkness. All my senses are on high alert. I scan the pit without making it obvious. No white people. I don't see anyone much bigger than I am, No immediate threat. I see the shit pile in the middle. Shit, piss, garbage and torn pieces of clothing, someone I guessed needed to wipe their ass.

I walked around the perimeter and it was 153 steps with my nine inch feet. The temperature dropped and the wind kicked up. I count 19 men down here. No one looks too ragged so I assume that they're here being extorted or held for ransom of some sort. I don't know. I don't know if I'm still high from the cocaine or my adrenaline either way I will kill someone if I'm left in this shit hole. I don't know what's going to unfold and that starts to put me on edge. I need water.. I find a place to sit against the clay wall. I see and hear three guys sniffing something. I stay away but it's good to know whose holding. I see the sky getting brighter. I do the math in my head; I've been detained for three and a half hours. Fuck me. I need water. "I need Agua." I yell to no one. I just yell it. Now I can see what a real shit hole this place is. I didn't notice the two half dead guys lying near the shit pile. The stench is fucking insane. I wonder if Nick is going to leave me. I have no one I want to call plus I don't see a fucking phone in this ces pool. I need sleep and a shower but that's not going to happen. It starting to get hot out and my insides are shriveling up. I desperately need water.

I could tell what time it is by the shadow the sun casts in the hole. It's 8:30 in the morning. 2 more hours, maybe. This is getting ridiculous. I hate fucking cops. I hate corrupt cops. Pieces of shit.

For the first time in a long time my head isn't clogged with sadness or depression. It's filled with hate for man. I'm being taken advantage of because of my skin and where I'm from. These ignorant fucks think I'm rich. I wouldn't care if that was true but it's not and these motherfuckers want what's the last of my money. I just got my blood boiling and I need some water. "Can I get some fucking Aqua. You hear me! Aqua. Aqua. I need water!!" No one response to me.

My thoughts are creeping up on me. Bad thoughts. I think about Karma and what did I do to deserve this. Then I think about praying and I chuckle. I would be a hypocrite. I'm smarter than religion. I don't fear what I don't know. Religion is based on fear of the unknown. Man made up fucking Religion. Man made up god, the devil, allah, jesus and all the rest of that bullshit. I am stardust; it's up to me if I want to be positive energy or negative energy. The church is a racquet just like this situation I'm in now. These cops are trying to put fear in me, threatening me with jail if I do not pay. Little do

326

they know I can leave this planet at any time and I can also take people with me.

Every motherfucker is fighting for the shade around the perimeter of the hole. I so need water. I'm lying up against the wall. My upper body is in the shade my legs are in the sun. It's so fucking hot. What if he doesn't show? How long do I wait before I plot my escape? The last time I've seen clay like this I was jackhammering holes in San Diego. My 20 year high school Reunion is coming up. I wonder if I'll be going. I might be dead but I won't be in here? I wonder if Elizabeth would go. What the fuck am I doing involved with corrupt Peruvian Police? I need water. I need water. I need water. I don't think anyone knows where I am. I just told my folks I was going to Peru. I need water water water. I didn't give them a name or number. I wish I could piss but I've got nothing.

Time is slow. My heart goes from racing one moment to calm the next. I need to manifest myself out of here. I need fucking water. I'm amazed that no one else in the pit is asking for water. I've got nothing left to sweat. My emotions are all over the place but I stay solid as a stone. At least my depression hasn't come back…yet. This is some sort of test and I will not fail. All my friends are sitting home with their beautiful wives and children. I'm all alone in a pit in Peru. Something got fucked up along the way.

I sent the vibe out and then I sent it out again. The calmness and numbness just settled into me, I no longer felt anything. I wasn't tired or hungry and my thirst went away. I felt good and kept building on this. I made eye contact with everyone in there and in a quick look I gave them the same respect I wanted. I had nothing to worry about. I haven't seen a cop in hours now and according to the sun it's noon and probably 100 degrees in the sun. I'm sunburned. I can feel Nick getting closer, I'm confident he is on his way.
"Mate, Mate wake up." I must have dozed off.
"Nick.?" I yell and stand up, I have to block the sun from my eyes but I can see his tall body standing at the edge of the pit.
"Come on you're all set, let's get the fuck out of here." He says.
"Really, what time is it?" I say as I walk up the clay steps.
"2 in the afternoon."

After I shower I meet Nick in the kitchen. We are back in Mira Flores.
"Get your shit man, we are going to Iquitos. Hurry up before my girl comes home."
"Are you kidding me I was just in a hole in the ground, and now you want me to go the Amazon?"

"You don't need any change of clothes Mate we are going for a couple of days. Come on now."
"Really just like that."

I shut the door behind me and reach into my jeans and pull out some little baggie. I fling it onto the hallway floor. I don't give a fuck who finds it. This shit is getting crazy. I'm in Peru.

My depression has not set foot in my brain yet.
Adrenaline is the cure.

He told me flying over this part of the amazon is like flying over the Bermuda triangle. Except here there is no water, the trees eat you up.
We land at a landing strip that appears to be the only airport. Burnt out planes make for barriers along the runway. The sun just set.

Nothing but motorbikes and no white people. No tourists I see.
We check in to a two star room in the center of the city. The television was 10 feet on the wall and you had to operate it by a pool stick. No toilet seat, no shower head or curtain, a window from the shower to the outside world. No glass. No bars. Open. Open for any savage to squirm his way in and cut our throats. After we check in we walk to the river. Everyone is trying to sell me shit again. We turn them down and find a place to eat, I get the crocodile burger. I feel uneasy but I like it. I'm in the amazon and I haven't seen any police.

This kid who looks like he's fourteen but probably 21 keeps making small talk to us while we eat. I'm in no mood.
"What's your name?" I say to him as he is riding his bike back and forth.
"John."
"John,.. John? O.K John. You speak English? poquito?" I say as I stare him down. He nods and I immediately say "cocaine" and touch my nose. Like that's the universal sign.

John stops and Nick speaks Spanish to him. I pay no attention and pull out 16 American dollars and put it on the table. Nick grabs it and puts it in Johns hand then takes his shitty cell phone as collateral.
We don't speak because we don't need too.

The crocodile burger was rubbery and the roll sucked. John pulls up on his stolen bmx bike and throws down a handful of yellowish pink, depending what light you're looking at it powder, Rocket fuel.

I don't even know what to say, Nick is dazed for a moment. Then I grab the crocodile wrapper, with chunks of meat and roughly100 grams of pure heaven. I pull all the sides together and twist the top. It's the size of an orange. I jam it into my pocket and stand up. Nick throws cash on the table.

About 180 people saw what just unfolded as they were eyeing us as they sold their shit along the river.

At any moment I felt like I could be attacked. I'm inside my room and it doesn't make me feel safe. The blow is on the night stand, on the floor, in different piles on the plastic chair, and since the bag broke I had powder all over my jeans and the inside right front pocket. I literally would lick my fingers and stick them in my pocket and a pile of coke would appear. Much too much too much.

I did so much coke I end up thinking what a bad son I am. I got the heebie jeebies and tried to sleep underneath a bug infested blanket. No chance. Nick is talking but I can't understand him so I block him out.

My life came to this? I like this.

Forget sleep. The sun is up and we negotiate with some drunk drugged out locals to take up the amazon in their canoe. But it's not a canoe.
The best fifty bucks I ever spent.
I got ounces of the best blow. I'm my pocket.
I got cash. A total of a hundred and fifty buck. I'm loaded.
I'm wearing designer jeans and sun glasses.
I'm putting my life in the hands of strangers in the Amazon jungle.
I forgot about clean water.

We're all on something and as the sun dipped behind the trees I tried to have a beautiful moment. Then the walls of the jungle started talking and I did more blow so the voices in my head will drain out the death calls from the jungle. It didn't work.
Where the fuck am I? No, for real.

Four hours up the Amazon Proper is what they called it. First we went to visit their family. It was a little town built on the river. Built on the river. Little shanties floating on the water, we had to lift up electrical lines as we floated under them. Poor has a new meaning to me now.

Everyone's eyes have this glaze over them. Plus they are blood shot. I don't understand shit and I can see big brave Nick getting uncomfortable as we travel in pitch black on the amazon with a couple of strung out drunks. I look at Nick and we both give a short cackle. Fuck we are strung out drunks. No more worries.

My mind is clear. I think about nothing but the moment.

I'm so dehydrated, but not bi- polar, all my senses work. We land in the jungle of course, I see a bunch people running over in a single file. The moon is the only light. I think I'm normal.

I'm not hallucinating; the Bora Bora tribe came to meet us. It's some sort of racquet in the jungle. It's dark and I'm thirsty. We follow. I'm too numb to freak out. They sit us down at their hut. I forgot what they call it. Hut.

About 17 females topless, of all ages and one glazed out dude decked out in tribal garb. All my senses are heightened. We decline the brown water in the used plastic bottle instead we ask for the sweetbark. Moonshine in the jungle with no water. Nick hasn't said much in a while; I can see the cocaine has finally affected him.

I don't understand a word these people are saying to me. I take out the cash in my pocket and throw it. I lay down in the mud facing the sky. The opening in the trees lets me see the moon. I have a moment of clarity. I feel free. Truly free. No money and left in the middle of the amazon I finally feel free. I leave my body.
I don't think I slept I just became more aware.
"Mate. You up?" Nick speaks.
"I need water dude." I sit up. My whole back is black and wet. "Let's get the fuck out of here. Here" I give Nick the bag of blow. "Go wake up that fucker and put some coke in his nose and tell him to take us back. I got to take a piss."

We quietly paddle out of there. The sun is hot and the humidity is ripe. Four hours of sitting on a piece of wood and my ass is dying. We continue to pass the bag of blow amongst the four of us and never speak. When I get back to the shitty hotel I see all the coke that was spilled all over swept up in nice neat piles. I don't bother to shower but I glance in the mirror and notice now that my eyes are glazed over and blood shot.

"You're not brining that on the plane."
"Yeah I am. Look at all this shit I'm not leaving it, this is gold."
"Mate fuck you. You'll get arrested. Look at yourself, go look" I walk into the bathroom.
"O.K, o.k I get the point." I stuff 3 grams into my little key pocket.
I walk out and throw Nick the big bag,
"I don't trust you Mate. "
"Nick fuck you I'm not going to go thru the shit I just went thru. Come on now." We stare at each other and he knows.

No one at the airport wants to touch me, The dried up mud works. I walk right on by wearing my shades. When I get on the plane I'm handed a towel so sit on. Nick shakes his head and we take off.

I got rid of the depression gene. I found the cure. Cocaine.

Back at Nicks flat I pull out the 3 grams and throw it on the table.
"Fucker I don't know where my girl is. What are you doing?"
"I'm going to shower. Look at me."

The hot water feels good and makes me rejuvenated. I can't sit around and talk to his straight girlfriend I need to bust out.

"I'm getting a room for tonight and going to Cusco in the morning."
"Good. Get out of here. I got to act straight for a bit while my girl is here.
"When are you coming back?"
"Four or five days. I'll email you." I grab the bag of coke off the table and walk to the lobby. I have the doorman hail me a cab.
"Do you speak English ?" I say to the cabbie. He nods.
"Good now bring me to Park Kennedy and find me some whores."

I'm not feeling so right. The fumes at the airport are killing me plus the Black market Jack Daniels I drank last night isn't helping.

I can't think about anything but the moment. The minute I realize I'm alone in this world I start to freak. Its true feelings not the drugs. I want to cry. I want to cry because I'm free. I'm free and I have no one to share it with.
I land in Cusco and go to the party hostel. More blow and a bunch of Australians, good folk but I'm old or older, no one can tell. I have my own room and host a little party. It's June and the temperature drops 40 degrees plus at night. I don't sleep but snuggle with this New Zealand chick. It's cold as hell. I hear the horn for the bus to Machu Pitchu and I just remember that I bought a ticket earlier in the night. This chick is hard to leave, she's so warm. I give her my key and leave what little clothes I have left on the floor.
I'm wearing a white Hanes neck t-shirt, 527 Levis and engineer boots. My head was shaved 3 weeks ago. The bus holds 22 people. I take the seat touching the rear of the bus, this way I can see everything that's going on. To my left is a sliding glass window to my right is a young lesbian couple from New Zealand. I am just told that the bus ride is 9 hours and my seat doesn't recline. The landscape makes you wonder.

We start climbing up the mountains and the switchback is making me nausea. The Peruvian music playing over the speakers became hypnotizing, when I look out the window and notice a foot from the dirt road we're on is a 2000 foot drop. I don't see any guard rails. Some parts we are hugging the side of the cliff because part of the road fell away. I'm just a little bit freaked out; no one else seems to be bothered.

I grab my little draw string back pack and put it on my lap. I untie it. I stick my head in and breathe in as much cocaine as possible. Then I look back out the window to make sure I wasn't dreaming.

"Are you shittin me. No one else is looking out the window?" I scream. I look to my right and the dread lock lesbian smiles.

"Have you looked out the window? It's gotta be 2000 feet down, what the fuck man? No one told me about a suicide ride."

She laughs and extends her hand "My name is Carmen and that's Lindsay."

"Hi I'm Wolfgang." I whisper "do you guys want to do some coke?" and place my bag on Carmen's lap. They both laugh and Carmen wipes my nose and chin with her sleeve. I didn't know I had salt all over my face.

"This ride is the most fucked up thing I've been on, look at all the crosses." The girls are passing my bag back and forth. I'm about to jump out of my skin. This isn't how I planned to die.

We stop in some one-road Town for lunch. I buy wine and ignore the guide. I don't eat the pre-paid lunch and jump back on the bus. Me and the two lesbians down the bottles and eventually pass out. When we arrive at the base of Machu Picchu, I talk the chicks into going to the hot springs and the guide is starting to become a pain in my ass and tells me I'm not following the rules. I ask him if he would like some boxed wine. He's not amused and tells me the bus up to Machu Picchu leaves at four in the morning but first I have to wait in line and get a ticket, first come first serve. Wait, what?

The temperature and the boxed wine was no match for these girls, they did everything short of dying in the springs. Everyone from the bus looks at me as the guide and staff are pulling the girls out. I can't help but laugh as I walk away to my room. I put my clothes back on and go to the cheesy disco. I'm still doing blow and I can't remember the last time I ate. I feel fine or at least I think I do. I close the bar and head over to get a massage. I can see by the look in their eyes that they are terrified of me. I'm just smiling.

"Come on. Come on I pay double." I say this as I'm pulling on the door while they lock it. I pull out a wad of cash. "See double." I point.

They unlock the door and tell me 40 dolla. I thought it would be more so no problem. I awake after 45 minutes and this little fat Peruvian lady is massaging the hell out of me. The best massage I ever got. I flip over on my back and point down to my cock and make the hand motion for hand job. She smiled and slap my bare cock open fisted. That was the end of the session. I retreat back to my room and just lay on the bed. My mind hasn't slowed down. I don't even think about being depressed. I can't believe that I was even ever. I don't have a care in the world and I drink two quarts of passion fruit juice. I hear the rumble of people in the hallway so I guess it's time to get up. The first come first serve line was no joke. They only hand out 400 passes a day and I was number 70.

"Wolfgang." I hear from the lesbians eight people behind me. I leave my spot and walk back towards them.

"Hey Guys."

"You made it. We thought for sure you would be sleeping. Did you get in trouble last night?"

"Come on now. I don't get in trouble. I haven't slept yet and my body is pushing through. How are you girls doing?"

"Not as good as you, are we going to hike up together?"

"Yeah I like that"

"Wolfgang we are going to take a picture together as the sun rises over Machu Picchu."

"Who's we?"

"You, me and Lindsay, there is no one else here I would rather spend the sunrise with." She smiles at me and I feel like crying.

It's cold out and I'm starting to fade. I don't know if I can make it. I'm standing in line and the wait is freaking me out.

"Carmen save my spot I got to piss so bad. I'm going to run over the hill to the restroom."

"Do you think you'll have time? The line is moving quickly."

"I don't have a choice." I say as I go running to the men's room. I'm out of breath when I reach the door I already have the little tied up bag of blow ready in hand. I wait for the old man to get out then I lock the door behind me. I can't untie the little knot so I bite it off. I'm starting to shake. I pour it out into the palm of my hand and stick it in my nose. I go running back and make it just in time to go thru the turnstiles with the lesbians. We have our picture taken overlooking the mountains and sunrise. My eyes are beady and bloodshot.

I'm impressed. I have never seen anything like it. I'm speechless. After the tour around Machu Picchu, the girls decide to climb the mountain next to it called wannapichu. I think it's a good idea so I follow.

We start walking up and I notice the steps are steep and no rails. I continue and we climb higher. My breathing is getting difficult and the steps turned into terrain. Things aren't looking to safe. I find myself on a ledge with my lips pressed up against the rock. I have to slide my feet because there is no room to take a step. I have about four inches of ledge and then a thousand foot drop. I can't look and I freeze up.

I could end it all here. Close my eyes and take a step back. My body will never be found. I'm frozen in thought, should I do It. Don't be a pussy the voices say in my head say. The numb warm feeling is coming over me. My body wants to melt. Maybe it's all a dream? I drift off for a moment that seemed like forever; when I come to I have the courage to take one more step up and slide on to the peak.

"Wolfgang..Wolfgang" I hear the voices and recognize them as the lesbians but I can't see them I can't see anyone.

"Yeah. Hey, I'm up here. On the top." I yell.

"Wolfgang you're not supposed to go up there."

"Whatt!?"

"You can't be up there Wolfgang, come down."

"Howw!!?

I never saw signs. I start crying I cry helplessly. I breathe in the air and continue to cry. All my emotions let loose at once; I can't control this feeling of ecstasy. No one can see me except the sky. For once I don't feel any guilt or shame. I don't feel lonely or sad. I'm not angry or tired. I'm free. I control my own destiny. I'm done carrying mind baggage.

I stay on top of the peak for 20 minutes by myself. I renew my soul. I climb down with confidence and never hesitate. The girls greet me and show me photographs they took while I was standing on the ledge. The best gift anyone ever gave me.

We had enough and make our way to the bottom. Carmen wants to grab a bite to eat so we grab our shit from the hostel we were at and walk toward the café. As I pass the bus driver he tells me the bus is leaving in fifteen minutes because of the rain. I tell the girls and they get food to go and wait in line at the bus. I remember it's a 9 hour bus ride on narrow dirt roads in the dark of night. I tell the girls I will meet them in line. I go running to the main strip and look for a pharmacy. I enter this small little Rx store and behind the counter is this old fat Peruvian lady. I start to speak and she says "No English." We just stare at each other.

I take my finger and tap on my forehead then I smile and stick out my arm and make it shake. She doesn't take her eyes off me. I then make the gun sign and point it to my temple and pull the trigger. I stick out my tongue. The little fat lady takes four steps back to her jacket that was hanging on a chair. She pulls out these pills wrapped separately. I look on the wrapper and I notice something that looks like diazepam I tell her I will take two strips of ten. She doesn't understand and I throw down an American 20 dollar bill and take them out of her hand.

I walk back to the bus and I eat six of them I gave the girls 2 each, before the bus pulled out I was fast asleep. No other way I could take that ride. I get back to Cusco and someone is waking me at my Hostel. I slept straight thru. I party for two more days before I head back to Mira Flores.
I feel good I feel accomplished.

I recoup for 3 days at Nicks, I spend one day with his girlfriend and we try to teach each other our language. She's real nice and Nick is a lucky man. I spend some quality time with my friend because I don't plan on seeing him again.
I jump on a plane to Argentina.
I 'm not done yet and my money will go a bit farther.

I have the cab driver from the airport get me all the weed and blow I needed then he drops me off at a hostel in the Palermo section of Buenos Aries. I rage for a week. Fuck young 20 something year old girls from France I don't sleep. I take a 14 hour bus ride to Mendoza and chill with relatives of my cousin's husband. I stay a month before I head back to Peru and take my flight to New York.

It's now or Never.

6 months and 18 days of sobriety. I needed a change the voices came back louder than ever. I battle them daily. It sucks. When I came back from South America I immediately landed a gig in New York City as a stagehand on an off Broadway show. Some reason Bud hooked it up for me. It's decent money but only enough to survive in the big city. I find an illegal warehouse loft to rent in Brooklyn, two girls live in this 3500 sq. foot loft, it has two bathrooms and 3 bedrooms, one in each corner.

Susan and Stephanie are in their late 20's and one is in ballet and the other is a trapeze artist. Avi is the Landlord a wealthy Jew about 30 years old. He owns the whole building. He dresses like a hipster and tells me he used to have a drug problem. I don't know why he felt comfortable telling me this. I just nod.

The rent is $750 a month and it has to be cash, I'm cool with that I tell him. He shows me a slot in the sheetrock behind the washing machine and tells me to put the cash in an envelope with my name on it and put it in the slot. I don't think twice about it and say "Yeah. No problem."

I've been reflecting on my past and came to the conclusion that being sober blows. I'm more depressed now than ever. I have no self-esteem. I'm just another slob in the system. Each day that goes by I become more bitter. I'm 38 years old and I have roommates. Pathetic. All my friends have gone onto another life and I don't make enough money to keep a girlfriend. Something's not right.

I go days without talking to anyone of substance. The thought of suicide floats around in my head. I'm getting the urges again. I want to kill someone or I am going to explode. I need to go on the hunt I need to fuck. I need chaos. I need my adrenaline back. I need the animal inside of me.

My roommates are leaving for the Holiday but before she leaves she tells me Avi has been looking for me and hands me an Envelope.
"He has my number. Why didn't he call me?"
"He says he has been and you don't pick up or listen to your messages."
"That could be true Susanne. Well you guys have fun and I'll see you in a week or so right?"
"Merry Christmas Wolfgang, See you after the new year." Susan says. I don't know it at this point but that was the last time I ever spoke to her.

I have fourteen hundred saved, not much but it's slow time after the Holidays so I need to hold on to it. I have 4 days before I have to show up at my Aunts house in Stamford Connecticut for Christmas Eve dinner with about 40 relatives.

I shut my phone off and go out, its 11am and I'm dressed well with a Michael Korrs pea coat and scarf. My hair is longer than the norm. I haven't shaved in two days. I look good.

I settle in at the Blackbird, it's a coffee shop slash bar. Very hip and eclectic. The back wall is filled with books and everything else looks hand crafted. It's cool. I eat the pumpkin soup and order my first beer. I don't care anymore. After about five beers and two hours later this chick sits next to me and immediately starts chatting with me.
She's young 25, 26.

After we say hello I buy her a drink. My state of depression is fading. I feel brave and order a shot of Jack Daniels. This chic is now getting touchy feely with me. She brought in a lamp and told me she found it on the side of the street and it would look great in her apartment. I agree, it's not a bad looking lamp. She must weigh 100 pounds and I could see the gin and tonic she ordered is taking affect. She leans into my ear and asks me if I do coke.
"It's one thirty in the afternoon. Why do you have any?" I whisper back.
She licks her lips and smiles. She's hot and crazy I like this young chick.
"Come to my apartment its two blocks away and you can carry the lamp."
"Yes." I don't hesitate.
I pay the 70 dollar tab and leave with the lamp.
Her studio apartment is tiny but nice. I place the lamp on the table and turn around. She jumps into my arms and starts making out with me.
I can't remember her name for the life of me.

She pulls down my pants and goes straight for my cock; I'm still wearing my coat. I lift up her skirt and she is not wearing any panties. I fall back on the couch and she jumps on me and starts riding me. I can't believe this shit, it's fucking Tuesday afternoon. As she is screaming and getting off I can't hold my own and release inside of her. I don't say anything and she climbs off me.
"Do you know I made a suicide pact with my cat?"
"What?"
"Do you know that I made a suicide pact with my cat?"
"Yeah yeah I heard you, I wasn't sure. So I guess that's a good thing right. You and your cat are that tight. Did the cat tell you this…Never mind."
I'm losing my buzz and this chic is freaking me out and I just fucked her with no condom in Brooklyn. Fuck I need a drink.
"I forgot to pay my tab at the Blackbird so I'm gonna head over there now."
"I thought I saw you pay it when we left." She says as she lights up a smoke.

"Uh that was a different tab, well than meet me there. Hey, what about the coke?"

"It's in the bathroom medicine cabinet."

I walk straight to the bathroom and take her vile of blow and put it my pocket and I beeline to the door.

"O.K. thanks meet me at the bar." I say as the door is about to slam.

As soon as I'm in the stairwell I take it out and start doing small little key bumps. I push open the doors and the sunshine hits me in the face. I walk back to the Blackbird.

The bartender just stares at me and pours me a pint from the tap.

"Where did you go?" He asks me.

"Why? I ran out for a minute."

"Did you go with that girl?"

"Why?" I can't say it without smirking.

"You did, didn't you?"

"Why guy what's the problem?"

"You fucked her didn't you?"

"I don't know what you're talking about I just brought that lamp to her pad."

"You fucked her, I know."

"What do you mean you know, what the fuck is going on here?"

"Wolfgang she's crazy."

"I sort of figured that."

"No. She is nuts. Crazy. She belongs in a home."

"Why? Wait I don't want to know."

"You fucked her."

"Fuck you."

"I hope you wore a boot."

"What guy? I didn't fuck her."

"Whatever, I just hope you protected yourself."

"Why? What do you know? Forget it you're making me crazy. I'm going to take a piss."

I walk into the bathroom and do a few more key bumps.

When I walk back out I see crazy girl sitting on my stool.

"Wow you made it back quick." I say.

"Oh I think you mistakenly took something that didn't belong to you." She says quietly but to the point.

"Oh yeah I forgot, here." I put it in her hand and she kisses me. The bartender smiles and shakes his head.

"Let's get out of here I got to go to my apartment anyway."

I grab her hand and lead her out the door.

"Why is that guy telling me you're crazy? He's bugging me out."
"Who the bartender?"
"Yeah the bartender he's knows you fucked me."
"He's my ex-boyfriend, he's just jealous."
"That's the shit you pull in front of your ex. Who acts that way?"
"Wolfgang when I saw you I knew we connected."
"Fuck you, now I know you're crazy"
"Wolfgang don't say that, you know you hurt people's feelings."
" Crazy. You are. Five hours ago I walked in here to get some pumpkin soup and now I think I'm in some sort of soap opera."
"You don't care."
"What should I care about, some chic I met in a bar. It's still daylight out damn it, this is too much drama lets go chill at my pad." The cocaine just hit me and I felt like being nice.

   She grabs my hand and we walk together back to my pad. I have 3 beers and offer her one. She pours out the coke on a magazine and cuts into six lines.
"This has been an interesting day so far to say the least." I say as I sit next to her. "You never told me what you do Wolfgang?"
"Oh I guess I didn't. I work for the United States Government."
She leans back on the couch and throws this look at me.
I bend over to do a rail.
"What do you want to know? I'm not a mailman."
"What do you do for the government smart ass?"
"I kill people."
She laughs and laughs then says "Me too."
What the fuck? She is crazy.
"Oh really you also work for the government. Do you carry a weapon?" I say fucking around.
She pulls a 9mm out her little bag.
"What the fuck? Is that loaded? Put it away. Do you have a license for that?" I say as I grab it out her hand. I wipe off my fingerprints and put it her purse.
"You really are nuts. I don't want to know anything else about you. I think this is where we part ways. Take your coke or I'll give you money, whatever, but you got to go."
"Oh Wolfgang don't be mean. I told you I work for the government."
"You don't work for the government you nut. Get out."
"Wolfgang just calm down and let me rub your shoulders. You're so tense and maybe the coke is too much for you."
I think about it and a back rub does sound good.

"Should we go in my room and get naked for this massage?" I say.

"Sure I would like that."

"Wait no what the fuck am I doing? You really got to go."

She grabs my hand and pulls me up off the couch and into my bedroom. This is a bad idea. 2 minutes of a lame back rub and she's on top of me again. I don't remember her name. No condom again. Fuck it I say to myself and fuck her all over the apartment. My roommates would not be happy.

"It's ten o'clock do you want to grab a bite to eat?" She asks me.

"How can you eat? You been doing coke all day."

"I don't know but I'm hungry and you are coming with me."

"I don't know if I want to go in public with you and that gun."

"Wolfgang don't make me mad. Let's go now."

"Don't make you mad? Are you nuts? Are you threatening me?" I laugh.

"Wolfgang you promised."

"What. No, when the fuck did I promise. You're delusional too?"

"Oh come on I'm buying."

"In that case fine." I grab my jacket and lock up behind her; I don't trust this whack job.

We take the subway into Manhattan and I'm getting sober and starting to think what I got myself into with this chick. We are at restaurant in the west village its dark and quaint. This chick starts ordering 250 dollar bottles of wine not one but two. I don't say anything and chug the first glass.

"Your nuts are you really going to pay for this?"

"Wolfgang I told you not to worry."

"I don't trust you. How do I know you're not going to open fire in this place?"

"Wolfgang stop. I'm not crazy and you keep saying that, it's going to make me crazy. And fuck you who are you to judge you're right here beside me."

Oh fuck she's right.

"Ok let's start over. I'm sorry if you took my sarcasm the wrong way."

"I like that better Wolfgang."

"I'm afraid to ask your background and where you're from? I don't think I want to know."

"I'm Iranian."

"What? Now you're fucking with me. You're pretty white to be Iranian."

"I'm Iranian you dumb ass and that's a racist comment."

"No it's not. I thought all Persians were dark in skin color."

She doesn't blink.

"O.K so you're Iranian and…"

"And nothing. Most of my family is still there."

"O.k and you're here going to school?"

"Nooo I told you I work for the government."

"Alright I'm not going to ask you any more questions. I'm just going to sit here and drink this expensive wine."

She smiles and tells me to follow her to the ladies room.

"Noo. Not here look around it's pretty quiet and very posh and you're very loud. No. No way am I having sex with you."

"Wolfgang you idiot I was going to ask you if you wanted the last of the candy"

"Sshhh. People can hear you. Alright give it to me and I'll be right back."

When I come back the bill is paid and they package up the second bottle of wine.

"Come on lets go back to your pad."

"Really we just got here. Whatever."

We walk down to Soho to Miladys. It's a classic dive bar.

"I have to go in here and drink tequila I'm to amped up. Please tell me that you don't have any more of that shit left. I can't handle it."

She smiles and doesn't respond. I order six shots of tequila. Before the Bartender is done pouring them she knocks back three of them.

"What the fuck really? What's wrong with you?"

"What's wrong with you? She says. And bursts out giggling.

"I'm not carrying you back to Brooklyn. I say and she says it right back to me. "You're crazy."

WHACK. I never saw it coming she belted me in the eye. I can feel it blow up immediately and my vision is a bit blurred in the left eye.

I throw back the three remaining and ask for three more, the bartender pours and tells me my eye is cut. She hands me a bill for 55 bucks and laughs and shakes her head.

"O.k I'm sorry. I forgot about that word. O.k. Are we cool? Can we be friends now? She jumps on me and starts kissing my neck.

"O.K, O.K O.K Wait let me pay the bill."

I want to puke and I can't find a cab anywhere. This chic is killing me but I'm not depressed or lonely anymore.

We get back to my apartment and she takes off all her clothes and pops the bottle and drinks from it. I like this and I take off my clothes. She turns up the chili peppers and plays air guitar. I like this but now she looks Indian to me. We kill the bottle and go to bed. Six months of sobriety and now this.

I only slept 4 hours but I feel good. I got this naked Persian whack job lying next to me. I get up and make breakfast and I fix myself a stiff bloody Mary.

Round 2.

"Wolfgang can you make me a bloody Mary?" How the fuck did she know.

"Yeah you're up."

"Come see your girl."

"What? My girl. " I walk into the room" You're my girl now? Really. Do I have a say in this?"

"Nope and thank you for the drink boyfriend."

"Boyfriend? I don't think so." I lay down next to her.

"Do you have to go home and change?"

"No I'm going shower with you and then we are going shopping."

"We are? I don't think anything is open now."

"Good then we will lie naked and drink bloody marys." She says smiling.

I like this crazy chic, I just don't know her name.

   We bounce around the city buying new clothes; she buys shit like she has an addiction problem. I spend 340 bucks on a suit on sale. I put on the jacket and don't take it off. We look good along with all the holiday shoppers bustling in the city. How funny two days ago I wanted to kill myself now I'm happier than a pig in shit. We drink and can't keep our hands off each other. We make a scene in every restaurant and bar. The animal is loose.

   I give the cab driver 50 bucks to drive us back to Brooklyn. We put our bags in my pad and run out to her blow dealer's apartment. She tells me she doesn't have any cash so I give her 200 bucks. I don't think about my funds, I'm going to keep spending until it's all gone and deal with being broke like I always do. I buy more bottles of wine and we return to my apartment and rip off our clothes again.

"I'm going to kill the Bartender at the Blackbird." I say this at four in the morning when I wake up out of a dead sleep.

"Wolfgang I can hear you."

"I want you to hear me. I'm talking to you."

"Go back to sleep."

I can't sleep my chemical balance is off and I'm obsessed on hurting this man. Who the fuck is he to play with me.

I can't sleep and don't.

She wakes up around nine and I ask her if she is ever going home and she asks me why. I'm cool with it. I turn my phone off.

"Let's go for brunch on the lower east side I know this cool joint."

I cab it there and immediately order a Vodka. I'm not feeling right. She asks me what I'm thinking about and I tell her I'm thinking on how I'm going to dispose of her body. She laughs.

I still don't know her name I've been calling her "Hey."

"Where are you going for Christmas?" I ask her

"I'm jewish."

"You're an Iranian Jew? Is that possible?"

"Yes Wolfgang. What are you doing?"

"I am going to Connecticut for Christmas Eve dinner and then I'm racing back."

"Are you going to take me with you Mr. Wolfgang?"

"Uhh.No."

"Wolfgang you're not being nice. You need to introduce me to your family if I'm your girlfriend."

"Girlfriend I don't think so. I don't even know you. I thought we were just having fun."

"Wolfgang you wanted this. You asked for it."

"Uh What? What did I ask for?"

"Me."

"Ok. Who did I ask?"

"The Universe dummy. You wanted this. You put it out there and I answered. You always get what you want once you focus on it. You know this I don't have to tell you. I came into your life because you wanted me. I know you like me; otherwise you would have left a long time ago."

"Wow. Now I am really freaked out. The Universe huh?"

"Wolfgang you're taking me to your dinner tomorrow as your girlfriend. I will make you look good."

"I don't know about that. I have to think about it. You can't bring the gun."

We decide to go bowl a few games. She doesn't put the bowling shoes on she slides in her socks and when she is not bowling she's dancing to her own beat. I like her. I'm chugging pitchers of beer and get the itch again.

"Hey did you bring any of that white stuff?"

"Wolfgang don't you think you should calm down if we are going to see your family tomorrow."

"Let the universe handle it. Do you or don't you."

"I do but I'm not doing any. Here it's all yours."

"Good." I grab it and walk into the bathroom.

When I return she is sitting and tells me to come over. I do and she plants a kiss on me. "Do you love me yet?"

She says.

"I'm not in the right frame of mind to answer that. You're…..Beautiful." I stopped myself from saying nuts.

"Wolfgang I'm hungry and I want to go uptown."

"Why uptown I never go uptown. Fuck uptown. I feel whacked."

"Then let's go to the Soho Grand and eat something you're starting to worry me. I've seen you eat and it's like a little bird. You need to slow down on the drinks and blow."

"Whatever you say woman." We jump into a cab downtown and I'm starting to fade. I'm talking nonsense and when we get out of the cab I piss right there on the street..

"You asked the universe for the animal well now you got him baby!"

"Wolfgang I'm not going anywhere, don't get so crazy. Don't forget you're in public."

"Fuck public. You better tell me the truth."

"About what Wolfgang? I told you everything."

"I want to know about this universe shit. I think your fucking nuts and you're playing games with me. I'm vulnerable. Are you fucking with me because I'm starting to feel for you? I like you. Is this some sort of joke.?"

She pulls me out of the road and into a doorway and hugs me. She whispers in my ear.

"I'm here because you want me here. I'm here because I want to be here. Now straighten up before I shoot you."

I push away from her and we just look into each other's eyes. I believe her because she Iranian.

She doesn't drink at dinner I do. I order a salad and a scotch. The voices are back and my life savings in my pocket is getting very low. The buzz is dying and chaos is entering my head. I'm beyond drunk and talking to people that aren't there. She laughs and acts like everything is normal. I don't get this girl I can't figure her out.

The next thing I remember is waking up naked and going to take a piss in my apartment. Everything is trashed. The couches are flipped over. My paintings are ripped off the wall the bathroom door has a hole in it. The TV screen is cracked and it's not mine.

"What happened?"

"You had an episode." I hear from the bedroom.

I walk back in.

"You started trashing things at the Soho Grand and then you threatened the cab driver. Then you came back here retrieved your gun and put to my head. I knew it was unloaded so I let you rant and rave and destroy your pad. I made some Jell-O it's in the fridge." She says as she is playing with her phone on my bed.

"Yeah. Wow. And you stuck around for all that."

"I told you dummy, you want me here. You did for me. In your twisted mind you thought you were impressing me."

"You're killing me with this talk. Who the fuck are you?"

"Wolfgang what time are we expected at your Families dinner."

"Leave at 4. Get there at five eat at six and leave at seven."

"I'm going back to sleep for a few hours come with." She says as she pulls the sheets off her body. I jump in bed and we make love then she falls asleep. I'm hungover and dehydrated.

I'm angry at myself. I get up and check my pockets; I have 230 dollars left to my name. No rent money. And how am I going to explain the television and bathroom door. Fuck me. I go back to bed.

"Wolfgang wake up we've over slept. Its 330 and I have to get ready, I'm jumping in the shower and then can you swing by my apartment for me? I have to grab something."

"I don't feel so good I might just cancel."

"Wolfgang get up you're going. It's your family!" I hear from the bathroom.

She looks stunning but I still don't know her name. I don't remember any questions I asked her either. I don't know if she told me about her family or anything. I'm not going to bother asking and look like a fool. I will listen closely when my relatives ask her all sorts of questions.

We jump into my truck and see 4 fucking parking tickets on my windshield I throw them in the back and swing by the Iranian's apartment. She returns to my car with a violin case.

"What is that?" I ask

"What does it look like Wolfgang?"

"It looks like a violin case but what do you have inside that there case is what worries me."

She laughs. "I will show you."

She pulls the violin.

"Thank God I thought you had some arsenal in there and you were going to mow down my family."

"Wolfgang, you're funny. Do you remember what you told me last night?"

"Umm Noo. Do I want to know?"

"You said You loved me?"

"I don't think so I don't say those words."

"And then you told me you will kill for me."

"Yeah, then what?"

"You start breaking shit and told me you're going down to the Blackbird to kill the bartender."

"O.K. now it all makes sense. Great"

"And Wolfgang, you never gave me a chance to reply. I love you too." She leans over and kisses me.

We pull into my cousin's house. I'm wearing the same clothes for 3 days unshowered and unshaved. I didn't even brush my teeth and I can smell myself. She looks beautiful. We reach the door and she plants a kiss on me. The door opens and I'm greeted by everyone. I don't get a chance to introduce her before my aunt asks her name. I ignore everyone and turn my head towards her. She looks directly at me and says "Penelope. My name is Penelope." Penelope? I would have remembered that. What Iranian is named Penelope? She is fucking lying.

When I see my parents my mother doesn't acknowledge me but says hello to Penelope. My Father pulls me aside and says "I thought you got you're shit together. What happened? You couldn't clean yourself up and who's this nice girl you got involved with?"

"Relax Dad. She is a terrorist from Iran and she is here to kill the President and I told her I'm going to help her. I'm going to get some wine. Would you like some Pops?"

My old man is disgusted with me, but what does he know. We sit at two tables for dinner. I happen to be placed at the adult table. I never sit at the adult table I hang with my much younger cousins at the kids table. Always. I didn't know Penelope spoke fluent Spanish until she engaged in conversation with my cousin's husband from Spain. I didn't know she came from Texas. I didn't know she had four brothers. I didn't know she worked for the wall street journal. I keep drinking wine and keep my mouth shut. How do I know she's not lying? Is she crazy or am I?

The attention was taken off of me; it was a good idea to bring her. After dinner she pulls her violin and everyone gathers in the living room. Everyone was mesmerized. I was in awe and immediately fell in love again. She played for 25 minutes and no one wanted her to stop. I notice at the end when she was putting her instrument away she was crying. She cried a lot of tears. I walked over to her and hugged her and she cried even more. Now my relatives are catching wind of this so I bring her into the kitchen.

"Baby don't cry. Why are you crying? Everyone loved you. You're great." I hug her again.

"I'm just happy Wolfgang. You make me happy and you have a wonderful family and I'm happy you waited for me."

I don't know what she means but I go with it.

We end up staying later than I expected because everyone is enjoying Penelope's company. I steal a bottle of wine and put it in my truck. No one kisses me but they all kiss her when we leave.

I don't know if this girl is crazy. Everything is nuts, four days ago I was sober and lonely now I'm the animal with a woman, I can't have a happy Medium. I manage to pop the cork while I'm driving. Penelope is fast asleep and reclined. My mind is flip flopping from joy to sadness to anger. I keep swigging the bottle until its empty and throw it out on the BQE. I don't want to be sober I have too much shit to deal with.

Penelope wakes up two blocks away from the loft.

My vision is not right which makes my walking abit fucked up.

"You drove like that?" she snips.

"Yeah I need glasses." I hand her the key. We walk in and she goes to take a shower and I pour myself a Vodka and look for any crumbs of cocaine. It dawns on me I don't have her phone number. I'll get it later. I manage to scrape up enough junk for myself and blow a huge rail then I down the vodka and go to my bedroom. She's not in the room yet and I'm freaking out already about the damage and the rent and I have no money or work for at least 5-6 weeks.

She smells clean as she lies next to me, I smell like a bum.

"Wolfgang, do you want to marry me?"

I look at her, half crazed. "I do, I want to. When?"

"Haahaa Soon Baby. You really want to marry me?"

"Yes, I want you. I need you in my life."

"Good Baby now just spoon me and go to sleep I will wake you early for morning sex." She kisses me.

"Good night Baby." Is the last thing I said.

Christmas morning, I wake to silence. No traffic. No water pipes burping. No doors slamming. No dogs barking. I turn over and she's gone. I get up and piss, I don't see a note but I'm not concerned. I go back to sleep and wake back up at noon. I check my phone and nothing. We never exchanged numbers. I clean up my apartment and everything looks good except the television and door. I keep checking my phone for some reason. It's 4 in the afternoon where is she? Where did she have to go?

I put on my coat and walk to her apartment building. There is no doorman, so I check the buzzer list. I don't know her last name but I think she lives on the 3rd or 4th floor. I hit all eight buttons and wait till I hear a woman's voice. 3 don't answer 2 men answer and then 3 three old ladies. I walk away and stand across the street and wait and wait. The temperature dropped and I walk home. I continue to drink and pass out. I wake right up at 4:17 am and check my phone. Nothing. My heart sinks and I start thinking the worst. What if she got hurt? What if she got raped or kidnapped or murdered. Then I think what if she played me? But for what?

I get up and put on my clothes and walk back to her apartment. I know nothing's going to happen but I go anyway because I can't sit still with my thoughts. I'm tempted to ring the buzzers again but I don't. It's still dark out. I'm starting to panic. I don't panic ever. I go back home and lay down under the covers with all my clothes on. I sleep 2 hours and have a dream that she left me a note on the front door. I get up and run downstairs. Nothing. I'm starting to lose it. I have no one to call. Am I dreaming? Did I dream all this crap? Nothing makes sense. I can't control my emotions and break down. What is going on? How did I deserve this? I pace all around my apartment. It won't sink in. What happened? She kissed me before bed.

It's 11 am and I buy a 9 dollar bottle of wine and walk up and down her block thinking I might run into her.

I don't. Its been two days what the fuck why wouldn't she tell me if she had to go somewhere. I don't eat. I'm getting depressed. What the fuck happened. I try to sit in a bar and drink what little money I have left I can't sit and the bar is empty. I walk home. I check my phone to see if maybe she called. Nothing. I pull out the vodka because I can't stand this state I'm in. I'm useless. My mind won't shut off. I take deep breaths and try to calm down, I can't. I race back to her apartment and wait, I'm there 20 minutes and I see a couple come out of the building.
"Excuse me guys do you know a Penelope that lives on the third or fourth floor?"
"We live on the third floor and there is no Penelope on that floor. Sorry."
My heart keeps sinking and I'm fucked up. Why would you do that to me? What the fuck did I do? I buy another bottle of wine and walk to the bridge. I got to get out of here I say to myself out loud.
Four beautiful days turned into hell.
I really want to kill myself.

December 27th. I wake up and I don't feel anything. I 'm numb. Any bit of heart I had left she took. It's just an empty black hole now. I can see I'm starting to shake as I brush my teeth. I jump in the shower and then I shave my beard. Then I shave my head. I make a drink and by pass breakfast. The T.V doesn't work so I can't watch it. What friends I have are with Family. I have no food in this place and 73 dollars to my name. I keep going over and over in my head. Where is she? I hope nothing bad happened to her.

I call the Brooklyn and Manhattan Hospitals. No one by her description was admitted they tell me to call the morgue. First I call the police to see if she was locked up. Nothing. I hesitate then I call the Morgue. The dispatcher checks for me. She says no females fitting her description in the last three days. Good.

Where the FUCK are YOUU!!!!
Where are you Where are you Where are you.

I destroy all my paintings, I bust them into kindling. I rip the bathroom door off the hinges it had to be removed any way. The bottle is almost empty and I'm lost. I don't know what to do.
"Mom."
"Wolfgang. Hi. Is everything all right... Wolfgang?"
"Ma I'm not doing too well something is wrong with me. I need help."
"Wolfgang did you take something? Are you crying? What's wrong son."
"Mom you saw me Christmas Eve right?"
"Yes I saw you."
"Did I bring someone with me?"
"Wolfgang, yes you brought your friend Penelope. What's going on Wolfgang? Hold on I'm going to get your father."
"No mom wait. She was real right? She came with me. You talked to her right mom. She is real mom. You touched her, you shook her hand right? I'm not imagining it am I? She was nice, right? And beautiful. She played the violin do you remember she played the violin? She was real mom. She was real." I can't control myself and I start whimpering like a pussy.
"Wolfgang where are you?"
"I'm in Brooklyn and she's gone, she disappeared Christmas morning and I can't find her anywhere and I've been losing it ever since. I can't fucking find her. Is this a fucking game because I want out!"
"Wolfgang come home we never got to talk the other night, come home. Don't be by yourself."
"I don't think so mom I'm not gonna make it up to Connecticut. And guess what I'm always alone so what does it matter now." I take a deep breath and wipe my eyes and clear my throat. I'll be fine mom I didn't mean to call." I hang up before she can say anything. Then my phone rings.
"Mom I sorry I didn't mean to hang up I'll be fine, I don't want you to worry about me. "
"Wolfgang, just come home. We want you home."
"O.k O.k Tomorrow, traffic is a bitch right now. I will call you in the morning."

"Wolfgang get some sleep and we will see you tomorrow. We love you."
"I love you too mom." I hang up the phone and smash it on the ground. I don't need a phone because she doesn't have my fucking number.

I have to get a grip. I'm the animal I shouldn't care. I won. Fuck her. Fuck her Fuck her Fuck her. I get angry then I get worried. I don't want anything bad to happen to her.

I sit on my stoop and kill the bottle. My eyes are bloodshot from crying. The rage just peeked.

I need my mind right. I need a good sleep. I need Penelope.
I kick around the clothes on my floor and come across my gun. It's not loaded but bullets are all over the floor. I pick one up and put in the chamber and spin it. Fuck you. I put it to my temple and pull. Nothing just like I thought. I still have it. I can call it. My instincts are on par. I spin it again. I wait. I'm not going to do it. I take the gun and point it at the wall and pull the trigger. It goes off and I was right my instincts are in check. I empty the shell on the floor and rush out of the building. I take deep breaths and put the gun inside my coat pocket. I walk past her apartment and I can't control myself. I ring each buzzer on the fourth floor. I ask politely for Penelope. 3 out of the four answer and tell me that they don't know a Penelope.

I'm starting to shake. I'm getting obsessive. I don't know how to think anymore. I don't know what's real. I don't what's bullshit. I can't take it any more I can't take it anymore I can't take it anymore I can't take it anymore.
I want to kill myself.
Fuck you god.
I'm not here for this.
Where is this girl I'm fucking scared.

Nothing meant anything before now. I wasn't paying attention when she spoke. She said she waited for me. She said I wanted her and so she came. She met my family. She said I asked for all this. My mom said it was real. All my emotions flipped to anger, I'm being fucked with. I walk briskly in the cold down Metropolitan ave. The sidewalks are still filled with holiday cheer, I want to cry.

The lights are dim and the atmosphere is cozy and pleasant among the happy customers. He doesn't recognize me with a shaved head. I don't sit I stand between two girls on stools at the bar.
"What can I get you? Oh Wolfgang I didn't know it was you."
"Did you see her? Has she been here?" I don't order a drink I'm visibly shaken.

"Who?"

"The girl I was in here with four Days ago. Don't fuck with me. Did you see her?"

"Calm down Wolfgang." I can see the guests getting frightened and moving away from me.

"No. she hasn't been here."

"Tell me her name. Is her name Penelope? Where the fuck is she?"

"Whoa calm down. Her name isn't Penelope." He chuckles. Her name is Ashari. Man I told you she was crazy. What she do now?"

I look to my left. I don't see anything. I look to my right and nothing. In one second I pull my gun from the inside of my coat and point it at the smart ass bartender. Its 12 inches from his face. It's not loaded but he doesn't know this. His hands go quick in the air.

"Say it again. I yell. "Say it one more time." I have tunnel vision. "Tell me she's crazy one more time." I pull back the hammer.

I'm breathing so heavy my chest is moving. I hear nothing. Silence. I don't see anything. Everything becomes bright.

I was whole for that second I was no longer broken.

I don't take my eyes off him and I slowly put the hammer back and place the gun back inside coat pocket. I turn and walk out the door. I take a left and I run up Broad.

Now I did it. That dude knows me.

I run all the way down Hope St. under the overpass and towards The Marcy projects. I'm fucked. If they find me I'm definitely getting arrested. I will be sitting in the pen for a while. Fuck that. I run back towards the bridge.

I pass a sewer grate and let the gun slide out of my coat and down my leg until I heard the clink. I then shuffle around my feet and kicked it thru. No one notices. I then cross the street and make a loop around the block. Just to see. I sit on a bench overlooking the east river. Where is this girl? What the fuck just happened?

If I go back to the bar and apologize. I will still be arrested. I'm fucked. I grab a cab and have him drive me around my building and block. I don't see anyone looking like cops. I pay the cabbie and get out.

I'm fucked, this place is trashed. I have no phone. No money. No rent.

I'm numb; I'm too drained to keep having breakdowns. I grab a bag and I'm stuffing my clothes in sub consciously. I see a white envelope and I instantly think it's from Penelope. I'm wrong. I open it.

Wolfgang;
I have been trying to reach via cell phone and left repeated messages. I have not received payment from you in the last five months. I know we have different schedules but that is no excuse. I will be back on the 3rd of January and hopefully we can resolve this then.

Have a good Holiday
Avi.

I crumble it up and toss it. Fuck him. I paid. Wait. That stupid fuck doesn't remember telling me to put the rent behind the washer in the wall? Was he on drugs?

I move the washer from the back wall. I stare at this slit in the sheetrock. My money is behind that wall. I put my boot thru it and then I rip out pieces with my hand. I feel an envelope then I reach down abit more and I grab five of them. Holy fuck. Cash. My cash. $3750.
I thought something was strange about that guy.

Fuck the apartment. I leave everything. All I own now is a bag of clothes. I lock the door and leave the keys in the mailslot. I take a cab to Manhattan. I get out downtown and walk to my bank. It's closed but I make a deposit at the ATM. I'm over drawn $129.

I walk to the internet café and sit quietly in the corner. I'm searching the internet for a place to escape. I'm thinking Panama and I come across Bocas Del Toro. I could hide out there for a while. It's cheap. Then I come across Puerto Viejo Costa Rica. The voices told me to get there and I booked my ticket to San Jose right then. $742. I have time to kill but no phone. I walk to Chelsea and get a drink. Then I get seven more. Five days ago things were great. Then this chic came into my life and turned it upside down. I'm mad and pissed and hurt, but I hope she is alright. My eyes keep tearing up. I'm losing it again and the bartender asks me if everything is O.K
"Yeah everything is fine I'm waiting for a cab to the airport I have to go to L.A. A friend of mine died." She feels bad I can see. She walks over and gives me a hug. The next 2 drinks are free.
My emotions no longer exist.

I have the cab driver drop me at JFK at three in the morning and I sleep in the terminal until 6 my flight is at 8:30 am. I carry on my bag and I end up sitting next to this Costa Rican couple.

I wake from a sweat. I take my Pea coat off and also My Michael Brandon Shirt. I'm wearing a white v neck and jeans. I leave the coat and shirt on the plane.

The couple smile at me and the woman in her fifties asks me. "Where are you going in Costa Rica?"

"The jungle. Puerto Viejo, Limon."

They look at each other. "Are you aware that's the most dangerous place in Costa Rica?"

"I was not aware. I didn't read the travel advisory."

"It's very beautiful but also very violent, crime is widespread. Have you been there before?"

"No. First time."

"Are you taking the bus?"

"I didn't give it much thought."

"The bus ride takes about 5 hours and cost 8 dollars. If you get a cab you can negotiate for 120 dollars. Do you speak Spanish?

"No."

"We can tell you how to get to the bus station once we land or we can point you in the direction of the taxis. If you like."

"Thank you, I'm going to think about it."

    I fall back asleep. When I exit to the terminal I immediately feel the heat. The couple point to the taxis and I walk outside. It just hit me I'm in Costa Rica. Why did that couple say it's the most dangerous place? I jump in a cab and ask if he speaks English. Not really but we can communicate. I tell him Puerto Viejo Limon. He tells me 150 dollars and 4 hours. Fuck it. I jump in and tell him I'll pay when we get there. He takes off out of the city.

    I'm not going back; I want no part of the States. I'll send my parents a postcard. My mind is already clear and I have only been in the country for a couple of hours. I'm dehydrated and I can't piss. The sun is setting and the ride is taking longer than I expected. I don't think the cab driver knows where he is going; we are thick in the jungle. We stop in Limon and he asks for directions. He tells me not to get out of the car and locks it. I get the feeling we are not in a safe place. He jumps in and tells me 35 miles. We take off on the dark dirt road all I can see is the moon reflecting off the ocean on my left. We pull up to Kayas place a surfers hotel/hostel. The cab driver charges me an extra hundred and I don't feel like hassling so I give it to him. I slam the door and say "Adios."

Animalsdontpray.com